LISA HELEN GRAY
MAVERICK
A CARTERS BROTHER NOVEL BOOK FIVE

©
Copyrights reserved
2017
Lisa Helen Gray
Edited by Hot Tree Editing
No part of this publication may be reproduced or transmitted in any form or by any means, electronic or mechanical, including photocopy, recording, or any information storage and retrieval system without the prior written consent from the publisher, except in the instance of quotes for reviews. No part of this book may be scanned, uploaded, or distributed via the Internet without the publisher's permission and is a violation of the international copyright law, which subjects the violator to severe fines and imprisonment.

This book is licensed for your enjoyment. E-book copies may not be resold or given away to other people. If you would like to share with a friend, please buy an extra copy. Thank you for respecting the author's work.

This is a work of fiction. Any names, characters, places and events are all product of the author's imagination. Any resemblance to actual persons, living or dead, business or establishments is purely coincidental.

DEDICATION

You are not alone....
"The scars you can't see are the hardest to heal."

MAVERICK

ONE

MAVERICK

THERE COMES A TIME WHEN YOU reflect back on your life and know you need to make some changes.

Serious changes.

I was barely out of nappies when my dad first started beating me. It wasn't long after that started when my mum left, walking out on me and my four brothers.

Then, not even a teenager, I was used for something far worse than beatings. They were a breeze in comparison to what I endured. I was torn apart from the inside out, and each and every time a part of my soul disappeared.

I'd like to be able to say my childhood doesn't reflect on who I am, that is doesn't define me.

But that would be a lie.

I'm very rarely with it lately, the fight having left me. My heart and body are being pulled in two different directions: one half clings to my past, the other fighting for a future, the same one my brothers have. Each has a woman in their lives, and not just as lovers, but as friends—partners.

And it wasn't until I watched Max, the most unlikely of my brothers to fall in love, that it hit me.

They don't need me anymore.

For years, raising my brothers has kept me from drowning in my own sorrow and guilt. It's helped block out my past and forget about the future because I never deserved one for what they went through, right under my nose. But now, seeing them happy, it's making me want more. I've realised just how lonely I am, how much I crave to love and be loved. I want someone who completes me the same way my brothers' girls complete them.

The thought alone terrifies me because I've never wanted anything like that. Not for myself, at least.

I don't trust women, my mum a prime example as to why. But it also has to do with my past and the women I had to deal with. My dad is to blame for that part. He's the one who brought them into my life, forcing me to do things no kid that age ever should.

He's the reason I can't stand to be touched, especially when I'm fucking some random chick for a quick release.

Speaking of, I've been having a dry spell for a few months now. I've not had the time, and if I'm honest, one-night stands really aren't doing it for me anymore. I never thought those words would enter my mind but it's true. It doesn't hold the same satisfaction for me as it used to.

The first woman to pique my interest for more than a one-night stand also happens to be my new tenant, Teagan.

She's the other reason why I've been so fucked up, thinking things I never used to think about, and it scares me. From the second I saw her, I've not been able to get her out of my mind.

Our first encounter wasn't even a great one—or much of one at all, if I'm honest. Some dickhead attacked her, tried to steal her purse or something. I went after him, but he was gone the minute he rounded the corner.

When I made my way back over to the group, I had been too focused on the scared little girl to notice anyone else. Her face struck a chord with me and I couldn't help but react, wanting to protect her.

Then I looked up and my eyes connected with Teagan's. Something resembling an electric shock ran through my chest in that moment, stunning me speechless.

She had to be the most beautiful woman I'd ever seen. And her body... fuck, her body was pure perfection. She had an hourglass figure, curves in all the right places and legs that went on for days. But it was her eyes that sucked me in.

They were a startling deep blue, with lashes so thick and long they fanned her cheeks. I'd gotten so lost gazing at her that I turned into a blubbering fool. I rushed off not long after Max introduced her and said she was my new tenant. I couldn't breathe.

She's been in every one of my fantasies every time I wanked one off, but soon I know my hand won't be good enough. I'll want the real thing.

The fact that she has a kid hasn't put me off in any way; if anything, it pisses me off knowing there's a man out there somewhere, probably still in the picture. Although, in the stupid interview Max conducted, she stated there wasn't one.

A knock on the door startles me and I thrust the weight bar up above me one last time, clicking it in place.

Sweat trickles down my back, my arms aching and back burning as I glance over at the time, and I can see why. I've been here for four hours after waking from another nightmare.

Coming to the makeshift gym I built in one of the empty storage rooms usually helps me blow off some steam and burn away the images still floating around in my head from the nightmares, but lately, I've had too much going on to clear it. I've ended up coming here every night for the past two weeks, working out until my body passes out from exhaustion.

My attention goes to the door when Matt, my assistant manager, walks in, looking pissed. Swiping the bottle of water from the floor, I gulp down the contents before facing him, knowing I'm going to need to be prepared.

"What's happened?" I ask, breathing heavily as I wipe my face and neck free from sweat.

"Dore hasn't turned up for her shift again. And the place is a shithole since the night staff didn't bother doing clean-up," he grumbles.

None of us like cleaning, especially on a weekend when we have mostly dickheads coming in. V.I.P. is supposed to be a restricted club. You can't just walk in off the streets in a pair of trainers; you need to be dressed to impress and have enough money to pay our high entrance fee. However, weekends we've been letting the public in, but only if they're following the dress code.

Dore, our regular cleaning lady, has failed to show up for work several times over the past few weeks, always giving us some lame-ass excuse. She had her final warning last week, meaning I'm now going to have to go through the hassle of finding someone else. Hopefully I'll be able to talk Max into finding someone.

Actually, I'll see if Lake wants the job of hiring a new cleaning lady. After the tenant interviews and having more complaints than I get from drunken customers, I'm thinking she's the safest bet.

"I'll have to do it," I sigh, angry. "First, I'm going to leave Dore a message, let her know she's fired."

"Rather you than me. That bitch is fucking crazy." He sniggers, telling me something I already know; it's the reason I hired Dore in the first place. I knew she could handle the customers when she came in during rush hour to clean the toilets and again at dinner time to hit the backstage area, making sure the work stations were ready for the next group of dancers.

"I hear ya." I nod, getting up and grabbing a T-shirt.

Matt leaves, grabbing a crate of bottles from outside the door before heading to the bar. Walking into my office, I find her contact information, wasting no time in dialling. The quicker I do this, the less I risk her coming in and having to do it face-to-face. Matt wasn't joking when he said she was crazy.

After ringing for the third time she finally answers, her voice filled with sleep and slightly slurred.

"Ello?"

"Dore! You're alive! I've been so worried I went and called the police to search for your body. I'm so glad that this isn't one of those missing girl cases and that you're really just a lazy employee. Oh, and in case you were wondering, you're fired," I bite out sarcastically.

"What? Why? I clean—"

"No, Dore, you don't. You were meant to be here an hour ago and what do you know? You're not here," I snap, my voice hard and cold.

"But I need the money. I have bills, I have—"

"You had your last warning last week, so now you're gone. You're fired. I'd tell you it was a pleasure working with you, but it would be a lie, and I hate liars. *Loathe* them actually," I tell her brightly, though my voice is still tight. "I best get going, as I've got cleaning to do. Oh, and don't bother asking for a letter of recommendation. You won't like what I have to say," I warn her before ending the call, ignoring the word "bastard" before it cuts off.

Lovely!

I don't bother putting my T-shirt back on as I walk down the hall to the cleaning cupboard. Instead, I throw it on the shelf before grabbing some black bags and bleach.

"Fuck, this is going to be a long ass day," I groan to myself, then head back towards the club.

GRABBING THE BLACK bags full of crap, I walk outside to the back of the club, making my way over to the bins. My joggers ride low on my hips and when I lift the bags, throwing the trash into the bin, they drop farther, exposing more skin.

Something hits one of the tin bins behind me, gaining my attention. Glancing over my shoulder, I freeze.

"Um... hi," Teagan waves, looking down at her Ugg slippers and back up at me, her cheeks a rosy red. "I'm just putting the bin in the rubbish," she rambles, then shakes her head. I chuckle, amused. "I mean, I'm just putting the rubbish in the bin."

"I can see." I grin, not able to help it. She's adorable, and my dick twitches seeing her all flustered with her bare legs on show. They're longer than I remember. She's wearing sleep clothes from the looks of it. As I continue checking her out, I find she's not wearing a bra. Her nipples are puckered, a rosy red colour from what I can see through her white, nearly see-through tank top.

Fuck!

I want to suck on them, taste them and see if I can make her come just by playing with them. They appear to be a perfect handful, the size I love. I can picture it now, my cum smeared all over her tits, over her tight puckered nipples.

I groan at the image, biting my bottom lip.

She crosses her arms over her chest, feeding my fantasy even more, especially seeing them pushed together the way they are. Now all I can think about is my dick pressed between them, her squeezing them together whilst licking the tip of my dick as I fuck them.

She looks down at my crotch and a squeak leaves her mouth, her face turning redder. I don't bother covering the hard on I'm sporting; there's no point. I'm not wearing any boxers and I like the fact that she's checking me out.

"Moommmmyyyy, I want some of my princess cereal," Teagan's little girl calls from the top of the stairs. My heart stops seeing her hang her head out of the bars.

"Hey, move back a little, squirt," I warn. She startles, falling through the gap one that shouldn't have been big enough for her to fit through, but some fucker broke one of the panels by swinging from it when he was drunk.

"Faith!" Teagan screams in fright behind me.

Sprinting forward, I catch the little girl in my arms, my heart pounding in my chest.

Fuck, I don't even like kids all that much. I love my niece, don't get me wrong, but any other kid and I'm gone. Something about Faith is different though. Fuck knows why, as she looks like any other kid. Just cuter.

"You're Superman," Faith whispers, looking up at me with wide, trusting eyes.

"Nah, kid, just Maverick."

"Are you okay? Are you hurt? Oh, Faith, what did I tell you? I said not by the stairs," Teagan fusses, grabbing Faith out of my arms and holding her tight. All of a sudden I feel cold from not having her in my arms.

"I'm okay, Mummy. Superman saved me." Faith blinks, touching her mother's cheek lovingly.

"You're not hurt anywhere?" Teagan asks again, still trying to look for injuries.

Fuck, she's white as a sheet, worry plastered all over her face. A burning pain hits my chest, witnessing her distress. All I want to do is pull her into my arms and comfort her.

"She's good, aren't you, squirt?" I interrupt, rubbing the back of my neck, feeling like I'm intruding.

"Yep." Faith giggles, squirming to be put down.

"Thank you. Thank you so much. If you weren't here...." Teagan trails off before throwing herself at me.

Her arms wrap around my neck, her body pressed flush against mine. Instead of the normal dirty thoughts I'd usually be thinking—like how good her nipples feel, hard against my chest—all I can think about is how right it feels to have her there.

I know the only reason she's hugging me is because she's grateful I just saved her daughter from cracking her skull open, but a part of me wonders if she's thinking about how good it feels to be in my arms too.

"Kiss, kiss, kiss," Faith starts chanting, giggling her little head off.

Teagan pushes away, a deep red flush covering her face and neck. She doesn't look at me as she nervously laughs at Faith's giddiness.

In all fairness, I'm all for her kissing me. It definitely wouldn't be the worst thing to happen.

"Come on, I thought you wanted cereal," Teagan teases, her voice raspy. She gives me a quick glance, her eyes soft. For a moment, an intense look passes between us, causing the hairs on the back of my neck to stand on end. She seems to snap out of it quickly, trying to mask how affected she was or how she just tilted my world on its axis.

"Thank you again." Teagan smiles.

"See you later," I promise, knowing there is nothing I wouldn't do to have this woman in my life and in my bed. It's not even about how hot she is either—it's her. Her personality, the way she makes me feel when she looks at me and how she interacts with her daughter.

She gives me one last lingering look before shutting the door behind her. I'm still staring at her closed door when a body jumps on my back, scaring the shit out of me.

"Guess who?" Lake says in a deep voice, her hands covering my eyes.

"I want to say the Wicked Witch of the West, but I'm scared of getting my ass kicked." I spin around and smile, happy to see her. I haven't seen much of her since she and Max announced Teagan was my new tenant. I think they've been avoiding me.

She huffs, jumping down and walking to stand by my side. She's staring up at Teagan's front door like I am, looking amused.

Please don't let her have seen me make a fool of myself in front of Teagan.

"Is there a reason you're staring at Teagan's front door?" she asks, her eyebrows scrunched together.

"No!" I cough uncomfortably, shifting so I'm facing the tiny little thing. "Why do I have the pleasure of your presence this early?" I ask, hoping she forgets I was staring at Teagan's door like a creeper.

Still watching her, I can't help but see the change, not only in her appearance but in her behaviour and personality. She was so withdrawn and closed off from the world when we first met her; it's hard to believe this is the same girl standing in front of me. Hell, she couldn't even eat a cooked meal without looking broken and torn up over it.

But she's changed. Her life has changed, the outcome happy for once.

Her eyes are brighter nowadays, and she's happier with herself, more relaxed.

"Matt called Max to come in and help with the cleaning," she answers. I raise my eyebrow, wondering if that's really her explanation.

"That doesn't answer my question." I chuckle, walking to the bins and grabbing another bag to throw in.

"Yeah, well, it should. As soon as Matt mentioned 'work' Max passed me the phone, saying it was an emergency. He's an asshole. He tried using the spot he has on his back as an excuse for why he couldn't come in, said he needed to get more beauty sleep," she says, rolling her eyes.

I laugh. "It's better than the whole 'I can't clean, it makes my skin dry' excuse."

"He's going to pop by later to 'help'. Looks like you're done though," she says, looking at the bags.

I smile, my eyes softening. She really is a rare gem, always ready to help others. She's good for Max, sometimes too good, but I couldn't picture either of them with someone else.

"Nope, still got the toilets, tables and vacuuming to do. Matt's stocking the shelves, so after you finished cleaning, you can wash last night's glasses, if you'd like," I offer, grinning.

"What will you be doing?" she asks as she walks beside me down the hallway.

"I need to fix a little problem," I tell her evasively, not wanting to admit that I'm fixing that goddamn railing. She'll probably read more into it. Or maybe *I'm* reading too much into it, making it out to be a bigger deal than what it is. I've never done anything for anyone other than family, but with *her*, I find myself wanting to do everything to impress her. And I've never needed to impress anyone before in my life.

"*Oookay*, Mr Avoid The Question." She snickers, walking into the cleaning closest.

If only she knew how much I do avoid.

TWO

TEAGAN

MONDAYS AT THE FLOWER SHOP MY nan owns are usually peaceful.

Not today.

My nan has slowly been driving me nuts all morning about my new accommodation. It doesn't matter that the place is in a better neighbourhood; that it's closer to Faith's, my five-year-old daughter's, school; or that we finally have fully functioning central heating and other appliances. Not only that, but Faith has her own bedroom, something she's been begging me to have.

"Please, Nan, just drop it. We've settled in nicely and Faith loves it."

"You got attacked," she deadpans.

She has me there.

As scary as that day was for me, I've been through a lot worse in my life. I was concerned for Faith's safety more than anything else. She'd been so scared, so terrified of the drunken man who attacked me that it took me days to calm her down. I wasn't even planning on telling my nan; I knew she'd freak the hell out, like she's done ever since Faith blurted it out to her.

"Nan, the neighbourhood is better than where we lived before. Plus, it can't be that bad. How long have you owned this place?" I ask, gesturing to her small but perky flower shop. It's only a ten-minute walk from here to mine, so she doesn't have a leg to stand on.

"Thirty-six years," she tuts, picking up a bucket of roses. "Teagan, it's above a strip club, and Colene said it's been in the paper for drug raids."

Glancing up from the morning's deliveries I was going over, I roll my eyes at her. Colene is an old gossip who makes it her business to know everyone else's. Half the time it's true. Other times... not so much. I've told Nan to stop listening to everything she tells her on more than one occasion; it's getting old. Hell, she knows most things before it's even posted on Facebook. I'd warn Nan to stay away from her, but out of all my Nan's friends, Colene is actually the tamest.

"Possible raids," I correct, going back to work.

Hearing her sigh, I glance over, watching her snip away at the rose stems furiously. "Okay, I'll let it be. Maybe now you can stop working at the doctor's office."

Ah, my job at the doctor's.

I'm only a receptionist, but the job is taxing. I don't even work that many hours, yet when I'm there time drags and I'm utterly miserable. The place drains the life out of me.

The women who work with me are cruel and judgemental, and a few times since I started there over a year ago, I've heard them trash talk me. We've never clicked; even the doctors look down their noses at me. The only reason I've put up with it for so long is because I needed the money to support Faith and me. Having a kid and bills isn't cheap.

But now I have a more affordable place, so I won't need the job. I've also saved a ton since I moved in by not having to eat out every day.

"Yeah, maybe," I tell her absently, going over ways to tender my resignation. I'd love to be the person who can throw it in their faces, make a scene by telling them what I really think, but it's not who I am. I hate confrontation of all sorts. I'm the quiet one, always have been. The wildest thing I've ever done is lose my virginity, and even then, that wasn't by choice but from necessity.

"How's me bitch?" Tish, my best friend, booms as she walks through the door. With her wild black afro, huge knockers, hourglass figure and out-there personality, she certainly makes an impression. Her hair is her best feature for me, anyway. It still astounds me how many ways she can have it. She's always getting something different.

My smile brightens at seeing her. There's never a dull moment when she's around, and I've missed her.

I've hardly seen her since the move. We've both been busy, but secretly, I think she's still pissed at me for moving away. We only lived a few streets from each other before. She hates it.

"Language," Nan scolds her, but there's no heat in her tone. Plus, she swears more than anyone I know—except maybe her friends.

"My bad, Connie," Tish says, then glances at me, winking, a grin spreading across her face.

And that is why I love her.

Tish and I have been best friends from the moment we met six years ago. She literally bounced into Nan's house without knocking, walked right up to me and said, "Yeah, you'll do." After that we became inseparable.

She lived next door with her grandparents, situated in a small old people's housing community. When I arrived, she was stoked about having another kid around.

She never judged me for my lack of fashion, which consisted of clothes two sizes too small, stained and worn out. Nor did she judge me when I found out I was pregnant. She was there every step of the way.

"Hey, Tish. How are you doing?" I smile, finally getting a word in. Leaning over the counter, I kiss her cheek.

"I've come to get the deets. I was speaking to my girl, Ronnie, and she said the manager at V.I.P. is hot. As in H.O.T. Spill it, girlfriend."

She winks at me, and jumps up on the counter, swinging her legs. I try to push her off, but she doesn't budge. Instead, she ignores my attempt and just stares at me, waiting for an answer.

"He's all right," I shrug, looking down at the order forms like they hold the answers to world peace. I can't tell her that he's more than hot—he's beautiful. She'll be staking the place out until she gets an eyeful. And if the package tenting in his joggers this morning is anything to go by, then she'll get more than she bargained for.

I wouldn't put it past her to start stalking him. She's done it before.

My face flushes as I remember the intense stare-off we shared this morning. He looked right at me with those mocha chocolate eyes and I felt like he was staring into my soul. It's the first time I've felt like anyone actually saw *me*. It unbalanced me.

I'd been taking the rubbish out, minding my own business when I noticed a bare, muscled, tattooed back glistening with sweat. I'd been so startled to see someone there and so caught up ogling the way his back strained and arms flexed as he lifted his own rubbish bags that I hadn't been watching my step. I ended up kicking one of the bins, bringing his attention on me.

The air left my lungs when I saw it was Maverick, my landlord, the same person who had chased down my attacker on the day of my interview. He had the same effect on me as he did that day, only this time I had a chance to really check him out.

He had muscle everywhere, places I never even knew muscles could exist. I've only ever seen bodies like his on the front of book covers, or in magazines, but even they don't compare to his.

And his tattoos… they're drool-worthy, totally completing the bad boy image he has going on.

I'd slowly taken him in, tracing every line, every dip and ridge of muscle on his glorious body.

It was then I realised my body was responding to him, tingling all over and coming alive in ways I've never felt or experienced before. But there it was in the pit of my stomach, pulling me towards him.

I wasn't the only one. No, he was certainly checking me out too. At least I think he was. Although, for all I know he could have been gawking at the fact that I was only wearing a pair of bed shorts and a thin white tank top that showed my muffin top and stretch marks.

I'd frozen, becoming so self-conscious that I'd ended up embarrassing myself. But I think the fact that I wasn't wearing a bra and the top was basically see-through made the whole situation more awkward.

He must have gotten a right eyeful.

He didn't appear to be disgusted though; if anything, he seemed to be turned on. His eyes were molten, pupils dilated when he finally looked up, and I couldn't help the thrill that ran through my body. It made me feel indestructible, sexy.

Then he saved my little girl and my attraction skyrocketed. There was no way I could've gotten there in time to catch her, let alone react as quickly as he did. The fall would have done some serious damage.

Which reminds me, I need to pop into the DIY shop tomorrow, since it's my day off, and see if I can find something to put there to make it safe.

"I know that look. Get it out, girl." Tish grins, clapping her hands.

"What?" Feigning innocence, I look away, unable to meet her eyes.

She grins wider, looking to my Nan with a wink. "This is going to be so much fun. Our little Teegy has a crush."

"No, I do not," I snap, feeling my cheeks heat.

She scoffs. "If you don't tell me, I'll just go round there. Maybe I'll even give him a strip tease," she jokes, messing with me.

"Don't," I warn her, pointing a rose stem at her. "He's…. Crap. He's hot, okay? He's gorgeous, like Chris Hemsworth gorgeous, just better-looking. I saw him…." I shake my head, waving away my thoughts. I can't let her know how I perved on him this morning, checking out his rock-hard, delicious body, or that when he looks at me my stomach flutters like crazy. She'd be there in a flash.

"You saw him what?" she asks, leaning in, her eyes lighting up.

"He was shirtless and I saw him. Now shut up," I tell her, wanting to die of embarrassment.

"You like him?" she asks, all teasing gone.

I look up at her, my expression serious. "Yeah, I do."

Her eyes soften and I try to blink away the pain. She knows why I don't date. It's not just because I have a daughter to think about, or a busy schedule, but because I don't trust people—mostly men.

After my mum died, I was sent to live with my uncle. It was a living nightmare, my own prison full of torture.

He ruined the last part of my childhood and made me lose faith in men altogether. Hell, I've only ever had sex once, which ended up with me being pregnant with Faith.

But there's something about Maverick that makes me want to try.

"Just ask him out on a date. What do you have to lose?" Tish asks.

"No!" There is no way she is going to talk me into this. Tish has a strong personality and could convince anyone to do almost anything. She blames her strong nature on her ethnicity, but really it's all her. She's as wild as they come, just like her hair.

"Why not?" she whines as she grabs a nail file out of her bag and starts nail filling her claws. Jesus, they get longer every time she has them done.

"Because…." I pause, not actually able to come up with a good excuse.

"Oh hell, girl, you need to get some lovin', clean the cobwebs and all that shit. If he's as hot as you say he is, what's your problem? Does he have funny-lookin' teeth?"

Teeth?

What on earth!

"Tish, his teeth are fine." I roll my eyes.

"Just checkin'. The blind date I went on last night? The dude had teeth that looked like he ate glass for breakfast." She shudders, looking disgusted as she points her manicured hand my way. "So, why not ask him?"

"I... I don't know him, okay? Maybe if we knew each other." I'm totally lying. There would be a zombie apocalypse happening before I gained enough courage to ask someone out, especially a man that good-looking.

Tish opens her mouth, but Nan butts in. "Latisha, go make an old lady a hot brew, will you," she orders. That's my nan, always bossing others around.

"Okay," she moans, never able to say no to Nan.

I laugh, earning a smack on the arse from Tish. Turning back to Nan, I'm about to thank her for saving me from the third degree, but from the look in her eye, I can see I'm in for a lecture from her too.

"You need to start trusting men some-time," she tells me, placing her hand over mind.

I smile sadly. "Maybe. I just... He's really nice, and I wasn't joking about the hotness, Nan. He's freakishly hot. I don't stand a chance. Plus, he works in a strip club. Why would he want frumpy me when he can have hot girls with big knockers?"

Nan smiles back, shaking her head. "Oh, darling girl, you look just like your mother. You're beautiful, inside and out, and if he can't see that, then he isn't the man you should place your heart and trust with."

"I guess," I whisper, wondering if I should tell her about the darkness I saw in his eyes. That he holds a sadness inside him so strong that when he looks at me, I feel it to the depths of my soul. It hurt my heart to see his internal suffering fill those eyes.

Although, there's no denying the overwhelming sense of safety I felt both times I've been with him. I knew the first time I laid eyes on him that he's the type of person to protect those he loves. I envy those people.

It also added to the major crush I have.

"Right, bitch, we're talking about me now and my horrendous date last night," Tish announces as she prances back into the room, and I shake Maverick from my thoughts.

Nan shakes her head as she walks back to the window, rearranging the flowers on display with a smile on her face.

"Okay." I laugh, grabbing my mug off Tish, enjoying the smell of fresh brew as I stand back and listen to my bestie fill me in on one of her many dates.

I HOLD FAITH'S HAND as we walk side by side across the car park, listening to her chat about her day at school.

"The teacher said I was the bestest one to read out loud," she tells me again.

I look down at her and give her a bright smile. "I'm so proud of you. You do read brilliantly, baby."

My heart melts when she rewards me with a wide smile. Her face splits into an even bigger grin when we reach our place.

Max, the weird, overactive lad who interviewed me, is standing at the bottom of the stairs to my place, holding a plank of thick wood up for Maverick.

My gaze flickers only briefly across Maverick, but that damn flutter in my belly is still there, going crazy mad.

Instead, I glance back at Max, trying to suss him out. I'm still unsure whether he's sane or not. I wanted to ask his girlfriend, Lake, more about him, but I felt like it would be rude to, especially if he's not all there in the head.

The jury is still out on that one.

Okay, now I feel like a complete bitch for judging him. There has to be a reasonable explanation.

"Maxy," Faith shouts as she starts running over to him. He drops the plank of wood he was holding, causing Maverick to curse down at him. Now my eyes are glued to Maverick, greedily taking everything in.

I'm glad to find he's wearing a shirt this time; I don't think my heart could have taken it if he wasn't. My eyes roam over his body, taking in every delicious inch before reaching his handsome face. His eyes light up as he watches Faith run into Max's arms, and I stare, mesmerised.

When I notice what he's doing outside my door, my heart flips over, pounding hard in my chest. I take a step forward, gobsmacked. My eyes begin to sting, my throat tightening at the kind and considerate gesture.

"What are you doing?" I ask, needing him to clarify, even though it's blatantly obvious.

Pulling his eyes away from Faith, he glances my way, then to the wood in his hand before finally looking back at me, his forehead creasing. "I'm making the stairs safe for Faith. I didn't want her to have another accident. It's no big deal. It was already on my list of things to do," he explains while rubbing the back of his neck, looking nervous.

He did this to protect my daughter. He cared enough about her well-being to go out and buy the correct supplies.

"Thank you. I was going to get it done," I rush out before I choke up.

He raises a sceptical brow at me, amusement lighting his eyes. "And how was a tiny thing like you going to lift this up here, hold it, and nail it in place?" he asks, his gaze raking me up and down, making me feel naked under his inspection.

"I... I don't know," I admit, sighing. I hadn't gotten that far. I just wanted to make sure Faith wouldn't have another accident. "Thank you. It's very thoughtful."

Seeming uncomfortable, he shifts on his feet, looking down at me. "It's no big deal."

Max scoffs at my side, holding Faith upside down. "No big deal?" he says, shaking his head, a smirk teasing his lips. "He had to drive all the way to Warrington to get the right wood because B&Q didn't have any in stock."

"She's going to get nauseas," I warn Max, and he grins, as if just remembering he has my daughter hanging upside down. Turning to Maverick and seeing him in a new light, I give him a shy smile. "Thank you. You really didn't need to go out of your way."

"It's all good," he mutters, banging a nail into the wood before wiping sweat off his forehead.

Christ, how can someone look so gorgeous when they're all sweaty? It should repulse me, yet all I want to do is lick him and see if he's as tasty as he looks.

And now my mind is in the gutter.

A dirty gutter.

Sheesh, I've been hanging around Tish too long.

"You little rascal," Max mutters, chasing Faith around the bins. "Where'd you go?" he calls, teasing her, pretending not to know where she is. Although I'm still unsure about his sanity, he really is good with Faith. He seems to have a knack for making her laugh uncontrollably.

Faith squeals and runs over to the stairs, making her way up to Maverick where she clings to his legs. He looks down at her, grinning, ruffling her hair. "You can't get me now. Maverick will protect me," she tells Max, giggling before sticking her tongue out at him.

I'm beaming like a mad woman. When I look up to see how Maverick is taking her admission, I find him staring at me, his eyes soft. Flushing, I turn away, fixing my gaze on Max.

"Such a cheat," he pouts, glancing between Maverick and me with a mischievous look in his eye. "So, Mav, don't you think T looks *fine* today?"

"It's Teagan," I correct him, which is all I ever seem to do.

"Should I be worried?" Lake teases as she walks out of the back entrance of the club.

"No, babe, never." He chuckles. "So, Mav? Answer or it's going to get awkward real quick."

Maverick glares at him before scanning over me once more. "Yeah, beautiful," he chokes out.

"Hey, Lake," I wave, wanting to change the subject and fill in the awkward silence. Although there's nothing I can do about my flushed face or the way my belly flutters from hearing him call me beautiful, even if it was pushed on him.

"Hey, Teagan. Hi, Faith." She waves back, standing next to Max who pulls her into his side, kissing her temple.

"Oh, that reminds me. Did you get a date for the wedding? Denny and Mason were on my ass to find someone for you, but because I'm in a relationship, it's hard. All the girls think I'm asking for myself and my girl… she won't be happy," he states, smirking up at Maverick, that glint still in his eyes.

"You know I haven't," Mav growls at him, his eyes narrowed into slits.

"I can be a date. What's a date, mummy?" Faith calls, sitting on the top step near Maverick, picking up the nails that have fallen and putting them back for him.

We all laugh, and I decide to be the one to answer. I tell myself it's because I'm a good mum, but really it's the wide-eyed, scared look Maverick gets, seeming torn on what to say.

"It's when a man takes a woman he likes out for food, or somewhere fun," I explain, chuckling.

"Cool! I like food." She nods enthusiastically, thinking it over. "I can be your date." Maverick smiles tenderly down at her and I have to bite my bottom lip to keep myself from sighing.

That smile could seriously melt some panties straight off. His grin, his smirk—hell, even his laugh—have nothing on his smile, especially when his eyes go all soft like melted chocolate.

Yep, my knickers are soaked.

This is so embarrassing!

"Faith," I warn gently, not wanting her to push herself on them. It's hard to say no to the little madam. She's just too darn cute.

Besides, he probably has some super-model girlfriend lined up to take with him, anyway.

"How could you turn down the perfect date? Or shall I say dates? You're game, aren't ya, T?" Max grins—a little too widely if you ask me.

He's up to something.

"I-I... um...," I stutter, wondering what the hell I should say. I'm not normally shy, yet for some reason, Maverick makes me incredibly shy and on edge.

"See, she's game," Max announces, and my cheeks heat. I turn to Maverick to find him glaring at his little brother. "And how can you say no to this one?" Max coos, staring up at Faith who's still sitting at the top of the stairs. Maverick's moved so he's guarding the gap, making sure to keep an eye on her so she doesn't have another fall.

God, why couldn't he be someone who didn't make me so nervous?

Maverick coughs, looking uncomfortable. "I...."

"It's okay. Ignore him," I say, letting him get out of this without things becoming more awkward.

"It will be fun," Lake pouts, then smiles at me. "We'll finally be able to get to know each other better."

"I don't know who's getting married though," I answer, wondering why that came out of my mouth when I should be making up some excuse not to go.

"It's our brother," Max replies. "And you'll need to meet him sooner or later."

"Oookay," I say slowly, not following.

"So, it's a date? Can I wear a big princess dress? Please, pretty please," Faith gushes, and I can't help the smile that spreads across my face.

I notice Maverick staring at me again, an intense, broody expression on his face. Even while brooding he looks freakishly good.

I really need to get laid.

"It'll be good for us to get to know each other," Maverick agrees lamely. "You do rent a flat off me."

Ouch!

Great boost for my ego.

Although, I have to admit my heart still takes a sudden turn, beating wildly in my chest at the notion of spending time with him in an intimate setting instead of in this car park. The urge to get to know him is too strong to ignore.

"You don't have to," I tell him, feeling like we're being forced into it by his weird little brother.

"I want to. It'll be fun. They've been on my ass to get a date for weeks," he explains, sucker punching me once again.

"Yeesh, make a girl feel special, Mav." Max chuckles, shaking his head.

Faith makes her way down the stairs to me, pulling on my shirt. Leaning down so I'm eye level with her, I ask her what's wrong.

"Maverick said a naughty word," she whispers, her eyes wide as she stares back at Maverick.

He must have heard because a small smirk forms on his lips.

"Sorry, squirt, I didn't mean to," he tells her and she blushes, nodding at him. He turns back to face me. "I'll grab the information for the wedding and bring it over later. That's if you're okay with coming?" he asks.

"Well...."

"She'd love to," Max answers and I turn, narrowing my eyes at him.

"I'll get this finished, then. I'm just going to grab a drink." Maverick rushes down the stairs, giving me a quick, nervous nod as he passes, making sure to ruffle Faith's hair on the way inside the club.

I'm still staring after him, stunned and completely speechless, for almost a minute after he disappears.

How the hell did this happen? Am I really going on a date with Maverick? My landlord? The hottest man I've ever laid eyes on? One I have a serious crush on? He couldn't possibly have been serious. Could he?

"How cute," Lake sings. "They both have an issue with staring after each other."

I shake my head, my face heating. "I'll see you guys later." I force a smile, taking Faith's hand and getting us out of there as fast as our feet will take us.

I hear Max say something behind me. I'm pretty sure it was "See you at the wedding," but I can't be sure, not with my pulse pounding so hard in my ears.

I'm out of my element here. I don't even know what I should do. Deciding I need my best friend, I grab my phone, turn the TV on to occupy Faith and head towards the open kitchen, dialling Tish's number on the way. I need to hear her tell me this is all a joke, that it's not real and I should go back out there and make up some lame excuse as to why I can't make it.

But the second I finish blurting out the whole ordeal, she's screaming and hooting down the phone, rambling on about my vagina.

I'm so screwed.

THREE

MAVERICK

THE POLICE ARRIVING AT THE CLUB has become such a regular occurrence that I've given them their own parking spot out back.

It started the night V.I.P. was raided for drugs and underage drinking a few months back. What I first presumed was someone trying to ruin my club's reputation actually turned out to be a little more complicated. It seems the cops have been watching my club for a while now and, as I'm majority owner, keeping track of me. Luckily, they've ruled me out as a suspect for selling drugs.

The second time I met up with them was when they finally came in and filled me in on everything that was going on in *my* club. It was the first time I was informed of any wrongdoing.

Long story short, a number of patrons have overdosed on drugs that were sold to them here, at V.I.P.

In the beginning, I thought someone was just playing some huge prank on me. A sick one, but a prank nonetheless.

I was wrong.

Once I asked Evan, Denny's brother, to look into it, I got confirmation back that there was indeed someone selling drugs here. I've been working with the police ever since to find out who it is. It could be a patron who frequents the bar or someone who actually works here. I'll be seriously pissed if it turns out the latter is true. I've handpicked every member of our staff, knowing one wrong move could ruin the entire business. I wanted girls who genuinely wanted to dance, not because they're being forced to. I'm not that kind of boss—or a sick bastard.

We're not even close to finding out who's bringing the drugs into the bar, but hopefully after today's meeting, we'll be one step closer. It's been hard to ask around the club since I've been told to keep the investigation on the down-low.

The knock on the door gives me a second to prepare myself before it opens, and the two detectives working the case walk in with grim faces.

Fuck! This can't be good. Usually the moody fuckers walk in looking bored or a little pissed, so I can only imagine what news they're going to bring me today—especially if their sour expressions are anything to go by.

"Just get to it. I can already tell you're here to be the bearers of bad news," I say dryly, my patience with this whole fucking thing wearing thin.

The eldest of the two detectives, Paul Barrett, clears his throat, slapping a folder down on the desk in front of me.

Glancing away from Barrett, I eye the folder with mild curiosity before actually picking it up. "What's this?"

"A man was found dead this morning in his apartment by his girlfriend," he explains, then gestures for me to open the folder.

I do.

Fucking hell!

I've seen a dead body before—my dad's, to be exact, and I'd been the cause of it—but seeing the young lad in his early twenties, his eyes blood-shot, face pale and foam pouring from his blue lips, is just something else entirely. My stomach churns, this morning's breakfast threatening to make a reappearance the longer I stare.

Grabbing my water, I take a sip, slamming the folder closed as I do. I hand it back over to Barrett, using more force than necessary, my eyes narrowed. I swear the fucker gets off on showing me sick shit like this, trying to get a reaction out of me.

"He was here, I take it?"

I'm not really asking. If they're here about a dead body, then they must know he was here last night; they most likely just need it confirmed.

"We interviewed his girlfriend ourselves. She didn't understand how this could have happened and was adamant about the fact that he didn't do drugs and that this wasn't an overdose. The only reason she was there this morning is because she knew he couldn't handle his liquor and would need some help nursing his hangover," Barrett explains.

I scrub the scruff on my jaw, trying to remember if I had seen the lad or not, since I was working. We'd been busier than normal so it's hard to pick out a face from memory.

Calvin Grant, the other detective, much younger than Barrett, speaks up, leaning forward in his seat, elbows on his knees. "We're going to need to see your tapes from last night. We've got the names and addresses of everyone he was with, but when uniforms went out to interview them, none of them knew anything about any drugs. Either they're all lying to cover their asses or someone spiked his drink. Even the deceased's mother told us he wasn't the type of kid to do drugs and had always been against them. We'll need the security footage to see if their stories add up."

"Not to be a prick or anything, but everyone says their kid or friend was an angel when they die. No one likes to speak ill of the dead." I shrug, wishing I didn't have to deal with this shit right now. It's one thing for someone to willingly take drugs and overdose, but it's another when someone is spiked.

"True. Although we've done a background check on him and everything seems to add up with the mother's and girlfriend's statements."

"I'm thinking we need to put someone undercover," Calvin chimes in, sitting back in his chair.

I groan, looking up to the ceiling. Not getting any answers from there, I look back at Calvin, an idea forming. My gaze flickers between the two detectives, wondering if they'll agree to *my* terms.

"Let me sort something out. My sister-in-law's brother is a PI. He's been looking into my staff for me. We'll come up with something. It's not that I'm not comfortable with having someone come in from your team, but I need someone *I* can trust too. If you get someone to become a regular, get them to feel out the customers, I'll deal with backstage."

"We do think it's a staff member," Calvin admits, sounding superior.

Prick!

"How?" I ask, pissed that they haven't bothered to say anything until now. All this time they've made me think it could be anyone and now they drop this shit on me.

"If it was someone who frequented your bar or, hell, different people who came in to deal so it didn't look suspicious, then they would go upstairs and do it too. It's a large venue—more college kids, more sales—but whoever this person is has only sold drugs in *this* part of the club. It has to be a member of staff. What we don't know is if they sell to customers at random, or if people use this place as a way to pick up their supply."

Running my fingers through my hair, I want to pull at the strands. All of this is so fucking frustrating. Four hours in the gym again this morning didn't do me much good; I want to go pound my fists into the punching bag once again, this time until my knuckles bleed.

"I'll find someone. If it doesn't work out, we'll let you do this your way." I sigh.

"Okay. Can you get one of your staff to bring the tapes over to us as soon as they can?" Barrett asks, seeming to realise I need some space.

"I'll get Matt to bring it over later." I nod, knowing I can trust Matt with this. He's the only one who's been filled in, and he's just as shocked and appalled as I am.

"We'll get whoever is doing this, but in the mean-time we want to keep this quiet. We don't need to remind you to keep it low-key. We don't want to spook whoever it is."

"No," I grit out, really wishing Calvin wasn't an officer. Something about him gets me riled up. He's probably a stand-up guy, but the last few times he's been here I've wanted to smash my fists into his face.

"Good, keep us up to date," Barrett says as he shuts the door to my office behind them.

Groaning, I slam my fists down on the table. Why can't I find who the fuck is doing this? At the rate this investigation is going, my club will lose customers and be closed down before long.

I thought I could trust my staff implicitly—apart from Dore—and knowing one of them is betraying me is tearing me up inside. It's not like I don't pay enough either; I pay more than most bosses do in this business.

Kicking my feet up on my desk, I lean back, contemplating on who I can use to fish out the dealer. There's no way I can let the police come in undercover.

I'M A GROWN-ASS FUCKING man and yet it takes me two days to get the invitation to Teagan. The first day I'd forgotten, getting caught up in paperwork. The second day, I had all the shit with the cops going through my head. Now my nerves are getting the best of me.

Staring down at the invitation, I groan, wondering if I can just get away with posting it through her letterbox. It's an informal way to invite her, and by now she probably thinks I've changed my mind anyway.

But I also wanted to talk to her about some safety measures that might need to be put in place around the apartment for Faith. I've been worried about it ever since she fell off the ledge the other day. The knowledge that there could be something else that could cause her pain, plagues me. It's why I need to do something to prevent that from happening.

"Bro, you missing me already?" Max calls as he staggers into my office. He plops his ass down in the chair, kicking his feet up on my desk like he owns the place.

Could this day get any worse? Not that I'll voice that shit out loud; Max might take it as a challenge. No, I *know* he will.

Pushing his feet off the desk, I let out a frustrated sigh. "What are you doing here?" I glance over at the time, noticing it's ten at night. I can't see Lake being happy about him still being here, especially when the girls take the stage in ten minutes.

"Lake made me help her clean the dressing rooms. Apparently, make-up is a bitch to get out of the carpet," he mutters. "Women say men are messy, but have they seen the shit they leave while getting ready? I've seen cleaner bins."

"Been spending a lot of time in them?" I ask, half curious.

He looks confused for a second until he catches on, slow as ever. "Yeah, I've been bin diving once or twice this week." He shrugs and I roll my eyes.

"Seriously though, why are you still here?" I ask, tired and ready to go home.

"Lake sent me to make sure you take that invitation to Teagan's. When she asked Teagan yesterday if she'd gotten it, Lake was surprised to find out she hadn't. What's holding you back, Maverick?" he asks, sounding like Dr Phil.

"Nothing, I've just been busy with all of this shit going on," I tell him, not divulging in too much information. He'll try to investigate somehow and end up ruining the whole thing. He knows as much as he needs to, that's the main thing.

"True dat," he says, leaning back and folding his arms across his chest.

I give him a dry look. "What's with the gangster shit?"

"Trying new shit out with Lake, see what gets her hotter," he tells me, going *way* too far.

"Too much information, bro," I choke out, rolling my eyes again.

"Nah, never too much info." He chuckles, and leans forward, his bent elbows resting on his knees.

"Shouldn't you be going home before the show starts?" I ask, hinting again for him to leave already. I've had a banging headache all day and he's only adding to it.

"No, not until you leave to take the invitation to T's," he counters.

"What?" I ask, louder than intended. He can't force me to take it. Fuck no! "I'll take it when I've got time. I'm busy at the moment."

"Now is perfect, then. I spoke to Matt before coming in here and he said you don't need to be in tonight, it's quiet."

Why do I let him out of the house? Oh yeah, because he'd end up burning it down. He nearly did it once...okay, twice, but who's counting?

"I'm not going now. It's gone ten, Max." I give him a hard look, wishing he'd just drop it.

"I knew you'd say that. She's awake. Her lights are on."

I growl, giving him a murderous glare as I stand up, my chair scraping back on the floor and hitting the shelves behind me with a thud. He'd have to have gone up her stairs to know the lights were on.

"What the fuck are you doing, staring into her house?"

"Whoa, hold up. Calm down, calm down," he says slowly, patronising me. "I went to see if she was awake before I came down here. She is, so now you don't have a choice but to go and give her that fucking invitation."

"Stop laughing, this isn't fucking funny. She probably doesn't even want to go," I grumble, feeling like an idiot for even talking about this with Max. He's the worst gossip I know, and that's saying something with Mary and Joan in my life.

"Then you're the idiot of the family, because the sexual tension is fucking scorching between the two of you. Fuck, even I had trouble keeping my dick in my pants." He chuckles then winks.

I clench my hands into fists, ready to knock him the fuck out if he talks about Teagan that way again. If it weren't for the fact that he's my brother, he'd be sprawled out on the floor already.

"Get out, Max." I sigh, grabbing some files and locking them away. I'm ready to get home, start working on the new house and go to bed. I just need to get out of this club for a bit. I feel like I've been living here lately. I'm forgetting what daylight looks like; it's always so dark and dim down here.

"Like I said, Lake won't let me leave until she sees you're going to take that invitation to Teagan. You can't get out of this."

His grin is so fucking annoying, and I know he isn't going to leave until I give in. "Fuck's sake, okay! Anything to get you out of my hair."

"That's the spirit." He grins, jumps up from his seat as I grab my jacket.

Picking up the invite off my desk, I walk out, following Max as he meets up with Lake, who is outside the door waiting for him.

"Good luck." Lake smiles widely and I roll my eyes at the little woman, ruffling her hair.

We walk out together, waving goodbye to each other when we reach the car park. Once they're out of eyesight, I run up the stairs to Teagan's two at a time. I want to get this done as quickly as possible.

Taking a deep breath, I knock on her door and wait. When no one answers right away I turn around, facing the deserted car park, debating whether or not to post it and run or if I should wait and knock again. It's late, so she most likely forgot to turn the light off and is in bed asleep. Plus, my nan always drilled it into us that it was rude to call or knock for someone past nine o'clock. I feel like I'm going to get my ass kicked.

The decision is made for me when the door swings open a little bit. When I don't see anyone, I squint in confusion, but then, sensing movement, I look down. Standing in the doorway is Faith, wearing *Frozen* pyjamas.

"Faith? Where's your mum?" I ask worriedly, wondering why Teagan is letting her five-year-old daughter open the door alone at this time of night. *What the fuck is she thinking? Any fucker could be hanging around out here.* I grit my teeth, trying to control the anger surfacing, especially when Faith still looks half asleep, not awake enough to observe any danger she might have been in had it not been me at the door.

"Superman?" She rubs her eyes with her chubby hands.

"Where's your mummy?" I ask, stepping inside and taking the girl in my arms.

"Sleeping." She yawns, resting her head on my shoulder.

I look around the immaculate room, finding Teagan curled up in a ball on the sofa, sound asleep. She looks peaceful, rested. Her mouth is hanging open slightly, her mass of her hair wild and tangled in knots around her face, yet I've never seen anyone look more beautiful.

I know I should wake her or probably just leave, but there's no way in hell I'm leaving with the possibility of Faith opening the door again.

Looking down, I reach out to wake Teagan, but pause, not having the heart to disturb her.

Light snoring turns my attention to Faith who has fallen asleep, her head resting on my shoulder. A small smile slips past my lips, my heart softening at the sight. She looks cute as hell, and completely blissful sleeping in my arms.

Torn over what to do, I glance once more at Teagan, deciding to let her sleep. Sitting down on the end of the sofa, next to her feet, I pull the blanket from off the floor, keeping Faith secured to my chest before covering them both up.

Once I know they're settled and not going to wake up, I relax back into the sofa, switching the channel on the TV to the news, promising myself I'll wake her up in a bit. It's clear she's tired if she can sleep through the television playing some Disney song, knocking at her door and her daughter getting up to open said door.

I can't help but wince, remembering how judgemental I had been when I saw Faith. I should never have questioned Teagan's parenting. From what I've seen she's a great mum, and even she deserves a break. I was a prick to rush to conclusions.

Jumping the gun is something I've grown accustomed to when it involves parents. But who could blame me with the parents I had? Hell, Denny's and Kayla's parents were just as bad.

But with Teagan, I shouldn't have thought the worst. She's a single mum working two jobs to provide for her family. And looking around the room at all the toys and books lying around, Faith is certainly taken care of. We never even got a colouring book as a child, much less a box full of toys.

With Teagan lightly snoring and Faith doing the same while cuddled to my chest, I rest my eyes, more comfortable than I've been in my entire life.

As I start to fall into a deep slumber, I can't help but notice the ache I usually carry around in my chest is gone.

FOUR

TEAGAN

My neck is painfully stiff as I stir awake from what has to have been the best night's sleep I've had in ages. I finally feel well-rested, something I've not felt since I moved out of my nan's to give Faith and me the independence we needed.

Opening my eyes, I frown. The TV is on, playing cartoons, and I realise I fell asleep last night watching *Frozen* with Faith.

Crap, Faith!

Sitting up, a scream bubbles up from the back of my throat, pure terror raging through me as I take in a man holding my daughter, his face turned away from me.

He jumps, sitting up with a frantic, concerned expression, holding a very bored-looking Faith to his chest.

"Maverick?" I whisper once I'm able to calm down enough to stop screaming. "What are you doing here?"

I blink and rub my eyes, trying to figure out if he's here or if I'm dreaming. When he's still there, looking sexy as ever, I pinch myself and wince.

Nope, still there.

He looks dazed, still half asleep and, if I'm seeing correctly, a little embarrassed.

"I—" he starts, but Faith jumps in.

"He's my friend. He came for a sleepover," she mumbles over the thumb she's sucking, her eyes glued to the TV that's playing her favourite cartoon.

A small smile curves at his lips as he shakes his head, glancing over at me. When he does, I pull the sheet up higher, wishing I could hide beneath it. I already know my hair is going to look like a bird's nest. Nothing but a shower, blow-dry and my straightener will be able to sort that mess out.

"I came by last night to give you the invite to the wedding. I've had a lot going on at the club, so I haven't had the time to bring it round. When I saw your lights were on, I thought I'd pop it in. Then this little'n opened the door," he tells me, looking down at Faith.

I gasp, staring at her, horrified and panicked. "Baby, I've told you never to open the door, *ever*. Why would you do that?" I ask, pure underling fear creeping in. I feel sick. Anything could've happened to her. Anyone from the club could have drunkenly stumbled upon the door and knocked. What was I thinking moving here, above a place where there are drunken idiots coming in and out all times of the day?

Oh yeah, it was the only place I could afford and was available at such short notice. It was also the nicest one we looked at.

"I don't remember." She smiles, not seeming the least bit bothered by my scolding or the fact that I'm hyperventilating right in front of her. I don't know whether I should yell at her and shake some sense into her or cry, thankful she's safe and okay.

"Faith, darling, you don't open the door," I tell her again, needing her to really hear me, my voice stronger.

"I won't do it again, I promise," she tells me, her eyes glued to the cartoons. "Can we have breakfast now? I didn't want to wake you. You were snoring like a grizzly bear."

"I was not snoring." I snort, my cheeks flaming when Maverick begins to chuckle.

Crap, I forgot he was here.

"Yeah, you do," he agrees, tickling Faith and making her squirm and laugh in his lap.

Ahh, I wish I was my daughter right now.

Shaking off unwanted thoughts, I look back at Maverick and cringe. "I'm so sorry. I don't normally fall asleep like that. I've just been having trouble adjusting to the move and such. I swear, nothing like this has ever happened before." My eyes water, feeling like the worst mother in history.

God, what he must think of me now. Lord only knows what he thought when she opened the door and I was carelessly sleeping.

He slides across the sofa so he's closer to me, plopping Faith down where he was sitting before. Straightening, I curl my feet under me, wiping away my tears as I do. I'm so ashamed of myself right now. I've never done anything like this before.

"Hey, don't get upset. Things like this happen every day. She was half asleep, and had she been in her bed she wouldn't have heard me knocking, so it's not something you'll need to worry about happening again. It was my own fault for turning up so late," he tells me soothingly, his voice deep and raspy from sleep.

"You could've been anyone though," I admit, revealing my worst fear. And although I don't know anything about him, I do trust him.

His jaw hardens as he thinks about what I said, probably thinking the worst like me. He looks over to the door, his mind seeming to be working something over as he inspects every inch of it.

"I'm going to put a chain on the door which will be out of Faith's reach. I know it won't stop her from opening the door, but at least it will stop people from entering."

"You don't need to do that. I can go out today and get one myself," I tell him quietly, wishing I thought of doing it. We have a camera outside of our door already. It was there before we moved in, so putting in added security didn't even cross my mind, if I'm honest.

"No, I'll do it. It's another reason why I came by. I wanted to check the place out and see if there's anything I can do inside. The place was renovated last year, but I never thought to ask about childproofing. It was never intended for a child to move into," he admits.

I can understand that. If it weren't for the fact that this was the only place I could find and afford, Faith and I would have found somewhere just out of the town centre, somewhere with a garden she could play in.

Most bar owners raise their kids above pubs, so it's not like it can't be done. I guess I just want a safer environment for Faith to grow up in. Our last place was definitely not that, so this is a step up, at least.

"That's really kind of you." I smile, trying to tuck my untamed hair behind my ear but it just springs free.

One thing I'm glad about is the fact that I didn't have time to get ready for bed last night. I literally fell asleep in the clothes I was wearing yesterday. If he had seen me again in my normal bedtime attire—which is usually a white tank top, braless and only wearing a pair of boxer shorts—I would've died.

"Food," Faith grumbles as she mindlessly strokes her nose using the same hand she's sucking her thumb with. I've never been able to get her out of the dirty habit. And believe me I've tried. "Mavy is hungry too." She looks at me with an adorable, hopeful expression.

Maverick chuckles, his eyes crinkling at the corners as he looks at Faith, his expression soft.

"Would you like to stay for breakfast?" I wring my hands together nervously, trying to keep my gaze on him, but it's so hard when he's so incredibly hot this early in the morning.

"Um...," he starts, looking a little sheepish.

I'm still in shock at waking up and finding him asleep on the sofa with us. I don't think my heart has calmed down since, but I admit that it does feel good having him here, scare and all.

"Yes, we want bacon," Faith cheers, answering for him. I chuckle, biting my bottom lip.

"I guess that's a yes. Can I use your bathroom?" he asks politely.

"Of course you can, it's down—" I stop, grinning when I realise he already knows where the bathroom is.

Out of nowhere he reaches out for me, his fingers brushing along my cheek before tucking a wayward strand of hair behind my ear. My breath catches in my throat. Getting lost in his eyes once again, I feel the world around me come to a stop. Why does he have to be so goddamn gorgeous? I feel like I'd have a chance with him if he weren't. And knowing how incredibly sweet and gentle he can be isn't helping lessen the attraction.

"Bacon," Faith whines, breaking whatever spell Maverick and I were just under. I hadn't even realised either of us had moved, but somehow in our daze we ended up closer, our breaths mingling together as one.

"I'll, um, be back in a minute." I watch him jump up like his ass is on fire.

He's probably just realised he was about to make a huge mistake. I mean, it's not like he could be interested in someone like me.

Blowing out a breath, I get up, making sure to give Faith her good morning kiss before heading over to the kitchen. The first thing I do is flick the kettle on, craving my morning coffee. I don't know how anyone can function without having at least two cups once they get up. It's like a passage of life. You're just plain freaking weird in my book if you don't drink it.

Next, I pull out all the ingredients for mine and Faith's traditional Sunday breakfast, getting extra for Maverick. Ever since Faith was able to chew solid food, we've had a full English breakfast every Sunday. My girl has a thing for bacon, so there are times in the week when I have to make her bacon on toast. Nan blames it on the cravings I had when I was pregnant. I literally lived off bacon, eating it morning, noon, and night.

While everything's cooking, I go over to the cupboard and pull out two mugs just as Maverick finishes up in the bathroom. He walks in looking fresher, more awake and alert than he did going in.

"Coffee?"

"Please." He grins, coming to stand close, watching me move around the kitchen. Once it's done I hand him his drink before taking a sip of mine, making sure to blow enough to cool it down. A loud moan escapes my lips as the bitterness hits the back of my throat, causing my whole body to relax. There's nothing quite like the taste of fresh coffee first thing in the morning.

A throat clearing snaps me out of my coffee orgasm. I open my eyes to find Maverick's on me, a predatory gleam in them.

Good God, I'm in trouble.

"Sorry, I love coffee," I mumble, taking another sip. This time I keep the pleasure to myself, moaning on the inside.

"Anything I can help you with?" he asks, clearing his throat again as he turns to face the sink. That's when the lower half of him catches my attention, a fierce blush flames my cheeks as I take in the huge bulge straining the front of his jeans.

Dear Lord, he looks bigger than he did the other day when I caught a glimpse. How is that possible?

Tripping over my own feet, I just catch myself in time, feeling my face burning hotter than before. "Um, can you... can you watch this for a second and make sure it doesn't burn while I go freshen up?" I stammer, needing to put some distance between us.

"No problem," he says, keeping a close eye on me, causing a shiver to run through my body.

Forcing a smile, I rush away, practically running out of the room and down the small hallway that leads to the bedroom and downstairs bathroom.

My room is on the second floor, up a flight of stairs that reminds me of bookshelves, just tilted a little. Joining my room is an en suite with a small shower. The place isn't big, but it's enough for me and Faith. In fact, it's perfect for the two of us.

When I get into the bathroom I nearly die from embarrassment. Yesterday morning, Nan picked Faith up to give me time to clean up and get ready for the day. Since I had already cleaned up, I decided to spend the free time I had relaxing in the tub with a long hot bath. I left in a hurry when I realised how long I'd been soaking, leaving my dirty clothes in a heap on the bathroom floor.

So not only has Maverick now seen me in my pyjamas, braless, and woken up next to me looking like the bride of Chucky, but he also saw yesterday's washing. Meaning he saw the Hello Kitty boxers I wear for comfort.

Today just keeps getting better and better.

Throwing my hair up in a bun, I make quick work of washing my face and brushing my teeth before reluctantly leaving the sanctuary of the bathroom.

The smell of food hits me as soon as the door opens and my stomach rumbles, although thankfully not in hearing range of Maverick. I think I've already reached my embarrassment quota for the day.

"Hey, it's nearly done." He smiles, rolling the sausages over in the frying pan.

"You cook?" I squeak, noticing he's loaded the second frying pan with bacon and has the egg pan heating. He's also broken some eggs into a jug to make Faith's scrambled eggs.

He has to have some kind of flaw. He has to. No one can be this perfect. It's so frustrating.

"Hey, fed up of cartoons?" I ask my daughter, who's moved from the living area to the breakfast bar. Usually I have to drag her away from the television pouting and whining, but she seems happy enough to watch Maverick cook. Can't say I blame her either; it's a sight to behold.

"Maverick is going to let me meet his niece, Hope, one day soon," she tells me, smiling wide.

"Faith and Hope, huh? What are the odds?" Maverick muses, winking at me, and I blush. It's still bizarre seeing him look so carefree. He usually has worry lines around his eyes and a stony expression, making him unapproachable, but it's like I'm seeing a new him.

Either that or he's just really a morning person. Which is the worst kind of person. Nobody should be that cheerful in the morning.

I gave Faith her name because it's all I had when I was alone, scared, and worried for my youth. I hate thinking of where my life would be right now had I not had faith, or if I hadn't moved in with my nan when I did. It's something I don't like to think about.

I chuckle, moving to help Maverick with the food. "How old is your niece?"

"Sit down. I'll cook." He gently moves me out of the way. My mouth drops open and my skin burns from the small contact. "And she turned one last year."

"It's fine. I can help," I tell him, waving him off.

"Oh no, you don't." He grins and before I know what's happening, I'm up in the air, squealing when he effortlessly lifts me. Carrying me over to Faith, he plops me down on the stool next her. "Stay put. Let me cook." He winks, and I stop breathing altogether.

I'm too stunned to speak, so instead I sit staring at him in bewilderment as he moves through the kitchen, putting together our breakfasts with ease and grace.

By the time he's setting the plates down in front of us and taking his own seat opposite me, I'm a blathering mess. My heart is going crazy, and I'm pretty sure I'm turned on just from watching him cook. Him being domestic in my space stirs something deep inside me, something I've never felt before, and it scares me a little. I feel the beginning of an obsession coming on; it won't be long until he becomes someone I crave, something I need to breathe. He's already consuming my every waking thought and I've barely known him five minutes.

"So, there are three of you?" I ask, finally finding my voice and bringing up a safe topic for conversation.

He finishes chewing his food before answering. "No, there are five of us. I'm the eldest. Mason, the one who's getting married, is two years younger than me. Then there's Malik and the twins."

"Twins?" I ask, wondering where Max fits in. I'm sure he said they were brothers. Maybe they're step-brothers. There is no way on this earth that someone could survive if there were two of Max, surely.

I look at Maverick, noticing he doesn't have any grey hair, so there has to be an easier explanation. Maybe they gag Max and lock him in the basement when they're home, or maybe they let him out in public to get his weird behaviour off his chest before he goes home.

"Oh, Max and Myles. They're the youngest of us all," he explains.

"Twins?" I ask again, my eyes widening in horror.

"Yeah," he says, slower this time. He raises his eyebrows as if begging me to ask him again.

"There're two of Max?" *How the hell has he survived this long? The man deserves a medal.*

I'd normally at this time ask about his parents at this point, but I already know from when I asked Lake about something Max said in the interview to me that their parents weren't good people, and that they were raised by their granddad in the end.

"Yeah." He nods, a slow grin forming on his handsome face.

"How the hell did you survive this long?" I ask in all seriousness, beginning to wonder if he's actually a god and not someone who just looks like one.

He laughs, throwing his head back. I watch fascinated by the way his throat bobs up and down and the way his eyes crinkle at the corners; it's downright sexy.

"Myles is nothing like Max. Yeah, they look alike, but they're nothing alike."

"Maxy? I love Maxy. More bacon, please?" Faith mumbles around her food, tomato sauce all over her mouth.

I giggle and grab a towel to wipe it off, laughing when she tries to slap my hands away to stop me.

"Here, have mine." Maverick chuckles, transferring some of his bacon onto her plate.

There's a knock at the door and my eyes widen a little when I see what the time is.

Oh no! Please no!

Shit!

How the hell could I forget what day it is? Oh yeah, I know. It's because Tall, Dark and Dangerous has been playing house, filling my head with so many wild fantasies that I managed to forget my own name.

Damn Maverick!

"I'm really sorry for everything that's about to happen. I promise, she's okay normally," I warn Maverick briefly, leaving him looking confused. "I'm sorry."

With that, I jump off the stool and run to the front door. If I leave it unanswered I wouldn't put it past Tish to break the door down. She's always loved making an entrance, but she hates being ignored.

Opening the door, Tish barges her way in without looking up. Before I can warn her that we have company, she's opening her big mouth. I cringe, knowing what's coming; she's asked every time she's seen or spoken to me.

"You fucked that delicious landlord of yours yet?" She grins as she walks past me, towards the kitchen.

Someone shoot me, please.

Tish stops suddenly when she hears a strangled cough. I stumble into her back, groaning loudly when I realise Maverick just heard her.

"Tish," I warn, but there's no stopping her.

"Holy fucking crap! You move on quickly, my girl," she booms, waggling her eyebrows over her shoulder at me and grinning. "And who are you, hot stuff?" she flirts as she walks over to the breakfast bar. I stomp my foot, wishing the earth would swallow me whole, already wanting this day to be over.

"The delicious landlord?" He grins, looking at me and not Tish. His eyes are twinkling, a smouldering look aimed my way. For some reason, the fact that he's looking at me at all comforts me, boosting my confidence. Usually when people meet Tish, they never glance my way. I'm the one they normally ignore, the duff of the group. Normally I'm happy with that, but if Maverick had begun flirting back with her, it would've hurt, more than I care to admit.

"Oh God," I moan out loud, my face heating with embarrassment.

Tish turns around again, giving me a wink and mouthing "So hot" before turning back to the table and eyeing Maverick once again. "Hey little human," she greets, kissing my daughter's cheek.

"Hey, Aunt Tish," Faith returns, chewing her food.

"So, didn't take long." Tish grins, eyeing me and Maverick once I take my seat. I cringe when she sits next to him, taking his cup of coffee like they're old friends. Tish has no filter. She doesn't care what anyone thinks of her, and she has the confidence of twenty people, I swear. She's harmless though.

"Tish, *please* shut up," I beg, but it falls on death ears.

"So, how she do? Any cobwebs?" she asks Maverick.

"Tish!" I shout, covering my daughter's ears whilst contemplating the best way to kill my best friend.

Maverick chokes on his food, eyeing Tish like she's crazy before glancing at me, raising his eyebrows in a way that makes me melt. Why does he have to look so sexy all the time? Can't he have a mole on his face or a spot or two so I can at least point *something* out? I can't even pretend he has a small penis because I've seen the bulge he's packing and there's *nothing* small about it.

"I'm sorry," I tell him again, wincing when Tish begins to laugh. I give her a warning look but she ignores me, turning to Maverick with a wide smile.

"So... you gonna speak or keep ignoring me?" she asks, grabbing a slice of bacon off Faith's plate.

"Stop it! Maverick made this for me," Faith yells, slapping Tish's hand away, and I giggle. I love the way she says "Maverick"; it comes out "Mav-rick." It's adorable, and by the way his eyes soften when he looks down at my daughter, I believe he thinks so too.

"I've got to get going. It was... interesting meeting you," he says, giving Tish a wary look.

"I'm not nice," she scoffs, pulling his plate in front of her before digging in.

He looks at her with wide eyes, making me and Faith giggle openly. He looks so carefree in that moment; it makes my heart melt more towards him.

"It's okay, Maverick. Aunt Tish is cuckoo crazy." Faith giggles again, wiggling in her seat.

"I'll take your word for it." He chuckles, kissing the top of her head. I'm caught off guard by the open show of affection, and if Maverick's expression has anything to go by, he's just as surprised by his actions. "See you later, squirt."

"I'll walk you out," I tell him warily, feeling like we're actually doing the walk of shame.

"See you *later*." Tish winks suggestively and Maverick just shakes his head at her. When he reaches me, he takes my hand, startling me.

I jump when I feel his breath on my neck. "Don't let her and Max in the same room together. I predict trouble," he whispers, making me laugh. I never thought of Tish being anything like Max, but now he's said that, I can't help but compare the two.

She's always been Tish to me, my best friend. Her attitude, her reactions to certain situations and her personality are what makes her so amazing. And I love her for it. A lot of people judge her, thinking she's rude and stuck-up, but she's far from it. She's the most caring person I know; you just have to be on her good side to see it.

Now I can understand why no one batted an eye when Max asked me all of those ridiculous questions in the interview. Max wouldn't be Max if he didn't do the things he did. It actually makes me feel guilty for judging him.

"I won't," I promise, grinning.

"Good." He smiles. "Oh, here, I didn't get a chance to give it to you." He hands me a grey and silver invitation and I stare, stunned.

He's really taking me to the wedding. *Us* to the wedding, I should say.

My cheeks heat as I take the invitation, our fingers brushing together. My belly flutters at the contact. Something tells me that my body will always react this way when it comes to him. I haven't decided whether that's a good or bad thing yet.

"You really don't need to take us if you don't want to," I murmur, secretly hoping he still wants to.

He looks at me for a second, seeming hesitant about something. "No. I want to." He smiles, looking away. "More now than ever," he mumbles before turning back to me. The intense look we share causes my breath to hitch, and I wonder if he meant for me to hear that last part or not. It's hard to get a read on him.

"Okay." I nod, my hands shaking slightly.

"I'll see you later." He grins, leaning forward and kissing my forehead. Pulling away, he frowns a little before shaking his head, clearing the frown lines away.

"Bye," I tell him quietly, still stunned. I keep watching long after he leaves. It isn't until Tish walks up, slamming the door shut in front of me, that I come back to the present, struggling to catch my breath and get my fluttering stomach under control.

One look at Tish and I know I'm in for it. "Don't," I warn her. Before she can lecture me, I rush up to my room to get dressed, ignoring her peals of laughter behind me whilst I curse her under my breath the whole way.

FIVE

MAVERICK

"STOP!" MASON BOOMS, STARTLING me. Turning around in a daze, I pin him with a murderous glare.

"What?" I growl, looking around the bathroom, trying to figure out what's got him so worked up.

"You just nearly hammered into a fucking water pipe, you dickhead. What the hell has gotten into you? I told you that wall had water pipes inside it and you completely ignored me," he scolds, looking pissed.

Glancing back to the wall in question, I sigh. I drew up the plans, so I knew where the plumbing was located. I mentally scold myself, feeling even more agitated than I did before I started. I've just been lost in my own head, a tornado of thoughts swirling around.

Mostly of Teagan.

"Sorry, everything with the club is just getting to me," I grouch, sitting down on the toilet seat. I'm only half lying, but I don't want to tell him that my new tenant is driving me crazy.

I've not been able to get her out my head and I've been messing everything up because of it, from drink orders to remembering my own name. I have to talk myself out of finding more excuses to go round and see her. I've already fitted the new locks and made sure the windows all have child safety latches on them. I went a little overboard and even bought plug covers, plus fridge, cupboard, drawers and door locks, making sure I covered everything. The only thing I didn't get was a stair gate. I wasn't sure what they achieved, and when I asked Denny if Teagan would need one for Faith, she said she was old enough to climb over them or open it herself.

Telling my brothers about her will just make things worse; they'll tease me relentlessly until I ask her out for real. It wouldn't be a bad thing, but I just don't know what I could possibly offer her. She has a daughter, and if Teagan and I were to date, then Faith will be involved. I can't do that to her, because when I fuck up—which I will, I guarantee it—it means Faith getting hurt in the process. And the thought of Faith hurting because of me is indescribable. The squirt has already found a way under my skin, much like her drop-dead-gorgeous mother.

"I know you're lying. Whatever it is, you need to work it out and soon. I get married in a week and we've got loads to fucking do until then. Between Harlow and Denny, I'm about to lose my shit, so I'm counting on you to keep it together."

I chuckle and get up to finish screwing the blind in, this time in the right place. "What have they done now?"

"What *haven't* they done, you mean? We need to get these houses sorted already. Harlow wants to revamp the old house too so that it feels like it's theirs and not all of ours still."

"You decorated yours and Denny's to suit her so she would feel at home. That's all Harlow wants. You can't blame her for that," I tell him. "What has Denny done?"

"Moaning at me to get the houses done because she can't listen to Harlow bitch much longer." He chuckles.

"Food has arrived," Max shouts from the next floor down before we hear him stomp his way down the stairs.

"Thank the gods," Mason mutters cryptically, following Max downstairs. I quickly finish the blind before going after them.

The house is a decent size. Downstairs you have the front room, dining room and kitchen, set up pretty much like Joan's house, only here we have a downstairs toilet under the stairs instead of a storage room.

On the first floor there are two rooms and a bathroom, and on the third floor are two other rooms, one with an en suite, which is the room I'll be in. I'll have the whole top floor to myself. Max and Myles each wanted the rooms on the first floor, nearer the kitchen—Max's words.

Kayla meets me on the first floor, walking out of hers and Myles's room. I'm thrilled to bits that she'll be moving in with us. When they broke the news to me and Max, I could have done a happy dance. One thing I've learnt about my brothers since they've been in relationships is that they keep their shit clean when the girls stay over. Now that she'll be living with us, I'm hoping I won't have to live in a pigsty anymore. Hopefully it'll also force the twins to start acting like the mature adults I raised them to be.

The other reason I'm grateful she'll be here is because of her dad. As much as the fucker has tried to make amends with her after her mother tried to kill her and he was blind to the abuse, he still neglects her, both as a person and as a daughter. Kayla needs people around her who will support and love her no matter how alone she likes to be at times. I've picked up on it a lot since she started staying over more. She's more relaxed with us than she is at the mention of going home to her dad's place, where he's moved his new girlfriend in.

"Hey." She grins, waving at me.

"You still painting?" I ask with a raised eyebrow. I thought they'd finished decorating yesterday and that the kitchen was the only room left to paint. It's the room that needed the most work. The dirty scumbags who lived here before us made sure to leave as much damage as possible. Luckily for us, the previous owner knocked the price down, covering the cost of the work that needed to be done.

"Yeah." She sighs. "We decided to put up wallpaper instead and it went wrong."

"What am I missing?" I glance over grinning as we make our way downstairs.

"We couldn't line the wallpaper up. The flowers ended up looking deformed, so now we're painting again." She giggles, shaking her head. "Myles kept losing his temper with it and ended up just shredding all the paper."

Laughing at the image of Myles losing his temper, we head into the front room. The laughter dies in my throat as I walk into in to World War Three.

"But I ordered the bucket for myself," Max growls, looking down at Harlow, who's sitting on our new sofa, her rounded stomach sticking out like a sore thumb. It looks like a football has been shoved under her top. If the poor girl gets any bigger I'm worried she won't be able to stand without tipping forward.

"So? I'm hungry, and I want chicken," Harlow snaps, pulling the KFC bucket box towards her.

"It's mine." Max growls, pulling it back. "You have two meals, extra popcorn chicken and corn on the cob. *And* you ate not even an hour ago."

"I want some chicken," she repeats angrily.

"Lake, tell her," Max whines, looking at his girlfriend with puppy dog eyes.

"Let her have the chicken," Malik seethes, trying to step between them.

"No. I'm hungry."

"It's an eight-piece chicken bucket, Max," Denny tells him. She looks frustrated—at who, I'm not entirely sure.

"I'm hungry," Max growls again, pulling the bucket harder so it falls out of Harlow's grip.

Oh shit!

Tears fill Harlow's eyes and Malik shoves Max out the way, giving him a murderous look.

"Ah crap." Max grabs a chicken leg out of the box, shoving it in his trap. I roll my eyes and take a seat on the floor next to the fireplace, watching everything play out. It's what I do; I watch everything that happens and when the time is needed, I intervene.

"I just want some food." Harlow sniffles and my body tenses, hearing her sound so broken.

"Max," I warn, giving him a pointed look, my voice holding authority.

"What?" he yells, throwing his hands up in frustration.

"Here, have mine," Malik offers, handing her his meal box.

"No. I want *that* box," she yells through a broken sob, pointing to the box Max is clutching to his chest.

"I've got some chicken. Here, have mine." Lake smiles softly at Harlow as she holds out her box of chicken.

"I want *that* chicken," she sobs.

Malik, clearly finding it hard to see her so upset, gets up and snatches the box out of Max's grip. Harlow's head jerks up, taking the bucket of chicken quickly before Max has a chance to take it back from her. She guards it with her life as she hugs it to her chest, wasting no time in eating her chicken. She sighs blissfully, her tears subsiding.

"Malik!" Max yells, moving forward to get his food.

"No, eat this," Malik snaps, handing him his meal box.

"Fuck's sake," Max mumbles, moving to sit next to Lake as he sulks. She pats his leg, smiling slyly behind her burger.

"Is that better? Do you want anything else?" Malik asks gently, rubbing Harlow's shoulder.

Sniffling, Harlow wipes her nose on her sleeve before looking up at Malik with wide, watery eyes. "Is there any coleslaw?"

Malik glances around the room, searching in various bags, and I grin when I see Max trying to hide the tub of coleslaw behind him when he thinks no one is looking. Malik sees and narrows his eyes.

"No. Fuck no!" Max snaps, giving Malik a death glare.

"Max," Malik snarls, holding his hand out.

Lake's quick, snatching it from behind Max's back. I nearly choke on my food at Max's wounded expression.

"Here you go, babe," Malik soothes, moving over to sit next to Harlow. Her mouth is stuffed with food, the bucket of chicken resting on her stomach and a meal box on her knees. She gives Malik one of her adorable smiles, her eyes glistening with tears.

Denny laughs, shaking her head. "The way you're eating, you'd think you were having triplets."

"I'm not fat," Harlow cries, throwing her chicken bone in the box, looking angry. "I am eating for two."

"Yeah, and the way you act, you'd think it was *my* fault," Max mumbles, still in a sour mood over his stolen food.

"I'm just hungry," she defends, stuffing her mouth.

"Yeah, for *my* food. You've done nothing but eat all of *my* food. Don't think I didn't know it was you who ate my chocolate gâteau from the fridge."

"I had one slice." The glare she sends him signifies his death.

"It was a whole cake, Harlow. It wasn't in slices," Max says, exclaims.

She shrugs, not seeming to care. I've always loved listening to them argue back and forth like this. I miss most of it because I work long hours. When I get the rundown later on, it's not the same.

"And it's not just *your* food," Myles laughs.

"Yes it is," Max responds, ducking behind his box to eat his takeaway, making sure Harlow can't see.

"No it's not," Malik tells him dryly, rolling his eyes.

"*Yes*, it fucking *is*. This morning Joan made us *all* breakfast, but Harlow didn't want her plate, she wanted *mine*. It had a few extra hash browns, that was all. She could have asked Joan for more or gotten some, but no! She had to have *my* food. In the end I had to sneak some extra hash browns off the side. I could have starved."

"Stop being dramatic," Malik snaps, defending Harlow who has started sniffling again.

"I'm just so hungry," she tells everyone apologetically.

"You're eating for three. Of course you're hungry," I tell her gently. She beams over at me, looking grateful.

"She doesn't need to eat my food though. I've lost so much weight. I'm skin and bones. People are gonna start thinking I'm neglected. Even Lake's mom noticed how much weight I'm losing," Max barks, trying to sound hard done by.

Lake nods, laughing. "No, she says that about everyone. She likes making you her beef stew."

"That sounds yummy," Harlow moans, her eyes wide with hunger. I burst out laughing when Max looks ready to cry.

"See?" Max yells, glancing around the room.

"Sit down and eat," I tell him, trying to breathe through my laughter.

"Does anyone have any more popcorn chicken?" Harlow mumbles, looking around the room. Everyone's eyes go to Max, and we all laugh when we see him tipping the whole box into his mouth before Malik has a chance to snatch it from him.

When the laughter dies down, I turn to Mason. "Are we still closing the bar for the wedding?" I ask, double-checking so I can let Matt know.

"Yeah, I was gonna tell Matt to put up an announcement in the window tonight so people know beforehand."

"Oh, Evan called earlier asking if I'd seen you. I forgot to mention it. He said to call him as soon as you can," Denny tells me, interrupting the conversation.

"Cheers," I say, forcing a smile as I grab my phone out of my pocket.

MAVERICK: Denny said you called. Can't talk right now, I'm at home. Was it important?

A few minutes pass before Evan replies, my phone beeping with a message alert.

EVAN: Yeah. Meet me at the club tonight, around nine. I've got some work shit to sort out before I can get to you. See you later.

MAVERICK: Is everything okay?

MAX: hu u txtin?

I groan, giving Max an exasperated look. He shrugs before eyeing my phone, demanding me to answer.

MAVERICK: Evan. Why the fuck are you texting me? We're in the same fucking room.

MAX: I'm worried Harlow will wnt 2 eat me nxt if she keeps hearing me voice.

MAVERICK: You're a fucking weirdo. And will you spell fucking properly. You were brought up, not dragged up.

MAX: I don't know. If memory serves me correctly, I was dragged around a lot. LOL Is dat betta?

MAVERICK: You aren't funny. And you were only dropped on the head a few times.

EVAN: Yeah, but it is urgent. I think I have a plan.

MAX: Did me good then since I'm better-looking than you ugly fuckers.

MAVERICK: Myles looks just like you! Twat. And I'm not sure. You're texting me when we're in the same fucking room.

MAX: HAHA but you're replying so wat's dat say bout u?

"Who the hell are you texting with a grin on your face? You look scary," Lake tells Max, and I burst out laughing.

"Your mum. She told me to wear those silk boxers to bed tonight," he tells her, winking.

"Eww, you dickhead. That's gross." Lake scrunches her face up in disgust, sliding away from him.

"Not what you said last night," he teases, pulling her to his side.

"Oh my God, I meant the whole mum part," she laughs.

"Ah, I knew you thought I was sexy in those boxers." He chuckles, playfully kissing the tip of her nose.

I look away, shaking my head. I don't think he'll ever be right in the head but for some reason, you can always count on Max to cheer you up.

Now I just have to make it until nine tonight without killing him so I can see what the hell Evan wants.

I LOOK AT THE STACKS of files piled on my desk and sigh in frustration. One of my staff could very well be selling drugs laced with some chemical that's killing the people taking them, and I can't for the life of me figure out who would do such a thing. Every staff member went through full background checks before I hired them. I made sure their credentials were all up to date and interviewed each and every one of them myself. But still, it was one of them. Their file is sitting there in front of me, taunting me.

Matt peeks his head around the door, a grim look on his face, knowing I'm not in the mood for any more bullshit where the club's concerned.

"What's up?" I ask, closing the file I was looking at.

"Laura Ashley is here to see you," he tells me, his expression unreadable.

"Who?" I scrunch my brows together as I try to put the name to a face, coming up blank.

"The girl of the dude who died," he whisper-yells, looking apologetic.

My eyes widen and I gesture for him to let her come in. None of the other victims' families have come here, but I think that has more to do with the fact that they aren't sure where their sons or daughters died.

"Laura." I greet her when she appears in the doorway, getting up and gesturing for her to take a seat. She's wearing a baggy hoody far too big for her small frame, so I can only presume it belongs to the deceased boyfriend. Her eyes are red and swollen, and she sniffles as she takes a seat, glancing around nervously. "Can I get you something? A drink?"

Matt leaves, giving me one last apologetic look before closing the door behind him.

"No. No, thank you," she chokes out, a few tears escaping and rolling down her cheeks. "I... I don't know why I came. It's stupid, really. I guess I just wanted you to know that Luke, he wasn't a druggie. He never touched them, not even as a teen."

"I didn't think he was," I whisper gently, hating that this woman is so distraught over something one of *my* staff members did, something we could have prevented if we could just figure out who it is.

As much as I don't trust women, seeing one of them upset guts me. I just wish there was something I could do make her feel better, to take away her pain.

"He didn't even want to go to the stupid stag party, but they made him. He doesn't drink much. The most he could handle was half a pint." She chuckles sadly, her eyes tearing up and looking distant for a second. "But the police, they said... they said he bought them. The drugs, I mean. Please, I need you to help me prove that he didn't, that one of the lads with him spiked his drink or something."

"Laura, I don't.... The police are doing everything they can."

"No, they're not," she snaps furiously. "They have the tapes from that night but said they can't see anything incriminating. I've asked and pleaded with them to let me look at the tapes to see if I can find anything, but they keep refusing."

I hold my hand up to stop her, realising where she's heading with this. "Laura, I don't have the tapes," I lie. "The police are the only ones with a copy. Let them do their job, and I promise you they'll find out what happened to Luke. We're working non-stop to make sure this doesn't happen again. In the meantime, go home and get some rest." I soften my voice by the end, knowing she needs to be handled with care.

She nods, rubbing at her tired eyes. "Okay. Please, just.... Please get to the bottom of it."

Seeing her crumble is killing me. No one should have to go through this much pain. When she gets up, I follow, walking her to the door where we bump into Evan.

"Oh hey, I didn't realise you had company." He looks at Laura with worried eyes. "Is everything okay?"

"This is Laura. She's the girlfriend of the young man who recently passed away," I tell him, giving him a look to not question it any further.

"I better go," Laura mumbles.

We watch her go with matching worried expressions. "Is she going to be okay?" he asks, reading my mind.

"No idea," I tell him honestly, walking back into my office and taking a seat. "She's really torn up over her boyfriend. All of this is starting to piss me off. It's been months and no matter how hard we try, this fucker keeps slipping through our fingers. All of the bouncers are on watch, but now it's making me wonder if it's one of them."

"About that.... It's not one of the doormen," Evan sighs.

"How do you know?" I ask, sitting up straighter.

"Because when I went over their background checks, I also spoke to their old bosses. They all said how good each one was at getting the riff-raff out of their clubs. Also, your main doorman was a Marine. Can you really see someone with honour killing innocent people with drugs, for money?"

"True. I just feel like we're missing something big."

"That's because we are," he admits gruffly, looking as tired and frustrated over the whole thing as I am.

"Stop talking in fucking riddles," I snap before sighing. "Sorry."

"No, it's okay. I don't have all the answers yet, but I do know there's a bigger picture we're not seeing. From what I could find out, there's someone new in town who owes some bigger dealer a lot of money. Whoever it is has managed to get a hold of more drugs from another dealer, local in town, and has started selling drugs again. But because they owe so much money, they're diluting everything with poisonous shit to make a profit."

"How does my club fit in? I mean, if this dealer owes a chunk of money and is new in town, then it can't be one of my staff." I sigh, wishing life would just give me a fucking break.

"I don't know how your club fits in, Mav, but if I had to guess, I'd say whoever is involved in selling the drugs either needs the money or is being blackmailed. They might just be related to whoever is doing it and they're selling inside as a favour. I don't fucking know. It's driving me insane not knowing, that's for sure. It's never taken me this long to solve a case, not one that should be straightforward and simple."

"I know how you feel." I groan. "I've got so much shit going on that I could've missed something vital. I've read these staff files over and over again, and nothing is popping out to me. There have been four new employees, all of whom were recommended and had background checks, but they seem fine. No problems."

"Which is why I think you should get someone in here to look over the girls. You need someone who can keep an eye on them."

"The police said exactly the same thing, but it's finding someone I trust to help. I can't use members of my family because everyone here already knows about them. They won't let their guard down if one or more of my family is here looking shifty."

"Kennedy said there's a new tenant living above the club. Denny mentioned her when she visited the other day. Do you think she has anything to do with this?"

Leaning forward, my jaw clenches, my voice hard and cold when I speak. "She has fuck all to do with any of this. Keep her out of it."

"Whoa! Hold the fucking phone. I didn't mean any harm. Sheesh, I didn't even think you knew her that well."

Feeling bad, I grunt, getting up and pouring us both a whiskey before sitting back down. "Sorry. I'm just strung up tight. No, she hasn't got anything to do with this. She has a daughter and from what I've seen, there's no reason for her to sell drugs. And she's not the kind of mum who would have that shit around her child."

"Hmm," he mumbles, looking deep in thought. I leave him to his thoughts for a few seconds, waiting for him to carry on. "Would she think about coming in for a few hours a night? No one here knows her, right? And if they have seen her, then they'll know she lives upstairs."

"Not many people know about her. They know someone moved in upstairs, but I don't think anyone has really seen her. I could ask," I tell him. I only want to ask for selfish reasons, needing to spend more time with her. It's also because Evan is right; we need someone who my staff haven't seen hanging around me. If anyone does question our friendship, then we have the tenant-landlord relationship as a cover.

"Ask her and let me know. I need to get back. Kennedy hasn't been feeling well."

"All right. I'll see you at the wedding. You'll meet Teagan then since Max has forced us into going together," I tell him, not admitting I'm glad Max did his weird shit where he gets his own way because it meant I get to take her out without feeling any pressure.

"Ah, so it's true." He chuckles, knocking his knuckles on the table. "Don't forget to let me know what's been decided. In the meantime I'm going to keep asking around, find out if anyone knows who this new dealer is. Maybe then we'll find a link from them to someone on your staff and finally put a stop to all of these deaths."

"True. Speak to you later." I nod, letting him walk himself out.

Once he's gone, I pull another file off the pile and settle back in my chair, reading through it.

I have to find something in one of these; otherwise, we've got nothing, and whoever this is will get away with it.

One of these files has to give us a clue on who is doing this.

People are dying.

Innocent people.

One way or another, I'm getting to the bottom of this. The fucker better pray it's the police who finds him first and not me.

SIX

TEAGAN

"My boobs are practically bursting out of this fucking dress," I snap at Tish, who stands there chuckling and shaking her head in amusement over my discomfort. I'm so nervous about today that I'm actually shaking and close to throwing up.

"You look real pretty, Mummy," Faith says, smiling as she twirls around in her puffy princess dress.

"So do you, sweetheart," I tell her, returning her smile before looking back to the mirror, fussing with my dress and frowning.

Tish made me go shopping with her on Thursday for a dress to wear to the wedding. I told her I was happy wearing a simple maxi dress, but she wouldn't hear any of it. When she threw a bunch at me, telling me to try them on, I dismissed every single one.

Defeated, we had come home empty-handed. But Tish, being a sly little dog, went back to the store and got me the dress I'd profusely refused, no matter how much she told me I looked stunning in it.

"It's supposed to look like that, you goof." She chuckles, adding another pin in my hair. The bottom part of the gown is filled with layers and layers of light, soft cotton voile. There's a split up one leg, leaving the rest to flow elegantly around me. The top half is thicker with glittered sequins and silver straps, the material dipping low between my breasts. I've topped it off with silver strappy sandals, the heel higher than I'm used to.

The one thing I do adore about my appearance, and actually agree with, is my hair. Tish has managed to curl the thick mass into loose waves, pinning it up into a messy bun before adding a silver headband with diamonds to it. It looks beautiful, especially with the natural-looking make-up she's applied. There's a little blush to my cheeks and dark, silver-shadowed eyes, providing a smoky effect.

"You sure it's not too much?" I ask, hating that I'll be flashing my cleavage all day and night.

"You think it's too much cleavage because you're not used to having those beauties out, but believe me, it doesn't look skanky. It's elegant and you really do look beautiful, girl. Listen to Tish. She knows all," she insists. "Plus, now you're defo gonna be gettin' some lovin'."

"What's lovin'?" Faith asks when she stops spinning. Her curls bounce around her face, sitting nicely at the small of her back. I added a butterfly headband, which probably won't stay on her head longer than five minutes.

"It's when your mum and—"

"It means snuggles. It means Mummy is going to get loads of snuggles off you today." I smile at Faith then glare at Tish who just laughs at my explanation.

"I love you Mummy," Faith squeals, happy with my answer.

"I love you too, bug. Now go get your shoes on. Maverick will be here any minute." My palms are sweating as nerves begin to sink in again.

"Calm down before you start to stink," Tish scolds. "You'll be fine. Plus, you have the little human to divert any unwanted attention. They'll be too busy 'oohing' and 'ahing' to even notice you."

I give her the finger before putting in my earrings, completing the outfit. Although I hate having my cleavage on show, I do have to admit that I feel empowered, sexy. I've never had a reason to get dressed up like this before, so it's refreshing.

"Mummy, someone's at the door. You told me I couldn't answer it, remember," Faith yells from downstairs.

I give Tish a scared, wide-eyed look, but she shakes my shoulders, ignoring my heavy breathing and my obvious panic.

"You're going to be fine. Stop panicking. Now let's go check him out in a suit. My panties are already wet thinking about it." She sighs dreamily and I slap her arm, astonished by her crudeness.

"Tish!" I squeal.

"Oh shush, like you weren't thinking about it." She grins as we make our way to the front door.

Opening the door, the air is knocked out of me and I stand frozen, taking in the magnificent sight before me.

Hands shoved in his trouser pockets, Maverick looks more like a model from a romance cover than a bar owner. He's decked out in a three-piece, dark grey suit, a silver tie hangs loosely around his neck. Instead of the usual, unkempt look, his hair is styled, gelled into place. His jaw is rough, making him even sexier, and don't even get me started on his cologne. My body sways towards him, his smell intoxicating as well as hypnotising.

When I finally reach his eyes, I'm taken aback by the smouldering heat blazing in them. He does a slow appraisal of me, his eyes darkening with every inch he takes in. I shudder, my throat dry as I suddenly become aware of my body's reaction. I can't help but wonder if his touch will have the same effect or if it will be more.

"Well, this isn't awkward at all," Tish mutters, sounding amused, snapping me out of it.

"Look at me, Maverick. Look at my pretty dress," Faith gushes, pulling on his hand.

He glances down at my daughter, his mouth pulling into a wide smile. His eyes twinkle with a softness I've only ever seen him show with Faith.

"You look just like a fairy princess," he tells her.

"I know, right. I need to get my shoes real quick." She giggles, running back into the living area.

My mouth is still hanging open in shock, my body buzzing with awareness. I can't seem to take my eyes off his stunning form. I've never seen anyone look so damn hot. He's completely breathtaking.

"I-I...," I start, at a loss for words.

"You look beautiful," he tells me, his voice hoarse and raspy, causing a tingle between my legs.

"She looks hot as fuck," Tish corrects and I shake my head, turning to glare at her. I'd forgotten she was even here. My cheeks flush when it registers what she said, wishing I could strangle her for it.

"Um, yeah," Maverick coughs out, looking slightly uncomfortable.

"You look good too," I tell him quickly, then realise how lame it sounded.

Shoot me! No, seriously, shoot me. It would be a lot nicer and more humane than the humiliation I'm feeling right now.

"Thanks." He chuckles. "You ready? I need to be at the church soon. I'm running late because of Max," he tells me, not needing to explain any further. Just saying Max's name is enough for me to realise something must have happened to put them behind. Instead of asking, I just nod, calling Faith over my shoulder.

MY JAW HAS BEEN hanging open for the past ten minutes from the sight in front of me. Standing next to each other at the front of the church are Maverick and his four brothers. And holy shit, are they something to look at.

I seriously wish Tish was here right now to see them. I've even contemplated snapping a few pictures to send her, but I don't want to come across as a creeper.

She's missing out big time though.

When Maverick introduced me, it was one at a time, but then the vicar called them to the front. Seeing them standing together, talking and laughing amongst themselves, kind of blew me away.

I kept waiting for some club song to come on and for them to start stripping when they first got up there. Honestly, my imagination becomes so vivid, I mentally checked what money I had in my purse.

Each and every one is unbelievably hot, but none hold the same power Maverick has over me.

The groom, who I was introduced to first and very briefly before he was called away, is a pretty boy, but with a dark edge to him. I imagine him to be a big softie, but still, he was different from who I pictured him to be. He also seemed fine with Maverick bringing a complete stranger to his wedding.

I met Myles next, and he's the mirror image of Max. That's as far as similarities go between the two though. It only took me a few minutes to realise how different they both were personality-wise. Myles is softer, less arrogant. And thank the gods they are. Two Maxes would be a handful for the sanest of people.

Now Malik—the middle child, so to speak—is completely different from the others. He's not as talkative for one, and if I'm honest, he seemed unapproachable, but I think that may be because of whatever is bothering him. He's been on edge from the moment I sat down, constantly fidgeting with his tie and mumbling under his breath. At one point I thought I'd mixed up who the groom was because he'd done nothing but look anxiously at the church doors.

"When is the princess bride coming?" Faith asks loudly, her voice echoing. A few guests chuckle at my daughter's frustrated outburst.

Maverick hears her and walks over, giving her a dashing smile.

"She'll be here in a minute, squirt. They're just waiting for the last of the guests to find their seats before they let her come in," he explains, kneeling in front of her. He looks up at me and winks, and I nearly choke on my saliva.

"Why does Malik look more nervous than the groom?" I ask, trying to be quiet, but the question echoes around the large hall of the church, making me cringe. Max booms out a laugh, Mason and Myles chuckling. Thankfully Malik doesn't hear me, or at least doesn't acknowledge me, his face staying impassive as he stares holes into the entrance doors.

Hopefully he didn't. First impressions and all.

"He's worried about Harlow. She didn't feel well this morning and he didn't like leaving her. She's pregnant with twins."

"Ouch!" I wince, feeling for the poor girl. "I remember it being hard when I was pregnant with Faith. I can't imagine carrying two in there. Hopefully it won't be long until she arrives so he can settle down."

He gives me a small smile. "It's why he's so stressed."

"If you could gather round, the bride has arrived," the priest announces and everyone stands. I shoo Maverick away out of instinct, but I only realise what I've done when he gives me an amused chuckle, his eyes crinkling.

The wedding march begins and all five men stand straighter as another man I haven't met yet joins them. They quickly greet him before turning their attention to the back of the church.

The priest asks us to stand, so we do, facing the back. I hold onto a giddy Faith, trying to keep her still so she doesn't disrupt the ceremony.

"Shush, remember," I warn her quietly, and she nods excitedly.

The most beautiful woman I've ever seen walks down the aisle, her dress flowing over her large rounded stomach, looking radiant. She's not even halfway down the aisle when a large figure moves past us. I chuckle when I realise its Malik rushing towards her.

The crowd begins to laugh as he walks up to the girl, holding her around the waist to support her. She smiles wide whilst staring up at him, her eyes shining with so much love and adoration that mine start to water. When my eyes flicker back to Malik, I see him differently for the first time since I met him. His facial expression has softened, his eyes filled with love for the girl he's holding, seeming more relaxed and approachable. It takes my breath away seeing how deeply in love they are. That kind of love is once in a lifetime, something I've dreamt of forever but know I'll never have. The only love I've ever been shown is from my mum, my nan, Tish and Faith, and for that, I'll be eternally grateful. But a part of me will always wish to have their kind of love.

A girl with fiery, red hair that falls in loose curls down to her waist starts down the aisle next, her green eyes sparkling bright like emeralds. Her gown is elegant, a lighter grey than the first girl's, and has one strap that crosses over her large chest. She's stunning. Even with her obvious shyness and unease she seems to capture everyone's attention in the room. I notice her eyes light up when she finally lifts her head, making eye contact with someone. Her smile is so wide, so full, that I have to turn to see who has her attention. It's obvious that whoever it is has captured the young girl's heart.

Myles's face is a complete picture as he eyes the girl walking towards him. Their gazes never falter and it's another bond that warms my heart. This family, although I don't know them, are loved, strong, and stick together. It's clear as day when they look into their loved ones' eyes as they walk down the aisle.

My attention returns to the back of the room. Lake is already nearing where Faith and I sit, her gown similar to the girl who just passed, but with two straps instead of one. Her long hair falls past her waist, silver flower clips scattered in the unruly mess of curls. She's breathtakingly beautiful, her skin practically glowing with happiness.

When I glance to see what Max's reaction is, I have to stifle a giggle that threatens to escape. He looks seconds away from jumping the poor girl, his eyes nearly dark as night. When he holds his hand up, gesturing for her to call him, he mouths the actual words "call me." A few guests snigger, as do I.

He's such a charmer.

I'm surprised when another girl walks out, holding a little girl in her arms in a white flowery princess dress. She's so small and dainty, reminding me of a Disney character. The little girl in her arms shouts, "Da da," and when I turn my attention back to the front, my eyes land on the man I haven't met yet. He's shaking his head at the girl, amused, but they heat as soon as looks at the woman holding the little girl. Clearly the two are together.

When the young woman reaches the front, she passes the tiny girl into an older woman's arms, kissing the girl's head before walking over to the group of bridesmaids.

The wedding march starts and yet again, I turn my attention to the back of the room, my eyes filling with tears as I watch the most beautiful bride I have ever seen walk down the aisle.

Her blonde locks are up in some fancy hairdo, silver flower clips added to the mass of twist and twirls. And, if my eyes aren't deceiving me, that dress has to be Flora's. She's a wedding dress designer who has won awards for her creativity. Just seeing one in person has taken my breath away and I can't seem to pull my eyes away, from the exquisite dress. It fits her perfectly, and I know before I leave today that I'll be getting some pictures of her to show Tish when I get back. She is going to throw a fit when I tell her.

The man walking her down the aisle, clearly her father, looks down at her with adoration and love, his eyes brimming with unleashed tears. It causes my chest to tighten, knowing I'll never have that. My dad died while on duty when I was a toddler. I don't remember anything about him. I don't even have a grandpa to walk me down the aisle; he died before I was born.

My eyes bug out when I recognise the older woman walking in behind them, holding a little girl. Mary is one of my nan's closest friends, part of the 'trouble threesome' as I call them. They go to bingo every Sunday together, and nearly every Sunday I'll get a call from Sasha, the manager at the local bingo hall, telling me to come collect them. More times than not it's because they've caused trouble, drank too much or caused a scene. But because everyone at the place is in love with the group of ladies, none of them ban them from entering the bingo hall. Why, I don't know, since the last time I had to go and pick them up—which was three weeks ago—they were ready to strip on stage, saying the place needed livening up.

Walking by, Mary winks when she sees me and I smile, waving shyly. Feeling an intense stare burning through me, I turn to the front, my eyes meeting Maverick's. I'm taken off guard by the questioning look he's sending my way so I ignore him, knowing I'll explain later.

Glancing to the front, Denny and Mason join hands, their eyes locked, staring at one another in a way that makes me believe they've forgotten there's a room full of people watching them.

It occurs to me then that Maverick never had anyone walking towards him. All of the others up there were waiting for their loved one, their soulmate, and it confuses me as to why he didn't. He could have any woman he wanted.

This bit of startling news has me wanting to know more about him. It also makes me feel better about coming today, knowing if I weren't here he'd have been on his own.

Time seems to still as the bride and groom gaze into each other's eyes, like neither of them are in a rush to be anywhere else but here, where they will say their vows, promising each other the world in return.

My eyes find Maverick's once again, and he's staring at me with a heated gaze. Unable to look away, I end up picturing what his lips would feel like against mine, my skin burns as my mind conjures up image after image of what it would feel like to be loved by him, to be touched by him.

I'm losing my mind.

At that moment his intense gaze burns hotter, his eyes darkening and his jaw clenching. He looks like it's taking all his physical restraint not to take me right here in front of the eyes of God and all the wedding guests.

My legs squeeze together in response. I just hope my arousal isn't as obvious to everyone else as it is to him.

Needing to snap myself out of it, I remember where I am and shake the dirty thoughts away, facing the loveable couple at the front to keep my mind from steering off in the wrong direction again. I must have been staring a while because listening, I realise they're about to exchange vows.

"Denny, today, I take you to be my wife, my lover, my best friend, and my home. Today, I pledge my love to you without reservation, to grow with you in spirit and mind, to cherish and worship you for eternity.

"You showed me that love isn't someone you can see a future with, but someone you know you can't live without. You've made me see light when all I could see was darkness.

"So with this ring, I give you my heart, my soul, my spirit. I promise to shower you with love, pepper you with kisses, and remind you each and every day that our love is once in a lifetime... *and* that you're stuck with me," Mason vows, grinning when he says the last part. I choke up, the back of my throat burning.

Denny has tears running down her face, not caring one single bit about ruining her make-up, and I can't blame her. There's not a dry eye in the house. Luckily, it seems Denny was prepared for tears and wore waterproof mascara.

"Mason, when I first met you, my soul called out to me. It told me you were *the one*. Very rarely does a woman get to feel the love I have for you and feel it in return," Denny starts, choking up so much she has to pause, taking a minute to catch her breath. Mason wipes at her tears with the pads of his thumbs, looking at her with tenderness and love. I have to bite my lip, the overwhelming love passing between the two making it hard for me to stay composed.

"It's okay," he whispers, yet clear enough for us in the front row to hear.

She shakes her head, standing up straighter and squeezing Mason's hand tighter.

"You are my many firsts, my very beginning, and I vow to be with you till the very end. I promise to hold you when you're down, to light a candle when you lose your way, to comfort you when you're in need and to keep score even though I'm winning." She chuckles, and we all laugh lightly with her. "I promise from this day forward that you will never walk alone, that my heart and soul will be your shelter and that my arms will be your home.

"You are my home, my hope and my every dream. No matter what happens between now and forever, I know that every day I'll get to spend with you will be the greatest day of my life.

"I will always be yours," she whispers, finishing her vows. Opening my handbag, I grab the stash of tissues I thankfully remembered to pack and begin wiping away the tears falling down my cheeks.

I don't hear the priest as he talks; I can only feel the overpowering bond of love they've made, my heart filling with love right along with theirs.

Everyone rises, clapping their hands as the newlyweds kiss, sealing their vows forever. I can only hope, dream, that one day I can feel that kind of love for someone and that I will stand where they are, proclaiming my love to my soulmate for eternity.

If only dreams came true and wishes were always granted.

SEVEN

MAVERICK

It's official—I've turned into a creeper. I've not been able to keep my eyes away from Teagan since I picked her up this afternoon. Even when someone starts a conversation with me, my gaze has drifted towards her, seeking her out. It's like I'm in my own little world that only consists of Teagan.

I've never laid eyes on anyone so beautiful in my life. She quite literally knocked the wind out of me the second she opened the door, revealing her outfit. Fuck, just knowing the split up her leg goes far enough for my hands to explore her heat is enough to undo me like some horny teenager.

It's more than just her appearance though. I've found myself really enjoying her company. Even when she's nervously chatting my ear off, I find her endearing and cute.

It's new for me. I don't normally do the whole conversation thing.

"Will you just fucking smile so I can go grope my smoking-hot girlfriend," Max hisses under his breath. I shake my head, glancing away from Teagan to look over at him in annoyance.

We had some pictures taken back at the church, so why the fuck they're making us do more here in Joan's back garden is beyond me. Isn't one fucking picture enough?

It's one of the reasons I keep spacing out, bored as fuck. The other is because of my infatuation with Teagan and how her body looks in that incredible dress.

"What?" I ask defensively. I just pray he hasn't caught my ogling because I'll never hear the end of it.

"We're waiting for you to fucking smile. Smile like you just got laid by Megan Fox," he snaps.

I glare over at him before turning back to the cameraman—who is seconds away from getting the lens smashed down his throat—and grit my together in a fucking smile.

"Maybe you shouldn't smile. That's just creepy," Max whispers under his breath, and I growl.

A giggle to my right grabs my attention and I turn to find Teagan covering her mouth. My lips twitch and I subtly shake my head, wondering what the hell has gotten into me. I've smiled more today than I have in my entire life, and it's all because of that sinfully sexy woman.

"Okay, that's enough," the photographer shouts and we all sag with relief, thankful to finally move.

"Come to Daddy," Max shouts, making his way over to Lake.

"He's her daddy?" Faith asks, looking wide-eyed between Lake and Max. She steps closer to her mum, taking her hand. "But he kisses her."

"No." I chuckle. "He's just being silly."

Her cute face relaxes and she nods like she understands. Denny walks over to Mason and pulls him in for a hug.

"You having fun, *wife?*" he asks, staring down at her with a loving expression. I have to look away but before I do, I catch Denny grin wide and nod.

"Where the hell has Harlow gone now?" Malik hisses, looking around the impressive garden for her.

The girls did a good job at helping to set it all up. A giant white tent takes up most of the garden, covered in silver and cream balloons with flowers matching Denny's bouquet decorating the entrance. White round tables surround the lawn, silver candle lanterns as table decorations. They've had matching chairs covered in white cloth, a huge silver bow tied to the back of each one.

The only thing that doesn't match the decor is the outdoor heaters Mason demanded they have. And thank fuck he did; the temperature has slowly been creeping down since we arrived back.

"She's... there." Denny giggles, pointing towards the tent. One by one we look over, finding Harlow at the buffet table sneaking food while she thinks no one's looking. It's hard not to laugh. Malik seriously has his hands full with that one. Not that she isn't worth it. I'd do anything for her, for any of my brothers' girlfriends, but Harlow pregnant is like dealing with... well, like Max.

"Harlow?" Malik booms across the lawn. Everyone around us stops talking and turns our way, but Malik doesn't notice, his eyes never leaving Harlow.

She jumps a mile, dropping a few sausage rolls and whatever else she had crammed into her hands. She glares at Malik, her mouth full of food, but once she notices we're all watching she forces a smile. Everyone around us, including the people who stopped to see who Malik was shouting at, bursts out laughing. Quickly, she grabs a few more finger foods before anyone can scold her, then walks over to the group with a sheepish smile on her face.

"Faith, it's rude to stare," Teagan scolds softly. I look down, my lips twitching when I find Faith watching Denny with an awestruck expression. Her cheeks have turned pink from her mum's scolding and everyone's sudden attention.

"She's fine." Denny giggles, leaning against Mason as she stares down at Faith.

"I want to be just like you when I'm older. I want to be a princess and marry my prince charming," Faith gushes just as Max walks over to the group, Lake at his side.

"You're too young," Max tells her, his eyes deadly serious.

Seems like someone other than me is smitten with the rugrat.

Hands on her hips, Faith narrows her eyes at my stupid brother, looking cute as hell. "I *am* going to marry my prince, *and* I'm going to wear a pretty pink princess dress."

Max's brows rise as he takes a step back, putting Lake in front of him. "Okay, Faith, whatever you want," he tells her slowly.

Chickenshit. I grin.

"Who's going to be your prince?" Teagan pouts playfully. "And why didn't you tell me?"

By now, Faith has gained pretty much everyone's attention. Even Mary and Joan have joined the group, wanting to hear the pretty little girl's answer.

"Maxy," she states proudly. She points her finger at Max and he chokes on his beer, nearly spraying it all over Lake's back. We all laugh again, but it doesn't seem to bother Faith in the least; she just keeps looking at Max.

"Eww, Max," Lake snaps, moving away from him. She wipes away the specks of beer he managed to catch her with, her eyes narrowed.

"I'm a bit old for you, kid," Max wheezes out. His face pales, seeming scared, and I chuckle under my breath.

"I'll be old too. I will eat *all* my vegetables and grow up big and pretty like my mummy. We can get married then." It seems like she's put a lot of thought into this, which only makes it even funnier.

The idea of her marrying someone or even growing up gives my heart a jolt. I hardly know the squirt and already I'm planning on ripping off anyone's head who dares go near her. She can't date until she's at least thirty. Well, as long as I know her she's not allowed to date. Hopefully in that time I can warn her away from boys.

"Max already has a girlfriend. He has Lake," Teagan reminds her.

Faith seems to think that over before nodding like she's not too bothered about it and turning to Myles next. She smiles so bright it lights up her whole face. "I'll marry you, then. You look like Maxy."

Myles moves away from Kayla, bending down on one knee so he can get eye level with Faith. "I'd love to be your prince charming, because any prince would be lucky to have a pretty little girl like you as his princess someday, but I promised Kayla forever. I love her. She's *my* princess," he whispers conspicuously. She looks up at Kayla, seeming to eye the young woman closely.

"She is real pretty." Faith nods like she's approving of his choice, which only makes us laugh. "He's already married to a princess," Faith says, looking at Mason with a pout.

"You'd be my second choice." He winks and Faith giggles, turning to Malik with bright eyes.

"Do you want to be my prince?" she asks quietly, seeming shy all of a sudden.

"Shit, she picked the wrong family to find a prince," Max mutters, earning an elbow to the ribs from Lake. "Ouch, woman! I just don't want her to be heartbroken. We Carter boys have that effect on women."

Malik smiles down at her, his eyes softening in the way they do only when he looks at Harlow. "I've already got my princess, kid. You shouldn't rush into finding a prince. You should find one who is going to protect you, love you, cherish you—"

"And feeds you," Harlow adds quickly. Malik turns around, shaking his head at her, amused.

"And feeds you loads of chocolate," he finishes, smiling. "Only when he's proven himself worthy can you marry your prince charming."

Eyes wide, she looks at Malik with an understanding that I clearly didn't think she'd pick up. But she has, and she seems perfectly fine with waiting. Then a thought occurs to me and before I can shut my mouth, I'm speaking, word-vomiting all over the place.

"I'm feeling kind of unworthy and left out. How come I didn't get asked?" I ask, smiling down at her.

She looks up at me with a serious expression and my heart does a little flip, wanting to lift her in my arms and hold her close. God, her eyes are just like her mother's—large, round, and hazel.

Under her scrutiny, I begin to feel nervous, wondering if she can see the darkness behind the facade I put on for those around me.

I become aware of everyone watching me, watching us, all of them waiting to hear her reasoning, and I gulp.

"That's because you're going to be mummy's prince. I want a brother, by the way." She smiles, giddy with the idea of a brother. "Mummy, can I play? Please?" she begs, pointing over to where Granddad and Denny's dad are playing with Hope and Imogen.

My mouth hangs open at her admission and I stare down at her in shock. I hear a few people giggling, my brothers teasing me, but I can still hear the sound of Teagan's gasp echoing in my ear. She hadn't expected her daughter to say that and was taken aback just as much as I was.

Clearing her throat, Teagan answers, "Yeah, just stay close, and don't move from out of the garden." Her face is red with embarrassment as she avoids looking at anyone, including me, and I find myself not liking it. I stare, waiting for her to look at me, but she doesn't.

No one says anything about Faith's confession, everyone standing in awkward silence. Well, that is until Max opens his big trap.

"Thank fuck we're getting a nephew," he says, filling the silence.

Everyone bursts out laughing. Teagan and I, on the other hand, can only force a chuckle each. I'm still stunned, no idea what to do or say.

The thought of having a kid makes my stomach turn, but the more I picture what our kid would look like, the more I wonder if it really would be such a bad thing.

You just fucking met her, you fucked-up asshole.

My inner conscience is right, yet oddly enough, it feels like I've known her longer. However, with my past and my present, there's no way it can ever be more than this. There can never be an us—not the way she wants, anyway.

"She's a really good kid, isn't she," I say to Teagan, sounding lame. I just don't know what else to say.

"Nice." Max chuckles behind his hand.

I turn, glaring at him, then sigh gratefully when Joan asks him to help her bring some more drinks out for everyone. As much as I love my brother, I can only take him in small doses.

"Yeah, she is," Teagan answers me. All I do is nod in return, and I want to bang my head against a wall. Mason must read my expression because he smirks behind his beer, the cocky bastard.

"How's your nan, dear?" Mary asks Teagan. Then I remember the look that passed between them in church and wonder how they know each other.

"Wait! You know each other?" I ask. I move to stand closer to Teagan, my body drawn to hers, but mostly because I know how crazy Joan and Mary can be.

"Yes," Teagan answers sweetly. "My nan goes to bingo every Sunday with her." She stares at me a minute longer, lost in my gaze before turning those beautiful eyes back to Mary. Her smile is wide and beautiful like her daughter's. I wish she'd aim that smile my way. "Unless they get banned, which they haven't. *Yet.*"

Mary's eyes twinkle and peals of laughter escape her as she places her hand on Teagan's bicep. "That bingo hall would be boring without us there, dear. We're going dressed up as goddesses at their annual prime member party. Liven the place up a little."

I sputter out a curse, closing my eyes. I really didn't need that image in my head.

Teagan's eyes widen with horror and she groans. Her head rests on my arm, startling me; my muscles lock up, causing her to jump. Her face turns bright red as she moves away, realising what she'd done. I clench my hand into a fist at my side to stop from reaching out and pulling her into my arms. I want her—no, *need* her close.

"That's why she wanted me to pick up some white and gold cotton from

Fabric Factory the other day. I thought she was just making a new bed duvet," she says, cringing. She shakes her head in dismay and I chuckle.

"We're going to look so darn good. Joan even went out and got some gold glitter to cover ourselves in. Maybe we can get some of the men to put it on us." Mary sighs wistfully, making *me* cringe this time. There's no way that can be unheard.

"Oh God! Nan, please don't say any more. You can't go out dressed like that. You're too old," Denny scolds, looking as pale as the rest of us. I'm glad I'm not the only one who would rather pluck their eyes out with a spoon at the image. Fuck, at this rate I'll be heading into the kitchen and *bleaching* my eyes out for letting myself picture it.

"Hush, child. I'm still in my prime. I have a lot of years left in me before my ticker stops ticking."

"They aren't going to let you go back in there if you go dressed like that, Nan," Denny warns, glaring at Mason when he begins to chuckle. "I wouldn't laugh, Mase. It's your bar they're planning on going to after," she tells him, and his expression turns to one of horror.

"What am I missing?" I ask out loud, earning a chuckle from Malik. I'm glad I'm not the one who has to deal with MC5. It's not like they're going to come down into... *Shit!*

Don't mention V.I.P.

It will only give the bunch of old crazy ladies ideas, and they already have enough of their own. They don't need me giving them more.

"Nearly every Sunday I get a call to pick them up from the bingo hall. They're always up to no good. Thankfully, the last time was three weeks ago. They started to strip an item of clothing every time one of them got a full house," Teagan explains, wincing at the thought. "They were on a winning streak," she whispers.

The blood drains from my face. I've never prayed before, never believed in *Him*, but I'm actually contemplating going to church to pray they don't come anywhere near our club or V.I.P.

She couldn't be serious though. Could she? I keep waiting for her to burst out laughing, shouting, "I'm joking," but when that doesn't come, I realise she's deadly serious. I stare at Joan in horror as she walks up to us.

Does Granddad know what she gets up to?

"No, it was last Sunday, actually. I had to go and get them because Nan accused some woman of cheating," Denny says, rolling her eyes.

"She did cheat," Mary snaps. I turn to face her, watching as an angry expression crosses her face. Surely bingo can't be that bad.

"It's bingo. I'm pretty sure the only people who can cheat are... well, are the bingo hall," Myles explains, earning glares from both Joan and Mary. Wisely, he takes a step back, shutting up.

"No! That dreaded woman has had a thing going on with the new bingo caller. No one wins that many times in one night," Joan spits, taking up for Mary. "Even I wanted to throttle the woman. She was too smug for her own good."

"Joan, she was in a wheelchair," Denny reminds her, trying hard to fight a grin.

"She doesn't even need the thing. She's as fit as a fiddle."

"True, she was okay on her knees when—" Mary starts.

"Please don't finish that sentence Nan," Denny shouts, her face flushed, earning curious stares from the other guests. Not many people were invited back to the reception. Denny wanted it kept small since she didn't want a big, full-on wedding. Bet she's glad about it now.

"Sorry."

"I can't believe you pick them up too," Teagan says, suddenly waking up from whatever daydream she had been in.

"I do too. Malik has made me stop though. He turns my phone off every Sunday now because the last time I went, I nearly got taken out by a trolley they were racing in on the bingo's car park," Harlow explains, laughing lightly. My eyes catch Malik's narrowing, clearly none too pleased with the reminder of someone nearly hurting his girlfriend, even if it was her nan and friends.

Mary and Joan start grinning, their expressions glowing with happiness. "That night was so fun. Someone left them in the bingo car park so we decided to have some fun before Harlow picked us up," Joan explains.

"You weren't even there half an hour before the manager called me and said you were damaging cars. He also said—heatedly, I may add—that if I didn't come and get you he was going to have to call the police," Harlow reminds them.

"They shouldn't have parked there, then," Mary says, waving Harlow off.

"Did you notice he didn't mention banning us? Told you they loved us," Joan grins.

"I'm so having words with my nan tomorrow," Teagan whispers, shaking her head.

"Looks like we've got something in common, Teagan," Denny grins.

Teagan gasps and shakes her head. I wrap my arm around her shoulders, worried. "What? What's wrong?" I ask, looking around for Faith in a panic. When I find her playing nicely with Hope and Imogen, I glance down at Teagan, confused. My heart had started racing thinking something had happened to her.

Shit! I need to get a grip.

She ignores me, turning to Denny, looking almost shy. "I'm so rude. I've come to your wedding when you don't even know me, and I don't even introduce myself. I'm Teagan, and my daughter's name is Faith. Thank you for having us," she says, her cheeks turning pink. "But you already knew that."

I'm starting to find her behaviour and personality really fucking hot. *Maybe if I fuck her I'll be able to get her out of my system. Yeah... not likely to happen.*

But something tells me I'll need more than one night to get her out of my system. She's not the type of girl you move on from. She's a forever kind of girl.

"It's fine. I was going to introduce myself to you earlier, but everyone got sidetracked," Denny muses. "It seems you already know Nan and Joan, so I'll just introduce us. I'm Denny, obviously, and this is my *husband*, Mason. The pregnant one is Harlow, and the moody one who looks like he's ready to commit murder is Malik. You already know Max and Lake, and then there's Myles and Kayla."

"Hey, everyone." Teagan waves as if she really is just meeting them for the first time instead of acknowledging the fact that she's been speaking to them for a while. I chuckle, finding the whole thing adorable. When she glares up at me, I want to kiss her pouty lips and soothe those frown lines away, but I stop myself before I do something stupid.

"Thanks for coming too," Denny adds quickly. "We'll have to all meet up soon, fill you in on what these get up to."

"I know." Teagan laughs looking at Joan and Mary. "I feel like I've been played. I never knew they had someone else picking them up. Nan made me believe they only let loose once every so often and that I needed to give them a break."

"Trust me, that is *not* the case." Harlow giggles. "They have everyone on speed dial, I swear."

"Can the bride and groom make their way to the dance floor?" the DJ announces, and Denny starts grinning and jumping on the balls of her feet in excitement.

"Our first dance," she gushes before dragging Mason away to the makeshift dance floor.

My lips twitch, happy for my brother, and for Denny. I follow them into the tent, guiding Teagan with my hand at her back. "A Thousand Years" starts playing and Mason spins Denny into his arms, which has her throwing her head back laughing.

I watch as the cameraman steps out onto the dance floor and gets into their personal space. When he starts snapping photo after photo, I narrow my eyes. Something about him being there pisses me off and I grind my teeth together, wanting to pull the little bastard away so I can give them back their intimate moment.

"Why do you look like you're about to murder someone?" Teagan whispers, rising on her tiptoes to reach my ear. Her head only reaches my shoulder.

"What?" I ask, shaking the violent thoughts away as I concentrate on Teagan.

"You look like you want to murder someone," she repeats, her lips twitching. My gaze seems to zoom in on her perfect, plump lips, and I focus on them for a moment too long.

I laugh, the sound awkward and gruff. "Sorry. It's just... I thought this was meant to be a big thing," I blurt out, gesturing to the dance floor, where Denny is laughing at whatever rude comment my brother is no doubt whispering in her ear.

"It is," she says, her eyebrows scrunching in confusion.

"Yeah, I know," I grumble, feeling like a total dickhead for not explaining myself better. "I just think the photo guy is rude. He's walked out there like he owns the place. This is *their* moment," I explain, and she laughs. Her laughter rings beautifully in my ears and I can't help but stare down at her, fixating on her slender neck and the way her smile pulls in her tiny dimples, which you can't see unless she's smiling. She's fucking stunning and I don't even think she knows it.

"Maverick." She laughs, softly this time as her eyes lock on mine. "He's *capturing* their special moment so Denny and Mason can frame it, keep it, and cherish it. He's not doing anything wrong."

"I just don't like him." I shrug, feeling like an idiot. Why didn't I think about that? No, instead, my thoughts turned dark, as always. It's just another reminder as to why I could never be with Teagan. She deserves light, good, and a bright, happy future.

Listen to me, getting all sentimental and shit.

"Okay." She giggles, leaning in closer. Her feminine scent, sweet like lilacs surrounds my senses, the aroma intoxicating.

When Joan pulls Mark onto the dance floor, leaving the kids with one of Denny's cousins and Mary, my face must look irritable again, or confused because Teagan starts giggling. My lips twitch into a small smirk, knowing I'm being irrational.

"What now?" I ask, trying to sound scolding, but failing.

"You look like you want to rip your own Granddad away from the dance floor." Her giggles turn into full-on laughter and I shake my head in amusement. "They're supposed to move in for the last part of the dance. All couples are," she explains. That part doesn't make sense, but I nod like I understand. When I turn back to the crowd, I notice more couples getting up to dance. Even the people who turned up on their own are grabbing someone, sharing their moment.

I turn back to Teagan, wondering if this is something she wants to do. My question is answered when I find her eyes sparkling with happiness as she watches everyone dance with their partners, a wistful expression flashing across her face as her body sways side to side with the music.

Before I can chicken out, I clear my throat. "Do you... do you want to dance?" I ask, holding my hand out while trying to hide how vulnerable I am of her answer.

"I would love to." Taking my hand, her smile is so wide that my chest begins to burn. I swear that smile could make the hardest of men fall for her.

I frown at my trail of thoughts. I don't know where all this is coming from. I've had woman after woman sharing my bed, my desk, or the sofa in my office, but not one has ever made me think of a future or of more. It surprises me how someone so small could affect me so much.

Pulling her into my arms, I wrap them around her slender waist, sighing contently when she puts hers around my neck. We both step closer, our bodies flush together as we sway back and forth to the music, my pulse skyrocketing at the sensation.

My dick stirs, twitching, and it shocks the fucking hell out of me. So much so that I nearly trip over my own feet. I haven't lost control over my own body's reactions since I was younger. Since I was made to....

Shaking away my thoughts, I scold myself for even thinking about the past on a day like this. It never does me any good and only puts me in a mood for days, if not weeks. Denny and Mason don't deserve to have a cloud like that over them on their wedding day.

I inwardly groan at the feel of her body under my fingertips. The top of her waist is narrow, her body flaring out at the hips and curving in all the right places. I can't help but enjoy the touch. I only wish I could control my body's reaction to her, hating that she's making me lose control. But mostly I hate it because a part of me is enjoying it.

A little too much.

Shivers race down my spine and I pull her closer.

My breath catches as I look down at her. I don't know if it's the soft song playing, the way her eyes seem to stare up at me longingly or the feel of her body pressed against mine that makes me lean forward.

My eyes focus in on her lips, my pulse spiking in my chest as I debate on whether or not to take a chance. I lean in a little more, gauging her reaction. When she freezes, I pause, waiting to see if she'll push me away. When she doesn't, I grip her hips tightly. No longer swaying to the music, I press my lips to hers, the thread holding me together snapping.

The second our lips connect, everything around me melts away. I can no longer hear the music or the people around me. All I can feel is her, the way my body hums to life at her touch.

Fucking hell.

Deepening the kiss, I cup her jaw, the taste of her intoxicating as well as addicting. A kiss has never felt this good, and never has a kiss made me hard as rock.

Pulling away, I keep my eyes on her, watching her chest rise and fall heavily as she struggles to catch her breath. It's nice to know she's just as affected by the kiss as I am, her cheeks flushed and her lips swollen.

I've never wanted a girl like this before, and never has one made me feel anywhere as close to how Teagan makes me feel when I'm around her.

And now that I know what she tastes like, sounds like when she mewls in pleasure, it's going to be hard as hell not to pull her away to a quiet place and fuck her senseless.

I'm so fucking screwed.

It's going to be one helluva long night.

EIGHT

TEAGAN

Holy crap! I'm drunk, but not drunk enough to not know what I'm doing. I guess I just have more confidence since I'm buzzed. And after the scorching kiss Maverick and I shared earlier this evening, who could blame me for wanting a drink.

I can still feel his lips on mine, so soft, so tender, yet demanding at the same time. I don't even know how it happened. One minute we were swaying to the beautiful melody of Christina Perri and the next I couldn't look away from his dark predatory gaze, my eyes only once flickering to his luscious lips. It was so intense, my heart going crazy, and before I could blink, he was kissing me.

And it was by far the best kiss I've ever had—not that I have a lot to go on.

"What is this drink?" I giggle, holding the cocktail glass up. I'd talk about anything right now if it would distract my wondrous thoughts away from Maverick.

"Gavin's speciality," everyone says simultaneously.

I arch my eyebrow when everyone looks horrified at the jug sitting in the middle of the table. There has to be a story there. It can't be that bad; everyone seems to be drinking it.

"What? What's wrong with it?" I ask, looking into the glass—for what, I'm not sure. Bugs? Pills? Sugar? Who the hell knows?

Maverick boldly pulls me down onto his lap, laughing at my hesitation to take another sip. I'm not even surprised at his open affection; he's been touchy-feely since our dance, although he hasn't tried to kiss me again. I don't know whether to be disappointed by that or not. The jury's still out.

Spending the day with him has been really amazing. I've gotten to know the real him. He's more relaxed around his family, the lines around his eyes gone. The one thing that hasn't changed is his lack of conversation. Don't get me wrong, he's spoken to me just fine, but when someone else has walked up to him, he resorts to a one-word vocabulary. I actually find it endearing, and kinda hot.

"Don't have more than one glass. One will be enough to give you a hangover," he warns, smiling up at me.

"I don't really get hangovers," I admit. I always stop drinking once I've reached my limit, unless it's a special occasion; then I go crazy.

"Trust me, you will," Lake says, a faraway look in her eyes.

"Yeah, listen to Mav. You'll end up stripping, or worse," Max shudders.

"What am I missing?" I giggle, looking between everyone. "It can't be that bad if you're all drinking it."

"Trust me, it's bad," Lake groans, taking a sip. "I've learnt my lesson and now know never to drink more than one glass."

"Why?"

"Denny got on stage in a hooker outfit the night of her hen party when she drank it. She wanted to strip for Mason," Harlow tells me matter-of-factly.

Harlow and Malik are the only sober ones here. She's done nothing but eat all day and the poor girl is *still* eating.

I actually really like her. She's bubbly, fun, and a lovely woman. Earlier she had me in tears from making me laugh so hard. She was moaning and whining for some salmon sandwiches, practically begging anyone and everyone to make her one. She even went as far as promising to name her first-born after them. But when we looked, there wasn't any salmon left. Then, like she could sniff him out, she found Max sitting under the table scoffing down the rest of the sandwiches. Thankfully, Malik moved quickly and snatched the last sandwich off him. Harlow looked ten seconds away from losing it, and I felt so sorry for her. Max took it pretty hard, which surprised me, especially when he seems like the type to move heaven and earth for the young woman.

"She what?" I laugh, remembering what Harlow said. I look to Denny, who smiles. "What else happened?"

"We got tattoos," Kayla adds, grinning.

"No way," I gasp. I've always wanted a tattoo, but I'm too much of a chicken-shit. I had to be pinned down when the doctors took my bloods during my pregnancy, so there's no way I'd willingly walk into a tattoo parlour and let them stick a needle in me.

"And Max got arrested for indecent exposure. He also slept on a farm," Lake giggles.

"And don't forget you passed out," Maverick reminds Lake, causing her to stop giggling.

"Maybe I'll just stick to Malibu," she adds slowly, putting her cocktail down.

I laugh at her expression, loving the easy conversation flowing between us. There aren't many guests remaining, leaving us and a few others in the garden.

Faith and Hope are now inside the house. They both fell asleep around ten, tuckered out from all the dancing and fun they were having. I'm grateful Joan offered to take Faith inside so I could stay with Maverick and his family a little longer. I'm enjoying myself far too much.

I've gotten to know more about the group, falling in love with all of them. I wish I had brothers and sisters, or even a best friend who was like a sister growing up. I didn't have anyone, not until I ran away. I had no friends, no family, no one who cared about me.

My nan was ill when my mom died so I was made to move in with my uncle, who was a total stranger to me. He refused to take me to see her, so I had no one.

My uncle was a violent man and had already made a name for himself in the small town we lived in. No one would talk or look at me, not unless it was to call me names.

At first I thought it was because I was new, but once my uncle showed me his true colours, I realised all of the hostile behaviour and vile name-calling was because of him. So when I started school, I was pretty much ignored. I kept to myself after that, didn't even *try* to make friends.

The only time I ever interacted with my classmates was the night I got pregnant with Faith.

Watching Maverick with his family, listening to how close they are and how long they've known each other, has me longing for more. I have Tish and my nan now, but seeing these guys as a unit, as a family who would die for each other... I wish I had that.

Harlow yawns loudly, food halfway to her mouth when Malik gets up, pulling her to her feet. "Come on. It's late, and you need to rest. Everyone's leaving anyway," he tells her when she goes to protest.

I turn, glancing around the garden to find the last of the guests packing their stuff away. I hadn't even noticed. Time has flown right by.

Yawning, I take my phone off the table, gasping when I see it's one in the morning.

"Crap! I need to go home and get Faith to bed," I splutter loudly, jumping off Maverick. I sway slightly at the sudden movement and reach out for the back of the chair to keep myself steady.

"Calm down." Maverick chuckles, getting up and standing behind me. "We'll see you all tomorrow," he tells the group. They all wave before getting pulled back into whatever topic of conversation they were on.

"Where's Faith?" I ask as we step inside Joan's house. The place is quiet, so my voice echoes in the hallway. Joan startles me when she steps out from the living room, holding her finger across her mouth.

"Shush, the kids are asleep upstairs."

"I need to get Faith home to bed," I tell her, feeling the effects of the alcohol.

"Nonsense. She's asleep with Hope in Lake's old bedroom. She's perfectly fine, and I have the baby monitor on. You two get going, and you can come pick her up tomorrow. Mark and I are going to bed. It's been a long day."

"No, I can't leave her," I rush out, never having left her with anyone other than Tish or my nan.

"She's safe here, my darling, and you'll only be a few doors down."

"Huh?" I ask, wondering if I heard her right.

"Night. See you tomorrow." She waves, ignoring me as she walks upstairs without looking back.

What the hell just happened?

"Did she just kidnap my daughter?" I ask Maverick, kind of awestruck at how easily she manipulated the entire conversation.

"She has a way of getting her own way," he tells me, wincing.

I giggle but then remember the kids are in bed and snap my mouth shut. "Whoops. We should go before I wake them up. I'll get a taxi back to mine and come pick her up in the morning."

"You're not going home," he rumbles, his deep voice sending shivers down my spine. My body heats from the sound of the promise in his voice, the night's cool air soothing my heated skin when we step outside.

"W-what?" I ask, turning to him.

"You're staying with me." He takes my hand, pulling me against him, and I gasp in surprise. I melt against him, and the feel of his hard body pressed against mine has my thighs clenching together.

Suddenly, before my brain can comprehend what's happening or process what he's doing, his soft, full lips press forcefully against mine, his tongue demanding access. I give it to him.

The kiss is by far the most intense I've ever experienced. I fall into it with as much passion as I can muster, feeling light-headed from my heart beating rapidly in my chest. His tongue caresses mine, the strokes firm and slow, and I moan into his mouth.

He totally held back earlier.

He pulls me between his legs, his hands making their way down to my lower back, grabbing my ass, and squeezing the soft flesh.

I moan louder from the demanding, possessive touch and try to step back, needing to take a breath. He only lets me take one, watching me closely before kissing me again with ferocity.

His hands move from my ass to grip my hips, his hold firm before he lifts me off my feet. I wrap my legs around his toned waist, knowing if I don't let myself experience this kind of need, this kind of desire at least once in my life, I'll forever regret it. I'm fed up of living with regrets and 'what-ifs.' Now is the time for doing, for living. I don't know whether it's the drink talking or not, and I don't really care; I just know I'll never regret giving myself to this man. I've only really known him for a day but I'm that sure of him, I'm willingly giving myself to him. It might make me a slut, but I don't care, because at the end of the day I want this. I want this more than anything. The connection between us is blinding, intense, passionate, and I know he feels it too.

I hadn't even realised we had moved until he sets me down outside what appears to be an abandoned house. The wind blows, whipping my hair into my face. A cloud of doubt hits me for a second, but it's gone the minute his eyes land on mine. His gaze is filled with desire, lust and a primal need. I've never been on the receiving end of a look that intense before. I feel special, sexy and wanted.

"I've wanted to do that again all day." His voice is raspy, and the look he gives me sends tingles all the way down to my toes. I melt against him, my eyes softening at his declaration.

"W-where are we?"

"Mine," he growls, pushing the door open before pulling me back into his arms.

We're all mouths, tongues and hands as he carries me up the stairs, neither of us willing to let go. The minute we hit what feels like the tenth floor, I'm back on my feet and slammed against the closed door in seconds. His hands run up my bare leg beneath the dress's split and my skin burns at the touch. I throw my head back against the door, moaning.

"Oh God," I cry when he licks the inside of my thigh. "Please."

A deep guttural sound comes from Maverick as he lifts the dress higher, bunching it up around my waist. His hot breath brushes against my soaked knickers and I want to die right there, knowing he can not only feel how wet I am but see it too. His teeth scrape across my sex, his tongue rough against the sensitive spot. I reach out, grabbing his hair to keep my balance as he continues to drive me wild. I've never felt anything like this before.

I never knew anything *could* feel like this.

The sound of fabric ripping gains my attention and I look down, finding him tucking the scrap of my lace knickers into his pocket. His eyes reach mine, dark from what I can see in the dimly lit room. My breath hitches when he kneels before me. Without taking his eyes off me, he pulls my lips apart, opening the most private part of my body, making me feel vulnerable. I've never done this before and if I'm honest, I'm nervous as hell. But as soon as I see his tongue snake out, all thoughts are lost. Pleasure consumes me as he licks my slit, the pad of his tongue sending delicious sparks through my sex and all the way to my toes.

"Yes," I sigh, then again when his finger circles my entrance, making me gasp in surprise.

Yes, I could definitely get used to this.

My hips buck towards him of their own accord and my cheeks heat, more so when Maverick growls against me, lifting my leg and placing it over his shoulder, giving him better access. Puffs of air leave me in pants as I try to control what I'm feeling, but it's no use; he's manipulating my body with that talented tongue of his, driving me closer and closer to what I can only describe as heaven.

"Oh, God, yes," I scream. My hips move faster, my movements jerky, but I don't care. *I just need a little*—Maverick's fingers curl inside me and another scream bubbles out of my mouth. My whole body coils so tightly that my back arches away from the door as my lower half continues to spasm. The sensations are overwhelming, becoming too much and yet not enough at the same time.

All too soon the pleasure starts to ease, leaving a low ache in my core and my clit sensitive. Maverick takes one last lick before rising, his mouth glistening with my juices, and I find myself thinking how hot he looks and wondering how I taste all at the same time.

Without thinking, I step forward, grabbing his tie. I balance on my tiptoes, licking the corner of his mouth before reaching his lips. It doesn't take long for him to take control of the kiss, an animalistic growl rumbling from his chest.

"Fuck, I need you so badly," he grunts, picking me up. His free hand comes between us, and then a deafening cry tears from my throat as he enters me in one punishing thrust. I should be disappointed that he's still mostly clothed, his trousers only pulled down enough to free himself, but nothing matters apart from the feel of him sliding inside me.

Nothing could ever compare to this—*to him.*

"Kiss me," I whisper.

His dark eyes catch mine in a heated stare, his thrusts slower, hesitant. When I bite my lip, waiting patiently to see what he'll do, he groans, closing his eyes like he's in pain. His kiss is hard, forceful, and the minute I have his tongue on me again, I moan. This kiss is nothing compared to the intensity of our earlier one. This time it's more powerful and I cling to him, devouring him as he claims me.

He lifts me higher up the door, the new angle making my eyes roll and my toes curl. He's been rough, something I never thought I'd like, but I do and with Maverick, I want more. My hands go to move down his back, wanting to feel him, but he startles me when he roughly grabs my wrists and pushes them against the wall. He holds them there in one hand while the other slides down to my hips, gripping me there tightly as he continues to thrust. I feel completely and utterly fucked. The pleasure begins to build again, this time more intense, and a garbled sound escapes me.

"No touching," he rasps. A part of me knows I should be asking why, but his mouth is on my neck, nipping and biting, and I lose all sense of thought.

"Please," I beg, feeling closer to the edge.

"Fuck," he curses and starts slamming inside me, his thrusts becoming painful but nevertheless pleasurable.

This is what I've been missing out on all these years. Good to know.

My first time wasn't exactly memorable or even pleasurable, and something tells me this isn't something I can experience with just anybody.

This is *all* Maverick.

He's incredible.

He feels incredible.

I've never felt anything like this and I want more—*need* more.

The pleasure keeps building and when my orgasm tears through me without any warning, I slam my head back against the door, screaming out my release.

Maverick keeps thrusting, his body slick with sweat before he stills. Groaning out his own release, his eyes never leave mine, the intensity filling them nearly blinding me.

He lets go of my wrists to hold onto my hips, keeping me upright. Our breathing is heavy, his breaths blowing against my ear when he drops his head into the crook of my neck. My eyes close as sparks of pleasure continue shooting through my body, my sex twitching.

I can't believe I've just been fucked against a door. Seriously, could I be any more of a slut?

I wince when Maverick pulls out and am thankful he keeps a hold of me as he carries me to the huge bed in the middle of the room and lays me down. My legs are the consistency of jelly and I'm pretty sure I've lost all feeling in them, but I feel awkward just lying here.

Do I talk? Thank him? Give him a thumbs up? What the hell am I supposed to do?

"Um...," I mumble as I climb under the blanket, covering myself up.

Maverick chuckles, looking down at me with eyes filled with lust and desire. From the time it took him to carry me to the bed, he's tucked himself back in, leaving his button and zip undone. He unbuttons his shirt and my eyes widen.

"We're not finished, and covering yourself isn't going to stop me from consuming you, fucking you until you can't remember your own name," he warns huskily.

Okay. "I'm pretty sure I've already forgotten my name," I gulp and he chuckles again, shaking his head.

When he lifts the blanket off me, I shiver, watching his eyes skim slowly over my body. His tongue snakes out, wetting his bottom lip, and my heart stops, my body already primed and ready for him.

Paralysed by the look he gives me, I don't argue when he sits me up and lifts my dress over my head, never once taking his eyes off me. I'm only wearing a strapless bra and I want to cover up, hide my stretch marks and Buddha belly, but something in his gaze has me pausing, shifting slightly.

A primal look flashes across his face as he continues to strip out of his tux. He kicks off his trousers and I'm left staring at the magnificent body in front of me. Tattoos cover his chest—a dragon on his ribs, breathing fire, and a tribal tattoo which reaches from his neck down his bicep. He has many others, but it's the scripted quote below his heart that has me pausing.

I've always known there was more to Maverick, more than he let on, and seeing his tattoo proves my theory.

'*You did not break me for I am not what happened to me.*'

My eyes sting from seeing the tender, heartbreaking words on a strong, dominant man. It just adds to his allure, his mystery, which is something he has in bucketloads.

He sees where I'm looking and a dark expression passes over his face. Instead of staring and questioning, I further inspect his tattoos, smiling when I see '*My brothers' keeper,*' scrolled into his bicep.

"You really are your brothers' keeper."

A sad smile forms on his lips.

"No more talking. You're mine," he growls before kissing me.

He keeps his promise, making me forget about his tattoos, my own name and everything else in my life.

This has without a doubt been the best night of my life.

NINE

TEAGAN

Stretching, I can't help but groan out loud at the delicious ache running through me. Last night, after round two, I passed out, but then was woken up in the early hours of the morning to Maverick entering me. It was different, slower, but dynamic nonetheless.

I've never felt so connected to anyone in all my life. The moment he entered me, time stopped, and it felt magical. There's no other way to explain the feeling or rush that passed through us in that moment; it was everything I dreamt my first time to be—perfect.

He was perfect.

I've never wanted anyone the way I want him—and boy, do I want him.

Now my body craves him.

I turn to his side of the bed, frowning when I find it empty. The bed is cold where he slept, and disappointment rings through me. I had hoped he would be here when I woke up so we could maybe have a shower together or whatever two people do after a night of hot, sweaty sex.

Sitting up, I find a pile of clothes at the end of the bed with a note on them. Picking it up with a smile, I read over the simple words, my smile slipping.

Meet me downstairs.

His cold words send a shiver down my spine as tears gather behind my eyelids. Why he's acting this way, I have no idea, but I'm determined to find out. He can't deny we had a connection last night. Even when he fucked me against the wall, I felt it, but when he woke me up, making love to me, something I've never felt before blossomed in the very pit of my stomach and a magnetic force pulled us together. It was too powerful to ignore.

Grabbing my phone, I see it's nine and decide to hurry up and catch him before everyone else wakes up—if they're not already awake, that is. Plus, I really need to get Faith since she'll be waking up in a strange place, wondering where the hell I am.

The clothes are my size and thankfully, he managed to get me some new underwear, the tags still attached to them. This has me adding more questions to the list I want to ask him. I mean, does he have a stash of girl's clothes somewhere in different sizes for all his conquests, or am I special?

The sarcasm isn't lost on me and I groan, walking over to the en-suite bathroom to take a shower.

THE SIMPLE PAIR OF BLACK leggings and loose, baggy T-shirt left for me fit perfectly. Even the trainers I didn't see before because they were left on the floor fit well. I don't know whether to find the whole act sweet or disturbing. Either way, I'm going to get some answers out of him.

Walking down the stairs, I hear voices and immediately want to run back upstairs and hide. There's no way I can confront Maverick with his whole family around, especially when I'm doing the walk of shame. I'm just glad I'm not in yesterday's clothes.

"Go and wake her," Max snaps, sounding grouchy. "Harlow will have eaten all the food by now."

"Will you shut up," Maverick growls as I round the corner and step into the room. Everyone pauses what they're doing to look at me. Max is the first to speak, a small smirk playing on his lips.

"Well, don't you look like you just got fucked."

My face heats and I look away, embarrassed. Hearing a yelp, I snap my eyes up as Maverick steps away from Max, who is rubbing the back of his head, his eyes narrowed warily on Maverick.

"Can we go eat now?" Max whines.

"Yes." Lake smiles, jumping up.

Max moves so quickly he knocks his chair back. I chuckle, earning a look from him that says 'shut up.' I do, but I find it hard to hide my smirk.

"Come on, we should go with them. Joan is waiting to feed us," Maverick says, startling me. It's the first time he's looked at me since I walked into the room, and the blank look in his eyes has my hands shaking and my cheeks burning.

"Can we talk first?" I ask, my voice small and hesitant, which I hate. I'm usually more confident with myself to be able to speak my mind, but as per usual, Maverick has me in a jumbled mess.

"Look... last night was really fun, but I have a lot going on...." He trails off and it feels like he's kicked me in the stomach.

Embarrassed I even asked, or thought someone like him would be interested in more than one night with me, I nod, fighting tears. How could I have been so stupid? The thought of him blowing me off never even crossed my mind.

"I need to go and get Faith anyway," I tell him, my voice hoarse from talking past the lump in my throat.

"Yeah," he says, then clears his throat, gesturing me to follow him. I fold up my dress, holding it to my chest as I follow him out.

The walk to Joan's house is awkward and silent. I shouldn't have expected anything less, but he could have at least said *something*. "I'm sorry" would've been sufficient.

When we walk in, I'm surprised to find everyone in the living area. All the furniture has been moved to the sides of the room to make space for the large table they have in the middle.

I find my way over to Faith, smiling down at her. "Hey, beautiful. Did you sleep okay?"

She beams, jumping off her chair and lifting her arms up to me. I groan when I pick her up. She's getting too old for this, and a lot heavier than she used to be, but I don't care. I love our cuddles and she'll always be my baby girl.

"I had the best night *ever*! I went to bed *really* late. All my friends are going to be so jealous at school. I'm going to tell them all about Hope and Imogen. They'll be so jealous, Mummy. Joan said I can come back and sleep over all the time. Even tonight. *And* she said I could go out with her and Nanny together," she rushes out so fast I'm pretty sure I missed half of it.

I smile, but then it registers what she said. "I think day trips with Nanny and Joan should be supervised," I tell her. Denny and Harlow giggle, covering their mouths, and I shake my head at their antics.

"It's been so cool," Faith gushes, ignoring what I said since she pretty much knows she rules me.

"I'm glad you've had a good time, baby, but we have to go. Why don't you go say goodbye to your friends?"

Everyone in the room goes silent and I close my eyes, wishing I was invisible.

"Go?" Faith asks, her bottom lip trembling. I want to groan, but with everyone watching I act neutral.

"Sweetie, we have to go back."

"No! I promised Hope I'd stay, and Nanny Joan said I could have as much bacon as I wanted." Her eyes begin to water. I hate upsetting her.

I'd rather cut off my own arm than ever hurt her.

"Come on, dear. Take a seat and eat some breakfast. I'm sure you can spare twenty minutes," Joan says and I look up, finding everyone staring at me. The only one who isn't is Maverick, but that doesn't surprise me.

He really regrets last night. He might not have said it, but he's sure as hell thinking it if he can't even stomach looking at me now.

Defeated, I sigh. Faith, knowing what the sigh means, starts jumping in my arms, squealing, "You're the best mum ever!"

I chuckle, putting her down. "Glad you think so," I mutter.

"Did you sleep okay?" Joan asks, looking at me with concern. Max sniggers, earning everyone's attention.

"Hmm, it was all right. Just a little uncomfortable," I say, my words having a different meaning to the one she's thinking of.

"I thought you bought a new mattress," Joan says, looking over to Maverick. I could die right here, hating that she knows where I slept and just announced it to the whole room—including my daughter.

Maverick's eyes have hardened a touch, narrowed on me, but I straighten and take a seat next to Faith.

"It is new. There's nothing wrong with the mattress," he states.

"I don't know what it was, then. It just wasn't the best night's sleep. I've had better. The bed seemed a little hard and springy," I lie, smiling tightly at Maverick, hoping he gets my meaning.

"We'll have to look into that," Joan says worriedly. "I'll get the breakfast now that everyone's here."

Faith squeals, setting Hope off, who is sitting on the other side of her in a high chair. I smile, watching as Faith hands Hope a napkin, laying it on her lap. It doesn't stay there long as the little girl picks it up and shoves it in her mouth.

"Ood," Hope squeals and I laugh before turning my attention back to the table, feeling eyes on me.

Maverick sits opposite, staring holes into me while the rest of them talk amongst themselves, seeming to give us a wide birth.

My eyes once again find Maverick's. When his darken, I have to look away, squeezing my thighs together.

How can someone be such a jerk, yet still manage to turn me on? It's not fair. He doesn't play fair, and it makes me want to throw a tantrum and demand he talk to me. He could at least be an adult about it. But I don't think it's worth arguing over. Not if he'll treat me like this every time we spend a night together.

Then why does it feel like my heart is breaking?

"When do you go on your honeymoon?" I ask Denny, breaking the uncomfortable silence. I also want something to distract me from Maverick's burning stare.

"We leave tonight for two weeks." Denny grins giddily.

I smile softly. "Where are you off to?"

"We're going to Spain. I can't wait. The last time I went abroad, I was nine or ten. Mason hasn't even been on a plane." She giggles, looking at her husband.

"Neither have I. I'd be scared shitless. I mean, what keeps something that heavy up in the air? The speed? Because if that were the case, wouldn't racing cars fly? It reminds me of fast rides. I hate them. I don't think I could do it without throwing up or something," I ramble nervously.

Food is set in front of me, snapping me out of it. When I look up, everyone is hiding their amusement whilst Mason looks at me with a pale and panicked expression.

"What?"

"Way to make him feel better about flying, T," Max chokes out before booming out a heavy laugh.

My head snaps to Mason and I wince. "My bad."

He nods, understanding, still looking pale before he turns to Denny. "We'll google that shit later, before we go."

"Yeah, baby," Denny giggles again and I feel my face heat.

In all fairness, I've only known them all of five minutes; how was I supposed to know he had a fear of flying?

"Bacon," Faith squeals, clapping her hands when a plateful of food is placed in front of her. "Thank you, Nanny Joan."

"Nanny Joan?" I mumble to my daughter. She'd said the same thing earlier, but I'd been too busy having a stare-off with Maverick to question it.

"Hope you don't mind. I did try to get her to call me Grandma like Harlow does, but she said Nanny sounded better," Joan says, smiling adorably down at Faith.

"No, it's fine." To be honest, I didn't think it would take them this long to ask Faith to call them Nan. Joan was first, obviously, but it won't take long for Mary to order Faith to call her the same thing.

BREAKFAST WENT PLEASANTLY. No one mentioned me or Maverick again, but it didn't stop them watching us with a careful eye, or stop me from wanting to leave. Which reminds me…

"We really do have to be going. Whosoever these clothes are, I'll bring them back freshly washed and ironed. I promise," I tell the room, since I don't know whose they are.

"They're mine." Kayla smiles. "And it's fine. Keep them, throw them out. It's no big deal."

"Thank you." I smile in return.

Kayla is the quietest out of the group and is a perfect fit for Myles. The two are a match made in heaven. She's such a lovely girl.

"My pleasure."

"I'll give you a lift home," Maverick says, moving to get up.

My head snaps in his direction. "No. I'll get a taxi, thank you. Wouldn't want you putting yourself out for me, now would we?" I bite out, and the atmosphere in the room tenses.

"You're not putting me out." He narrows his eyes on me.

"I'll get a taxi, thanks. I know what I'll be getting, then."

"Ooohhh," Max says, grinning from ear to ear.

"Shut up, Max," the whole room snaps at the same time, and my face flames.

"Come on, baby. Let's get your coat," I tell Faith, and she looks between Maverick and me in confusion. Instantly, I feel guilty. I know if we argue she'll get seriously upset; she's fallen in love with him already.

"Are you and Mummy not friends anymore?" she asks him softly, pouting.

Maverick's face pinches together like he's in pain, but somehow he manages to soften his expression for my daughter.

"Of course we are," he answers, smiling.

"I'll call you a taxi," Max snorts.

"No, *I'll* take her," Maverick says, glancing quickly at his brother.

"Thank you, Max. That would be great," I tell him, ignoring Maverick.

He stands up, ready to make the call, but Maverick shoots him a warning glare and he sits back down.

"I said I'm taking her."

I sigh, glaring at Maverick. "And I said no, *you're not*."

"Why not?" he says, throwing his hands up in frustration.

"Why? Why?" I screech. "Maybe because I don't want to—" I notice Faith looking between us, her eyes wide, so I lean over and cover her ears before turning back to Maverick. "Maybe I don't want to sit in a car with a J.E.R.K for ten minutes," I whisper-yell.

He glances to Faith before turning back to me. "Let me take your crazy ass home. I'm still your landlord."

I scoff. "Yeah, because landlords take all their tenants to weddings, spend the night with them and don't even bother to talk to them the next morning." I hiss in a breath when I realise what I just revealed in front of everyone. They're all trying not to look—okay, Max is point-blank staring—but the damage is done.

"Teagan," he starts, looking frustrated and a little annoyed, but something else flashes across his features that I can't quite read. It just makes the entire situation even more humiliating.

"Don't. We're going to get a taxi. You can stay here and finish your breakfast or whatever it is you normally do on a Sunday morning," I snap, taking Faith's hand in mine. We walk out and thankfully, he doesn't try to stop me.

I'm grabbing my phone out of my bag to call a taxi when the door opens behind me and Harlow and Malik walk out.

"We'll give you a lift back," he says gruffly.

Tears spring to my eyes. "It's okay. We can grab a taxi."

"We'll give you a lift," he repeats, then shocks me when he reaches down, takes Faith into his arms and starts walking. He only pauses when he checks to see if Harlow is following him.

"C'mon, it'll be okay," Harlow whispers, taking my hand.

I sniffle, wiping my nose with the back of my free hand. "Okay."

The word tastes bitter in my mouth because I don't think I can ever trust myself or him again. The second person I sleep with and it's not in a relationship or as special as I thought it was. I could have dealt with a one-night stand if I knew it meant something, but I was just another notch on his bedpost.

I want someone in my life who wants me for me. I want what Denny and Mason have, what Malik and Harlow have—hell, what Max and Lake have. Something that special, unique and rare, is something I've always wished for. The kind of love that only comes once in a lifetime.

I was stupid to think Maverick might be that for me. Even for a split second.

TEN

MAVERICK

Frustration doesn't even begin to describe what I'm feeling right now. For two weeks Teagan has successfully avoided and ignored me. And for those two weeks I've done nothing but lose my ever-loving mind over a girl I spent one night with.

One night.

One night where I let all my self-doubt and rules fly out of the window.

I let her touch me, kiss me—something I've never let any other woman do when I fuck them. It's too intimate, too personal, and reminds me too much of my past.

But worse, I made love to her. Something I said I'd never do. I'd been half asleep when I felt her warm, naked body pressed against mine and I'd become instantly hard. Her skin was smooth and soft as I snaked my hand over the curve of her hip before sliding my fingers through her silky folds. Fuck, she felt so good, but it was the pleasurable mewing sounds she made when I circled her clit that had me losing my mind.

But what made me pause, what made me take her slow and gentle like she deserved, was the content, sleepy look she gave me when I entered her. I'll never be able to get her expression out of my head, or the way she whispered my name in a soft plea.

The whole night fucking scared me, and not because I made love to her. I'd slept for the first time since I can remember without waking up from a nightmare and covered in my own sweat.

When I woke up with her in my arms, I smiled, my heart squeezed by an emotion I've never felt before. It was like I'd woken up and everything from my past, my present, had all but gone, and the only person who mattered was the woman in my arms.

That's when I froze. I woke up, looked down at her sleeping form and I got scared. For the first time since I was a child, I got fucking scared. And because of that, I ran and acted cold towards her. It's what I do when things go wrong; I deflect what I'm really feeling and hide behind a cold facade. I acted like a complete prick to her, all because I was in defence mode.

She didn't deserve waking up to that. And I've been paying for it every day since, kicking myself for treating her like she was nothing. No matter what I've tried to do to fix it, nothing has paid off.

She's been ignoring me and dodging me at every turn. She's not answering her phone or her door, and now I'm out of options. Hell, when I've gotten lucky and the door *has* been opened, it's only been slammed in my face seconds later. Tish, her crazy-ass friend, was the worst. She literally slammed the door *into* my face, causing a nose bleed. Twice. I've learnt to step back since.

I groan into my hands, needing to figure out a way to get her to speak to me. I shouldn't have been such a dickhead, I realise that, but I wish she'd give me a chance to explain. Explain everything. I've never wanted to talk to someone as much as I do when I'm with her.

"You look like shit," Evan tells me from the doorway of my office. He walks in without invitation and I give him a dry look.

"Come on in," I reply sarcastically.

He grins at me, shrugging. "Don't mind if I do."

I watch as he drops himself into the chair directly opposite me, all cocky and smug.

I really don't need to be dealing with any more bad news, not today. I've got enough occupying my mind right now; anything more and I'll explode.

"Get it over with. I've got a kicker of a headache and I just want to get home."

"Translation: I fucked my tenant, fucked it up with her, and now I don't know how to make it right with her. Did I miss anything?" he asks, smirking.

With narrowed eyes pointed solely on Evan, I sit forward in my seat. "Never talk about her like that, ever!" I warn.

He raises his eyebrows at the seriousness in my tone but doesn't seem vexed or irked by my behaviour. If anything, he looks smug.

I groan. I'm usually good at controlling my emotions, but yet again, Teagan is unravelling me. I'm losing it.

"We need her," he says, all joking aside. He's all business now and it has me straightening.

"Teagan?" An unsettling feeling hits me in the stomach.

"Yeah, man. Another body was found last night. And although the police can't prove he got the drugs from here, the symptoms were the same. They'll probably be around sometime tomorrow for the CCTV footage. When they do, you're going to want to have *something* to please them."

"Fuck! She isn't even talking to me, and I'm not sure I want her involved in this shit, anyway. There's too much at stake and it's getting worse. She's got a kid."

"I know, man, but what other choice do we have? It's the perfect setup."

"But she won't talk to me," I groan.

"Maybe asking her to do this for you will give you a chance to make it up to her. She seemed like an all right chick to me. And you seemed different with her," he says, catching me off guard.

"You gonna start spilling your feelings?"

He laughs. "No. But get your head out of your ass. It's obvious she likes you and you like her. I don't see what the problem is."

I want to say "me," that I'm the problem, but having a heart-to-heart with my sister-in-law's brother? Yep, not going to happen.

"What am I going to do?"

"Go fucking talk to her. Grovel. If that doesn't work, then make up some sob story. Fuck, just tell her about the case. That will get her talking to you." He shrugs.

"Yeah, because she'll want to hear all that shit," I reply dryly.

He rolls his eyes and gets up. "You've got until tomorrow to think of something to tell the cops. They're getting anxious, and there's even word of them closing you down," he reveals and I stand up, shoving my chair back.

"What the fuck! You couldn't fuckin' *start* with that? They can't close this place down. It's paying for two fucking houses and a set of renovations. Malik has twins on the way. If this place gets shut down, we lose business and if we lose business, I can't fucking keep up with house payments," I growl, my chest tightening.

"Then get something set up to find the assholes who are doing this. It would've been over by now if we had someone on the inside."

"You don't think I've tried?" I roar. I grab the beer bottle off my desk, throwing it across the room. It smashes against the wall, tiny shards of glass flying all over the place.

"Fuck, man. I didn't think. I just…. I want this sorted out as much as you do." He sighs. "I have a mate who works at the local police station. I'll have a word with him and see if there's anything he can do for it not to happen. I'm sorry," he says and I nod, running a hand over my face.

"I'm gonna go talk to her now. But I swear to God, Evan, I'll go fucking apeshit if this place closes down."

"All right, man."

I walk out with him through the back exit. I wave him off before running up the stairs to Teagan's place. It's late, but not late enough that she'll be asleep. I hope. It also gives me a chance to tell her what I need to without Faith around, listening in.

I knock, but instead of taking a step back like I've learnt to do in the past week, I stay close.

The door opens quickly, surprising me, but it's the look Teagan gives me that nearly has me taking a step back. It kills me, more than I care to admit, but also because I know I deserve her hatred.

The second I see her decision to slam the door in my face, I step forward, putting my foot in the doorway.

"Teagan, please. Just hear me out," I plead, staring into her eyes and letting her see how desperate I am.

She sighs and steps to the side to let me in, not looking happy about it. "Why should I listen to anything you have to say? You treated me like a whore."

She stands up straighter, appearing unaffected by my presence and coming off cold. It doesn't suit her. And as much as she wants to pretend she doesn't care, I know she does. I see the pain and hurt in her eyes, the anguish I've caused her. I wince, ashamed of myself for causing her so much stress.

"Look, that morning—"

"I don't want to talk about it," she snaps, not looking at me. "I get it. I was just a hookup, an easy one-night stand for you. You don't need to explain anything, and I don't want your pity, so you can go now."

"Fuck." I start pacing in the living area. "Look, there are things about me that you don't know about. Things you wouldn't understand. I was raised by an abusive father and the shit he did, what he made me do, it would turn your stomach.

"I was never shown love, not from anyone but my brothers, for most of my life. The love I *was* shown... fuck! It was sick, twisted. It wasn't love, but back then, I was young, naïve and it was the closest thing to kindness I was shown." I don't even know why I'm telling her all of this; I don't even talk to my brothers about it. I just know I need her to understand because seeing her now, I realise what a huge mistake I've truly made. I want her, have from the very beginning, but I let my insecurities get in the way of that. I'm desperate for her to see me, the *real* me, not the jerk I was to her that morning.

"I've fucked a lot of women, sometimes once, sometimes twice. I've always been upfront about what I want, and I've never once promised them tomorrow. But I've never gotten close to any other female. None apart from my brother's girlfriends and even then, I couldn't trust them at first. I've never gone on a date before, ever. Hell, I've never even taken a woman to meet my family before, much less take one to my brother's wedding. I've never kissed while I'm fucking and I've never, not once, let anyone touch me while I'm fucking them either, but with you, it was different. *I* was different," I rush out, still pacing. I turn to face her, to see her reaction, and I find her watching me, her eyes filled with unleashed tears.

"Why are you telling me all of this?" she whispers.

"Because... because I need you to know why I acted like a jerk. I was fucking scared."

"Why? How did I scare you?" she asks, shaking her head as she moves to take a seat on the sofa. I stay standing, needing some higher ground since I just spilled my guts and she isn't saying anything about it.

"Because kissing to me is personal, intimate. I swore I'd never kiss or let anyone kiss me while we were fucking, early on in life. You scared me because you touched me...." I trail off, feeling like I've cut myself wide open for the woman in front of me. The woman I haven't been able to stop thinking about since I chased after the mugger who was hurting her. She's consumed me, day and night, and I barely know anything about her.

"What do you mean by touch you? I don't remember touching you." She blushes, looking down at her lap.

I still, turning back to face her. Everything in me comes rushing to the surface and I give her everything. "When I woke you up that last time, you got to me in a way that no one else has. You touched something inside me no other has ever gotten close to reaching. You owned me, all of me. It's never happened to me before and it was overwhelming, hitting me all at once.

"And you literally touched me. You touched my shoulders, my back, my ass," I say, my voice teasing, hoping to make her smile.

"Okay, I get it." Her cheeks have turned redder, if that's even possible. "I just.... I don't know what to say to that. You hurt me so badly. Before you, I've only had one sexual encounter. After that... I promised myself the next time I gave myself to someone it would be in a committed, loving relationship, or I'd at least have some sort of connection with them. I thought *we* had a connection, but I was wrong."

I sigh, taking a seat on the other end of the sofa. I knew I screwed up, but hearing firsthand just how much... it fucking sucks. Guilt gnaws at me and I wish I knew how to make this right, how to help her understand.

I repeat her words over in my head and turn to her, curious about something she said.

"You mean one partner? You've only been with one person? Faith's father, right?"

Her face reddens and she nods once, not looking at me. "I've only ever had sex once in my life. Before you, I mean," she rushes out.

My eyes bug out and a lump forms in my throat as I turn towards her. "How the fuck is that possible? I mean, Faith.... How? You're fucking gorgeous." I'm utterly baffled, shocked that no one ever swept her up.

"We all have a past," she whispers. She has a point, but what I don't understand is how she's stayed single. She's not only fucking gorgeous, but she's funny. She's also sassy and so easy to get along with. How has she not been fighting lads off her whole life? They must have been queuing up to date her.

"So explain Faith to me, and how someone like you only has sex one time."

"Because," she starts, blushing, but a flash of pain crosses her face. For some reason it has me on edge.

"That's not an answer," I point out, needing to know the meaning behind her look.

She sighs, giving me quick glance before looking away, twiddling her thumbs.

"I... I don't even know where to start. I'll give you the shortened version, okay?"

I nod, too shocked that she isn't telling me to fuck off to argue about getting the full story. Anything that will help me understand her a little better is better than nothing.

She tucks her knees to her chest, curling her arms around her legs as she stares blankly at the switched-off television.

Watching her tuck herself into a ball, as small as possible, has me wanting to reach out and hold her. Whatever has her curling into herself and looking shaken, like she'd rather be anywhere but here, has my protective instincts rising to the surface.

"My dad died when I was a baby, so I only had my mum and Nan growing up. My mum died of breast cancer when I was a teenager and I was sent to live with my uncle from my dad's side. I guess he was a little like your dad—an abusive asshole. He was violent, hostile and loved using his fists. It was bad," she whispers.

I clench my hands into fists, wanting to find the fucker and kill him. I want to track him down and see how he likes taking a beating off someone stronger than him. People who prey on the weak deserve to be punished.

"Why didn't you live with your nan? I thought you two were close?"

With her cheek now resting on the top of her knee, she opens her eyes, and I'm taken aback at the sheer pain and sadness that reflect back at me.

"She was really ill at the time, so social services wouldn't even consider me staying with her. They were worried I'd end up caring for her and not the other way around. But I'd rather have looked after her. It's not like she was ill for long," she breathes out, clearly upset over it. "They forced me to move in with an uncle I hadn't even met before. My mum never spoke about my dad's family. And when I moved there, my nan couldn't even visit because of the distance. She couldn't travel. I guess I could have visited her, but at the time I didn't know how. Travis didn't give me any money and he never let me use the phone, so I lost touch. By the time I was old enough to read the bus and train times, I didn't even know if she'd still be living in the same place."

I nod, trying to process everything she's told me, but it's hard to get past the blinding rage towards her uncle.

I have a new level of respect towards her now. She's been alone, a young girl with no family, and was treated badly. Yet, you'd never know by looking at her. She doesn't seem jaded, not like me and my brothers. She seems happy, content with her life.

She's fucking strong, I'll give her that. I just hate that she was alone going through it. That she had to go through it at all.

Teagan snaps me out of it when she starts talking again, her voice soft, lost in thought.

"I'd pretty much distanced myself from everyone—not that it was hard to do, since the whole town where I lived hated my uncle. I never really knew why at first, but once I got to know him, I didn't have to guess. His actions, along with all of the rumours, were enough.

"Anyway, it's why I never dated. I lost my virginity by choice after I crashed a kid's party from school. I left the day after and three months into living with Nan, I found out I was pregnant. Since then, dating hasn't been top of my agenda."

Her tone leaves no room for argument, which confuses me. During the first part of her admission, she seemed lost in the memory, speaking the truth and talking in detail. But the last part was like listening to someone check off a shopping list. She listed facts, yes, but she didn't speak in detail. Although I know she hasn't lied about any of it, I can tell there's more to the story. She's left a hell of a lot out and I don't understand why, not when she's already told me so much.

"What about Faith's dad? Does he see her?" I ask. I've not seen or heard about anyone of the male persuasion coming or going, and it makes me sick when I think of Faith being abandoned like that.

"He's dead. I went back a few weeks after I found out I was pregnant and was told he died in a pile-up on the motorway," she says, her eyes closing.

Fuck! She's been through so much. And Faith, the poor kid; she's at the age now where she'll start asking where her dad is and why she doesn't have one. It fucking pains me to know the tiny squirt will one day have to be told her dad is dead, and deal with that loss.

"What about his parents? Do they see her?"

She shrugs, more tears gathering in those beautiful eyes of hers—eyes that are filled with so much pain and sorrow at the moment. It's hard to keep it together and not break the face of whoever put that look there.

"They didn't want to be associated with the town scumbag's niece. They called me a whore, a liar and told me never to contact them again before they slammed the door right in my face." Her voice is void of any emotion, but I can tell what they said and did affected her.

Nobody deserves to be treated like that.

I also know firsthand how shit it feels when someone judges you for who your parents or relatives are.

All through school, adults judged me and my brothers, warned their kids—mostly daughters—away from us. Although I tried not to let it bother me, it did.

"Fuck!" I fall back on the sofa, overwhelmed by everything she's just revealed. "If it's any consolation, they're missing out on watching an incredible, beautiful little girl grow up."

She looks tired, worn out, and I feel bad for bringing up bad memories for her, but then she turns, smiling wistfully. Her eyes open, appreciation filling them. "Yeah, they really are."

She leans back on the sofa and we stay quiet for a few moments, both of us lost in our own thoughts. When I realise I still haven't accomplished what I came here to do, I turn to her.

"I really am sorry for the way I treated you. I acted like a complete prick. This"—I gesture between the two of us—"is new for me. That connection you spoke about earlier? Heaven help me, but I felt it—feel it. I... I can't keep living my life scared of letting someone good in, worried I'm going to tarnish them. I've got a dark past, Teagan, I won't lie. It haunts me every day, and every night in my dreams, and because of that, I've never been able to let anyone in. No one. But if you can find it in your heart to forgive me, I promise to try. I'd like to try, with you," I tell her.

And for the first time since I was sixteen years old, I feel unsure of myself, vulnerable. I've never put myself out there or put myself in a position where I've let someone have the potential to hurt me.

"You really hurt me," she whispers, and my heart clenches painfully.

"One date. Give me one date. If you're not interested after one date, I promise I'll leave you alone."

"And if I don't?"

Her demeanour changes right before my very eyes. She looks stronger, more sure of the situation now that she's in control and holds all of the cards.

"I won't stop until I get what I want, and babe, I've always gotten what I wanted. But word of warning—I've never gone after anything I truly wanted before, so I won't hold back." Her eyes widen, her breath coming in sharp and heavy pants as we stare into each other's eyes. "So, Teagan, what do you say? Would you like to go out on a date with me? Which would also be another first for me," I remind her, smiling a little.

"Yes," she blurts out, startling me. I was certain she wouldn't give me another chance. But then, she always manages to blow my mind.

"Really?" I smirk.

"Yes," she giggles.

"Okay. Good. Yeah," I stammer.

She laughs, and her body finally relaxes for the first time since I arrived.

"When will this date be?" she asks, looking almost shy.

"Um, are you free, say... next week? Oh wait, crap. There's actually another reason I came to see you," I tell her, wincing.

"Oh yeah?" she asks, eyeing me warily.

I gulp, knowing I have a lot riding on this. If she says no, I'm fucked. But I'm also fucked if she thinks I only came around here to butter her up before asking for a favour. I don't want her to think that of me.

Don't let me fuck this up.

"Yeah, I need a huge favour, and you might not like it...."

ELEVEN

TEAGAN

"You can do this," I whisper to myself, staring at my reflection in the floor-length mirror.

It's been a week since Maverick turned up late at my door, giving me a touching apology—well, tried to. He was so flustered and, being me, I couldn't stand to see him so torn up, even if he did deserve to squirm a bit. Then he dropped a huge bomb on me, asking if I'd do him a favour. A favour I couldn't possibly say no to, not when people are dying.

He mentioned the trouble going on inside his club briefly at the wedding, but I never knew the full extent until that night. Someone he works with is selling drugs and he's not been able to find out who—which is where I come in. Knowing that families are losing loved ones and more lives are in danger, I agreed to go undercover to find out who it is. My role is to clean the place, help the strippers get changed between their performances and some grunt work in between. The dancers and waitresses alternate nights, so I'll be able to get to know all of them one-on-one and weed out the culprit—I hope.

Drugs have played a huge role in my life. My uncle had a bad habit of taking them, but mostly, he sold them. He tried to get me to sell to kids at my school, but when I would come back from school still holding his stash, he got tired of asking me. I didn't even try to sell them, though he didn't need to know that. So I'd take my beating, get back up and move on to the next day, praying for something better to happen in my life. Every night I went to sleep wishing for an escape.

If helping catch one drug dealer makes up for all the crap I should have snitched on my uncle for, then I'll do it. The one thing I always regretted was not going to the police about all the crimes he was committing.

My nan has Faith for a sleepover tonight, as I didn't want her to be around if something bad were to happen. Not that I think something will, but you can never be too sure.

I've had officer after officer go through what's expected of me, what I should look out for, and what I should and shouldn't say. It took two hours for the first cop to go through it.

Maybe I should have taken notes!

My breathing grows heavy and I grip the sink, trying to take in deep, steady breaths.

"Teagan, you in there?" Maverick calls softly, knocking on the bathroom door. I don't answer since I'm too busy hyperventilating.

He lets himself in and takes one look at me before his jaw clenches. "You're not doing it. You're not up for something like this and I shouldn't have asked you in the first place." He curses, running his fingers through his hair. The motion causes the muscles in his biceps to flex and my mouth waters.

Ever since our night together, I've done nothing but fantasise about the man. Every morning I wake up in the middle of a dream orgasm and want to scream in frustration. I know what he can do to me, how it feels, and I want it to happen again *so* badly. But since he asked me out on a date, I've only seen him on a few occasions for a short amount of time. He's taking me out tomorrow, surprising me when he asked if there was a favourite place Faith liked to go. It melted my heart and I have to admit, it's made me fall for him a little. Not that I thought I wouldn't. Deep down, I think I've already fallen for him. It's bizarre, since I hardly know him. It's too soon to have feelings for him, right?

"It's fine. Just... please don't leave me if there's trouble," I plead. "Or if I'm a lousy liar and they figure me out."

He grins, walking over and wrapping his muscled arms around my waist, looking down at me with eyes filled with a deep yearning before kissing the tip of my nose.

"You won't screw up, babe," he says, kissing the corner of my mouth next. I love these fleeting moments with him; moments where he doesn't act like the man who has the weight of the world on his shoulders, or the stress of finding out the cure to cancer. He's so attentive, soft and easy-going when he's with me, but there are times when I still see the darkness in his eyes, reminding me he has a hidden past.

"You sure?"

"Positive. You should be more worried about me." He smirks.

I bite my bottom lip worriedly, my eyes filling with concern. "What? Why? Are you okay? Did something happen?"

"Yeah, my girl looks fucking hot in the work uniform I gave her. I'm gonna find it hard to keep my hands off her," he says lustfully and I grin, by belly fluttering at hearing him call me his girl.

"Wouldn't want to get done for sexual harassment to your new staff member," I tease.

"What if she likes it?"

I pretend to think about it, my lips in a side pout before I look into his eyes. "How do you know she will?"

"Well, will you?" He grins, his eyes full of amusement and laughter. The combination is a rare thing to see.

"Most definitely," I whisper, my core already clenching in anticipation. The need for him to touch me again is as frightening as it is consuming.

"There you have it. I won't have to worry about misconduct, now will I?"

"Nope. Just don't make promises you can't keep," I flirt, lifting onto the balls of my feet so we're face-to-face.

"Oh, I don't intend to," he says, right before he captures my lips in a fiercely hot kiss. My skin burns, my whole body alighting for him. I move forward so our hips are flush against each other's, wanting him closer.

Someone clears their throat in the bathroom doorway, which has us pulling apart. I straighten the short V-neck dress Maverick supplied me with and look to the door, my cheeks heating. Evan—who I found out is a PI, and also Denny's older brother—stands there, a smirk plastered across his handsome face.

Maverick pulls me against him and Evan's eyes shoot up in surprise, a teasing glint there. "Are you ready?" he asks, and Maverick grunts.

I look between them before turning back to Evan, nodding. "Y-yeah," I croak out, my voice filled with lust. When I close my eyes in embarrassment, Evan chuckles. Maverick growls something before I hear Evan step away, his footsteps echoing down the hallway.

"I can't believe he just caught us snogging each other's faces off," I groan.

He laughs, pulling me tighter against him. "Come on, before he comes back," he says, pulling me towards the door. Before we get to the living area, he leans forward, his breath against my ear. "We'll finish this later."

His promise has me clenching my thighs together and I narrow my eyes at him. I'm seriously wondering if they'll give me time to go change my underwear, because I'm incredibly wet and it's embarrassing. I'm just glad the dress is black and not white. My cheeks flush at the thought.

"So, you know what you're doing?" Officer Paul Barrett says when I step into the living area.

I nod. "Yeah. Today, I just do the job. Get to know everyone, but not be *too* friendly. Basically, treat this as a real job. Don't ask questions unless they approach me and start asking them." I repeat the rules they've drummed into my head for four days now, wanting to moan and groan. I'm fed up with them thinking I'm an imbecile.

I like Officer Barrett, but his partner, Calvin Grant? Not so much. He seems like a person who doesn't really want to make the world a better place, choosing to rank the highest in his division instead. He's a complete joke, and the way he keeps eyeing me is starting to creep me out.

"Good. We're not going to set you up with a wire, but the next shift we will. Today is going to be a trial run to see how you fit in, how they react to you. Fortunately for us, they won't be suspicious of a new staff member starting since Maverick really did fire someone a few weeks back," Calvin Grant says, nodding in Maverick's direction.

"So, I can go? You don't need me to keep in touch, ring you or anything?" I ask, confused. I thought they'd be more involved—this is serious, after all.

"No. We'll be by tomorrow, mid-morning to get the full details. If anything suspicious happens, or you see a member of staff selling drugs, go to Maverick. Just try not to be conspicuous about it in case you're wrong," Officer Grant says, a bite in his tone. I swear, he looks at me like I'm a woman yet treats me like I'm a kid who isn't listening. He's an aggravating jerk who I desperately want to punch.

"Watch your tone," Maverick warns, his tone deadly, and Officer Grant's eyes narrow on him.

Stepping between them, I block their view of each other. I glare at Evan's amused expression as he watches my manoeuvre, seeming to find it funny, then turn to the issue at hand.

"Want to walk me to work?" I ask Maverick.

He looks down at me, his eyes softening. "Yeah, c'mon. I can introduce you to everyone, show you around and let you get to it."

"I better be getting paid overtime," I joke. He looks taken aback for a second and it has me pausing, worried if I said something wrong.

"Um, you are getting paid, Teagan. I thought you knew that. You'll be getting paid triple the hourly rate," he says, looking to the officers behind me. "You didn't tell her?"

What?

"I thought we did," Officer Grant remarks, sounding annoyed. He gives me a sour look before dismissing me in a huff. I glance at each man, waiting for an explanation, but get none.

"I bet," Maverick mutters before turning to me. "They'll be paying you to do this, and so will I. It's not up for negotiation."

"But I was only joking."

I went into this thinking I was doing him a favour, not getting paid in the process. Although, a little extra cash definitely wouldn't hurt.

"We won't pay more than we agreed," Officer Grant says, and I hear Barrett snap something at him.

"I presumed you knew. Plus, you said you left your job at the doctor's, so at least you'll have some extra cash. Maybe we can take Faith to the seaside," he says and I smile, melting once again. It's not the first time he's mentioned taking me and Faith somewhere, and each time it's sent my belly fluttering.

He really does know the way to a young woman's heart.

And the seaside does sound really good right now. Faith and I have never been on holiday. We've never even been to the seaside. I'm not about to voice that though; otherwise, we'll never get out of here. Knowing Maverick the way I do, he'll demand we go now.

"We'll catch up tomorrow," Officer Barrett says, and Maverick nods before we follow them out, heading inside the club.

"You're coming?" I ask when Evan doesn't leave like the others.

"Only for a bit. I just want to go over something with Maverick before I head home. Why?"

"I was just making sure you weren't going to watch the dancers. I wouldn't want your wife finding out." I grin, teasingly.

He laughs. "You two will get on fine," he says, and then walks towards Maverick's office. "See you in a bit. Don't be long."

I SWEAR, AFTER I had Faith, all pride and dignity went straight out the window. Spreading your legs as wide as you can manage, pushing out a baby the size of a watermelon whilst having a bunch of midwives and doctors staring down at the most intimate part of your body will do that to you. *But* seeing a bunch of women topless, bottomless, well... it's hard to look past. I've lost count of how many times I've been smacked in the face by Holly's, Sophie's and Marley's boobs. I'm surprised I don't have nipple imprints with how hard they've hit me.

Damn fake boobs.

So far, I haven't seen anything out of the ordinary, but I have managed to narrow down a list of suspects. There's Holly who is twenty-six, a single mum to a little girl and is currently looking for another job. There's April who is twenty-four and a student. She's only on my list because of how bubbly and outgoing she is; no one should be that happy about taking their clothes off for a living. Sophie, who is the mum of the group at thirty-three, and a single mum to three kids, is also on the list. I've only added her because she seems to know all the girls on a personal level. Somewhat, anyway. I'm hoping I can get her to open up and talk about the other staff members.

There's only one girl everyone steers clear of and that's Marley, who I've labelled the bitch of the group. She doesn't really get on with anyone, and if that doesn't have suspicion written all over it, I don't know what does. Then there's Kathy, twenty-five, quiet student who has kept to herself pretty much the entire shift. The only reason she's on the list is because they say to always watch out for the quiet ones.

I haven't seen Maverick since he left after showing me around, but I'm tired and my feet are killing me. He also promised me pizza—amongst other things.

I rap my knuckle on the office door and walk in, finding him sitting at his desk wearing his light blue shirt with the top few buttons undone. He looks incredibly sexy and I can't help the grin that spreads across my face, my belly doing that crazy flutter thing again.

"Hey." He smiles, looking up from his paperwork. "How's everything going?"

I shrug, watching as he gets up and starts making his way over to me. I smile, lifting my head as he gets closer.

"Great, but I'm hungry. You promised me pizza," I remind him, pouting.

"Ahh, so I did," he says, pulling me close to him. "I'm pretty sure I promised something else too," he whispers against my neck. I move my head to the side, giving him better access as he peppers kisses across my skin. Shivers race down my spine and I sigh. It feels like heaven.

"You did, huh?" I whisper back, lost in the feel of his soft lips.

"Mmhmm," he mumbles, and I hear the lock on the door click in place. A squeal escapes when he lifts me, carrying me towards his desk. I swing my legs around his waist and lean back, capturing his lips in a deep kiss.

Yes!

This is what I've craved ever since our first night together.

"Fuck me," I whisper, feeling bold as he sets me down on his desk.

His eyes darken as he moves between my legs, jerking me forward so I'm pressed against him. "My pleasure," he says huskily.

I'm so turned on I can feel the heat of my arousal between my legs, seeping down my thighs. His hands come between us and seconds later, he yanks up my dress, exposing my damp knickers. My breathing comes in heavy pants as he leans forward, kissing me with promise and raw passion as he tears my knickers off my body.

"Please," I breathe against his mouth.

He drops his trousers enough to free his cock, not giving me any kind of warning before slamming inside me. I throw my head back screaming, and he grunts, pulling out and slamming back inside me with powerful, forceful thrusts, driving me closer and closer to the edge.

It's embarrassing how close I am already. And based on the sound coming from Maverick, it's clear he's struggling to hold on too. My fingers dig into his shoulders, my legs widening as he thrusts deeper, filling me. I start clenching around him, squeezing him tightly in a vice grip.

"Fuck!" Maverick rasps, his hold on my hips tightening as he shifts me forward, slamming into me over and over until I can't take it anymore.

"Maverick," I scream, clinging to him as the most powerful orgasm tears through me, pleasure consuming my entire body.

"Fuck," he pants, his cock pulsing inside me.

We take a few moments to catch our breaths, still clinging to one another. My hands fall limp around his neck and I drop my forehead to his shoulder.

I'll never get enough of him.

"So, pizza?" I breathe out and he chuckles deeply, kissing the top of my head.

"Yeah, baby, I'll get you some pizza."

Yep, I'll never be able to get enough of him.

TWELVE

TEAGAN

"So you've forgiven him, just like that?" Tish says from where she's perched on my bed.

I look at her through the mirror and sigh.

Since I told her about Maverick turning up at my door nearly two weeks ago apologising, she's been riding my ass about forgiving him so easily. She's not a second chance kind of girl; if you screw up with her, you never get another shot.

I can't exactly tell her what made me change my mind about him. It's no business of hers to know about his personal life or his past. And from the depth of Maverick's confession, I know he hasn't told another soul what he told me that night. His apology meant everything to me.

"Yeah, Tish, just like that. You won't understand, but trust *me*, please. When I say he's sorry, I genuinely mean it. You know I'm not the kind of girl to be walked all over. I don't trust many people, but I trust him."

"I don't get why you can't tell me what he said to make you all gaga for him," she huffs, leaning back against the pillows. "Can I use this?" she asks, picking up the midnight blue nail varnish.

I barely nod before she's picking it up and painting her toes.

"Because it's private. Now, which one?" I ask, holding up two dresses. The first dress is a purple skater-style dress with a deep V in the front; it's dressy but casual. The second is black and fitted with a deep V at the front. This one is more dressy than casual. Both reach above my knee and fit great, but I have no idea where Maverick is taking me. He wouldn't tell me or give me the slightest clue.

"I'd go with the purple. You don't know where that fucker is taking you, so you don't want to look stupid wearing the little black dress at McDonald's."

"He's not taking me to McDonald's," I scoff before taking off my dressing gown. "He just said to be ready by seven and look pretty."

"Yeah, like you ain't nothing but pretty, girl."

"Tish, please, just be happy for me."

"Oh, girl, I am happy for you, especially for your vajayjay. I was starting to worry you grew your hymen back." She snickers.

I look over my shoulder at her, my eyes widening at her words. I finish pulling the dress over my head and then stare at her in disbelief. Her tongue hangs out of her mouth as she concentrates on her toes, so she doesn't notice I'm staring or haven't replied to her comment.

"What, girl? I feel your eyes bugging into me from over here," she snaps, not looking up from her toes.

"I didn't grow back my hymen and my vajayjay is just fine, thank you very much. I'm beginning to have anxiety over some of the stuff that comes out of your mouth," I admit.

She looks up at me, grinning. "You should be worrying about what's going in it."

"Ew, too much information, Tish. Could you at least pretend to tone it down?"

"Sorry, no can do. Where's the little human tonight?"

"You make her sound like an alien," I huff, putting in the pearl earrings my nan gave me.

"She is to me. Damn, she tried making me watch that freaky fairy show." She shudders and I chuckle.

"It's called *Tinker Bell* and it's not as bad as you going to watch *Paranormal Activity* with her," I remind her.

"I didn't know she wasn't allowed to watch horror movies. She didn't come with a manual."

I love my best friend, I really do, but her and kids? They just don't mix. But even with all her faults, I know she loves Faith and would do anything for her. Which is why I know she watched *Tinker Bell* with her, whether she wants to admit it or not.

Tish was by my side throughout my pregnancy, and during the birth. She screamed at any nurse or midwife who went near my vajayjay or came at me with any funny-looking instrument. She also pinched my gas and air because she couldn't cope with the stress—her words, not mine. But she's always been there for me. I guess that's why she's finding it so hard to accept Maverick.

She was there when I got back from Maverick's after the wedding breakfast, and it only took one look for her to know something had happened. And the fact that Faith told her everything before we even fully reached her.

She held me while I cried, went to the shop to get some junk food, and spent the day watching films with me. She also bitched about how all men are wankers and should be burned.

"I love you," I blurt out, knowing I don't tell her enough.

She looks up at me, seeming taken aback. "You on something, girl?"

"No." I laugh. "I just want you to know I love you and I'm thankful for everything you do. You're always here for me, protecting me, and would be my alibi if I ever needed one. You're like a sister I never had." I smile.

"You need to be black to be my sister." She chuckles, shaking her head. "Stop getting all emotional on me. It's making me uncomfortable."

I notice her eyes water before she blinks, ducking her head. One thing I've learnt over the years is you don't upset Tish. She hates emotional shit, or any kind of touchy-feely. She avoids it like the plague.

"It's seven. He late, girl," she says, kissing her teeth. I hate it when she makes that noise only because I can't do it for the life of me. She tried to teach me but said I couldn't do it because I'm white. It drives me mad that I can't.

"He's not late," I scold, looking at my phone, which reads one minute past seven.

There's a knock at the door and I look to Tish, giving her a smug smile.

"So, where's the little human at?"

"She's in her room watching a film. I'll go say bye, so let Maverick in. And be nice," I warn as I head downstairs, moving towards Faith's bedroom.

I hear Tish interrogating Maverick and roll my eyes. I should have known she wouldn't listen.

Faith looks up when I walk in, and then smiles.

"You look so pretty," she gushes before yawning.

"Thank you, gorgeous." I sit down next to her on the bed. "I'm going out now, but I'll be back later. Be good for Tish. Make sure she doesn't eat all the chocolate, watch scary movies and she behaves, okay?"

She giggles, nodding. "I promise to have her in bed by eighty ninety," she says.

I shake my head at her reference to time and lean down to kiss her head. "Be good. Love you."

"Love you more."

"To the moon..."

"... and back," she finishes, and I smile softly down at her.

I wave goodbye and shut her door too, knowing she hates it completely shut. Maverick's standing by the door with a stoned-face expression as he listens to what Tish is saying. He looks bored and ready to kill at the same time.

Knowing I need to step in, I move quickly. Maverick notices me first and his eyes widen with appreciation. The heat in them as he takes in my outfit reminds me of the time he looked at me when I first wore the work outfit he supplied me with. Since then, we've made good use of that outfit, *and* his office.

I grin when his eyes reach mine, raising my eyebrow. "Hey."

"Hey. You look beautiful." He smiles, a dimple showing in his left cheek.

"Hell yeah, she does, and if you don't treat her good or you take her sexy MILF ass to McDonald's, we're gonna be having words, boy," Tish scolds, all sass and attitude.

I groan, grabbing my coat off the back of the sofa, slipping it on.

"McDonald's?" he asks.

I shake my head at him, silently warning him not to go there.

I don't wait for Tish to explain, I take Maverick's hand, pulling him out of the door.

"Hold up." He chuckles, stopping me at the bottom of the stairs.

"Sorry. She can be a little overprotective."

"I gathered that when she started threatening my balls if I didn't treat you right."

I wince, but he doesn't seem bothered by her behaviour at all. Instead, he pulls me against him and kisses me. I sigh into the kiss and put my arms around his neck, leaning on my toes for better access.

"I've been dying to kiss you all day." He grins when he pulls away.

I smile. "You have, huh?"

"Sure have. You ready?"

I nod, still smiling. "Where are you taking me?"

"We'll be going to Numero 38 for a starter, Sam's Grill for our main and Millie's, for dessert," he tells me.

"Three places?" I ask in awe, not just because it's the most romantic date I've ever heard of, but because all three restaurants are hard to get a table at. I'm flattered and blessed to have met such a charming man. He really does have some hidden attributes.

"Yeah. I've never been on a date before, but from what I know, it's always dinner and a movie. Well, if we go to a restaurant for two hours, we'll get a dead ass, and backache from crappy chairs, and end up getting drunk. At a movie, we won't be able to talk to each other. Yeah, I could cop a feel, but where's the fun in that if I can't finish what I started," he says, winking at me as he helps me into his car.

I wait for him to get in before turning to him, a huge smile on my face. He's put a lot of thought into this date, which tells me he's taking us seriously and wants to try. We were meant to go out last Saturday but I had to cancel because I couldn't get a babysitter. I felt so bad, but then he brought round pizza and a movie, spending the night with me and Faith. It was brilliant, but this... this is something else entirely.

"I don't kiss on the first date," I tease.

"You've never been on a date," he teases back, leaning forward to kiss me. "So, did I do well?"

"With three yummy restaurants, three types of food? Hell yeah, you did. But what I want to know is what replaced the movie?"

His face flushes. "You'll have to wait and find out."

I smile as I fall back into my seat. I wish everyone could see this side to Maverick, not just the moody, unapproachable man he usually is. He comes across as intimidating, but I've seen the real him now to ever feel like that around him again. Plus, he only ever makes me feel special, sexy, and loved.

"You brought me to an aquarium?" I gush excitedly.

He flushes, looking unsure as he nods down at me. "A friend of mine is the manager and he gave me a key. He's here but he'll be working in his office. He said we have the place to ourselves until eleven."

"This is unbelievable. You brought me to an aquarium for our first date and three different restaurants. This is incredible. Are you sure you've never been on a date? Because you sure know how to pursue a woman." I grin, jumping out of the car.

"So I did well?" He smirks, amused at my excitement.

"You did fantastically," I add, smiling huge. I love going to the aquarium. I've not been in a while because of money being so tight and because Faith doesn't like the underwater tunnel. She prefers the zoo.

Tonight has been surreal. Not only did our dinner taste delicious, but we also talked until we were blue in the face. Some bits were a little sad to hear but when he spoke about his brothers, their girlfriends and other people close to him, his eyes lit up. I could see the love he has for each and every one of them, and I hope one day he'll look like that when he talks about me. Because there's no doubt about it—I'm falling in love with Maverick Carter.

"I'm so fucking glad I didn't listen to Max." He chuckles as we enter the aquarium. All the overhead lights are off but the ones in the tanks are on, illuminating the room in a warm glow.

"Why, what did Max say?"

"He told me to take you to the park, grab a bottle of cider and play kiss or oral," he says.

"You're kidding, right?"

"I wish. He was so dead set on the idea that he's asked Lake if she wants to do it," he says, cringing.

"I bet that went down well. I'm so glad you didn't plan that."

"She put him in his place like she always does." He chuckles before turning to me. "So, does this mean I get to kiss you on our first date," he flirts, bringing me in for another kiss.

"Oh, handsome, you would have gotten a lot more if Faith weren't at home." I grin and he kisses me once more.

"C'mon." He grabs my hand, taking me down a path.

I'm in awe as we walk around. The place is beautiful but seeing it in the dark, with only the fish and tank lights on, is something else altogether.

We're walking into a darker part of the building, through a small tunnel before coming out to the most amazing view I've ever seen.

We're in what I can only describe as a fish bowl, except we're the ones inside and the fish are swimming all around us. But they're not ordinary fish. No, they glow in the dark. It's the most beautiful sight I've ever seen and I can't help but turn in a circle, taking everything in. Glow-in-the-dark fish in star-fire red, cosmic blue, electric green, sunburst orange, galactic purple, and moonrise pink. They're all swimming around, illuminating the place in a soft, warm glow. Ripples of water reflect on the floor and when I look to the centre, I gasp, spinning to Maverick.

"You did this?" I ask. On the floor is a mass of blankets and pillows. A bottle of wine rests in a tin bucket of ice, and a few candles surround the edges of the small dome shape we're in.

Maverick shifts, looking uncomfortable before clearing his throat. "Um, yeah."

"This is beautiful," I tell him, still in awe. Needing to take a photo, I take my phone out and start snapping away, including some of the beautiful fish swimming around in their tank. When I'm finished, I turn to Maverick shyly. "Can we take one together?"

"Yeah," he croaks out. I can tell he's not a picture person, but he's doing this for me which makes me like him all the more. He's incredibly sweet, something you wouldn't guess looking at his tattooed and rough exterior.

He steps next to me, wrapping his arm around my waist and pulling me against him. I relax into him, loving the feel of his hard body. With shaky hands, I hold my phone up and look up to Maverick to see if he's ready. He's looking down at me, his eyes full of heat and warmth and I smile, ducking my head shyly. At the same time, my finger slips on my phone, snapping the picture.

"Whoops, let me try one more time."

I hold it up again, this time resting my head against his chest and smiling. I snap the photo and turn to take a look, making sure I didn't cut us out.

My mouth falls open when I see the look Maverick is giving me. His face is full of wonder and I can't help but think he feels more for me than he lets on. It makes me giddy with excitement.

"C'mon, let's open the bottle of wine. I hear it's your favourite." He smiles as I look over to the bottle of white chardonnay, a smile spreading across my face.

"It is. How did you know?" I tease, already knowing the answer. I often pinch a bottle from the fridge in his bar—after he gives me his permission, of course.

"Come on." He chuckles, shaking his head as he directs me over to the blankets.

I sit, sighing against the comfort the blankets and pillows give me. Tonight has been brilliant. Maverick has been brilliant. Never in a million years did I think he was capable of organising such a romantic date.

Taking a sip of wine, I moan. It's the second glass I've had, not wanting to get drunk for my first-ever date. I can only imagine how that would turn out.

"I still can't believe you did all of this." I lie back on the cushions, watching the glowing fish swimming around. It's so peaceful, so beautiful, and the last place I thought I'd be brought on a date.

"It's my first date. I didn't want to ruin it," Maverick mumbles, leaning over me.

Smiling, I look up into his deep, brown eyes. God, he's beautiful. Strong jaw line, almost perfectly straight nose—I think it's been broken a few times in the past—and he has the most kissable lips I've ever seen. The top one is plumper than the bottom, and it's sexy as hell.

"You didn't ruin anything." I smile, cupping his jaw.

He flashes his pearly whites at me and leans towards me, kissing me softly. My arms wrap around his neck, pulling him further down, his body falling easily between my thighs.

I moan when I feel his thickness between my legs, pressing against my core. God, he's so big, so hard. I want more.

Forgetting where I am, I move my hands down his body, rubbing the palm of my hand against his thick bulge.

He pulls away, breathless. "Fuck, Teagan."

I feel the rumble of his voice straight down to my toes. He glances over my head, his eyes sparking with desire. I'm about to go all cuckoo on him and demand how fish could turn him on, but then he reaches over my head for something. I hear the bucket of ice move and my heart picks up speed.

Is he going to...?

My eyes scrunch in confusion when he pulls back with a red ribbon. It's the same red ribbon that was tied around the bucket.

"Do you trust me?" he asks.

I nod because I do trust him, I'm just a little... confused.

He rests up on his knees, the ribbon discarded to the side. His touch on my bare legs has goosebumps rising on my skin. His fingers grip the bottom of my dress and, with a hungry desire shining in his eyes, he lifts it up my body and over my head.

I gasp, looking around in horror.

"It's okay. There're no cameras. Shush," he whispers, leaning down to kiss me. I get lost in the kiss, running my fingers through his hair. My knickers are already damp from just the thought of getting caught. Anyone could walk in here. Okay, not anyone, but the thrill of the unknown is turning me on.

He swallows my moan before kissing his way down my neck, over my shoulder and between my breasts.

He lifts me back up, his eyes darker as he unclips my bra, slowly pulling the straps down my arms. My skin breaks out in chills, my eyes never once leaving his. He shifts, coming back with the red ribbon once again. My eyes widen in realisation. He lifts my arms, leaning down and hovering over my lips.

"Trust me," he whispers.

I nod, holding my wrists together to make it easier for him, the thick ribbon like silk against the sensitive skin. I shift, a torturous ache pulsing between my legs.

The knot he ties takes him a few seconds before he's back to kissing me. His hands are now between us, undoing his shirt expertly. I pant, wiggling my hips, wanting him to touch me, devour me.

My lips part when his magnificent chest comes into view. The fish and candles give off a warm glow, but it's this man in front of me who has me burning up, my skin on fire as sweat beads between my breasts from nerves.

We've had sex five times in total. Each and every time he's dominated me, owned me. I've never had to worry that I'm doing something wrong because every time we're together, he's always taken control of my body, bending it to his will.

This time it feels different. He's not just controlling my body; he's possessing it. With each second I look up into his dark brown, soulful eyes, the more I hunger for him, the more I want him to own every part of me.

Without a doubt, I'd do anything for this man.

His warm, bare chest hits mine and I arch my back, craving more. Before I have a chance to voice my desire, his lips are back on mine, his jean-clad thighs pressing against my bare ones, the texture rough, yet exotic. He presses his erection against my core and I moan, my hands fighting to be free so I can touch him. The need to touch him is far greater than anything I want right now.

"Please," I beg him.

"Jesus," he breathes, his lips hovering over mine. His eyes stay locked on mine, silent yet powerful, like he's trying to tell me something with one look. I try my hardest to look away, the intensity becoming too much.

Before I can make out the meaning of the look, it's gone, his head dips and his breathing is shallow and uneven. He licks his way down my neck and I tip my head back, giving him better access. With my arms tied above my head, my breasts pushed out for his pleasure. He lavishes them, paying each enough attention to drive me wilder.

"More, please, Maverick."

"Patience," he warns, his voice deep and thick with lust.

My body jerks when his rips my knickers off in one pull. "You need to stop doing that. I won't have any left," I gasp, teasingly.

"I'll buy you more," he growls.

He moves again, taking his body heat with him. A small whimper escapes me as he smirks.

He kicks his shoes off before removing his jeans and I notice he's gone commando. I shouldn't be surprised by that, yet I am. It's also incredibly hot.

His body looms over mine as he holds his weight off me. He looks down, his eyes sharp like razor blades, hungry with desire and need. The look burns through me, making me feel alive. My heart beats faster, taking my breath away.

And in one powerful surge...

One commanding stroke...

He's inside me.

He drives into me with such force, such fervour, my back bows and my mouth opens in a silent scream.

"Mine," he whispers before pushing himself inside me once more.

THIRTEEN

MAVERICK

A SMALL SMILE FORMS ON MY LIPS AS I shift through the papers on my desk. I decided to bring them home last night so I could be free tonight for Teagan, who will hopefully find out who's selling drugs in my club. We might not know who's doing this, but we do have a plan set in motion. We've been building it from the start.

One thing we have found out in the time Teagan has worked for me is that the money isn't being exchanged inside the club. It's why we can never pick up the deal on the CCTV footage. It was Teagan who actually questioned us over it, coming up with an outside handler of sorts, and she was right. But picking up whoever is taking the money would be like picking a needle out of a haystack. I wouldn't even know where to begin.

By tonight though, it won't matter because there won't be anyone in my club handing the drugs out for them anymore.

I throw my pen down on the stack of invoices, rubbing my hands over my face. I can't stop thinking about Teagan. She's in my head. Even now, thinking about work, she's there. It's like my mind finds reasons to conjure up her image, wanting me to suffer. In pain or pleasure, I don't know; I just know I can't give her up. Not for anyone, not even for my dark, unwanted past that's like a cloudy storm hanging over us. There's nothing I can do about it and I'll live with those burdens, those secrets and the lies for the rest of my life.

But I know what I can't live with and that's losing her. I can't even go a day without seeing or hearing her in my mind. She brings light into my life.

I love my brothers. I'd die for them. But they're a constant reminder of my past, of what I know, of what I keep hidden. But when I'm with Teagan, I'm just me, Maverick Carter. I can finally let my demons rest and just feel. No other woman has ever evoked these feelings inside me. They've only ever served one purpose for me in the past, and that was on a physical level. I know not all women are the same, but growing up around the cruel, vindictive women I did, it was bound to make me wary.

My feelings for Joan, Harlow, Denny, Kayla and Lake are different. They're different. I love Joan like she's my own nan and the girls are like sisters—which I guess they are. They're family, something my mother never knew the meaning of when she—

"What the fuck is going on, Maverick? I've just been told another kid died. Is it true?" Mason says as he walks into my room, livid and frustrated. I don't blame him, not really, but I do wish he'd let me deal with it.

"Yeah."

"And you didn't think to fucking tell me?" he snaps, sitting on the edge of my bed.

"You were on your honeymoon, Mase. Was I meant to disrupt your holiday for no reason? What were you going to do? Come back? To do what?" I snap back, frustrated myself. I've been dealing with everything since I was eleven years old. I was the reason they got fed, bathed and went to school. I've been trying to fix everything, mend what was broken and make sure none of the bad ever touched them.

I failed once and I left, making sure I didn't return until I could make sure they never had to suffer another day in their lives. I've been keeping that promise ever since.

"I don't fucking know. But I'm back now. You should have said something."

"You just got back," I say, throwing my hands up in the air. "I'm trying to protect you. I have no idea who the fuck is selling drugs in V.I.P. People are dying and it's all blowing back on me. You deal with MC5, not V.I.P. You don't need to be burdened with all this crap. You have a daughter, a *wife*."

"I also have a brother, a friend, a business partner. You're my family. Don't separate me, Denny and Hope from you and our other brothers. You're all my family. I'd do anything for any one of you. You've been carrying all of our burdens for far too long. You need to let us help. You need to let someone in. I mean, what about this Teagan chick? Are you serious about her?"

I look to my brother, knowing that, out of all of us, he knows my pain. He went through something so much similar to me, never having a choice.

"I know. Old habits and all that," I tell him, forcing a smile. "And Teagan... is Teagan." I don't want to divulge too much about her. She's mine. No one else needs to know anything else.

"That's not what I meant, but I can see you don't want to talk about her. But you will tell me about tonight. What's going on?"

I sigh, my elbows on my knees as I lean forward, looking at my brother. "It's Teagan's last shift, whether she finds out who's doing this or not. She doesn't belong there."

"You make it sound like a seedy strip club you'd find down some backstreet alley." Mason chuckles, shaking his head with disbelief.

"It's not that. She's just.... Fuck! When did this become a heart-to-heart? When you said your vows, did you turn into a pussy?"

He laughs. Full-on laughs. "Mav, you'll be right where I am one day. And you're the one getting all sentimental and crap. Want me to get Max to check if you have any balls left?"

"Why Max?"

"He's the only fucker crazy enough to get near you."

I laugh, this time because he's right. I'd never hurt any of my brothers. I'd rather die. Not that we haven't had our scraps, we did, but we've never hurt each other out of hate.

"True."

"So tonight...."

My eyes close for a moment, gathering all of my thoughts before addressing him. "She'll go in wired. They'll give her a phone, a bunch of fucking code words and a script."

"A script? How the fuck is she gonna find someone going by a script?"

"It's not a script like a play. She'll have certain things to add into conversation.

I just have a sinking feeling about it. Not that I think something bad is going to happen to her—I'll be there, the police will be there—but what happens after?"

"What do you mean?" Mason asks, more serious this time.

"Well, whoever is getting a member of staff to hand out the drugs, what are they going to do? Send someone else in? Is it personal, or was my club just an easy target because they knew someone who worked there? It's been driving me nuts. All my staff have worked for me for over two years now. Not once in that time have we had drugs brought into the club or a drug problem until nine months ago. I have so many questions and little to no answers. It's driving me fucking nuts. I don't want any of it to blow back on Teagan. She has a daughter. She's nothing like our...." I pause, shaking my head. I hadn't realised where my words were going until I said them, and now I feel like I've caught myself in a trap.

"Mother," Mason finishes.

I nod. "She loves Faith. She doesn't want her hurt, and has never raised a hand to her. She doesn't get involved in petty shit. She's everything our fucking mother wasn't. And I've gone and got her involved in something that she has no business with."

"Maverick, she said yes. She didn't have to. It's clear Teagan likes you and wanted to help you, so let her. You know if anything does blow back we'd never let her get hurt," he says, trying to come off casual, but he's anything but.

"You're right, but—"

"Is this a mothers meeting or can anyone join?" Max says as he barges into my room.

"Max." I roll my eyes.

"If you've come to moan about Harlow eating something you think belongs to you, then piss off. She's pregnant with your nephews," Mason snaps. There's no heat in his words, but I know he's as frustrated as we are. We all want her happy, and Harlow isn't happy unless she has food in her hands.

"Denny was never like her. I swear, you'd think she was having triplets. But that's not why I'm here. Joan's friend Hazel is here—"

"Did you want us to throw a party?" Mason asks sarcastically.

Max grins. "If you want to. I'm always up for a party, but I thought since Hazel is Teagan's nan and is here—"

"Why is she here? Is Teagan okay?" I ask, standing up.

"Fuck me! If you either of you'd let me fucking finish, I'd tell you. She came because of Faith. She can't calm her down. She wants you. I tried to calm her down but I'm feeling a little out of it," he says, puffing his chest out.

Which means he couldn't calm her down and if Max can't calm someone down and make them laugh, then something is really wrong with Faith.

"Are they at Joan's?" I ask as I slip on my trainers.

"Yeah. I'll come. I need food now that Mason's mentioned it."

"Fuck's sake. C'mon, then," I say, letting him follow me out.

"Fuck it, Denny's there. I'm coming too." Mason jumps up from his seat.

The three of us walk around. The second I reach the path, I hear Faith crying. I burst through the front door, giving Max a quick glance before rushing through to the front room.

She's on Hazel's lap, her back arched as she tries to get free, but Hazel, even with her old age, pins her down. My eyes narrow, my blood heating.

"Let her go," I say. My voice sounds dangerous, a clear warning, and both Hazel and Joan look at me warily. Hazel lets Faith go reluctantly. Faith stills when she hears my voice, and with red-rimmed eyes, she stares at me. Her cheeks are soaked from tears and my chest aches at the sight.

"What's wrong?" I ask, sitting down on the sofa. "Come here."

She runs over to me, jumping into my lap. She doesn't care that I sound mad, or pissed; she knows it's not aimed at her. I'm not really angry at her nan. I'm angry because I can't stand seeing a child being restrained, no matter how upset they are.

"I want Mummy. I want Mummy and Nanny won't take me back. Mummy needs me," Faith sobs.

"Mummy's working, sweet girl. I've told you this," Hazel says, glancing at me worriedly.

"I want Mummy. She's not safe," Faith cries again, and my back straightens.

"What? Why is Mummy not safe?" I ask, untangling her arms from around my neck.

"I had a bad dream."

I relax, and smile down at the girl who has already captured my heart. "I'd never let anyone hurt Mummy. If someone tried, I'd stop them," I tell her honestly.

"You would?" She sniffles, looking up at me all doe-eyed.

My features soften as I stare down at the most beautiful little girl I've ever laid eyes on. I'll never tell Hope that; she'd get jealous.

"Your Mummy is working for me tonight. How about Max babysits you at my house and I'll bring Mummy back to see you? Would you like that?" I ask her.

"Really? And you'll wake me up, even if it's really late? Mummy lets me stay up late. I stayed up till seven o'clock once."

Joan and Hazel chuckle as Mason, Max, Denny, Harlow and Malik walk in.

"Yeah, squirt. I'll wake you up. Mummy can say goodnight then." I smile, then realise my mistake and look to Hazel, wincing. "Is that okay?"

Her eyes water and I fear I've upset her, but then she smiles, placing her hand over her heart. "More than okay."

"What's okay?" Max mumbles, chewing on a slice of chocolate cake. Harlow sits next to me, placing a hand over her stomach, and I smile. She's getting bigger each day. I don't know how she's going to carry on to full term; whenever she stands up, I'm surprised she doesn't topple forward.

"You're babysitting Faith tonight so she can sleep at ours. I'll make a bed up in the spare room."

"Really?" he says, glaring at me. "I planned on—"

"We don't need to know what you planned to do tonight," Harlow yells, then winces, rubbing her stomach.

"You okay?" I ask, shifting Faith on my lap so I can turn fully to Harlow.

"Yeah. They're moving around a lot today. I've lost count of how many times I've been kicked in the bladder," she moans.

Faith giggles, leaning forward. "Can I touch?"

I watch with soft eyes as Faith places her hand on Harlow's stomach. The second she does, she snatches it back, her eyes wide with wonder.

"What?" I ask.

"Her belly moved. Is it the babies?"

"Yes." Harlow giggles, then looks to me with a wide smile. "Want to feel?"

My heart stops. I remember feeling Hope moving in Denny's stomach. It was the best feeling in the world. And heaven help me, I can't wait for the day I feel my baby in my woman's belly.

Fuck, I never thought I'd say that.

A picture of Teagan flashes in my mind. She's standing at the end of my bed in a dressing gown. Her breasts are full, her nipples large and pink, her stomach flared out, rounded, and carrying my child.

Beautiful.

My eyes must be as round as saucers because Harlow looks at me curiously. Then I remember she asked me a question.

"Yeah," I croak. I reach out, touching her stomach where Faith had before and smile when I feel the squirts kicking and moving.

"I still don't understand how that doesn't hurt," Max says, eyeing Harlow's stomach like it's alien.

"It does sometimes, but it's not painful."

Faith's hand comes beside mine and she giggles again. This time she doesn't pull away. She looks at me, still giggling, and something burns deep inside my heart. I don't know what passes through me in that moment but I know it's significant, far-reaching and vast.

The minute I laid eyes on Teagan I knew there was something special about her. I knew she wouldn't be a one-time fling. And as much as I've tried to fight my feelings for her, it's useless. I've come to care for her more than I realised, and seeing the little girl in front of me, looking at me like I've hung the moon, just seals it for me. I think I'm falling in love with her mum.

"Is the baby a boy or a girl?" Faith asks, snapping me out of it. My hand is still on Harlow's stomach so I pull away, noticing she's staring at me with deep curiosity still. I clear my throat, feeling as if she can read my thoughts, and look away.

"I don't know, sweetie. There are two babies in there, but we won't know if they're girls or boys until they arrive."

"When will they arrive?"

"In five to six weeks."

"*How* will they arrive?"

I look between them, uncomfortable, but Harlow seems content, her face relaxed and happy.

"They'll be born. I'll give birth to them."

"How will you birth them?" Faith asks, her head tilted to the side, studying Harlow's stomach.

This time Harlow shifts uncomfortably, her eyes meeting mine. I shrug, having no fucking clue what to say. I look around the room, my eyes finding Joan's but she just smiles.

"Maverick, do you know?" she asks and my eyes widen, taken back.

"Um… I…. Maybe we should ask mummy? She did give birth to you," I rush out.

Max chuckles. "Yeah, ask mummy, and then Maverick can sit you down and tell you all about the birds and the bees."

"Max," Denny snaps.

"Oh, blooming hell. I was kidding. He just put me on babysitting duty. He deserves more. He's lucky I like the kid."

"You said another naughty word. I'm telling mummy," Faith says, moving her hand off Harlow's stomach and back around my neck.

"Glad you're feeling better," Max mutters, looking horrified.

Denny laughs as my phone rings. I pull it out and see it's Evan. He's meeting with Teagan to go over everything with the police. I'd have been there—should be there—but if I were, I'd stop her from doing this. I know I would. So I decided to stay away until she started her shift. That way I can sneak in the back without having to see her.

"Hello?"

"It's time."

FOURTEEN

TEAGAN

I'M SUPPOSED TO ACT LIKE I'M having a bad day, only I'm not pretending. I really am having a bad day. Today has exhausted me, emotionally and physically. Faith woke up this morning in a clingy mood, looking sad, and demanding cuddles. She's followed me everywhere, including the bathroom. It's not unlike her; on occasions she does wake up sleepy, still in the midst of her dreams, wanting love and cuddles. It's one of my favourite times with her. She's always been quiet and softer in the morning. She normally snaps out of it after twenty minutes or so, but not today.

When the time came for my nan to pick Faith up, the child completely changed. She just lost it on me. My nan had to drag her out kicking and screaming, and it tore my hear apart. I've not been able to stop worrying all day about her, and countless of times I've wanted to ditch tonight and leave to go to her. I need to see her so badly. I hate how we left it.

I've never seen her so scared in all her life. Not even when she would have nightmares or thought the bogeyman was under her bed. God, her face....

"No! I don't want to go. I want to stay here with you," Faith cried.

"Sweetie, I have to go to work," I told her, my heart heavy as tears filled my own eyes.

"And we're coming back tomorrow," my nan whispered softly.

I pulled Faith closer in my arms, concern seeping into my pours. She looked so terrified, so scared for me, and it was so unlike her.

"No! No! I'm not going," she screamed louder, clinging tighter.

"What's wrong Faith? What has you so upset and acting up?" I asked, my voice soft yet firm.

I wanted to call Evan back, tell him I couldn't do it, that Faith needed me. But I knew Maverick was desperate to get this sorted. The quicker I found out who it was, the quicker it would be over and I could come home.

"You were hurt. They hurt my mummy and I have to protect you," she cried harder. Nan and I looked to each other with knowing expressions. She'd clearly had a bad dream where I'd been hurt and was worried about me. I began to relax, moving to appease her.

"No one is going to hurt me, silly. What's made you think that?"

"I had a bad dream," she told me, confirming my suspicions. She wrapped her arms around my neck, tightening them when nan tried to pull her off me. *"I don't want to go. I don't want you hurting."*

"Are you fucking listening?"

"Hey, are you okay?" Sophie asks, shaking my shoulder. Dazed, I look up, startled to realise I'd spaced out again.

"For the tenth time, can you pass me my fucking outfit? I'm on in ten minutes," Marley snarls.

I shake away thoughts of Faith, as hard as it is to do. I open my mouth, ready to apologise for my behaviour, when it occurs to me that this is my chance.

A scowl forms and I snap my head in Marley's direction, my eyes narrowing on her.

"What did your last slave fucking die of? Get it your fucking self." My words are heated and I have to fight the flinch that threatens to surface at being so cruel. It doesn't suit me. It also turns my stomach. And although I know this isn't real, that I'm only playing a part, Marley doesn't know that. And as much of a bitch as she can be, she didn't deserve that reply.

"Fuck me! What's gotten up your arse today?" Marley mutters before snatching her outfit from the table behind me.

"You do seem off," Sophie says, then gets distracted when Kathy calls for her.

"Sorry, I'm just stressed. I haven't been able to relax all week. I've got so much to do. I have to—" My voice reaches the level of hysteria before I break down, covering my face with my hands so they can't see that I'm not actually crying. I sit there, pretending to cry over stress I don't really have, although I am apprehensive about leaving Faith this evening. I feel like a fraud. I'm a liar, and I hate knowing not all of these women are bad and deserve my deception.

"Hey, it's okay, Teagan. If you need help you can always call me. If I'm not here or at college, then I'm free to help," Kathy says, Sophie at her side. I'm surprised Kathy even spoke to me. She's such a sweet, kind girl, but she's awfully quiet. She keeps to herself and doesn't get involved in the bitchiness that goes on behind the curtain. She's also the only girl who doesn't go topless. She's a dancer, a beautiful one, and seems to dance in a way that's tasteful, elegant. She moves so no one can see her breasts, covering her intimate parts, yet the crowd still goes wild for her. I always make sure I'm near the curtain so I can watch her performance.

"Thanks, Kathy. I guess I just need a little pick-me-up. It's been a *long* fucking week. I'll have to arrange a night out. Wind down for a night or something. I don't know how I'll survive any longer with all this stress."

"Back to work," Sophie calls as Tracey, another dancer, walks off one of the smaller stages. "Teagan, give me an hour. I'll finish what I'm doing and I'll let you take an extended break. Just make sure you come back in a better mood. I need you to go through outfits in the back. Make piles of which ones are in good condition and which aren't."

She walks off without a backwards glance. I sigh, falling back in my chair. She must think badly of me now. Sophie has three kids and has raised them on her own. She's kept two full-time jobs to keep her kids fed and clothed, and here I am, moaning that I can't cope with one when in all fairness, I've never struggled being a mother. Not once. I've never doubted myself either. But I'm doubting myself as a person right now.

If she doesn't think I'm a moaning Myrtle, then she most likely thinks I'm a lazy co-worker. Some of the other girls preach sobs stories to her, always making up some excuse as to why they were late. Now she's probably labelled me as one. I guess after today it won't matter because hopefully, it will all be over.

"Hey, if you—" Marley starts, but Sophie interrupts when she calls out her time. My eyes widen, wondering if this is it. Marley groans but reluctantly turns back. "I'll talk to you later. I may have a solution for you. It might help give you a boost."

I'm glad I'm sitting when she walks off because I would have stumbled. Not only has Marley just spoken to me without biting my head off, but I think she's going to offer me drugs. If I can get her to give them to me, then this is pretty much a done deal.

I'll have to pop into Maverick's office on my break, let him know what's happening. He's most likely with Evan who is in the empty supply room next to the office, listening to everything going on through the wire.

They wired me up an hour before my shift, then sat me down, going through everything I'd need to say and do. I thought everything would have taken longer, dragged out, or that I'd fail. But I'm close. I didn't expect that to happen.

I walk off into the back room to work until the time comes to talk to Marley. Plus, I can't wait to see Maverick. I've not been able to see him all day.

RUNNING A HAND OVER MY sweat-slicked head, I look at the time on my phone once more and sigh. The break Sophie promised me hasn't come, and it's been two and a half hours.

I've walked out to the dressing room a few times since being sent to the storage area. Each time Marley has tried to talk to me, but something or another calls her away, distracting her. It's starting to annoy me.

My phone beeps, alerting me of a message.

MAVERICK: Come to the office.

I smile down at the phone, giddy with excitement. I've wanted to see him since I arrived for my shift.

As I get up, the door is pushed open, revealing Sophie. "Hey, is everything okay?" I ask.

"I'm so sorry. We're down three waitresses tonight so I'm juggling all of the girls. Your break totally slipped my mind. You can go now if you like but first, there's something I'd like to talk to you about," she says.

My eyes scrunch together in wonder. I take a step forward, concerned by the expression on her face.

"You can talk to me about anything," I tell her softly.

"It's about—"

"Sophie, Tracey's fallen and twisted her ankle," someone shouts from the dressing room.

Sophie groans. She looks conflicted as she glances between me and the door before she sighs, giving in. "Take your break. I'll speak to you before your shift's over."

I nod, remaining silent as I watch her rush off to see to Tracey. Sophie's a wonderful person, a great mother. Whatever she has to talk to me about must be important. I just hope she has nothing to do with the drugs being sold on V.I.P premises. She doesn't seem like the type, but then again, none of the girls do.

Walking out, I head towards Maverick's office. I need to tell him about Marley and my suspicions before I go talk to her. I want him to be ready.

Before I can round the corner, I bump into Holly. She stumbles backwards, shocked. I reach out, steadying her before pulling away.

"Oh, hey, Teagan. How you feeling?"

"Tired," I lie, faking exhaustion. "I guess I'll have to get through it. I have no other choice."

"About that…. I don't normally do this, but I have something that could help you," she says, stepping closer, almost whispering.

Alarm bells ring in my head. I keep my expression impassive, knowing this is what we've been pursuing. If this is what I think it is.

"Oh yeah?" I say, feigning interested.

"Yeah. I just…. You need to keep it to yourself. Can I trust you?"

Who asks someone if they can trust someone? Stupid people, that's who. I know Maverick will be listening, along with Evan and whoever Officer Barrett and Grant has brought in with them.

"Of course you can. If you can get me out of this funk, I'll take whatever help you can give me." I force a smile, hoping she doesn't see through my lie.

"Good," she says, glancing down the hall to make sure no one is looking.. "These will give you the pick-me-up you're after. Take one, no more. I'll let you have these for free, but if you need more, you'll have to pay. You can't tell anyone about this though."

"What are they?" I whisper, taking the pills from her, my hands shaking.

She opens her mouth to answer, but before she can breathe a word, the hall is storming with uniformed and plainclothes police.

Her eyes widen in horror and fear, glancing to me before hardening. "You stupid bitch. You have no idea what you just did," she yells, coming for me. She grabs a chunk of my hair and the pills she gave me fall to the floor. I hold her wrist, crying out when I feel strands of hair fall free in her grip.

"Let me go," I yell, shaking.

"You'll pay for this. You have no idea what you've done. She'll know," she whisper-yells in my ear. I look behind me, my hair still in her grip. Her eyes are still wide, full of fear, but in a blink I see a flash of relief.

That can't be right. Why would she feel relief?

She lets go, pushing me to the floor. I land on my hands and knees before two strong arms come around me.

Maverick.

He stands me up, keeping me tucked into his side. I go willingly, shaken, breathing him in for comfort. His body turns rigid and I look up, finding the source. Holly stands there, her hands behind her back in handcuffs as the police read off her rights.

"How could you?" Maverick says, his voice hard, void of emotion, and cold.

"I had no choice. *No* fucking choice. You think I wanted to do this? That I wanted people to get hurt? No, I didn't. The police arresting me had always been a better option for me. Let's just hope these imbeciles get to my children before *they* do."

She's dead serious in what she's telling us, but it still doesn't make up for the fact that she helped kill people. She still sold those drugs and didn't care about the consequences. She could have gone to Maverick and asked for help, explained everything to him. I'm sure he would have helped her. No, I *know* he would have.

I can tell from the look on his face that he's hurt by her betrayal. Anyone who works for him knows he'll do anything to help any one of them. Hell, just the other day he gave Sophie a gift card for various shops so she could get her kids some much-needed clothes.

"You're an adult. You know right from wrong," he bites out before turning away, taking me with him. He stops when we reach Evan. "Check everything out about her. I want to know what she had for breakfast last week. I want to know every single one of her friends, visitors, and family. If the police need anything, tell them to call me tomorrow."

Evan nods and moves back into the office. I follow Maverick, staying silent. As we reach the back door, Holly's voice echoes down to us.

"You're going to pay for this. You're going to wish you never found out about me," she screams.

I visibly shake, and the hand Maverick holds becomes clammy. He looks down at me with a soft expression.

"It's okay."

"Where are we going?" I ask softly, looking back at all the police in the hallway.

"To see Faith," he says shortly, his tone clipped.

"Faith?" I ask, dragging him to a stop when we reach outside. "Stop! What's going on? Are you mad at me?"

He stops, sighing. When he turns to look at me, his eyes are sad, yet a fire burns there. "I can't believe her. She's worked here for three years. I don't get why she would do this. They get a fair wage."

I grip his face in my hands, leaning up on my toes so I'm somewhat eye level with him. "You couldn't have known she was going to do this to you. It's over. It's stopped."

"Yeah," he whispers. He brings his lips down, covering mine, and I sigh, contented.

"Now tell me. Why did you mention Faith?" I ask, kissing him once more.

"She's at mine. It's why I texted you earlier to come see me. She was upset at Granddad and Joan's house this afternoon. She wanted you, so I said she could stay with me. Max has her. I promised her you would tell her goodnight, so we should go."

I melt, my eyes softening as my lips pull into a smile. "You, Maverick Carter, surprise me."

"I surprise myself." He chuckles, picking me up and bringing me closer.

"Take me to my daughter, then." I wrap my legs around him, holding on tight. I never want to let go. Ever.

Maverick Carter isn't who he professes to be. He's more. Much more.

And he's mine.

FIFTEEN

TEAGAN

Why do Mondays always seem to drag? Every Monday is the fecking same. It's painful, tiring, and the day seems to move slower. I dread the day every Sunday. You know it's coming, like a killer in a horror movie, and there's nothing you can do to escape it.

God, the whole weekend seemed to drag for me. After the constant police interviews, them taking my statement and then explaining to the other members of staff why I was there, it's been exhausting and tiring. Most of them understood my reasons, but Sophie and a few other girls were a little hurt and pissed. They saw what I did as betrayal. Marley surprised me when she spoke up for me, telling them it was about time someone sorted out who was fucking with the club.

"I'll be off. Are you sure you're okay to lock up?" Nan asks, bringing me back to the present. She moves around the counter, grabbing her coat and handbag. She picks up the bunch of flowers she's made up for her friend before turning back to me, a worried expression on her face.

I lean against the counter, rolling my eyes. "I'm pretty sure I'll be fine on my own for one afternoon, Nan. No one has come in since this morning, so it's not like we're rushed off our feet. Go, I know Pat is waiting for you."

Her free, cold hand cups my cheek. She smiles sadly, shaking her head at what she sees. "I know that, my child. I'm not worried about you being rushed off your feet, but about *you*. You've had a long weekend." She sighs.

I let out a breath. Since Holly's arrest, I've been a little shaken up by her parting words. They've haunted me day and night ever since. It wasn't as much as the threat but the promise as she said them that has me wary.

I regret telling Nan. I knew she'd only worry but I wanted her to know before she read it somewhere or someone else told her. I told her the real reason why I was there and not the lie about needing some extra cash.

Although she was proud we saved lives and put away a criminal, she's also disappointed over the fact that I didn't tell her beforehand and that I put my life at risk doing it.

"I'm fine. I promise. Everything the other day was too much, too fresh, but I've had time to process it now. Stop worrying about me."

She glances at me for a minute or two before seeming satisfied with the truth in my eyes.

I step forward, mindful of the flowers she holds and hug her. I love my nan with all my heart. Without her, I don't know where I'd be. She picked me up when I was down and alone, and when I was scared and running from my past. She's helped me raise Faith and I'll be forever thankful to her, so knowing she's worrying over me makes me feel bad. She shouldn't have to anymore—not that she ever had to.

I'm stronger now. It should be me worrying about her.

"Okay. I'll see you tomorrow. Pat needs me to stay the night with her," she says, kissing my cheek.

"Tell her to get well soon and that we send our best wishes." I smile, kissing her cheek before pulling back.

"I will."

Once she's gone, I busy myself with idle chores. But after an hour they're done, so all I have to do is stand around being bored.

I'm walking back out to the front when the bell above the door dings. My head pops up, a smile plastered across my face, but it falls the second I see who's standing inside the door with two men at her side.

I stagger backwards, blood draining from my face. My mouth opens and closes, stuck on what to say or do. So many emotions are running through me.

Shock.

Despair.

Dismay.

A noise from behind me gains my attention. I turn, looking to the back entrance. Two more men step inside, sneers on their faces. My heart beats wildly against my chest.

"Teagan, it's been too long," she says in a sickeningly sweet voice.

My body recoils, flinching at the sound. I look at the woman who tried selling my body, my virginity, with narrowed eyes. She's still the cold, heartless bitch I remember from long ago. The years haven't been good to her by the looks of it, although she seems healthier in some aspects.

Lynn was my uncle's girlfriend... or a friend with benefits. Either way, she was his toy. She was a snake, a witch, and I hated her with a fiery passion.

"Lynn," I mutter, glancing behind me nervously.

The four men she has with her aren't like the usual pack of morons who do her bidding. Instead of the skinny, greasy-haired imbeciles willing to do anything for their next fix, these are sturdy, muscled and clearly know what they're doing.

"You've cost me, child," she says in a cringeworthy tone before turning around and flipping the door sign to Closed.

"As I recall, I stole from Travis, not you," I bite out. And the only reason I stole the money was because of this vile, evil woman. I needed to get as far away as possible from them. They were—*are*—toxic to anyone they come into contact with.

She's put on a little weight but her skin still looks worn, wrinkled and old. Before, she was skin and bone, looking fragile all the time. She reminded me a lot of the Wicked Witch of the West—but ready to break if you even blew on her.

She also seems to be doing well, if her appearance is anything to go by. Instead of the trashy-looking clothes she wore, she's wearing a pair of decent jeans, and a nice top.

She laughs at my remark. "You think that's why I'm here? Because of Travis?"

"Then why?" I ask, glancing at the two men standing behind me once again. I hate that I can't keep an eye on them without taking my eyes off the two in front of me. It's making me nervous.

"Well, as much as Travis would love to know where his darling niece is, I'm actually here because you took something from me, and *you're* going to replace it."

"How did I?"

I step to the side. I'm now able to get a clear view of both parties, but I've also pushed myself into a corner, the wall behind me.

"You see, Holly was working for me. She was my main distributor and *you* got her arrested. Now you, my darling, are going to fill her position. I need someone inside and my sources tell me you already work for Carter. I'm told you two are very close," she says, her lip curling.

Oh my God!

It's her!

"Why would I work for you?" I ask. She's crazy if she thinks I'm doing *anything* for her. I narrow my eyes, shaking my head. "Your drugs are killing people. Why on earth would I be a part of that?"

Her expression turns cold, her own eyes narrowing. She takes a step forward and before I can move, her hand connects with my face. I cry out, my eyes watering.

"You will. You will do as you're fucking told. You wouldn't want me to cut up your pretty little face, now would you? Maybe let my boys here see if you're still that sweet virgin? Maybe I'll get them to mess Carter up, the one you're so fond of," she sneers.

I grit my teeth, holding my stinging cheek. "I'll never work for you. Ever."

"Oh, you will. You won't like the consequences if you don't. I've lost money because of you, so to make it up to me you'll take a night's take from the club. I know their take for one night is a lot. You'll get it and bring it to me. In good faith, I won't set my boys on you."

I look to the men with her, all wearing blank expressions. From the way they looked at me when they first walked in, I knew they'd do anything without a care in the world or a backwards glance.

I force a laugh, trying to come across as brave when I'm no such thing. "I'll do no such thing."

She tilts her head to the side, regarding me. "You'd risk your life? Your lover's?"

"I'm not risking anything. I don't *owe* you anything. I'm not doing it, so go back from whatever gutter you came from," I snap.

She smirks, seeming amused and smug at the same time. "Very well. I'm due to speak to your uncle soon. I bet he'll love to know I've seen you."

I gulp, knowing if she tells him where I am, he'll come. There's no doubt about it; no one steals from him and lives to tell the tale. But if he comes, it'll be the end of me. I dread to think of what he'll do. I've watched him cut a man's finger off for digging into his stash of weed.

I stay silent, straightening my stance as I stare at her. Lynn seems to read my thoughts, a smug smirk forming on her lips.

"I see I've gotten your attention for once," she states calmly. "I'll be in touch in three days. You better have a night's take by then." She walks towards the door, but as she touches the handle, she stops, looking back at me over her shoulder. "Oh, and I shouldn't have to warn you to keep your mouth shut. If you go to the police, your nan will be arranging your funeral, or vice versa. I haven't decided."

I stay silent, frozen in place as Lynn leaves with her four goons. I'm shaking like a leaf, my body cold from her threat.

Tears fall before I even realise I'm crying. Then my brain unfreezes and I snap to attention. Rushing into the back, I grab my coat, bag, phone and keys.

I need Maverick.

I need to warn him.

I need to make sure he understands everything—who I am, who *she* is and how evil she is. I'll have to tell him the darkest time of my life. I just hope he can still care for me once he knows about my past, and the reason his club was in trouble in the first place. I don't think Lynn being at his club is a coincidence. I honestly believe it's because of me.

I TRIED TO CALL HIM BUT HE DIDN'T answer his phone, so I rush through MC5, ignoring the staff who try to stop me when I run into the back, using the staff entrance to V.I.P.

There are only a few staff members around when I storm in. They all look up from what they're doing to see what the ruckus is about.

Bet they think I've gone crazy.

Shouts from the MC5 staff can still be heard echoing down the hall behind me, but I carry on and ignore them. One of the girls from V.I.P looks up, confusion apparent before she glances behind me. When she sees the staff members, it must click what they're doing because she stands. I rush past her and I hear her tell the other members of staff that I work there, even though she knows I don't any longer. I'll have to remember to thank her later.

Maverick's office door is closed, but I don't let that deter me. I know he's working today, he told me he'd be stuck in his office doing paperwork.

I barge in unapologetically and he looks up from his desk. At first he seems annoyed, but when he sees it's me, his expression turns to one of concern and worry.

"Teagan? What's wrong? Are you okay? Where's Faith?" he asks, standing up and looking behind me, most likely for some kind of threat he can beat with his fists.

I struggle to catch my breath, but somehow I manage to push through, my words rushed.

"They want me to sell drugs. Rob from you. Kill innocent people. She's going to tell *him* where I am. She threatened to hurt you and Nan if I don't do as she asked."

More tears fall, blurring my vision. My voice is beyond hysterical and I find it hard to catch my breath once again. I jump, startled when a figure stands beside me, placing a hand on my shoulder. I hadn't even seen Evan when I arrived, I had been that frantic.

"Teagan, slow down. What happened?" he asks.

"Lynn...."

"Okay, who is Lynn?" Evan asks, looking alert.

"She was my uncle's girlfriend. I—" I start, but stop, choking on my words. My eyes fill with more tears, my throat tightening with emotion.

"You can tell us anything," Maverick whispers, pulling me into his arms.

He leads me over to the sofa, sitting me down and keeping me close. I let him, needing him right now. I didn't know how much I needed to feel his arms around me, comforting me, until I feel them come around me.

"Did I tell you my parents died?" I ask, forgetting everything we've ever talked about before. All I can think of is *her* promise to tell my uncle where I am.

"Yeah," he answers, looking confused.

"Well, I went to live with my uncle. He wasn't pleasant. He lashed out, liked using his fists, but he never did anything past that. Then Lynn came to live with us and he changed from worse to unbelievable. He could only think about money, sex, money, drugs, and more money.

"I overheard them one night talking about me. Lynn was organising a way to sell my body, *my virginity*, to the highest bidder," I choke out.

I watch as his jaw begins to tick, his hands clenching into fists. He takes a minute or two to calm himself down. It's not him who replies though, but Evan.

"Go on."

I turn to face him, no longer able to look at Maverick. "That weekend I went to a kid's party from school and lost my virginity. I didn't want her to take it from me. I knew Lynn enough to know she wasn't kidding around. And I knew my uncle would do almost anything for money.

"After I came home from the party, I started to clean up Travis's mess like I normally did when he had his friends round for a party. On the table was a wad of cash, three thousand. I stole it, packed a bag, and ran. I haven't seen Lynn or my uncle since. Not until today when she said I lost her money getting Holly arrested."

"What's her last name?" Maverick asks, taking my hand in his. It surprises me. I didn't think he'd want to know me once he knew I was a thief, and *why* I lost my virginity.

"I only know her as Lynn. We weren't BFFs. My uncle either ignored me or beat me, so he never talked enough to tell me." I shrug.

"What's your uncle's full name?" Evan asks.

I wipe my eyes, looking to him. "Travis Bellington. He doesn't have the same last name as my dad. They were brothers by marriage," I explain.

Evan types it into his phone. I sit, staring into space until I feel Maverick squeeze my hand.

"What does this Lynn want you to do?" Maverick asks.

"She wants me to take Holly's place, but first, I have to steal a night's take to make up for the loss she's taken. If I don't, she threatened to hurt you and Nan. She had four men with her. Big men. *And* she told me she'd tell Travis where I am. You don't understand what he'll do to me if he finds me. I stole a week's worth of money—money he probably owed to other drug dealers," I tell him, tears threatening to fall once again. I don't tell him she threatened to have her men hurt me. It will only fuel his anger, and I don't want him getting more worked up or doing something stupid, like giving in to her because he doesn't want to see me hurt. I'd rather take a beating any day of the week than sell drugs for some scumbag.

"No one's going to hurt me or your nan. And you won't be made to do anything that crazy bitch asks. Did she give you a number to get in touch with her?"

"No. She said she'll contact me in three days to get the money."

"Okay, if she contacts you, don't answer. We'll find out who she is. I'm sure Holly is talking to the police already, trying to get out of her charges. Don't worry. If she contacts your uncle, it won't matter. I won't let him get anywhere near you to hurt you."

I nod, sniffling once more.

"Does your nan have CCTV at her flower shop?" Evan asks, looking up from his phone. I'd question him how he knew about my nan owning a flower shop, but with Evan, I've found it's best not to ask questions. He always seems to know more about everyone else than they do about themselves.

I shake my head. "No."

"I'll ask at the shops nearby if I can check their footage. Maverick's right. If she contacts you, don't answer. She can't hurt you. We'll find her before she even thinks of doing anything stupid. It's what I do," he tells me, smiling. His calm demeanour reassures me, but deep down, a part of me has a sinking feeling that everything is about to go from bad to worse.

"Okay," I whisper, nodding.

"I'm gonna see what I can dig up about our new friend and inform the police of this new development."

He gives Maverick a look, a silent communication passing between the two before he gets up and leaves.

"Where's Faith?" Maverick asks.

I look at the clock on the wall, panicking when I see what time it is. "Shit! She's in after-school club. I'm gonna be late."

"I'll go get her. Call the school and tell them who I am, and that I'm picking her up. You go pack an overnight bag for you and Faith. You're staying at mine tonight."

"You sure?" I ask, not wanting to admit how shaken up I am at seeing a part of my past. Or how comforting it will be to be in his presence, in his arms, feeling warm, tender and safe. I'll take anything, even if it's only for a night.

"Yeah. I could do with a night away from this place too, and I can't think of two people I'd rather spend my time with," he says, pulling me to my feet. We both pause, staring at one another, lost in each other's gazes. Guilt gnaws at me and I bite my bottom lip.

"I can't believe it was someone from my past selling drugs in your bar. I'm so sorry. I feel like I'm the reason," I admit.

He sits on the arm of the sofa, pulling me between his legs, his arms around my hips. His expression is serious, focused, and sure when he looks up into my eyes. His thumbs start rubbing in slow circles on either side of my hips and I sigh, relaxed and content from that one touch.

"This isn't happening because of you. It *didn't* happen because of you. It was happening well before we even met and was an ongoing issue we couldn't deal with. Not until you came along and helped us. Don't shoulder that blame, Teagan. None of us could've known what was going to happen. Hell, I never thought Holly would be capable of doing what she did, especially when she knew the drugs were defective. So relax, don't let it get to you. Oh, and kiss me." He grins, his pearly whites and dimples on show.

I smile, leaning forward and capturing his lips in a deep kiss. They're soft, warm, and he tastes like peppermint. I could kiss him all day and never have enough.

My lips feel swollen when I pull away, blinking back the desire I have for the man in front of me. "We need to get Faith," I rasp, dropping my forehead to his. I close my eyes, my body swaying from desire.

His hands tighten on my hips, a groan escaping his mouth before he pulls back a little, putting some breathing room between us.

"Yeah," he says huskily, his pulse pounding at his temples. "We'll continue this tonight."

"Promise?" I smile, forgetting the day's events.

"Oh, it's a promise." He smirks, kissing me once more.

SIXTEEN

MAVERICK

A SMALL, HEAVY WEIGHT POUNCES on me, knocking the wind out of me at the same time I hear a squeaky meow.

That damn rat.

"Wake up," Faith whisper-yells, her breath blowing in my face.

I open my eyes, seeing a mass of wild brown, curly hair. Dark chocolate eyes shine down on me with a smile brightening up the dim-lit bedroom.

Looking down, I chuckle. "Faith, you're strangling Splinter." I pull him out of the chokehold she has him in, getting attacked in the process. "Ahhh, you little...." I stop, remembering Faith. Splinter runs off, but not before shoving his ass in my face, making me choke.

I swear that cat has the devil in him. When Joan first brought him home for Lake, I was a little apprehensive about the funny-looking creature. But when Joan explained how Lake needed routine, something to call hers so she would know this was home, I gave in. Then it attacked Max every chance it got. It would've been funny but the thing hates men. Literally. Not even Granddad can be around it without it attacking him somehow. But the worst part about it all is the fact that none of the girls see what it's really like. He's sweet as pie to them. It's annoying as hell.

"Why do you keep calling him Splinter? Max called him that too, and some other names, but he told me not to tell anyone he said naughty words. I thought his name was Thor," she whispers, careful not to wake her mum—who I kept up all night fucking.

"It is." I chuckle. I take in her school uniform and my eyes widen. "Shit! We need to get you to school."

Her eyes go round as saucers as she places her hand over her chubby, rosy cheeks, leaving her mouth hanging open.

"You can't say naughty words either. Mummy will be *so* mad."

I grin, giving her a wink. She's just too cute sometimes. "Don't tell your mum. And as long as you don't repeat the bad words, we're good."

"That's what Max said." She nods, seeming to be okay with it. "Ohhhh, guess what? Max said he's going to take me to school today."

"He is, is he?"

"Yeah. He said you owe him *big* money. He told me to come and ask you to do my hair so we can *crack on*."

"Crack on?"

"Yeah, Max said that too. He said it wasn't a naughty word. So, can you do my hair?"

I chuckle, shaking my head and look over to Teagan's sleeping form. She's lying on her side, her hands pressed together under her cheek. She's flat out, light snores coming from her mouth. I don't have the heart to wake her, knowing I exhausted her last night. And she looks sexy as fuck.

I glance back to Faith who holds her brush in my face, smiling wide. I sigh, giving in. I'll never be able to tell this girl no.

Sitting up in bed, I take the brush from her, noticing her eyes are glued to my chest.

"Can I have drawings on my chest?" Faith asks suddenly.

I grunt, amused. "Squirt, they're called tattoos. You can't get them until you're eighteen," I tell her, even though I was sixteen when I had my first one done. Pro of looking older than your years.

"I want Elsa and Cinderella. I want one here and one there." Smiling, she points to each of her skinny biceps.

I pick her up, turning her so she has her back to me. I hold the brush up, pulling it through her thick hair, struggling when it becomes knotty. She doesn't flinch but she does fidget, making the job much harder.

Once I have all the knots out, I pause, wondering what the fuck I'm supposed to do next. She hasn't moved so I'm taking it she wants it in a ponytail like the girls wear theirs.

"Um, squirt, how do I put your hair up?"

"Oh, sorry. You need this," she says, handing me a bobble. "And I have to wear it in a plait for school. Mum doesn't want me to get bugs. She said she hates trying to get the suckers out."

"Bugs?" I ask, giving her head a wide birth, leaning back.

"Yeah, nits," she states. "Come on, Maverick, I'm going to be soooo late."

I panic, looking back to Teagan. I have no idea what I'm doing or even what a plait is. We never really had females around growing up or cared to know how to do hairstyles. I'm completely out of my element.

"Um... is Kayla awake?"

"She's gone to the shop with Lake and Harlow."

Shit!

"Okay. I've got this.... Shoot. How do I plait it?"

She huffs in frustration, her tiny shoulders rising and falling in the process. "You take three pieces of hair and you do this thing."

"What thing?" I ask, dividing her hair into three sections.

"I don't know," she says, puffing out a breath. "Mummy does it."

Your mum is a freaking saint.

I'm still holding the outer sections of the hair I divided when the bed beside me moves.

"What are you doing to my daughter's hair?" Teagan asks, her voice still filled with sleep. It's husky, sexy, and if Faith weren't sitting in front of me, my dick would be hard and on its way to being inside Teagan. I can't get enough of her.

"I have no fucking clue." I chuckle and drop her hair, sighing with relief.

"Oh no, what time is it?" Teagan sits up, clutching the sheet to her bare chest.

"Are you naked, Mummy?" Faith snickers.

Teagan freezes, a red blush staining her cheeks as she stares at Faith. I'd laugh at her expression if the situation weren't so awkward.

"Turn back around," Teagan rushes out, ignoring her daughter's question. Faith giggles, doing as she's told. Teagan takes that moment to lean over the side of the bed, coming back up with the shirt I discarded last night.

"What time is it?" she asks me as she pulls my shirt over her head.

"It's fine, Max is—"

"Faith, c'mon, kid. I want to be back in time for breakfast," Max shouts up the stairs.

I glance at Teagan, who looks confused. "Max is taking her to school. And yeah, you should do her hair before he comes up here. He'll most likely try to get into bed with us," I deadpan.

She looks horrified at the thought and quickly grabs Faith, dragging her across the bed to her lap. Faith giggles as I chuckle, but Teagan ignores us, looking panicked.

I'm fascinated as I watch Teagan run her fingers through Faith's hair. She parts it, much like I did in three sections, but from the top instead of at the bottom. Then quicker than I can keep up with, she plaits Faith's hair.

I'm in awe. Shivers run up my spine as I watch the elegance, the smooth, skilful touch as her fingers twist and turn.

It almost makes me beg her to run her fingers through my hair.

"All done, baby," Teagan announces. She pulls Faith against her front, nuzzling her cheek and neck.

"Faith! C'mon.... Fuck's sake Splinter. Argh, Lake, come and get the rat. He's—" Max stops, a high-pitched screech echoing up the stairs. "Lake?"

Faith giggles, jumping off the bed. "I should go save Thor before Max gets hurt or realises Lake isn't here." She giggles to her mum. "Love you to the moon and back. Oh, and Mum," Faith says when she gets to the door. "Teach Maverick how to do girls' hair. He didn't know what to do," she says, rolling her eyes.

I open my mouth to defend myself but Teagan's abrupt laugh stops me. I turn, finding her laid back, her hands clutching her stomach.

"What?" I ask, my voice high and defenceless. I cough, clearing my throat, and narrow my eyes down at her.

"I just pictured you trying to do her hair. You looked so... so scared."

Her laugh has my lips twitching. "I didn't know what to do."

"I could tell. You even held her hair like it was an offensive object," she wheezes, still laughing. "I'd dread to think what she would have gone to school looking like had I not woken up."

"Stop laughing," I warn her, trying to sound stern.

"Nope! I'll have to teach you now. The lady has spoken." She laughs harder, shoving her head in the pillow to muffle the sound.

When I move she looks up, rolling onto her back. I fall between her silk thighs, pinning her arms above her head. The laughter dies from her lips, turning into a soft chuckle. The amusement is still clear on her face, shining brightly back at me through her eyes.

"Stop," I order.

She goes to protest so I lean down, pressing my lips to hers before she has a chance to speak. She moans into my mouth, her body arching beneath me. My dick twitches, hardening against her already wet folds.

She looks up at me from beneath her dark, long eyelashes, her hazel eyes sparkling back at me, strong with lust and desire.

That one look undoes me, tearing my heart wide open. Never in a million years did I ever imagine I'd feel like this about someone, that it would be *this* woman who would make me feel so alive, free, and unstoppable. Every time I'm with her I feel like I can finally have it all, baggage or no baggage.

"Mine," I growl as I slide inside her silk folds, a primal need for her taking over.

AFTER TAKING TEAGAN for the second time in the shower, we both leave freshly clean, yet the smell of sex still lingers. It doesn't help that her lips are swollen and bruised from kissing, and that her face is still flushed from her orgasms.

We're walking down the stairs after finally managing to get dressed. I've not been able to take my hands off her, especially since she has that 'just fucked' look going on. She works it well too.

In the midst of fantasising about her sweet body and her incredible mouth, I'm shaken out of it when I hear my brother's slightly raised voice.

"You're being emotional," I hear Malik say, sounding exasperated and exhausted. I can also detect a slight hint of sadness and pain.

"Uh-oh," Teagan mutters, eyes wide as we step into the kitchen.

"No, I'm not," Harlow argues. She's sitting at the table with her head down. Denny stands in Mason's arms by the sink, looking concerned for her friend. As do Lake, Kayla and Myles, who are watching the disaster play out in front of them.

"Then why are you talking about moving back in with Joan?" Malik yells. He looks panicked, pale, and frustrated.

Harlow starts sniffling, crying into her hands. I look back to my brother, the torment in his expression. Seeing her like this is killing him, I can tell.

Needing to fix whatever is going on, I take a step towards Harlow, who seems as fragile and broken as Malik. I grab the chair from the table and drag it so I'm sitting next to her. I give Malik a quick glance to see if he's okay with me being so close. One thing I've learnt about my brother since he's been with Harlow is that he hates people touching her, even if we're related. He doesn't even seem to notice me, his gaze fixated on her.

I have to fight not to go over there to reassure him that everything is going to be okay. But at this stage, I don't think it matters what I do or say to him; he won't see reason.

Turning my attention back to Harlow, I put my arm around her, rubbing my hand slowly down her back. Everyone watches, giving us a wide birth, but I can tell this has gotten to them too. This isn't like Harlow. She lives and breathes my brother; anyone can see that.

"What's up, Harlow? Why do you want to go back to Joan's?" I ask softly.

Her breath hitches at my question. She seems just as pained by the idea as Malik. It's hurting her, so I don't understand why she's saying it if it's not something she truly wants.

I'll never understand women.

She looks up at me, her eyes red and swollen from crying. "It's not going to work."

Malik steps forward, looking stricken at the idea. "What? Why? Harlow, what's really going on? I love you." He drops to his knees at her side, his face deathly pale.

"I want more," she cries, bending her head to look down at him. The second she does, another sob tears from her throat.

"Harlow, you're just emotional right now," Denny says softly. She goes to take a step towards her friend but Mason pulls her back, shaking his head.

"No, I'm serious," she cries, wiping her eyes.

Everyone looks sad. Even my own heart is cracking at their pain. It was these two who showed me what love was—what love *is*. Without them.... I shake my head. That's never going to happen. It's not a possibility. I won't let it.

"Why?" Malik asks, his voice cracking.

Fuck!

I've never seen him like this. Out of all of us, he's always kept his emotions hidden, pasting on a blank expression. Well, unless he's angry. He's never had a problem showing his anger.

"Because we don't have a future."

Her answer sounds grieved, anguished, her eyes filled with so much hurt and sorry it's gut-wrenching.

"We're having twins, Harlow. We love each other," he tells her, pleading now.

She shakes her head sadly, tears still falling as she hiccups. "But I want more. I want to get married, and I know how you feel about marriage. I understand why, but my parents wouldn't want me having kids when I'm not married. You could leave me at any given moment," she rushes out hysterically.

I start to piece it all together. Malik has always said he'd never get married because of our parents. A sickening feeling washes over me and guilt slams into me. What he or the others don't know, only Granddad, is that Mum and that piece of shit we called a dad weren't actually married. But telling Malik that now would cause more questions and I don't have all the answers. Most of the stuff I pieced together myself growing up.

"So we'll get fucking married," he responds, shocking us all. He's always been up front about his feelings about marriage, even when he and Harlow got together, so knowing he's willing to put all that aside to keep her happy is overwhelming.

"You don't believe in marriage," she yells, throwing her hands in the air before breaking out into another sob.

The front door slams shut in the middle of her outburst. We all turn in time to see Max running down the hallways towards us with a big grin on his face.

"I got attacked by a shit ton of MILFS at the school. Holy fuck, they wanted me. I'm the maaaan...," he says, just as he goes ass over tit. Literally.

He rushed in looking so cocky and self-assured that when he falls on his ass, I can't help but laugh. I watch in amusement as Lake walks over, looking down at him flat on his back. She tilts her head to the side, a look of worry and concern across her features. But I know Lake well enough to know she's laughing her ass off on the inside.

"I meant to do that," he groans, lightening the tension in the room. We laugh at his expense—well, everyone but Malik and Harlow who are in the middle of staring down at the floor.

"Are you okay?" Lake asks, helping him sit up.

"Good, I'm good." His words come out as a mumble as he rubs the back of his head, wincing.

"Good. How's your dignity?" she asks in all seriousness, which causes a burst of laughter to bubble out of my mouth.

He gives her a dry look before turning to the room, his eyes widening. I turn to in the direction he's looking, finding Harlow still crying into her hands and Malik staring at her helplessly.

"What's wrong with Harlow? I swear it wasn't me who ate all the chocolate bars.... Okay, I had like, three.... Fuck, I had the whole packet, but I'll replace them."

Everyone but Lake ignores him. She slaps him across the back of his head, shaking her head at him in warning. He shuts up, looking chastised.

"I swear, we'll get married whenever you want to, Harlow. You're not leaving me. I won't let you," Malik whispers, taking her hands in his.

"Marriage is a bit extreme, dude, and let's not mention incest. I'm not going anywhere," Max replies, his eyes drawing together in confusion and disgust.

Lake slaps him again and he winces, shaking his head as he glares at her. We all roll our eyes before turning back to Malik and Harlow, hoping they sort this out.

"But you don't want to get married. I'm not forcing you into something you don't want, then have you hate me." Harlow sniffles.

"You're not making me do anything. I'd marry you tomorrow, Harlow. I'm gonna spend the rest of my life *with you*. Nothing on this earth could force me into that, and if you need the piece of paper to rectify that, then we'll get the damn piece of paper. Either way, I'm not leaving you. I'm not going to walk away. You and I are forever," he says.

I've never heard him be so meaningful, so deep. He's an action person. Malik is not one for words, but as speeches and declaration of love goes, he did pretty fucking good.

She looks up, her eyes round with hope. "You really want to marry me?" she asks, like it's Malik bringing up the subject. She seems so surprised that he would, and she shouldn't. Malik loves her. He'd die for her. Anyone with a heartbeat knows that.

"Yes," he says, no hesitation.

"Before we have the twins?"

"Yes," he repeats, leaning down to cup her face.

"I love you," she cries, falling into his arms.

"Um, aren't the twins due in, like, five weeks?" Max asks slowly.

"Mase, get Joan here. We have a wedding to plan," I order.

"On it," Mason says, grabbing his phone. The relief on his face that Harlow and Malik aren't breaking up is evident. Even my shoulders have relaxed, the tension seeping from my body.

"Another wedding?" Max moans.

"Shut up. You'll be helping too," I warn him. "You okay now?" I ask Harlow.

She contemplates for a minute before shaking her head.

"No—" she starts, but Malik interrupts.

"Now what?" His once relaxed face is now tight again with tension. He looks ready to bust balls if it means keeping her happy.

"I'm really hungry," she says, looking away shyly.

"You saying the food isn't ready?" Max groans from where he's still sitting on the floor.

"Max," I start, not ready to have this conversation right now.

"I'll start it," Denny says hurriedly. She, better than all of us, knows how Harlow gets when she doesn't get her food.

"I'll help," Teagan offers quietly.

My eyes catch hers in a smouldering stare. I love how easily she gets on with my family and how much they've all taken to her and Faith. Not only that, but I love how easily she fits into my life. How nothing with her feels uncomfortable or forced. It feels right and until she walked in my life, everything felt wrong.

"Joan's on her way. She said she just needs Granddad to get her wedding albums down," Mason informs us as he walks back into the kitchen.

"Wedding albums?" I gulp.

"Plural?" Max swallows, looking scared.

"Um, yeah," Mason says.

"Oh God." Myles plops down into a chair.

"Oh God" is about right.

Maybe we should have kept Joan out of the loop until the actual day of the wedding.

"You only want something small though, right?" Malik asks, looking at Harlow, his face pale.

"Yeah, *small*," she says, staring down at him lovingly. "Small."

"Why do I have the feeling she's—" Myles starts.

"Lying," Max finishes.

The girls all giggle at our expressions. For Denny's wedding, we were all run ragged, doing jobs that were too girly and too stressful. The errands Mary had us on.... Fuck, I still think she did it for her own amusement.

None of us argue with Harlow though. Why? Because none of us want to be the reason she isn't smiling the way she is right now. Her whole face is lit up, glowing with happiness.

And I know each and every one of my brothers would kill anyone who tried to take that look away from her.

"*Small* it is, then," I say, thankful everything is right in the world now that they're okay.

SEVENTEEN

TEAGAN

I LAUGH AS ALL THE GIRLS TEASE Harlow relentlessly over the way she had Malik propose to her—even if it was unintentional. Watching that unfold in Maverick's kitchen broke my heart. You could see the two were torn up over it, that neither wanted to leave the other, yet Harlow's emotions got the best of her.

"I swear, you put us through something like that ever again, I'll strangle you myself," Denny tells Harlow.

"I told you it was that dream. It felt so real. I can still feel their touch and hear their voice," Harlow says softly, a sad expression crossing her face.

"What dream?" I ask, curling my feet under me. This is the first time I've heard about any dream.

Harlow turns towards me with a sad expression. "My mum and dad died two years ago. And the night before I went all hormonal on Malik, they came to me in a dream. They told me they wanted to see me married, that I would have a boy and a girl and that if I didn't get married, my future was ruined. But then the dream went back to Malik and the time he told me about his upbringing." She shrugs, trying to come across like it hasn't affected her, when we can all see the truth. It's gotten to her that much that she was willing to leave Malik, the man she loves and adores.

"Oh, Harlow," I say compassionately, knowing firsthand what those kinds of dreams can do to a person.

It was a dream I had of my mum and dad that led me to wake up and hear Lynn and Travis's talk about selling my body. They warned me to leave, to find Nan.

"It's fine," she says, her eyes watering. Her phone goes off, interrupting what I was about to say. "Malik is here. He's waiting outside for us. Thank you for tonight."

I giggle, watching her struggle to get up from the sofa, her round stomach getting in the way.

"It's fine," I tell her once again.

After last week's fiasco and her meltdown in the kitchen over Malik, Joan turned up with albums full of article cutouts from wedding magazines. When they got to the flowers, I finally had something to contribute, so I offered them to her for free. The minute my offer left my lips, Maverick and Harlow were quick to shut it down. Of course, I won in the end, reminding them that I work at a flower shop and can get them at cost, so it wasn't like it was going to break my bank balance. Plus, the chances of her getting another florist to see her on such short notice is not likely to happen, especially with the wedding in three weeks.

Denny takes pity on the heavily pregnant woman and helps her to her feet.

"Girl, after you drop them aliens, you're gonna be doing fanny exercises for years," Tish says, interrupting us.

I groan, looking apologetically at Harlow, who has taken everything that has come out of Tish's mouth in stride.

"Tish," I warn, narrowing my eyes at her before turning back to Harlow. "I'm sorry. Just ignore her. She's just jealous because hers looks like a soggy hamburger and is the size of the Mersey Tunnel."

"Bitch," Tish snaps, but there's no heat in her voice.

We all start laughing, including Tish, who doesn't care what I said. It's how we've always been together. She knows I'm only joking and would never say something malicious or hurtful.

Harlow's phone goes off again and she sighs, typing back.

"We have to go. Thank you so much for helping us with the flowers on such short notice. I do wish you'd take the money though," she says as she pulls her bag strap higher up her shoulder.

"Hush." I wave her off. "I'm just glad I could help. Plus, my nan will want to contribute when she finds out too."

"She loves this shit," Tish says before Harlow can say anything else. "And I best be getting an invite, girl. I've never been to a fancy wedding, or any for that matter. I wants to get all glammed up and shit."

I roll my eyes, but Harlow smiles big as she turns to Tish. "Of course you're invited. You both are."

The way she answers makes it sound like we should've already known we were going to be a part of the big day. I'm honestly shocked. I didn't offer to do the flowers to score an invite.

"I can't wait for you to meet Max." Lake giggles.

"He good-looking?" Tish asks, eyes sparkling with hope.

Oh Lord! She did not just say that.

"Max is her boyfriend," I tell Tish dryly.

Looking baffled and slightly disturbed, Tish rears her head back, looking at Lake. "Why the fuck you want me to meet yo man? I ain't into no threesomes. I did that shit once and shit the bed the next day."

I groan, covering my face with my hands. I know what she's talking about, and the fact that she's just spilled that crap to everyone is disturbing. No one else needed to be traumatised by that nightmare.

I move my hands slowly away from my face, seeing nearly everyone staring open-mouthed and shocked. Denny looks amused as she eyes her feet. Tish, damn her, is fine, like she's just announced she had cereal for breakfast.

"Um...." Lake blushes, not knowing where to look, which causes us all to start giggling. Feeling sorry for the poor girl, I help her out, putting her out of her misery.

"Tish, she meant because you're both nuts. I, for one, think you two should never meet. Maverick feels just as strongly," I clarify, amused.

"I ain't fuckin' nuts. And why, you ashamed of me, woman?"

I shake my head, amused at her bug-eyed expression.

"No, now shush. Malik is waiting for them," I tell her before turning back to the girls. Poor Lake still can't look at Tish, her cheeks bright red.

"I'll make another cuppa," Tish grumbles before shuffling her way over to the kitchen.

"Thank you for letting me help, and for coming here tonight. Nan was busy so I had no one to watch Faith. And Tish wouldn't let me go without her." I chuckle.

"No, thank you. You've done me a huge favour and I'll never be able to repay you," she says, hugging me.

"Do not fucking cry again," Tish shouts from across the room.

I roll my eyes and Harlow chuckles under her breath. We all hug each other goodbye, except for Tish. She just grunts, giving us all a 'don't fucking ask me to hug you' look from the kitchen. Tish isn't a hugger, never has been.

Exhausted after saying goodbye, I sit back down on the sofa, taking the fresh cup of tea Tish kindly made.

After a few moments of silence, I feel her eyes on me, so rolling my head to the side, I look in her direction. "What?"

"You really like this bloke, don't ya?" Tish asks, a concerned expression crossing her face.

I sigh, knowing how she feels about Maverick. As much as she wants me to have fun and clean the cobwebs—her words, not mine—she doesn't want to see me get hurt. And to her, relationships equal pain and hurt. She doesn't believe there are good men out there, thanks to her absent father.

"Yeah, I do. He's got a hard exterior, but I see inside him, Tish. He's soft as a teddy bear. I see the darkness swimming in the depths of his eyes, but I also see flashes, moments of vulnerability whenever we're together," I tell her, divulging more than I meant to. "He's not who you think he is, Tish. He's more. He's so much more."

She remains quiet for a few minutes before nodding, her eyes softening.

"Okay. I'll give the dude a chance, chica. I'm just worried about you. You go from not dating to hearing wedding bells within a short time."

"I'm not hearing wedding bells," I scoff.

"Whatever. I'll leave it be. I guess hearing the girls telling me about his whorish behaviour made me question what he was really after. But if you say I'm wrong, I believe you. Just know that if he messes with my girl, I'll cut his dick off and shove it up his arse."

The mere mention of Maverick with other girls causes a painful pang in my chest, like a hand around my heart, squeezing tightly.

I shake those thoughts away. I may not know everything about Maverick or his life, but I know *him*. Seeing him, knowing him, it's imprinted on me. The connection is as real as the air I breathe and nothing anyone, even Tish, can say will make me believe differently.

I'm not stupid. I know I'm not the only girl Maverick has ever been with, but there's no denying the powerful connection between us. I feel it with every inch of my body and soul.

My mouth opens, ready to defend him, but Faith starts crying, shouting for me from her room.

"I'll go and let you deal with the little human in peace," Tish says, getting up.

I give her a hug, even though I know it makes her uncomfortable. "Speak to you tomorrow. And Tish?" I wait until she looks up at me before continuing. "Thank you for always looking out for me. I love you."

"Shit, woman. Quit with the mushy fucking shit and go see to your kid," she says, looking like she has a thousand ants crawling over her.

"Shut up," I tease, shaking my head in amusement. Giving her a quick kiss on the cheek, I turn, rushing down the hall to a distressed little girl.

I run into the bedroom, finding her sitting in the far corner of her bed against the wall, clutching her Build-A-Bear Elsa to her chest. Her hair clings to her wet cheeks as more tears fall.

My heart stops at the sight of her looking so scared and upset.

"Hey, sweetheart. What's wrong?" I ask softly, pulling her into my lap.

"I had a bad dream, Mummy. It was—" She hiccups. "It was bad, and really scary." She sniffles, wrapping her arms around my neck.

"C'mon now. It's not real. It was just a bad dream. Mummy's here."

"A monster came and took you away from me." Her cries are louder as she clings to my chest, her tiny arms tightening around my neck.

I run my hand up and down her back soothingly. She relaxes somewhat, but not enough to stop crying.

"Calm down, baby. Everything is going to be fine," I assure her, feeling the last of her shakes start to subside. "How about a hot chocolate?"

She pulls away, her watery eyes mulling it over. "Could I have some warm milk instead?"

"Of course. Anything for you. Now, let's put on your fairy lights so you won't be in the dark."

She nods, seeming more relaxed. She climbs off my lap and helps me turn her lights on, lighting the room with a soft pink glow.

I smile to myself as I watch her tuck herself into the bed, making sure to do the same to Elsa. There's nothing in this world I love more than watching her. God, every time I look at her, *really* look at her, and see what I created, my heart feels so full, filled with so much love and happiness that I feel as if I could explode from the sheer intensity. There are times when I let myself think of what it would be like to lose her, and even the thought breaks me. The pain I feel from just that will be tenfold if I ever did lose her.

I give her one last look before walking back out into the living area. I smile when I realise Tish cleaned up after us.

I'm about to start on Faith's milk when a paper on the table catches my eye.

I love you too, girl. Always. T. X

A wide grin spreads across my face at Tish's note. I've never known anyone so reluctant to express their feelings before. Well, Maverick is similar but you can read the emotions in his eyes, no matter how hard he tries to mask it.

Walking into the kitchen, I pin it to the fridge. I'll make sure to tease her relentlessly over it. Hell, I may even get it framed.

Taking the saucepan out of the cupboard, I place it on the side, ready to pour milk in it, but as I go back to the fridge, there's a knock at the front door.

Grinning like a fool, I make my way over. It's probably Tish coming back to take the note, hoping I haven't already seen it.

I'm still grinning like the Cheshire cat when I open the door. The grin falls when I see the person on the other side.

Dressed all in black, I recognise the goon from Lynn's meeting last week at my nan's flower shop. The hairs on my arms rise and an alarming chill snakes down my spine at the sneer on his face.

Thinking quickly, I go to slam the door, fear worming its way under my skin, causing me to shake uncontrollably. The door doesn't even make it into the wood before it's flying towards me with such force that it sends me sailing through the air. I land with a sickening thud, sliding across the hardwood floor before finally coming to a stop when I smack into the sofa.

I'm too stunned to make a sound, my attention focused on the pain in my hip from taking the brunt of the fall.

I lift my head, a scream freezing in my throat as a hand comes towards me, punching me in the jaw.

Everything seems to happen slowly, yet quickly at the same time. When he moves towards me again, a frightened squeal slips past my lips. He pulls me up roughly by the scruff of my shirt. My head is barely off the ground but it feels like three feet when he slams my head against the floor. The force causes my vision to blur and a silent gasp of pain to slip free. My eyes water when the pain in my head becomes too much.

The ringing in my head gets louder and I groan. Then he shakes me, my teeth rattling. I bite my tongue, blood filling my mouth.

"Boss lady is gonna give you one last chance to get her money," he sneers.

Shaking my head, I glare up at him. I hate that woman now more than ever. "It's not her money," I bite out, clenching my teeth through the pain.

"I was hoping you'd say that," he says, an ugly smirk on his face.

I try to fight out of his grasp, but his fist rises once again, landing on my right cheek.

This time, I can't stop the scream from tumbling out. The pain is too much for my already swollen face. "Please, stop," I whisper, feeling pain explode in my stomach.

He grins, bringing his arm back for another hit. I scream. He's going to kill me and there's not a damn thing I can do about. Fighting is pointless; I'm not getting anywhere and he's too strong.

My eyes widen when I realise Faith will have heard me. She'll come to investigate—it's what she does—and he'll use her against me or worse, hurt her.

I can't let that happen.

A battle cry escapes my mouth and I kick out at the same time as I bite his hand, drawing blood. He cries out, smacking me harder across the face.

"Mummy," I hear Faith cry, and my heart pummels out of my chest.

The goon on top of me lifts his head, looking over the sofa. His eyes light up like he's just won some big prize. The distraction causes him to loosen his hold on me, giving me the open I needed.

"Run, Faith! Run! Go!" I scream, tears running down my face. He goes to make a move after her but I move, digging my fingers into his eyes. His scream fills my ears, deafening me.

I don't see if Faith makes it out the door because a burning pain in my ribs causes me to choke, fighting for air.

My eyes are barely open when I see him bring his fist back once again.

Faith!

Her name is the last thing I remember before everything goes black, the goon knocking me out.

EIGHTEEN

MAVERICK

EVAN: Still no last name. It's like this woman doesn't even exist. Does Teagan remember anything?

MAVERICK: Do you have that picture? And no, she doesn't.

EVAN: Yeah. Shit copy, but it's the best we could get. I'll email it over now. And damn. Let me know if she ever does.

MAVERICK: Cheers, mate.

Running my hands through my hair, I let out a groan. Whoever this bitch messing with Teagan is, she's fucking good at hiding and covering her tracks. We couldn't even get a picture of the men Teagan said were with her that day at the store. It's like they knew where every camera would be.

I'm just relieved I can trust Teagan not to fuck me over. She didn't have to tell me about Lynn, or the fact that she asked her to take money from me. She could easily have protected herself and taken it, but she didn't, and that shows me what a good person she truly is. It's something not many women in my life have shown me.

Speaking of Teagan, she's got the girls over tonight to look over some flower arrangements for Harlow and Malik's wedding. They all seem to have taken to her well, which please me to no fucking end. I'm only worried about the shit they could be telling her about me.

Opening our last messages, I go to text her to see how her night's going. My finger hovers over the screen when the door to my office flies open.

"What the fuck, Max?" I growl, gripping the phone tightly.

"What the fuck is about right. Why won't you let me hire the new waitresses?" he demands.

"Max, we've been through this once already. Fuck, even Lake has been through this with you. You had your chance," I remind him, pinching the bridge of my nose.

"I've got nothing to do until September when I can finally start college. I'm fucking bored."

"Get a job," I growl.

"Let me find you some new staff, or at least narrow it down to the best three," he whines.

"No!"

"Why?" he snaps.

"You know why," I tell him, giving him a pointed look.

"Oh my God, Mav. I asked questions you needed to know the answers to. It's not exactly a crime."

"You were asking them to pee in a cup," I growl. I can't even think about the lawsuit I could've gotten had Lake not stepped in.

He rolls his eyes. "Bit of a good job I did. The one girl was pregnant. Pretty sure I did her a fucking favour."

Frustrated, I lean forward, ready to rip him a new asshole. He always seems to know how to get on my nerves, and as much as I love the annoying fucker, sometimes I wish he'd act like a grown-up.

My mouth opens, but instead of me shouting at Max like I want to, a gasp escapes from the scream I hear echoing down the hall.

My eyes widen when I realise who it is. I fly out of my chair, jumping over my desk and knocking everything off in the process. All of this happens before Max even has a chance to blink.

"M-maverick," Faith screams, her sobs becoming louder.

My heart hammers in my chest when I reach the hallway. Before she can crash into me, I pick her up, holding her close.

"Faith, what's wrong? Where's Mummy?" I ask, trying not to show my panic. I feel Max behind me but I ignore him, concentrating on the little girl breaking apart in my arms.

"He's hurting Mummy," she cries, pointing down the hall. As hard as it is, I push her into Max's arms before racing down the hall and out of the building.

The rain is coming down in fucking sheets and it causes me to slip a little on the stairs as I race up them, taking two at a time.

I'll kill them if they've touched her.

The door is wide open so I rush straight in, coming to a barrelling stop when I see Teagan lying on the floor, unmoving.

I fall, skidding across the hardwood floor on my knees, stopping next to her. I go to touch her, but her face is covered in bruises and blood. I'm scared I'll only cause her more pain. The right side of her face is red, with purple mixed in around the edge of the swelling.

My hands shake as they hover over her. My breathing comes in hard, sharp pants, accompanied by a feeling inside my chest I'm not accustomed to. How my brothers coped when their other half's were hurt, is beyond me.

I'm scared for Faith.

I'm scared for Teagan.

But mostly I'm scared of fucking losing her.

Gently, I take her shoulders, shaking them. "Wake up, baby," I call out, my voice scratchy.

A noise from outside has me shooting to my feet, ready to attack. I'm by the door, hiding from view, when someone rounds the top step.

I move quickly, pinning them by their neck against the wall. My eyes widen when Max reaches through my blurred vision, his eyes filled with fear.

"Fuck, I could've killed you. Where's Faith?" I ask, ready to kill him if he's left her alone. We don't know if the person is still out there, looking for her.

He starts coughing, holding his throat. "I locked her in the office with Lake. She won't calm down. Where's—" he starts, his eyes rounding when he sees Teagan. "Holy fuck!"

I grab both the blankets she has folded on the back of the sofa, wrapping one over her body whilst placing the other under her head.

"C'mon, wake up," I plead, kissing her forehead. She stirs, and a painful breath escapes me.

"Faith," she whispers before falling unconscious once again.

"Call an ambulance," I tell Max, finally getting my head together.

"I've already called for one. They're on their way, along with the police. From what Faith was screaming, I knew it was going to be bad, just not *this* bad." He waves over Teagan, his eyes horrified at the sight of her.

"Thanks."

"Who would do this to her?" he asks, moving to stand by the door to look out.

"It's because of me. I'm bad blood," I whisper.

"What the fuck has this got to do with you?" he asks, looking back over and trying to read me. I blank my expression, not wanting him to see how guilty I feel for the sins I've made.

"It's no coincidence that she was hurt right after she was threatened because of something someone wants from *me*. I should've had someone watching her but I'm fucking stupid, thought I could protect her. I was wrong—again."

"Seems like you've been holding out, brother," Max grits out, looking at me through hardened eyes.

"Fuck," I breathe out, not taking my eyes off Teagan. I promised Max and the rest of my brothers that I'd never keep anything from them. Little do they know, I hold back a lot more than they'll ever realise. They can never know the truth. It would break them.

"Yeah, we'll be talking about this later," he says as we hear sirens off in the distance.

I look down at Teagan, watching her chest rise and fall. It's the only thing keeping me from going postal on everyone around me, knowing she's still breathing. She's still here.

"Ambulance and police have just pulled up," Max announces before running out into the rain to greet them.

"C'mon, Teagan. Faith needs her mum," I tell her, stroking her knotted hair.

The paramedics rush in after Max, coming straight over to Teagan. Another set of feet echo up the stairs, and by the time I pry my gaze away from Teagan's bloodied face, I see Evan rush in. His eyes widen when they land on Teagan before turning to me.

My hands ball into fists, my jaw clenching as I move towards him, my expression deadly.

"Who did this?" I grit out, holding onto my anger by a thread. I'm likely to attack him and he's not my enemy.

"I don't know, man. I scanned the picture through my database and had a friend at the station do the same with no such luck. It's why I emailed the picture we got to you. I wanted to see if you somehow knew her," he says, running a hand through his hair.

"How did you know?" I gulp, flicking my head towards Teagan being transferred to a chair, still unconscious.

"I heard it over the police scanner. I came when I heard an ambulance was called to the scene. I knew it was you."

I nod. "I need to find these fuckers. And when I do, I'm going to fucking kill every single last one of them," I hiss.

"You need to stay with your woman. Wait to find out what she knows first before you go and do something half-crazed," he says.

"She's not even conscious. Some fucker has beaten the shit out of her. I'm not gonna be some fucking pussy who sits around and does nothing. It's not in my nature. I want blood and I want theirs," I threaten, raging mad now.

All I see is red and the anger inside me—anger I try so fucking hard to keep at bay—surfaces, sparking brighter than ever before.

"Calm down. You can't lose it now," Evan warns me, his hands on my shoulders.

"Mav, they're ready to take her—" Max is cut short when his phone starts blasting "Too sexy". "Ello? Yeah. Fuck! K," he says, sighing and ending the call. "You need to go sort Faith out, bro. Lake can't calm her down."

I look to the paramedics, strapping Teagan in.

"I can't leave her," I tell him, torn. I know Teagan will hate me if she finds out I left her daughter in distress, but I also don't want to leave her when she needs me the most. Just the thought has my chest tightening.

"We need to go," the paramedic announces and I growl, wanting to rip his head off for interrupting.

"I'll go with her. Sort Faith out and meet us there," Max says.

I can count on one hand how many times Max has taken something seriously. Lake is one, and now this is the other.

"Go." I move out of the way, making sure I don't glance Teagan's way once. If I do, I won't go. The image of her battered face will be forever ingrained in my head.

At the bottom of the steps, I'm stopped by two cops. I sigh, wanting to plough through them. I just want to get Faith and get back to Teagan.

"I'll talk to them," Evan says, and I give him a grateful expression.

I move to the back door of the club, but when I get there, a thought occurs to me.

"Evan, Teagan's door is covered by a camera. You know the password," I call out. He nods, confirming her heard before turning back to the cops.

Rushing down the hall, I knock on the door. Faith's cries turn into scared screams from the other side.

"Who is it?" Lake answers, her voice shaky.

"Me, Mav."

There's a relieved sigh through the door before I hear it unlock. The sight of Faith crying and clinging to Lake breaks my fucking heart.

"Come 'ere." I tell Faith softly. Hearing my voice, she turns, throwing herself at me. I barely catch her in time, but when I do she cries harder, her tiny fingers digging into me.

"Is Mummy in heaven? I don't want her to leave me."

Her sobs and words rip my heart wide open, and tears of my own fill my eyes. I clutch her tighter against me, kissing her head.

"No, squirt. Mummy is going to be just fine. You need to calm down for me though. I need to get back to Mummy, so I'll need you to be a brave girl for a little longer. Lake will take you to my—"

"No!" she screams, clutching me tighter. "Don't leave me. Please don't leave me."

Fuck! She's breaking my fucking heart.

"I need to go to your mum, squirt."

"I'll come. I promise to be a good girl. I won't be naughty at all. I don't want you to leave me and I want my mummy," she rushes out, hiccupping at the end.

"I'll come with you. I'll keep an eye on her," Lake says, tears filling her eyes.

"Hey, it's okay," I tell her, leaning over to wipe her tears.

"We were just there. I only went into town to get you and Max some food. When I got back Max shoved me in here, telling me to lock the door and not let anyone in," she says, more tears falling. "We could've helped her."

"I'm glad you weren't there. C'mon, Max has gone in the ambulance with Teagan. I want to be there for when she wakes up—if she hasn't already."

I grab my keys off my desk, Faith still in my arms crying.

"Wait, was Tish still there?"

"Tish? I didn't see her," I tell her, worried. Not for the woman in general, but for Teagan. For some strange reason she loves the crazy chick and treats her like a sister. It would hurt Teagan something fierce if she knew she'd gotten hurt and I didn't do anything to get her help. "Faith, was Aunt Tish with Mummy?"

"No. I didn't see her there." She hiccups, burying her face into my neck. "I only saw the evil man hurting Mummy. I wanted to save her, but I was scared. Then she shouted at me to run."

Jesus fucking Christ. She saw it all.

"You are one tough cookie," Lake tells her softly.

"But I didn't save Mummy."

"Yeah you did, squirt. You helped her by coming to get me. Now, shall we go see Mummy?"

She nods, her bloodshot eyes and tear-streaked face turned to me, trusting me to take care of her.

After I find the fucker who hurt her, I'm never letting either of them out of my sight.

"SHE'S ASLEEP," LAKE TELLS me quietly, looking into the back seat.

"I'll take her," I rumble, pulling Faith into my arms. She whimpers but snuggles closer.

We make our way into the emergency room, finding Max standing against the vending machine fiddling with his phone.

"You said you'd stay with her," I growl when we reach him. He's fucking lucky I'm holding Faith right now or he'd be meeting my fist.

"They kicked me out "cause I'm not family," he explains, kicking off from the vending machine.

"We'll see about that," I mutter, cursing under my breath. I move to the reception desk, taking in the older lady sitting there. Her hair is pulled back in a tight bun, doing nothing to straighten out the wrinkles and frown lines on her face.

"Hey, I'm here for Teagan Williams. She was brought in not long ago, beaten badly. Can you tell me where she is?" I keep my tone light, hiding my anger and frustration as much as I can.

"Let me see. Ah, yes. Are you family?"

"I'm her fiancé," I tell her with no hesitation. Normally that word would cause me to lose my shit, but tonight, I'm thankful for it. Teagan is mine.

"Okay, well, she's not allowed visitors at the moment. The doctor is with her."

"Why not? I want to see her. Her daughter needs to see her. She watched her mother being beaten and right now, she needs to know that she's okay," I snap, lifting Faith higher up my chest.

The nurse looks at Faith, her eyes softening before she sighs, giving in. "Let me go see what her progress is. I was here when she was brought in."

I nod, my jaw clenched. Watching her leave, I turn to Max. "Call Joan, get her to call Hazel and fill her in. You might want to call Evan, get him to call her friend Tish. She'll want to know. Tell her I'll let her know how she is," I tell him before turning to Lake. "Call Mason. He should still be at work. Ask him to grab the girls' things from the flat and take them to mine. Oh, and to drop off some clothes and shit for Teagan here for when she wakes up."

They both nod, moving away with their phones in their hands.

"Are you Maverick?" the nurse from reception asks, walking up to me.

"Yeah."

"She's asking for you. She's in cubicle four," she tells me, smiling softly. It transforms her entire face, making her seem more approachable.

"She's awake?" I ask, sighing with relief. It's like a truck has been lifted from my shoulders.

"Yes, she is."

I nod, my nose stinging from tears trying to fight free. I pinch the bridge of my nose with my free hand, getting myself together before heading down the hall she gestured towards.

I shift Faith higher up my body once again, keeping her head resting in the crook of my shoulder.

"Where's my daughter? I need Maverick," I hear Teagan cry, and the anguish in her voice has me ripping back the curtain, nearly tearing it off the hooks. I send the doctor who is trying to stop Teagan from leaving her bed a murderous glare. She hasn't seen me yet, which is probably for the best since I'm about to put this doctor on his ass.

"Remove. Your. Hands. Now." The warning in my voice is deadly, a promise

I plan on keeping.

"Maverick," Teagan gasps, her body relaxing into the bed when she sees me holding Faith. A painful sob breaks free, and her face scrunches in pain.

"Hey, love. Calm down," I tell her.

Fuck! I feel so lame right now.

"Is she okay? Did he hurt her?" she asks, ignoring my demands to calm down as she continues to panic, looking her daughter over.

"She's just sleeping. She's fine, just shaken up a little," I tell her, walking farther into the room.

"Sorry to interrupt, but we've just got word that they're sending over a Detective Barrett to take Miss Williams's statement. Is it okay to send him in when he arrives?" the nurse asks the doctor, and I grunt in disapproval.

"How about you ask Teagan if it's okay for someone to come in," I snap.

"Maverick," Teagan says weakly.

"I'm sorry," the nurse replies, taken aback.

"Yeah, you should be." My voice is short, cold.

"Sir, I ask you to respect my nurses. We're here to help and if you use that tone again, I'll have you escorted from the hospital immediately," the doctor states.

I open my mouth, ready to tell him that I don't give a flying fuck, but a cold touch on my hand stops me.

"It's fine. *I'm* fine," Teagan tells me before turning to the nurse and doctor. "Detective Barrett can come in. I'm fine."

"You're not fine, Miss Williams. You've taken quite the beating. I'll be taking you down for an X-ray for your left cheek shortly. We want to rule out a possible fracture."

"A fracture? My cheek?" she asks with wide eyes, her hand going to her cheek, wincing at the slight touch.

"What does it mean if she has one? Will she be okay?" I ask, panicked.

"She'll be fine. It'll just take a lot longer to heal."

I nod, taking a seat next on the only chair in the small cubicle.

"I'll be back shortly to check in on you," the doctor says before walking out and pulling the curtain shut.

I watch him go, my heart beating rapidly as I turn back to Teagan, the woman who has consumed me, and now has the power to destroy me.

I can never lose her.

NINETEEN

TEAGAN

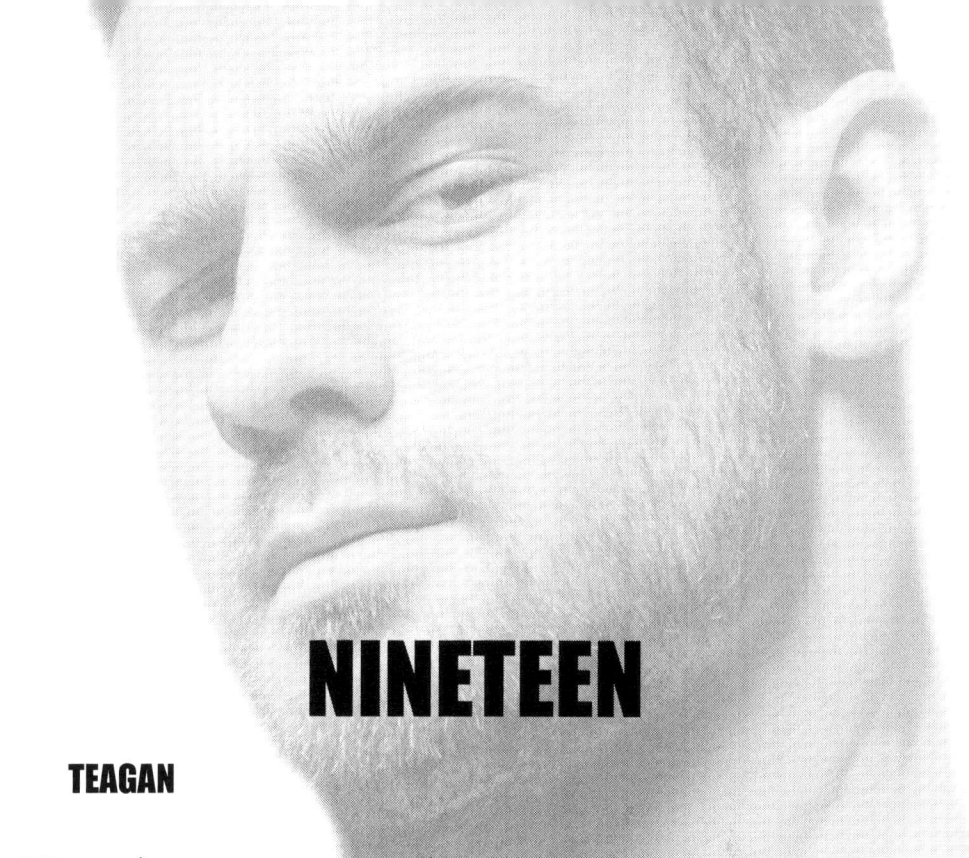

It didn't hurt this much when he was hitting me. In fact, I'm pretty sure I went numb at one point. But now everything aches. My vision is like looking through a kaleidoscope lens and my right jaw is the size of a golf ball.

Maverick is staring at me, his breathing heavy. It's hard to see what he's thinking when so many emotions are running across his face. I know he's scared. I also know he's relieved that I'm okay. But there's a spark of anger and frustration hiding in the depth of his eyes that he's been trying to keep hidden from me since I first took notice of him in the room. Whether it's aimed at me, because of me, or because of him, I'll never know. With Maverick, I don't think I ever will. He's kept his emotions close, never really sharing anything personal with me. And I let it be because I trust him—irrevocably.

"Have they caught who did this?" I ask. My stomach sinks at the thought of him still out there, roaming free. He could come back at any time to finish what he started. That notion has my eyes widening, panic setting in. "Please tell me they got him," I plead, staring at him through blurry vision.

He sighs, looking regretful as he shakes his head. "He was gone before I got there."

"No, no, no, no!" I cry, my hand covering my mouth.

"It's going to be okay," he says determinedly.

"No!" I snap, harshly, tears stinging my cut cheeks. "It's not going to be okay. He saw her, Maverick. He saw Faith. God, the way he looked at her. I could see he wouldn't care about hurting a child from the look in his eyes. What do you think he's going to do with that information? Leave her alone? No, he won't. He'll use it against me to get what he wants," I cry, sobbing into my hands.

If anything ever happened to her because of me, I'd never forgive myself. I've tried all her life to protect her from the world and the evil lurking in it.

I always knew my past would come back to bite me in the ass. I just didn't think it would be Lynn and her *friends*.

"No, he won't, because I'm going to find whoever did this to you and I'm going to end them."

The coldness in his voice has me losing my breath. I turn to him, noticing his eyes are just as cold, his pupils dilated. His expression should scare me, but it doesn't; maybe because he's only ever shown me love and care. And I know he'd never do anything to hurt me, not intentionally. Others? Well, I can't say the same for others, not at the moment.

Before I can question if he truly means it, Max is stepping through the gap in the curtain with Evan behind him.

"Thank fuck you're awake," he breathes when he sees me. It actually melts my heart seeing true concern in his expression. "For a minute back there, I thought I was going to walk in here and find Mav sedated on the bed."

"Um," I mumble, confused.

Max ignores me, turning to Maverick with curious eyes. "What did you do to piss the nurse off?"

Maverick ignores him, addressing Evan with a murderous expression. "Did you find him?"

"Someone managed to hack into your surveillance system and turn it off. It went off as her friend leaves and doesn't turn back on until Teagan leaves with the paramedics. I did get an image though, through one of the neighbouring shops. I don't know if it'll help, it's pretty blurry. Although, we managed to get a clear picture of a tattoo on his neck," he tells Mav before walking over to me. His pace is slow and unsure as he eyes Maverick warily.

He grabs his phone, pressing a few things before turning and showing me the picture. I gasp, more tears falling as I take in the man who attacked me. The picture is blurry, like he said, but I would recognise him anywhere, especially when he turns to the next picture of a scorpion tattoo on the bloke's neck.

"Is this the man who attacked you?" Evan asks and I nod, silently crying. It hurts to cry. The more tears that fall, the more it stings my cut cheeks. I can't even wipe my face because I can feel how swollen it is without even looking in a mirror.

I turn away from the picture to Maverick, who is handing Faith off to Max. She stirs and I stop breathing, hoping she doesn't wake up. I don't want her to see me like this. Thankfully she stays asleep, burying her head against Max's wide chest.

Maverick steps into my line of sight, blocking my view of them as he hands me a tissue. I take it gratefully, blowing my nose the best I can.

Sitting on the bed, he takes my hand, rubbing smoothly across my knuckles.

"Do you know him? Have you seen him before?" He asks the question like he already knows the answer. I'm guessing it didn't take him long to figure out who's behind this. I wish I paid more attention as a teen, picking up full names instead of dumb nicknames and first names. Maybe then this could have been prevented. I'd be able to give them more on Lynn.

"Yes," I answer, shakily. "He's one of the men who turned up at the shop with Lynn. They still want me to get them that money. I have one more chance," I scoff, wincing at the sudden movement. Everything hurts—mostly my face. He did a real number on me.

"They're not going to get a penny from me, and they're not going to touch you again. I'm going to find out who's doing this, I promise. And when I do, they're going to regret ever laying eyes on you," he says before turning to his brother. "Max, keep me updated on Teagan, and make sure she gets back to mine safe and sound. Evan, you're with me."

Evan nods, agreeing, but Max and I turn to Maverick with wide eyes. "Where are you going?" we ask in unison.

"To find the sick son of a bitch who hurt you," he says, leaving before I can protest.

"Stop him," I order, turning to Max.

He gives me a sad smile, shrugging. "I can't. Once he gets something in his head, he sees it through until it's done. Plus, the fucker deserves what he's got coming to him. He wants to pray the police get to him before Mav does. No one should ever lay a fucking hand on a woman, T."

"Yeah," I whisper, not knowing what else to say. Not when he's right. But still, the thought of Maverick getting into trouble over me doesn't sit right.

"Where the fuck is my girl," echoes down the hall, and I groan.

"Who called Tish?" I moan.

Lake barges into the room, shutting the curtain behind her quickly. "I told her not to come, but she wouldn't listen. I don't even know how she got here so quick," she says with wide eyes.

"Yo! You! Baldie, tell me where my girl is," Tish shouts.

"Funny chick." Max chuckles whilst shaking his head in amusement, his eyes sparkling with mischief.

The curtain flies back and Tish stares at me with wide eyes. "I'll fucking slice the prick. I'll fucking cut his dick off and shove it up his ass until he's spitting it out," she growls.

"Okay, not so funny now," Max mutters, pushing himself back in the chair so that he's farther away from her. I even notice Lake take a step backwards too.

"I'm fine."

"You don't look fine to me, girl. Please tell me they've got this fucker. And who the fuck are you?" she asks, turning to Max.

"Nobody," he answers quickly, shaking his head at me, his eyes bugging out.

"This is Max," I introduce, tired.

"Me rethinking that threesome. Hoowee, you are fine."

"Barely out of nappies," he tells her, eyes wide.

"Nah, you couldn't handle me."

"I don't doubt it. Lake, my darling love and best girlfriend in the world, did you get in touch with Mason?"

"Um, yeah," she says, her lips twitching.

"Girl, who the fuck did this?" Tish asks, ignoring Max and walking over to me.

"I don't know. It's someone who was with Lynn," I tell her, feeling my eyes water.

"I'll cut that bitch too for messing with my girl."

I chuckle but end up wincing because it hurts too much. "She won't know what's hit her."

"Sure won't, chica. Now, where the fuck are the doctors at? I wanna know what's going on. Nanna Hazel isn't answering her phone. That Mary chick said she had one too many at bingo tonight, so I doubt you'll hear anything from her till morning."

"You called Nan?" I ask, groaning. She'll freak out when she hears about this, more so when she finds out who's behind it.

"Of course I fucking did, *and* these guys did. Calm yo shit. I'm going to get me a doctor. Be back in five."

I nod, watching her walk out before relaxing back into the bed.

"Well, isn't she a breath of fresh air," Max mutters, still eyeing the curtain.

Lake and I chuckle, watching his face turn pale before I close my eyes, letting the exhaustion seep in.

"Thank you, Denny," I whisper, sitting down on Maverick's bed, my body aching.

After the doctors gave me the 'You're okay, but we'd like to keep you in overnight for observation' speech, I discharged myself. Faith needed me with her. She woke up once at the hospital screaming and sobbing, but exhausted herself back to sleep soon after. None of us could calm her down. Well, until Mason come to bring me some clothes. He turned up with Denny and the second he saw her, his eyes softened, taking her from Max since I couldn't really take her myself. She settled within five minutes. He was a star.

Now we're at Maverick's, Faith in the middle of his bed where Mason put her. Denny stayed a little longer to help me get in some pyjamas. I would've stayed in the clothes I changed into at the hospital, but they hurt my skin so badly it felt like I was tearing at fresh wounds.

"Are you sure there's nothing I can get you?" she whispers.

"No, I'm good. Thank you. I'm going to get some sleep. I'm so tired," I tell her, wanting to be left alone. I haven't been alone since I woke up at the hospital so I've not had time to process anything. Not really.

"Okay. Lake and Max are downstairs if you need anything. Myles and Kayla are at her dad's for the night. They left earlier. They did want to come back and see how you were, but we told them to let you rest." She hesitates, taking a deep breath. "I really am sorry this happened to you, but we're here if you ever need anything. We've all gone through our own demons, our own traumatic events that will stay with us forever, so we can understand on some level what you're going through."

Her voice is soft, yet the pain shows clear as day. "What do you mean? I'm sorry. You don't have to tell me anything."

"No. It's too long of a story, but short versions: Harlow was drugged and nearly raped. I was kidnapped by the brother of the lad who attacked her and held ransom in a burnt-down building with a dead body. Kayla was raped by the same person who tried to hurt Harlow but was also beaten by her mum for years and years. We also lost our close friend during her ordeal. Then Lake was a runaway who thought she was the reason her brother died. It turned out he didn't die, but he does have a brain problem. So you see, we've all had shit in our lives and I promise you, none of us would have pulled through without each other. Don't hold anything in. We're here for you. We've all got a broken past, including the boys, but together we fixed the pieces and became a family. We'd die for each other," she whispers, as tears run down my face.

"I'm so scared," I admit, knowing she'll understand. They've all been through much worse than what I ever did, and yet they've pulled through it.

"Come here," she whispers, holding her arms out. I fall into her them, sobbing into her shoulder. "We're here for you. You're family now, and family sticks together. None of us will ever let anyone hurt you."

I nod against her shoulder, clutching her as tightly as I can. "Thank you. For everything."

I'm too emotionally wrecked to say anything else. Hearing what they went through, even though it's only a small amount of information, still causes pain in my chest. None of them deserved to have any kind of darkness in their life. Sometimes life can be cruel, a bitch, but this time around I have something I never had before—I have a family. I have Tish, my nan, Faith and Maverick. With him comes his family.

"Get some rest," she tells me, pulling away.

I nod, struggling to talk past the lump in my throat. She walks out, shutting the door quietly behind her. The second I hear the click, I break down, sobbing into my hands.

Someone came into *my* home. They hurt me, beat me, and violated my safe haven.

My whole body shakes with sobs. The second I turn towards Faith's sleeping form, they grow stronger, louder.

He could've hurt her and there wouldn't have been anything I could've done. He was so strong, so brutal. God only knows what he would have done to her.

"Mummy?" Faith calls, her voice scared and wary. "Are you sad?"

I wipe my tears away, wincing at the stinging sensation. "I'm fine, sweetie." My voice is raspy, broken, and I know there's no hiding my red-rimmed eyes.

"Do you want a cuddle? Cuddles make *everything* better."

A soft laugh escapes me as tears run down my cheeks.

"I'd love nothing more than a cuddle from my favourite girl," I whisper before slipping into bed with her.

I wrap her in my arms, holding her close. I tense from the pain, gritting my teeth through the worst of it.

"Is the bad man gone, Mummy?" Her soft voice sounds scared, worried, and it tears my heart in two. I hate that she's carrying this burden, this nightmare. I wish I could erase her memories like they do in that vampire TV series Tish made me watch.

"Yeah, sweetie, he's gone," I lie. I still have no idea where he is, and that's what scares me the most. He could come back at any moment.

"Because Maverick scared him?"

My breath hitches when she mentions him. No one has heard anything from him since he left the hospital over six hours ago. He's reading messages; that much we do know. I haven't been able to check my phone. Mason said he packed it, but I'm too tired to search for it.

"Something like that," I murmur, absently running my fingers through her hair.

"He really is our guardian angel," she whispers.

"Huh?"

Where the hell did that come from?

"Nanny told me in my dreams that she sent us Maverick to protect us."

"Oh, sweet girl," I say, choked up as I pull her closer, ignoring the pain. Tears fall from my eyes so I close them tightly, trying to hold them back.

"Goodnight, Mummy. I love you."

"I love you too. Always."

TWENTY

MAVERICK

My office is dark, dim and cold, just like my current mood. Everything in here is disorganised, making it look more like a storage room than my office.

"It's been two days. You need to go home and get some proper sleep," Evan tells me, pacing the only clean spot in my office. "Max said you haven't been home, and Teagan's beginning to worry."

"I've slept. And I can't go back, not yet," I mumble, concentrating on the CCTV photos I had printed off, hoping I missed something before.

"Why?" he snaps. He takes the seat next to me on the sofa, but I keep my eyes on the task at hand, trying to ignore him. But I know ignoring him isn't going to cut it. He's not going to give up, not by a long shot. Explaining to him what exactly is bothering me though is like talking to a brick wall. He just doesn't get it. None of them do. I've had all my brothers trying to call me, leaving messages and voicemails, but my mind's been occupied with trying to find the fucker who attacked Teagan. I've wanted to go back home every time it's gone off, and time in between has been just as hard, if not worse, since all I've wanted to do is check in on Teagan.

But she's the reason I'm doing this. She's the reason I'm not going back until this is done.

"Because I can't go back there, not until that prick has been found. I won't be able to look Teagan in the eye and tell her he's still walking the streets. It'll break her. I'm not failing her. I just can't," I snap back.

"We'll find him—"

"Yeah? Looks like it." I throw the photos on the table and he flinches. "It's been two fucking days, Evan. Two fucking days and every time I think I'm close, I'm not. I'm back to the fucking start where I don't know shit. I've got everyone I know on this and they're finding fuck all."

He sighs, shaking his head like he doesn't know what to say.

"They just want you with them. From what Kennedy said, Faith is having trouble sleeping. She hasn't gone to school since the attack because she's too afraid to leave her mum alone. Oh, and she's wondering where the fuck you are."

I rub at my chest, above my heart. Hearing how hard this has been on both of them isn't making the guilt go away; it's just making the thirst for revenge heighten.

I know they need me, but I failed them. I failed my brothers once, leaving them to live in fear. I won't let that happen to those girls. I can't.

I open my mouth to tell him just that when my phone beeps. I look down at the screen, my pulse spiking when I see Darell's name flashing.

Darell is a friend of a friend who finds people, and not long lost relatives. When I was given his number, I called him, not hesitating or caring what it would cost me.

DARELL: Got a lead. That guy you're trying to find is hiding out at 45 Westcline Avenue.

"Fuck," I growl, ignoring Evan's curious stare. I get up, grabbing my jacket and car keys, not saying a word.

"Um, where the fuck are you going?"

"I've got something to do so I can get back to my girls," I answer, leaving him sitting there. By the time I exit the office, I hear him following, cursing about something under his breath.

"For fuck's sake, Mav. Are you going to tell me where we're going or what?" Evan asks, sounding more exasperated than he did the first time he asked.

I ignore him, skidding to a stop outside number forty-five. I turn off the car before getting out, slamming the door behind me.

"We're going to a party? You should have brought Max."

"Yeah, we're going to a party," I say, and instead of knocking, I kick the door in.

"What the fuck," Evan shouts as startled screams echo from the front room.

The place stinks and I grab the first bloke who tries to get in my face, pulling his jumper down to see if he has the tattoo. He doesn't, so I fling him across the room just as more people start to scream, startled.

I move through people, not caring if they're innocent or not. There are lines of coke on the table, along with other shit and the room is filled with smoke. It's fucking disgusting.

What has me pausing is the little girl in the corner, a blanket tucked up to her chest with her thumb in her mouth. Her tattered, unbrushed hair covers most of her face, but it's clear she's malnourished. She looks frightened, her large, brown eyes wide with fear. She can't be more than three. I glare at the motherfucker sitting next to her, presuming it's the kid's mum.

I walk over, grab the beer bottle out of her hand and throw it behind me. The woman looks stoned, high off whatever other drugs she's taken and I grunt, disgusted.

"Get your fucking kid out of here."

"M-my kid?" she asks, looking around in a daze.

"Yeah, her," I say, pointing to the kid still in the corner. She hasn't even blinked or run off, as if she's used to this scene playing out, and that breaks my fucking heart.

"That thing ain't mine. She's—"

"She's nothing to do with you. Who the fuck are you?"

I turn to the voice, my eyebrows rising in a challenge. His eye is bloodshot, a light bruising around the eyelid. My look down to his hand—Teagan mentioned biting him—and find teeth marks with angry bruising around the edge. He smirks, tilting his head and that's when I see it, confirming my suspicions. Evan must see the tattoo seconds after me because he curses, shouting my name.

"You're dead," I tell the bloke in front of me, my voice calm and deadly.

I push a drunken idiot who couldn't move quickly enough out of the way and fly at him, bending down low at the last second, surprising him. He grunts, falling onto the coffee table, causing it to collapse beneath us. Bringing my arm up, I slam my fist down, breaking his nose. Blood spurts out, splashing in my face, and I grin maliciously.

I'm gonna kill him.

"What the fuck?" he says, punching my side. I don't feel it, rage taking over and clouding my vision.

"Who sent you to hurt Teagan?" I ask, slamming his head against the splintered wood.

"You're *him*." He grins, blood staining his teeth.

I rear back, confused. It gives him the leverage he needs to push me off. He knocks me to the side, my hip banging against the shaggy carpet.

"Fuck," I roar when he lands a punch to the side of my face as he rolls above me. I spit out blood before landing a punch of my own to his jaw. The feeling of my fist connecting with his flesh brings some form of satisfaction, but not enough to pay for what he did to Teagan.

"This is going to be so much fun."

His response pisses me off. I kick him off me, my anger rising to the surface as strength I didn't know I had takes over. I pounce, landing on him, straddling his hips as I throw punch after punch until his head rolls to the side.

"Who the fuck sent you to hurt her?" I roar in his face.

"You'll find out soon enough," he sneers before coughing.

"Tell me or God help me, I will fucking kill you."

He laughs maniacally before headbutting me, catching me off guard. Stars explode behind my eyes, knocking me back on my ass. The prick goes to come at me, but before he can reach me, Evan steps in, pulling the bastard away.

That's when chaos erupts in the run-down house. Police swarm in and Evan announces who he is. Everyone—well, everyone who hasn't already run—starts to rush out of the house, avoiding the police officers who try to stop them.

"Pigs are here," one fool shouts, and footsteps upstairs are heard.

I sit back, wiping blood away from my split lip. Evan walks into my line of sight and I look up.

"Come on, bro. It's done."

"It's not done. It's not done until we find out who sent that tosser," I snarl.

An officer walks up behind Evan, clearing his throat. "Sir, do we have a problem here?"

"No, we don't," I snap.

"No. He's just... upset," Evan says, wincing when he sees the look on my face. I grunt, not looking amused. I'm more than fucking upset—I'm livid. I want to tear that fucker limb from limb until I get my answers.

"We'll need you to come down to the station."

"Um, no you don't. I'm going home, somewhere I should have gone two days ago," I say, standing up. This was a waste of fucking time. This Lynn bitch could just send someone else.

"If you don't come with us, we'll have to arrest you."

I open my mouth to argue, to tell him to go ahead, but Evan steps in, calming the situation. "How about I follow you to the station and give you my statement. You can come and get Maverick's tomorrow. He's been trying to find this man for days. He attacked Maverick's fiancée at her home while their child was there. All he wants to do is go back to her and let her know everything is safe," Evan partially lies.

"Okay, but we'll need to come and get a statement off you in the morning."

I nod, not trusting myself to talk. When he walks away, Evan turns to me, a scowl on his face. "You could have fucking killed him. What in the hell were you thinking?"

"He fucking deserved it. Hell, he deserves to fucking rot in hell for what he's done. Don't tell me you wouldn't do the same if it was Kennedy," I snarl, pushing past him and making my way outside.

"You're right. I would eliminate anyone who touched her. But he could press charges against you. There are too many witnesses."

"Let him. I don't give a fuck. Now if you've finished going all mum on me, I'll be going home."

"I'll see you in the morning. Oh, and Mav? Clean your face up before you see your girls," he calls back before walking over to the officers.

Fuck!

I never really thought about my face or what it might look like to Faith. Let's just pray I don't scare the shit out of her. I don't want her to be scared of me.

I thought I'd feel more... I don't know, relieved? But there's a tightness in my chest that won't go away. I feel like I've just opened Pandora's box and there's no telling what's going to come out of it.

Getting in my car, I sit back, running my fingers through my hair. This doesn't feel like the end. Nowhere near.

Starting the car, I drive the ten-minute journey before pulling up outside mine. Most of the lights are off except the kitchen, which means, one of my brothers is up.

Great!

Getting out, I head up the small path and let myself in as quietly as possible.

"You're back," Myles breathes, looking relieved. Then he sees my face and takes a step forward. "What happened to your face?"

"Got into it with someone who deserved it," I tell him, scrubbing a hand over my face.

"You found him?"

Looking at him, I see the exhaustion from worrying about me. I guess I've given him every reason to. Myles has always been the gentle one, the one who constantly worries about everyone else.

"Yeah, the police have him." He sighs in relief, dropping down onto the kitchen stool. "After I kicked his ass."

He looks up sharply. "Mav...."

"It's fine. They'll be here in the morning to take my statement."

"Will they arrest you?" he asks, panicked.

I shrug. "No. It's all good." I tell him, when I'm not actually sure what will happen. I just don't want him to worry. "Everyone else asleep?"

"If you're asking if Teagan and Faith are asleep, then they should be. Although, I did hear Faith crying over an hour ago."

I wince, feeling like shit for disappearing for two days. Now that my head is clear and I'm thinking straight, I'm worried about how she'll react when she does wake up. I just pray she'll understand my reasons.

"How are they?"

"They're getting there. I don't think it's really sunk in for them yet. Faith has been having trouble sleeping, but I think that's to be expected considering the circumstances."

"Yeah," I murmur, absently. "I'm gonna go up, clean up a bit."

"Yeah." He sighs tiredly. "I'm gonna lock up and do the same."

"Why *are* you up?"

"Harlow saw the lights on when Faith woke up and thought we were awake so she snuck over. I heard her and she made me go with her to McDonald's." He rolls his eyes, chuckling.

I shake my head, my lips twitching before telling him goodnight. I make my way upstairs, my body aching and calling for the shower.

Once I'm showered, finally washing all the blood and grime off me, I pull on a pair of joggers and head into the bedroom.

As soon as I enter, my eyes drift straight to Teagan and Faith who are asleep. The sight is beautiful and it takes my breath away. Faith, bless her heart, is cuddled up to her mum, her legs spread wide—one over her mum's stomach and the other taking up most of the bed. Teagan looks peaceful, her cherry-red lips shaped in a pout. The only signs that the incident took place are the bruises covering her face. I have to admit they look worse than they did two days ago, but at least the swelling has gone down. It still doesn't calm the raging inferno going on inside me over what happened to her.

Faith stirs in her sleep, shaking me from my thoughts. I watch, smiling as she untangles her legs from her mum and moves so she's cuddled up to her instead, her head on the same pillow.

Lack of sleep catches up to me, and with a yawn I contemplate where I should sleep since Faith is in my bed.

One more look at my girls and I know I need to be with them. Moving around the bed, I flick the light off and get into bed, keeping Faith between me and Teagan. Looking at them both, knowing they're mine, it feels like I have the whole world in the palm of my hand.

Gently, I kiss the top of Faith's head before leaning up on my elbow and sliding the hair out of Teagan's face.

"Maverick, is that you?" she whispers. In the moonlit room, I notice her eyes are still closed.

"Yeah, darlin'."

"Are we safe now?" she asks, still in the midst of sleep.

"Yeah, baby, you're safe now."

She sighs contently, hugging Faith tighter. "Thank you."

"I'd do anything for you," I whisper, not knowing if she can hear me or not.

"I love you," she mumbles before falling into a deep sleep.

My heart stops as I stare down at her, wondering if I really heard her whisper those words.

When I finally snap out of it, she's snoring lightly, while my heart is beating rapidly. I can say with utmost certainty that I'm fucked.

Severely fucked.

I think I may love her too.

TWENTY-ONE

MAVERICK

"Maverick? Maverick, are you awake?" I groan when I hear the whispered words against my ear and roll onto my stomach, trying to block her out. Not that it works, of course. She's persistent. "Maverick?"

This time when she calls me, my shoulder is being nudged lightly by tiny hands. Opening one eye, I find Faith a little too close for comfort and grimace. Biting the inside of my cheek does nothing to hide my amusement over her adorable face scrunched into a frown.

"Good, you're awake. I'm hungry."

Blinking away sleep and the bright morning sun shimmering through the windows, I roll onto my side, grabbing Faith around the waist. She squeals loudly as I pull her back against my front, holding her close.

"Shush, squirt. Let's get more sleep. Maverick's tired," I grumble hoarsely.

Faith giggles, wriggling her body to try and get out of my grasp. "Stop being silly, Maverick."

I sigh, coming to terms with the fact that she's never going let me go back to sleep. How Teagan always manages to sleep through her is beyond me. She really does sleep like the dead.

"Okay, squirt, you win this time. Give me five minutes to wake up and I'll make you some breakfast."

Turning in my arms, Faith looks up at me with her bright brown eyes, looking innocent like she always does, melting my heart. The wide, excited smile she had seconds ago slips, turning into a pout. Her chin wobbles, her eyes glistening with tears.

What the...?

"You have boo-boos."

Fuck!

"I fell down the stairs at work. I'm okay," I tell her, thinking quickly, hating the quiver in her voice.

"You've been gone a *really* long time."

"I know. I'm sorry," I tell her, kissing the tip of her nose.

"I didn't like you gone." She runs her finger along the length of my nose, tapping the tip.

Needing to cheer her up, I playfully nip her finger, causing her to giggle. "I didn't like being gone either."

"Then don't do it again." She shakes her head, looking serious.

"I won't." I chuckle.

"Hey, baby, who are you talking to?" Teagan asks, her voice filled with sleep as she rolls over. Her eyes find mine over the top of her daughter's head and she gasps, searching the injuries across my face no less. "Maverick?" she breathes, her eyes glistening with tears.

"Mummy, I'm hungry," Faith says, bouncing on the bed until she's facing her mum.

"You.... You're face," she whispers, not hearing Faith or even looking in her direction.

"He fell down the stairs."

"I'm fine. I'll explain later," I tell her, cutting my eyes to Faith who is looking between us curiously.

She nods, seeming to understand before she looks down at Faith, kissing her face all over. "Morning, bug."

Faith bats away her mum, moving back. She huffs, crossing her arms over her chest in a strop. I watch on in amusement, entertained by the little woman. "I'm going to wake Max up for breakfast. He feeds me bacon *all* the time."

"Faith, hun, Max doesn't like it when he's woken up, remember?"

"Yes he does," Faith argues, scowling. "Lake told me I'm his favourite part of the day. He likes waking up to my pretty face."

Teagan sighs whilst I chuckle, knowing what Lake was playing at. Only she could use a five-year-old to annoy my brother. It's one of the many reasons why she's perfect for him.

"She's right, squirt. So why don't you go down and wake up Uncle Max with a cheerful song and *really* make his morning."

"Yes!" She grins, pumping her fist in the air. Jumping from the bed, her tiny feet pad across the carpet as she runs from the room and down the stairs.

"You're evil," Teagan muses.

"He'll live." I grin, eyes still on the stairs, making sure Faith is out of earshot. Once I hear Max's door open, I face Teagan, wincing. "I'm so sorry for not being here for you. I should've been, but I couldn't, not until I found him."

"You found him?" she gasps, her eyes bugging out. Her body starts to shake so I pull her against me, rubbing my hand up and down her arm.

"Yeah," I answer, pointing to my face.

"Oh my God. *He* hurt you? Are you okay? What happened?" she rushes out, not taking a breath. She cups my jaw, sadness filling her eyes.

"I'm fine. You should be more worried about him."

"What did you do?"

"Gave him a taste of his own medicine before the cops showed up and arrested him."

"So they've got him, the man who hurt me?"

The relief on her face is evident, but I can also hear it in her voice. My eyes soften and, leaning forward, I take her mouth with mine in a soft, sensual kiss.

Fuck, I've missed her.

My whole body relaxes at the feel of her against me. All that built-up tension over the last few days starts to melt away from just a kiss and her presence.

This is where I belong.

Pulling away, our eyes connect and I get lost in them, my heart pounding.

"I've missed you," I admit unintentionally. I begin to shift, feeling uncomfortable, but then her eyes soften, shining brightly like I just handed her the moon, making the humiliation of blurting out my feelings worthwhile.

"I've missed you too."

"Really?"

"Yeah," she whispers.

"How are you feeling?" I ask. Seeing the bruising on her face in the fresh light of day makes me angry all over again. If only they'd lock me in a room with him for five minutes; I'd teach him some fucking manners.

"Better now that you're home." She gives me a shy smile, ducking her head. My chest swells with pride, but there's no denying the guilt I bear for leaving her for so long.

Grabbing her chin gently, I tilt her head until her eyes connect with mine. "I won't leave again, I promise. I should have called. I just.... Fuck! I wasn't in the right headspace."

"As much as I've missed you and wished you were here, I'm really glad he's been arrested. It's been hard to cope with thinking he was out there somewhere, so thank you for finding him. Did you find Lynn too?"

Wincing, I shake my head. "She wasn't there. I didn't see anyone her age or matching her description."

Fear flashes across her features as she bites her bottom lip worriedly.

"Don't be afraid. I'm not going to let anything happen to you or Faith. We'll find out who she is and stop this."

"You can't say that. We have to go back home at some point, and they know where we live. We could go back to my nan's, but then it's bringing trouble to her doorstep. Not that I'm okay with bringing it to yours," she says, her eyes frantic.

My forehead scrunches together as I tilt my head back, checking to make sure she's serious.

Fuck me! She is!

"Teagan, you aren't going back there. You and Faith are gonna live here."

"What?"

"Forever. I'm never letting either of you out of my sight."

"What?"

"I'll get Mase and Max to help me pack up your stuff," I carry on, rambling.

"Wow! Hold your horses, big guy. We are *not* living with you," she declares, her face stern yet stunned.

"Um, yes you are," I tell her, dumbfounded. I don't get it. She's saying no when it's the perfect arrangement. We'll get to see each other every day. I'll be able to wake up to her every morning, go to sleep with her every night and not have to worry, wondering what she's doing or if she's okay.

"You can't just move us in," she scoffs, trying to roll away, but I pull her back, pinning her in place.

"Give me one good reason why not."

"One," she says, holding her index finger up at me, "we haven't been dating very long. Two, you aren't the only person who lives here. Don't you think they should have some sort of say whether or not a five-year-old and your girlfriend move in? Three, you didn't even ask me—you told me. And four, it's too soon."

I roll my eyes at her reasoning and give her a quick kiss to shut her up before she comes up with more lame-ass excuses. "They won't mind. And no, it's not too soon. Maybe for other people it is, but not for me—for us. I've spent my whole life never believing in what we have, but then I met you and everything changed. *I* changed. Do you really think with the amount of women I've had that I wouldn't know when I had something special in front of me and not keep her?" I ask, tucking her hair behind her ear.

Her narrowed gaze burns into me, her eyes glistening with tears. "That was really sweet... until you mentioned how many women you've slept with."

I laugh, pulling her closer. "Teagan, I meant I've had choices and that this isn't something I've taken lightly. You're not a shiny new toy. You're mine. Faith's mine. Get used to it."

Her lips part, her eyes widening in shock. I smile, liking the fact that I've rendered her speechless.

Now this I can work with.

Tightening my arms around her, I press my hardness against her lower stomach. It's time to show her just how much I've missed her.

A throat clearing in the doorway makes me jump. My head snaps around, finding Max and Lake standing there.

Flopping back down on the bed, I stare up at the ceiling, wondering what I did so wrong in my past life to deserve this.

"Me, Tarzan. You, Jane," Max says, his voice deep and mocking.

"Max," Lake hisses, glaring at her boyfriend.

"What the fuck?" I growl, glaring at my brother.

He ignores me, addressing Lake with a smirk. "What? You have to admit it was funny. He went all caveman on her."

"Just shut up," she tells him, rolling her eyes.

"Yo! Is there a reason you're in my room?" I snap, still glaring at him.

"Um, yeah," Lake says, shifting on the balls of her feet before turning to Max, urging him with her eyes to say something. When he doesn't, she backhands his chest.

"Oh shit, yeah. Sorry, I was trying to come up with some caveman jokes, but I've got nothing." He laughs.

"Max," I warn, and Teagan giggles. I turn, finding her covered to her chin with the blanket. At least that's something. She's only wearing one of my T-shirts, and that's for my eyes only.

"Yeah, um, the police are downstairs waiting to speak to the both of you. I'd ask about the face, but Faith already told us you 'fell down the stairs'," he says. "Looks like you don't need me, so I guess I'll just go downstairs." He grabs Lake's hand, leaving abruptly before I have a chance to ask what all the hostility is about.

"Your brother can be so weird."

"He's pissed off with me," I tell her, getting out of bed to throw on some clothes. That's when I notice the place is clean. Like really clean. There're knick-knacks and framed pictures of me and my brothers on the windowsill that weren't there before. There's also one of me and Teagan from Denny and Mason's wedding.

Looking around, I notice more stuff. Her clothes are put away, no longer in the suitcase they came in, and she has her makeup on my desk in a black, gemmed box. Everything in here screams Teagan, and I like it—even the extra girly pillows I threw off the bed last night. And more to the point, I don't want to drink myself into oblivion, which has been done. A girl left her underwear once and I swear I had an aneurysm.

"How can you tell? He seemed happy to me, just a little weirder than usual," she says, snapping me out of it. When she climbs out of bed to get dressed, I want to tell her to get back in, to rest, but I know the police will want to talk to her. I'd rather just get this over and done with so we can finally be alone.

"He was being sarcastic at the end, which is why he left so suddenly. He only ever acts like that when he's pissed off and knows if he gets into it with me, he'll end up saying something he can't take back. He may seem easy-going, but he can also be hot-headed when he wants to be. What I can't tell you is why he's pissed. It could be anything with Max, but if I had to guess, I'd say it was either because I left for two days or because I beat the shit into the bloke who hit you without him."

"I'll never understand him," she says, bewildered.

"No one ever does." I laugh.

We get dressed, moving around each other like we've been doing this for years. It feels right, just like everything does with Teagan. It still astonishes me that we've only being seeing each other for a few months.

Sometimes, I wonder if my commitment issues really had anything to do with my past. As cliché and corny as it sounds, I really do believe I never connected with anyone, because I was waiting for her.

She's the one.

The only one.

My one.

"Let's get this over with," I say once we're dressed and standing by the bedroom door.

Teagan nods, looking scared and vulnerable. Taking her hand, I give her a reassuring squeeze, showing her I'm with her and not leaving.

TWENTY-TWO

TEAGAN

TWO UNIFORMED OFFICERS, PLUS DETECTIVE Barrett and Evan, are waiting for us in the living room when we get downstairs. Myles, Kayla, Lake, Faith, and Max are also there, Max glaring at the officers with a stubborn pout on his face.

What is that about?

I shake the thought away, knowing I can't deal with the inner workings of Max right now, and face the girls, who have kindly watched over Faith.

"We'll take Faith into the kitchen so you guys can talk," Kayla offers, taking her hand.

"Thank you," I whisper, unsure on what to do. I'm nervous, worried and, if I'm honest, I'm scared.

"I want bacon," I hear Faith tell Kayla, who giggles at my daughter and her love for bacon. I swear, she'd live off it if she could.

"We'll go with them," Lake says, having to drag a reluctant Max along with her.

Once they're out of the room, Maverick and I face the officers. I'm still unsure which direction this morning is going to go. Their expressions are unreadable, giving no indication on whether this is going to be good or bad news.

"Mr Carter, Miss Williams, this is PC Hart and PC Barnes. They're here to take a statement from you about last night, but first, I'd like to see if this is indeed the man who attacked Miss Williams at her home," Barrett says, addressing Maverick.

"What do you need me to do?" I ask, taking a seat on the sofa.

"We need you to pick out your attacker from a group of photos," he answers, all formal, which does nothing to calm my nerves.

"Why don't you all take a seat? I need to grab a coffee before we get into this. Would anyone else like one?" Maverick asks. They all shake their heads except Evan, who gives Mav a look I can't decipher.

"I'd love one. I'll even help, say hi to Denny," Evan tells him. Detective Barrett doesn't look happy about Evan following, and I feel like I'm missing something, especially when Maverick gives Evan a silent nod.

Whatever! I can't deal with that either. I'm giving myself a headache.

"I'll be back in a minute, babe," he tells me before addressing the officers. "Don't show her anything until I'm back. I don't want her to be alone when she sees them."

They nod, and my heart melts at how considerate he's been. He's always finding some way to look out for me. He must see the gratefulness in my expression because his face softens with a small smile as he runs a finger across my good cheek before he turns to leave the room.

"How are you?" Barrett asks once we're alone.

"I'm getting there. I'm just glad he's locked up. I've been living in constant fear the past two days knowing he's out there. I've not been able to sleep or eat."

"I'm sorry this happened to you, Teagan."

"What will happen to him now?"

"If you identify the suspect, then we'll be adding charges against him. He already had warrants out for his arrest, so he'll be going away for a very long time. You're safe now."

"I hope so."

An uncomfortable silence fills the room as I watch the two male officers sit on the sofa. They look tense in their bulky uniforms and I want to comment on how they should really lighten their load if they're going to be chasing bad guys. Their radios are the only sound you can hear, codes being called constantly, intriguing me. I'm so lost in trying to understand what's being said so I don't have to think about what's to come that I don't know Maverick and Evan have walked back into the room until a hand lands on my shoulder, causing me to jump.

"Holy crap, you scared me," I gasp, holding my hand to my chest.

"Shit, sorry," Maverick says softly, sitting down next to me. He puts his arm around me, handing me a cup of coffee with the other.

Lifting the cup, I breathe in the sweet aroma, sighing with contentment. "It's okay. And thank you."

"Shall we get started?" Barrett asks, stepping forward.

I gulp, my hands shaking around the cup, the heat doing nothing to warm my cold hands. "I'm ready."

He hands me a tablet, a picture of a man similar to the one who attacked me popping up on the screen.

"Flick through them and let me know if you see the man who attacked you."

I nod, sliding my finger across the screen. Picture after picture passes, all similar size and shape to the man who attacked me but none of them him.

Fidgeting, I start to become frustrated, unease settling in over the thought that they might not have him. But then I slide the screen again and my heart starts thumping in my chest.

Closing my eyes, I try to force the images from that night away, but all I can see are his eyes as he attacked me. They were so cold, so full of hatred and rage that I'll never forget them. Tears slip free and I wipe them away with a shaky hand.

"Take a deep breath. You can do this," Maverick says encouragingly, rubbing a hand up and down my back.

I do as he instructs, taking a deep breath before opening my eyes, holding out the tablet to Barrett. I can't bear to look at it a second longer; he's already haunting me enough.

"That's him. That's the man who attacked me."

"Are you sure?" Barrett asks, taking the tablet and looking down at the mugshot.

"I'll never be able to forget his face, or his eyes," I whisper, my voice raw with pain. Maverick pulls me closer and I soak in his warmth, needing him more than ever. He's the only person who has ever made me feel safe, and I don't want to lose that, or him.

"Thank you, Teagan," Barrett says, but I tune him and everyone else out as I stare into my coffee cup, wishing I could erase the whole ordeal.

I'm not sure I can describe what I'm feeling right now, knowing it's really him they've arrested. For a second there I believed they had the wrong man and that he was still out there, lurking, waiting to strike.

I've been so worked up and distracted over Faith and how much it's affected her that I never really gave myself time to process what it would actually mean if they caught him.

Does it mean it's over? That Maverick's club is safe? That Faith and I are safe?

Everything is swirling around inside my mind and I feel like I'm going to explode from the overcharge. I'd been so scared that night and every night since, but now I feel too much. I'm relieved, pleased, but the same dread and panic is there just as much as it was before, and I have no idea what to do about that. It's burning inside me, working its way through my system and suffocating me.

I just want this to be over. *Really* over.

"What about Lynn?" I blurt out, then blink, looking around the room. I must have spaced out for a while because Maverick is leaning forward, signing a piece of paper with his statement on it—one I completely missed him give.

I want to kick myself for letting Lynn slip through my mind. She's the mastermind behind all of this, the *reason* everything is happening. I should have remembered her.

Maverick's brothers and granddad walk in during my meltdown, scanning the room. No one seems to mind them being there, so I wonder if they asked them to come in when I was out of it. It's that or they wanted to witness my frantic breakdown.

"What do you mean?" Barrett asks from where he's sitting.

"Well, she's the one who started all of this. Where is she? Do you know her full name yet, or *why* she's even doing this? She was the one who got that thug to attack me in the first place. What's stopping her from sending someone else?"

"Calm down, baby," Maverick says softly.

"Unless Ian Richards, the man who attacked you, gives us something we can use, we have nothing to go on where Lynn is concerned. We'll continue our investigation, but we're at a dead end, Teagan."

"So what do you have?" I ask, getting up. I need to move, to do *something*. Pacing the floor, I glance at Barrett and Evan, knowing both have been working around the clock to try and find out who Lynn is.

"We have a photo, darlin'," Evan answers, concern written on his face as he watches me carefully, most likely thinking I'm crazy.

You are crazy.

"Let me see it. I mean, how do you know if it's the right person? It could be why you can't find her. You've probably been looking in the wrong place for the wrong person this whole time."

"Babe, come and sit down," Mav calls softly.

"I can't, not when she's out there. She only has to give the word and another one of her *friends* could come and finish the job, or worse, hurt you or Faith. I can't live like this. I can't breathe," I yell hysterically, trying to catch my breath. Maverick stands up, but before he can pull me into his arms, I push him away, crestfallen. "Please sit. Let me get through this."

"Let me hold you. I need to hold you," he says, looking helpless. Not able to see that look on his face, I step into his arms, dropping my head to his chest. "Do you have a picture?"

"I don't have it with me," Barrett says.

"Here, I have a copy on my phone," Evan says and I move out of Maverick's arms, taking the phone.

My breath hitches and my eyes fill with tears. The picture isn't the greatest, but it's most definitely Lynn. It's her. My shoulders slump with defeat, all hope fading slowly away. They have her picture, her first name, and *still* can't find her. They'll probably never find her. It's my worst fear coming alive.

"Is that her?" Evan asks as I wipe my tears away.

"Yeah," I whisper hoarsely. I hand him back the phone, but Maverick takes it, surprising me.

"I forgot about this. I don't think I even got the email that you sent me," he says, then looks down at the phone in his hands. His posture is rigid for a second before he staggers backwards, falling back down on the sofa. He turns a ghastly white, his eyes wide, looking shocked and freaked out.

"Holy fuck," he chokes out, his grip on the phone tightening.

Everyone pauses for a second, like time has stopped, but then chaos erupts as everyone starts firing questions at him, wanting to know what's going on.

Mark, Maverick's granddad, looks over Maverick's shoulder at the phone. I watch in confusion as he also pales, stepping back until he bumps into the wall.

"That can't be," he whispers, seeming absent. He looks like he's seeing the object of his worst fear standing in front of him.

"Granddad, who is it?" Mason asks, stepping to Mark's side, anxious.

Mark shakes his head, tears falling from his eyes when he glances at Mason. He doesn't say anything, and my stomach churns as unease fills me.

I step forward, completely baffled about what the hell is going on. A sick feeling hits me in the pit of my stomach when neither Maverick nor his granddad are able to talk, which can only mean it's *really* bad.

"Will someone please tell me what is going on? Do you know her?" I ask, my voice shaky.

Please don't let her end up being one of their exes, I think as I bite my nail. Not that she's in any of their age range, but then again, I don't think age as ever been a problem where she's concerned.

"This can't be happening," Mark whispers. He looks so lost, so sad. It's unlike him.

Maverick is just as bad, his eyes staring blankly down at the phone.

"Can someone please fucking explain," Max says, looking between the two men.

"C'mon, Granddad, snap out of it. Who is she?" Myles asks when they still don't get an answer.

My body heats, the back of my neck and palms beginning to sweat for reasons unbeknownst to me. My neck hurts and I start to feel a little dizzy, the colours in the room blending together.

I know whatever is going to happen next is going to be bad—life-changing bad. The looming dread is hanging over me like a storm cloud.

What hurts the most is that the answer to her identity is only a breath away, but neither man is telling us anything. Millions of scenarios are running through my mind, none of them good. I'm being irrational, I know, but not knowing is sending my emotions bouncing all over the place.

"Tell us!" I scream, tears running down my face as I stare Maverick down, willing him to answer me.

His head slowly rises and I gasp, taking a step back as his eyes come into view. He looks so haunted, so ashen and full of anguish; it's breaking my heart in two. It's with that look that I know he's going to answer, and I want to take back my words, wishing he never saw the picture in the first place. I'd do anything to get that look from out of his eyes. I feel like I just lost the man I've fallen in love with, and I'd do anything to get him back.

When the first tear falls from his eye, I cry out, covering my mouth with my hand. Nothing, and I mean nothing, could have prepared me for the words that leave his mouth.

"That's our mum, Maralynn."

TWENTY-THREE

MAVERICK

This can't be happening. It just can't. She's been gone for so long that I never thought we'd have to deal with her, especially like this.

I can't even look at my brothers because I know what I have to do.

I have to tell them everything.

And it's going to tear us apart.

It's like the ground is opening up beneath me and it's going to swallow me whole. My chest feels tight and I have to rub at the pain, hating that I could lose everything with one conversation, one big lie and secrets kept.

"They're gone," I hear Teagan say. She sounds distraught, broken, but I can't bring myself to reassure her that everything will be okay. Because, fuck... I have no idea if anything will ever be okay again.

There's so much to process, so much running through my mind. I don't even know where to begin.

"Joan and Mary have the kids," Harlow says gently. I can't bring myself to look up to see who she's talking to when no one answers, the room filled with an awkward silence.

"Will someone start fucking explaining," Malik explodes, and I look away from the floor to him. Harlow moves to his side, trying to calm him down. He doesn't, just keeps his fists clenched and his eyes narrowed into slits in my direction.

This isn't going to be good. I don't even know where to fucking start, so how the hell can I explain everything and keep them all calm? They're going to hate me, that's a certainty.

"I need to tell you something and it's not going to be easy for any of you to hear," I begin, my voice scratchy.

"So fucking tell us," Malik says, throwing his hands in the air.

"Malik," Harlow whispers, taking his hand.

"It might be best if it was just us," I say, not knowing how much they remember or have told the girls. And what I have to tell them is going change their lives; Mason more so than any of the others.

"No, I want Denny to stay. Whatever you have to tell us you can say in front of her," Mason says through gritted teeth.

"Are you sure?" I ask, looking to each of my brothers. They all nod in agreement, pulling their loved ones closer.

"Do you want me to go?" Teagan asks quietly, and I shake my head.

"Come here," I demand, needing her close. "I need you here."

"Okay."

"Granddad?" I call, looking over my shoulder.

He shakes himself out of it, clearing his throat. On shaky legs he walks over, sitting next to me on the sofa.

"Boys, before Maverick explains what's going on, you need to understand why we kept this from you. Your mum.... She wasn't well—"

"She was sick and twisted," I bite out, interrupting.

A sad smile reaches his lips as he gives me a short nod. I know she's his daughter but she's nothing to us, not after I learnt everything. She hasn't been since she walked out of our lives. It still blows my mind that he can act so surprised by her actions, especially considering everything he knows about his daughter and who she really is.

"You boys were going through a lot already when you came to live with me. I didn't want you going through anything else, so when we found out what we did, we decided it was best to keep it from you. It really was in your best interests. We just wanted you to be kids, to live your life and move on from what you endured."

"Just fucking tell us," Max snaps, getting impatient.

I nod, digging my nails into my palms to try and keep calm, drawing blood. "First, I should explain *why* she left."

"It was because dad was hitting her," Mason says, remembering the story I told him over and over. Not that our dad didn't knock her about because he did, constantly, but that wasn't the reason she left when she did. I think in a twisted way she liked the pain my dad inflicted, because not once did I ever see her look scared or cry over anything he did to her.

"Yeah he did, but that's not *why* she left, Mase. At the time, I wanted you to have what other kids had, so I made her up. Instead of describing our mum, I told you about a friend's mum. I made sure to drill it into your head that she was good and that she left because of Dad so you wouldn't remember what she was really like. You were all so young still."

"So why did she leave?" he asks, jaw clenched.

"She left because she was under a contract."

"Under a contract?" Myles repeats, sounding confused

I clear my throat, gulping. "She was to birth five kids for him—originally girls, but obviously she had all boys, messing with their plans."

"For fuck's sake, Maverick. Explain. Now!" Malik bites out, sitting down on the other sofa, resting his hands on his knees.

"I'm fucking trying to, but this is fucking hard to get out. Do you think it's been a laugh keeping this from you all? Do you? Well it hasn't. It's been a living nightmare for me. Each day I prayed that bitch would die from a drug overdose or some other cause so we'd never have to see her again. I never wanted her to come back," I roar, pulse racing.

"Son, calm down. They're just scared. They have no idea what's going on," Granddad tells me. I look to him, sighing in defeat. This has been my burden to bear for so long that I truly believed I'd never have to tell anyone, let alone my brothers.

Teagan runs her hand up and down my back soothingly. I flinch at first, feeling like I don't deserve the kind touch, but as always, she has a calming effect.

"I'm here," she whispers. Glancing her way, my expression softens. She's silently crying, her face pale as she gazes up at me. With the tip of my thumb, I wipe away the tears, mouthing, "thank you," to her. She rubs her cheek into the palm of my hand before giving my knee a squeeze.

Taking a deep breath, I face my brothers. "Mum and Dad weren't married. It was a ruse to keep Granddad from finding out the truth about her, about what she was up to and, in a way, to get money from him.

"From what I got out of Dad before he died and what I put together myself, we were a deal made between the two and an unknown third party. Mum got paid a chunk of money to have five kids with him, and in return, he would get to keep us, make a profit from us. The only reason we were biologically his was so no one would ask questions as to who we were, where we came from," I say quietly, yet loud enough so they can hear me.

"Holy fuck, the women he made me sleep with. It makes sense." Mason heaves, turning pale himself. Denny also pales, realisation dawning on her before she falls into silent sobs next to Mason, clutching his chest.

"What are you talking about?" Myles asks, looking close to freaking out.

"Most nights, Dad would come into my room—"

"No!" Max says, shaking his head in denial. "No! This isn't true."

"Listen, Max," Granddad tells him, his expression sombre and wan. His eyes are vacant when he turns back to me. I know he feels guilty over everything that happened, but in his defence, he only wanted to know his daughter. He couldn't see anything past that. "Go on."

"He would take me to the basement where he'd make me sleep with women." Mason's voice is dejected, cold. I know there's more to the story than he's saying; he's just sparing the others just like I wanted to do by keeping this secret.

He thought he kept this from everyone, but I knew. I knew because I was made to do the same—with men and women. It's the main reason I never liked been touched during sex. It revolted me to no end, always reminding me of their grimy hands all over me. It was better to keep women at a distance, not letting them close enough. Then Teagan came and changed that for me. Her touch is something I crave.

"Why didn't you tell us?" Myles asks, since the others are too shocked to speak. Mason gives him a dry, pointed look to which Myles nods, looking hurt.

"And how did he profit from him and his friends beating me nearly every night?" Malik grits out. The anger he's been able to tame since meeting Harlow threatens to surface. I can tell he's hanging by a thread.

"He recorded them like he did with me and Mason," I whisper, ashamed.

"I'm going to be sick," Harlow cries before rushing from the room.

"I'll go with her," Kayla says to Malik when he moves to go after her. Giving Myles a quick kiss, she leaves the room, following Harlow.

"And how do you know all of this?" Malik asks, finally looking at me. Torment and pain shine in his eyes, the hurt from my deception directing all of his emotions towards me. It's killing me to be on the receiving end of that look. We've all had our arguments over the years but nothing out of hatred, nothing like this.

"Because I found the tapes the week before he died. It's the reason he died."

"Now you're talking in more fucking riddles, Mav. Just tell us. We're not fucking kids anymore," Max snaps.

"I found a box of CDs one night when he locked me in the basement. I stole them and went to a friend's house to borrow a computer. That's how I found out it wasn't just me he was hurting, but you two too.

"The tapes went back to before we were born, and there was a little girl in most of them. She was so young and she went through the same. I looked up the name written on the tape online and she came up as a missing person. I... I... Fuck!"

Bile rises in my throat and I can't talk. I can't say the words I need to. I'm so ashamed. Every time I think of Hanna, what she went through and how she died, it sickens me. But what makes it worse is what I did instead of what I should have done.

"What Maverick is trying to tell you is that he found the girl's father. According to a police report I had a friend dig up, the girl was taken outside her home with no further leads as to who did it. Only later, we were told the dad owed money to a local gang member. When he didn't pay up, she was taken and sold to your dad," Granddad tells them.

"This can't be real," Max mutters, cursing.

"Instead of going to the police, I went to the dad," I whisper, grim-faced. "I should have gone to the police, but at the time all I wanted to do was hurt him. I wanted him gone. I didn't know at the time what was going to happen, just what I hoped." I take a breather, running my hands through my hair before looking directly at Malik, knowing this will hurt him the most. He was the one who watched Dad die, getting beaten and stabbed by the girl's father. "None of you were meant to be there. I didn't know you were there," I whisper.

"He's the bloke who killed Dad and that's why you left, isn't it? You didn't actually leave *us*," Malik says, everything coming together.

"Yeah," I whisper hoarsely.

"This is so fucking messed up," Max says.

"So why is she back, and how does she know Teagan?" Mason asks through gritted teeth, still trying to process everything.

"She—" Fuck! It all clicks into place. Never once since I looked at the picture of Mum did I realise why I was looking at it and who she was to Teagan. I'd been too focused and stunned over seeing her after all this time that I forgot she was the one who was going to sell Teagan's virginity.

It all makes sense, but at the same time, nothing does. It's all messed up.

"She was my uncle's girlfriend. I.... She...." She looks at me, pleading to explain and I sigh, pulling her against me before turning to my brothers. I explain what she had planned for Teagan, leaving out parts about Faith and how she left, knowing that's her story to tell if she wants to. Their eyes widen, looking at Teagan with a mix of sympathy and anguish.

"I need to go. I need to process all of this, to make sense of it in my head," Malik suddenly bursts out. Gently, I pull away from Teagan, standing to stop him.

"We need to talk about this—about *her*."

"I don't give a fuck about her. She's fucking dead to me. I'm gonna get Harlow and go home. If you try to stop me, I'll put you through the fucking window," he snarls, and I rear back in surprise, hurt by his threat.

"Malik, don't do this, please. If I knew you were being hurt I would have stopped it somehow. Everything I did was to protect you four. Fuck, I did *everything* he asked me because he said he'd leave you all alone if I did," I croak, my eyes filling with tears that threaten to fall.

Malik moves and at first, I think he's going to punch me, but instead, he brushes past me, turning to face me when he gets to the stairs. "I just need some time. I'm so fucking sorry you've had to keep this to yourself all this time, but you've had all this time to process it. We're just finding out and I can't deal, not yet."

I nod, looking to the floor. "Okay," I say, feeling the life drain out of me as I make my way back to the sofa, sitting down.

"He'll be okay. They just need time," Granddad says, choked up.

"Hope so. How the fuck are we going to find her?" I ask, running my hands through my hair again, pulling at the ends.

"Where's my brother?" Denny asks.

"He went into the kitchen to give you all some privacy," Lake answers.

I look around the room, finding all my brothers wearing the same broken expressions. I have to fix this.

"I'm sorry I kept this from you, I really am. And I'm sorry she's come back. I won't let her hurt you guys, not again. I just.... I don't know how to make this right."

"Are you keeping anything else from us?" Mason asks, his voice small and lost.

"No," I tell him, hurt at the cold treatment.

He runs a hand over his face before getting up. "Are those...? Shit, are those tapes still out there?"

My heart aches at the bleak and agonising sound of his voice. I get up, taking a step towards him, but he takes one back, holding his palm up to stop me, his eyes flashing with warning.

Pain like nothing before fills me, so much so my eyes burn with tears and I feel like I can't breathe. "The ones I found were all destroyed after Dad died."

"But there could be more copies?"

"Honestly? I don't fucking know. I know nothing about the dark web. I wouldn't even know where to start or even *want* to look," I admit, knowing there are more sick people in this world than just my mum and dad.

"I can ask Liam. He'll know how to," Max says, trying to be helpful.

"No!" Mason and I shout.

"Just trying to fucking help."

"I know, but those tapes.... I'd rather no one else knew, okay?"

Max nods before turning to Myles, giving him a helpless look.

"I need to go. I need to... I don't know what the fuck I need, but I know I can't stay here," Mason announces before looking at me. "I resent you for keeping this from me. There's only a few years between us, so there was no need for you to protect *me*, not when we should have been protecting each other. I'm furious that you let me spend years of my life believing I could have done something to prevent what happened when all along it was inevitable. Nothing you or I could have done would have changed what happened to us. There was always a bigger plan in play and it's that I can't understand, or wrap my head around, especially knowing my love for Hope.

"That said, I *know* this isn't your fault, but at the moment, my anger is zeroed in on you and I don't want to say something I'll regret later," he says, taking Denny's hand.

I watch them leave, already feeling the drift come between us, tearing us apart. This is what I've always been scared of—losing my brothers.

"Maverick, everything will be okay."

"Granddad, please, don't. Not now. I need to find her. I need to do something," I tell him, heading into the kitchen.

Evan sits on the stool, head in his hands. From the grave expression on his face, I can tell he heard our conversation.

"How much did you hear?"

"Everything," he whispers, turning to look at me, his expression filled with pity and concern. "I've heard some messed-up family shit in my time—hell, you've met *my* mother—but this is something else entirely."

"Yeah, well, nothing beats *my* psycho mum."

He chuckles dryly before his expression turns serious. "You do realise you're gonna have to talk to the police, right?"

"Evan—"

"No, Mav! I understand you not wanting to share, I really do, but this isn't just about you. You could potentially be helping thousands of other children out there by helping us find these guys."

"Fuck!" I roar, throwing a cup across the room. "Fuck." My voice is weaker, my body draining of energy as I fall into the stool next to him, putting my head in my hands.

"It's going to be okay."

"I'm getting fed up with people telling me that. Nothing feels right. You're right about talking to the police, and I will, but we need to stop her first. She can't get away with this any longer."

"I have a plan for that. We have her real name now, so we'll find her."

"I really fucking hope so. I can't lose my brothers over her."

Losing my brothers would be like losing a part of myself. Each one of them are a part of me. They're my life, my family, and my brothers.

I'm not going to let some low-life junkie who gave birth to us come between us.

Not again.

Not ever.

TWENTY-FOUR

MAVERICK

All my life I've dealt with one thing after another, always protecting my brothers and making sure they stayed out of trouble. Back then I had them by my side; now I'm not even sure if they can stand to be in the same room as me.

We've overcome so much as men, as brothers and as a family; however, this time it feels like the odds are against us, giving us no way out. I've never felt so useless or helpless in all my life.

It's been a week since my world blew up in my face, and we're no closer to finding where our mum is or what she's planning. There's been no word or sighting of her and it's concerning. Neither I, nor Evan, nor the police have been able to locate her, and we've been searching non-stop. It's like she foresaw us going to the police and planned the perfect disappearing act.

A part of me hopes we've scared her off, but I know we're not that lucky. Another part of me, the part burning for vengeance, wants her to rot in prison for the rest of her life.

I'm just unsure of what my brothers want. Things between us are still tense, and although I know it's because they've just had a huge bomb dropped on them, I'm also worried it's because we still have nothing on her.

It doesn't help that none of us have really spoken since it all happened. Max and Myles seem to be staying out of everyone's way, avoiding the tension between us other three. Malik and Mason, on the other hand, have kept to themselves, staying with their girls in their own space. I know this has been hard on them, but I wish they'd come to me and talk. The only reason I haven't pushed them to talk is because I've had a decade to come to terms with what happened, so I know it's not going to sink in overnight.

It's why I'm so stressed about today. We planned to take Malik to a motocross race for his stag party since he didn't want to go out drinking like we did for Mason's. Harlow and Denny both assured me that they were still coming since it had already been paid for, but a part of me feels like it's not going to be as simple as them turning up. We've hardly said two words the few times we did see each other the past week, so what makes the girls believe today is going to be a hit is beyond me.

I hate the distance between us; it's not who we are, and I feel like we'll never be the family we once were ever again. And it's all my fault.

"Hey, are you okay?"

My cup of coffee flies out of my hand, spilling all over this week's invoices. "Shit, Myles, you scared the fucking hell out of me," I tell him, grabbing some tissues to soak all the coffee up, not that it does a lot of good.

I'd been so lost in my own head I didn't even hear him walk in. It's another sign of how uneasy I am about today.

He winces. "Sorry, I thought you heard me knock."

I wave him off. "It's my own fault. I didn't think any of you would actually come, so I wasn't expecting you. The others *are* here, aren't they?"

He nods. "Yeah, they're all here. They got stopped by Matt and some other dude in the car park," he says, searching my face. "Are you sure you're okay?"

Isn't that the million-dollar question?

Getting up, I round my desk, scrubbing a hand down my face, yawning. "Yeah, I just have a lot going on."

"Mav," he starts, wringing his hands. I know he's going to say something meaningful or something to try and make this better, but there's nothing he could say that could make me feel any better about myself right now. I hate what I've done to us all.

"Don't, Myles," I say, my voice low and scratchy.

"No, you need to hear this, Mav. You're running yourself into the ground trying to fix everything. This isn't just your burden to bear," he says, stepping closer. "And I know everyone keeps saying this, but everything really will be okay."

"Will it?" I ask dryly, wondering how he can say that when he's seen the strain between me, Malik and Mason.

"Yeah it will, if everyone would get their heads out of their arses. She doesn't get to come back here and destroy our lives. She may have played a huge role in ruining our childhoods, but we got through it once as a family, as brothers. We're not the same kids we once were, Maverick. We can help."

"He's right," Max says as he steps into my office, Malik and Mason behind him looking grim. "We've all drifted apart this past week, and I don't know about any of you, but I feel like I'm missing a left nut."

"What he said," Myles adds, nodding.

"I didn't want to keep this secret from any of you, especially you two," I say, addressing Malik and Mason. "I knew this involved you, and that you deserved to know. I just never knew *how* to tell you. I fretted constantly about how you'd react. I never wanted this," I admit, gesturing to the distance between us. "I can't stand you all hating me."

I glance to the floor when the room falls silent. Malik can't even look at me, Mason's staring at the wall behind me, and the twins are watching their feet like they're the most fascinating thing in the world.

It's like we're no longer brothers, but strangers. We've always been so close, no boundaries between us crossed—Max's shenanigans notwithstanding. He doesn't count. I don't think there's a boundary that boy hasn't crossed.

Malik clears his throat, sagging down onto my desk. "Look, I'm not one to sit and talk about my feelings and shit, but I can't stand here and let you believe we hate you, because I don't. "I've been distracted the past week, lost in my own head. I've been trying to deal with everything the only way I know how to—by being broody and angry. My anger hasn't been aimed at you though. It's at them."

"You can talk to me about anything," I tell him, managing to keep eye contact.

"The whole situation is fucked up, more so for you two," he says, looking between Mason and me. "It's been a lot to digest. I also feel fucking guilty for being relieved. I've had this raging anger inside me for as long as I can remember. Fuck, I've lost count of the amount of fights I've been in, but it never bothered me until Harlow walked into my life. Then that anger morphed into fear—fear of hurting her like Dad hurt Mum and us. But it's taken me until now to realise that I'm nothing like him. I'd rather kill myself than ever hurt either Harlow or my babies. We're not to blame for what happened to us. *They* are."

Nodding, I look away, trying to absorb everything he's said, but it's so much to take in at one time. I never realised he looked at himself in that way; if I had known, I would've helped in some way.

"You've never been like him, Malik. *None* of us are like them," I tell him, my throat tightening.

"He's right, we aren't," Mason agrees before turning to me. "I'm sorry, bro. I really am. I never wanted you to think I hated you. I've been so consumed with my own past, my own demons, that I never even thought of how you'd be handling everything. Of course, I'm still pissed that you kept it from me since this is pretty fucking huge, but I also understand *why* now that I've had time to process everything. If you had told me this crap when we were younger, I dread to think what it would've done to me. I was already messed up in the head. Hell, I nearly lost Denny because my head was so screwed up. Who knows where my life would be if you hadn't protected me—us. So I guess we really should be thanking you instead of making you feel responsible."

My mouth falls open; I'm completely speechless. Out of everything I thought would happen or be said today, *that* was not it. If anything, I expected a full-on brawl between us, as well as a few choice words.

"I... I don't know what to say. I wasn't expecting...." I shake my head as I gesture between Malik and Mason. Their words mean everything and more.

"Shall we group hug now?" Max asks.

"Shut up," I tell him, rolling my eyes. "I really am sorry this is happening."

"And we're sorry for letting you deal with this on your own," Mason says.

"Yeah, any news on *mummy dearest?*" Max asks, his jaw clenching.

"No." I sigh, pinching the bridge of my nose.

"What are we going to do? She's got to have a plan, and we need to be ready for whatever that is. We do have one advantage on our side though—she doesn't know that we know who she is," Malik says, rubbing his jaw where he's grown a rough stubble over the past couple of days, aging him ten years.

"I don't know. She's nowhere to be found, so I think either she knows we're on to her or she's left town."

"But how? We only found out about her a week ago. Fuck, before that it was just about your club and Teagan. How could she know we fitted all the pieces together?" Myles asks, looking frustrated.

"That's the thing, I don't think we've got all the missing pieces. I feel like we're missing something. We know *why* she targeted the club, but what I'd like to know is why she never came directly to me. Why use Holly and then attack Teagan? None of it makes sense. And I'm not backing off until I find her. She's hurt too many people I love," I warn them.

"No arguments here. I want her to pay for everything she's ever done just as much as you do," Mason says, sitting on the arm of the sofa as he runs his fingers through his hair.

"What I'd like to know is why she hasn't shown her face yet. If we were the intended targets, shouldn't she be harassing us?" Malik asks, and rightly so.

"Not if she's only after money like Teagan said she is. She'd want to keep a low profile so she can make a clean getaway. For all she knows, we're just some low-life, fucked-up kids Dad raised. She might believe we're easy targets," I say, shrugging.

"*Or* she knew we'd never give her any money. She probably thought we were too dumb to figure out it was her, or thought we were too stupid to go to the police. It's not like we have a good track record when it comes to them," Max says, spacing out at the end.

"She clearly underestimated us."

"I certainly did, my boys."

TWENTY-FIVE

TEAGAN

So much for having a relaxing day at the spa. Even the masseuse couldn't massage the knotted tension from my body.

All I've done for the past week is worry, stress and worry some more. It's worked my body into a frenzy. Maverick and his brothers' pain is suffocating. I wish there was something I could do to take it away—Maverick's especially.

I've watched him become more withdrawn, more haunted as each day passes. There are moments where I think I'm losing him. The only reason I'm still holding onto hope is because even in those dark moments where he's lost in his own guilt and torment, I still see the Maverick I've fallen in love with.

I hate that he's hurting so much, and that his brothers can't see past their own pain to notice what it's doing to him. I wish they'd understand why he didn't tell them and just talk to him. The distance they've put between them is only making the whole situation worse and it's killing Maverick on the inside, even if he doesn't always show it.

I'm hoping today will help them come together and move forward with this whole catastrophe.

I pray he'll be okay and they go easy on him. He doesn't deserve their hostility.

"If who's okay?" Kayla asks from beside me. When no one answers, I wonder if they've gone to sleep, but then she calls my name. "Teagan?"

"What?" I ask, wishing I could relax for just five minutes. I'm strung up so tight.

"You said I hope he's okay. Who were you referring to?"

Removing the cucumbers from my eyes, I sit up, throwing them on the little table between me and Kayla, puffing out a breath.

"I'm worried about Maverick," I admit, watching as she and the others remove their own cucumber slices.

"Thank God! I can't relax, and faking it is tiring me out," Harlow huffs, grabbing the iced water next to her and taking a large gulp.

"He'll be fine," Denny says shortly. I know she's hurting for her husband, but there's no need for the attitude she's had towards Maverick all week.

"No, he won't. This is killing him, Denny. He's hardly slept or eaten this past week."

"That's called guilt," she says, looking away.

"Sorry, but fuck you. Did you—hell, any of you—or his brothers even bother to ask him why he didn't tell you? Or why he never said anything to them about what happened? I'm sorry about what happened to your men, I really am, but it happened to Maverick too and if you ask me, Malik and Mason got off fucking easy in comparison," I snap heatedly, my breathing harsh. Every time I think of what Mav told me the night we found out about Lynn, my stomach turns. But what hurts is that not one has asked him about what he went through, or even seems to care.

The room fills with an awkward silence, each of us thinking about what's just been said. I'm about to apologise for my behaviour, knowing it isn't my place, when Denny speaks.

"I'm sorry. I don't know what's wrong with me," she tells me, shamefaced.

"You're upset, just like everyone else is. Don't worry about it. And I'm sorry for biting your head off, but I'm just really worried about Mav. I know I've not known any of you long, nor do I have the history you share together, but from the very beginning I could tell you were all a close-knit family. But it was Mav who raised them, made sure they stuck together. He gave up everything just to make sure they had a happy life. Hell, he even let his father do what he did to him so they didn't have to go through it. And instead of being appreciated for his heroism, he gets shunned for *one* mistake. Can you understand why I'm so upset?"

They all seem to think it over, their faces a mix of shame and discomfort. "We've all been unfair, but none of us hate or blame him, Teagan. We love him," Harlow tells me softly. It's good to hear. I know it's one of the many things that Maverick has been worried sick over, even though he won't admit it. He respects his brothers and their girlfriends, so them having any ill feelings towards him matters greatly to him.

"I'm just being a bitch. Mase was messed up for years over what happened to him. Our relationship suffered because of it at one point, and I know he's never forgiven himself for it. He was starting to live with it, but having it all blow up again has brought back all those suppressed memories."

"Same with Malik. It brought back a lot of aggression towards his parents," Harlow says to Denny, understanding her concern for Mason.

"I think it's affected them all. I've never known Max to act like a normal human being in all the time I've known him. He's not cracked one joke all week," Lake informs us, something I already know.

"True. Faith was beginning to think he was sick," I remark.

"How is Myles doing?" Denny asks, looking at Kayla.

"He's been quiet, but I think that's because my sickness bug has kept him distracted," she explains.

"I didn't know you were sick. I thought you were avoiding us," I say softly.

"It wasn't bad. I just didn't want to risk anyone else getting it on top of everything else going on."

"You can always come to us," Denny says.

I watch the love and devotion pass through each woman. They might not be blood related, but they're family in every sense of the word. It's an honour to be a part of it.

Now I feel like shit for questioning where their loyalties lie. I look down to my lap, ashamed as I twiddle my fingers.

"You love him, don't you?" Kayla states softly, even though it comes out as a question.

Lifting my head, I take in her serious expression and slump backwards in my chair. There's no way they'll let me avoid the question; I can see written across their expressions.

"I really do," I admit, my eyes stinging from unleashed tears. I've not even told him because I'm scared he doesn't feel the same way. "I don't know what to do to make this right for him. I've only ever loved four people in my life—my mum, Nan, Tish and Faith. My dad doesn't count because I never knew him. It's not the same love. I'm struggling on what I'm supposed to be doing."

"Hey, take a deep breath. There isn't a rule book and if there were, I doubt it would cover what to do in our situation. What you're doing—being there—it's all you can do," Harlow tells me, her eyes filled with understanding.

"She's right. I've watched him with you the past week and can tell he's cherished every second of your presence. I think you help him more than you realise," Lake offers, her tone also gentle.

"Lord, I hope so. Some days I feel like I'm just getting in the way," I mutter, praying she's right. I can't lose him. My heart couldn't take it.

We fall into silence once again, but Tish storming into the room interrupts that. Her expression is thunderous, her wild hair covered in a bright orange bandana.

"Fucking arsehole," she fumes.

"What's wrong?" I ask, sitting up straighter. She's only been gone twenty minutes, what could of possibly have happened?

"Fucker, I didn't get the happy ending massage I asked for."

I gasp along with the others, who stare at her open-mouthed, stunned by her outburst.

"Tish, we're not in a bloody movie. Oh my God, have they called the police?"

"No, I gave *him* a happy ending instead." She winks, sitting down next to me. "Would have got mine too, but his boss interrupted," she pouts.

"Tish," I screech, shaking my head at her.

"What?" she yells, covering her ears. "Don't ruin my bliss."

I don't know why her behaviour still gets to me anymore; I should be immune to it. She's never been one to shy away from expressing what she's thinking. I don't even think she has a filter.

"I cannot believe you," I splutter, but she waves me off, uncaring.

"Whatever. I'm going for a swim to cool off," she tells us, dropping her dressing gown as she gets up.

"Tish, put them away!" I yell. She has on an orange Lycra bikini that barely covers her large breasts.

"Wow," Kayla mutters and I glance her way, laughing when her cheeks redden, looking anywhere but at Tish.

"I know, right? Got me a bargain at New Look last week. Makes my boobs look fantastic. They're large and in charge." She grins, bouncing them.

"Just go." I laugh, unable to hide my amusement.

She leaves without a backwards glance. As soon as she's out of sight, I turn slowly back to the girls, grinning sheepishly.

"I swear she does act normal... occasionally."

"It's scary knowing there's a female version of Max," Harlow says with wide eyes, still watching the door Tish walked through.

"Hey, Max isn't *that* bad," Lake protests.

"No?" Denny questions. "Pretty sure it was Max who showed the whole school his mangina."

"He's changed," Lake says, defends.

"He has," Denny giggles.

We all sober up, our laughter dying off as our earlier conversation comes back, the air around us thickening.

"Can I ask you something personal?" Harlow asks, looking down at her stomach as she rubs her bump affectionately.

"Of course," I find myself saying, although I'm wary. I hate talking about my past. I prefer for it to stay buried, where it belongs.

"What was she like? Their mum?"

I close my eyes, feeling a migraine coming. I knew this moment would come eventually. In fact, I expected to be asked by one of the brothers, but not Harlow.

Opening my eyes, I give them a grave look, trying to blink away the pain.

"She was pure evil," I whisper. "From the moment she turned up on our doorstep, things with my uncle went from bad to worse. She manipulated him, had him wrapped around her little finger. He loved her enough to let her, and I thought he was incapable of feeling anything. She didn't love him back though. There's a coldness in her eyes that I've never seen in anyone else. She was soulless, unfeeling."

"Did she ever talk about the lads?" Denny whispers sadly.

I've raked my mind over this since I found out our pasts are connected, but I've come up with nothing every single time.

"No, nada. You wouldn't have even thought she'd ever had kids by looking at her because she was skinny from all the drugs she took, but also because there wasn't a maternal bone in her body. The way she spoke to me, looked at me—hell, the way she treated me in general—was sinister. She was cruel in every way you can imagine," I tell them, gulping.

"I can't believe the woman you're describing birthed someone as good as Myles and his brothers," Kayla says, wiping away her tears.

"I'm glad they weren't raised by her," Denny mutters, her face pale.

"I just wish we knew how to get rid of her once and for all. If it's money she wants, she can have it. I have my parents' inheritance. Malik's never let me use it," Harlow says, shrugging.

"She'd just come back for more once she runs out," I tell her, knowing that much about Lynn.

"Why is she doing this? Doesn't she realise she's caused enough problems?" Kayla says, her shoulders slumping.

"I'd like to know why she hasn't gone to them," Denny adds, voicing her own concerns.

I'm thinking that over when Lake speaks up, stopping me short. "Maybe she doesn't know they're there, or who they are. She's been gone over a decade, nearly two. This has to be about money. Trying to get Teagan involved and using the club could just be a coincidence."

"No!" I say, my eyes rounding when something occurs to me. Why hadn't I remembered this before now?

Because you've had a lot going on with getting the life beaten out of you.

"She does know who the club belongs to. When she came to the flower shop she called him Carter, like she knew who he was. It didn't even click or seem important until now. I think she used the club to sell drugs because she *knew* the owner," I tell them, everything clicking into place.

"So why not use MC5? Why did she target V.I.P.?" Harlow muses.

"Because Mason is rarely ever there for night shifts anymore," Denny answers.

"What does that have to do with it?" Harlow asks, not following, but I am.

"Because if he were there, he'd want to keep the club's reputation clean," Denny answers, but poor Harlow still isn't following, so I interrupt, hoping I can explain better.

"If you were working a night shift and were acting manager and saw someone selling drugs, what would you do?" I ask.

"Go to the police," she answers, giving me a 'duh' look, but then realisation dawns on her. "Oh."

"Exactly, you'd call attention to the problem. She had an in with Holly, but thinking back, I think Holly was being blackmailed somehow. It could mean she's here for something bigger than selling drugs. We just have to figure out what that is."

"I still think it's money. It's always about money. She clearly knew where to come to get it because didn't you live five hours away before you moved in with your nan?" Lake asks.

I nod, my expression grim. "That means she has some sort of leverage over them to ensure she gets what she wants. She just hasn't needed to use it yet."

"Oh God," Denny gasps, her eyes watering.

"What?" We all ask, sitting forward in our seats.

"The tapes," she whispers, looking around at each of us.

I stare wide-eyed, everything starting to make sense. "We need to tell Maverick," I rush out, getting up to find my clothes.

"I need to talk to Evan," Denny says.

We all turn to see her pale, her expression full of guilt.

"I know that face. What did you do?" Harlow asks warily.

"I asked Evan to make sure those tapes were really gone. He knows a few people who work on special victim cases just like this. He said he'll call in a favour for me and find out what he can. I know it's not my place, but I couldn't look my husband in the eye every day, see that haunted look, knowing there was something I could do. The first three nights he had nightmares and he'd scream out for those tapes," she shares before she begins to sob into her hands.

Her bitchiness from earlier begins to make more sense. I move over to comfort her, unable to see her in this state and do nothing.

"It will be fine, Denny," Harlow whispers, her own tears falling.

"If I had those connections, I'd have done the same," I tell Denny, holding her hands in her lap. "If we're right about this, then it's good we got a head start. But as of right now, we're going on wild speculation.

"Let's go to the men, tell them what we've come up with and go from there. Text your brother, tell him to meet us at the club."

Denny nods, wiping her eyes before grabbing her phone off the table between her and Harlow.

If we're right about this—and I hope we're not—their whole life is about to blow up for the second time in a week.

Please let me be wrong.

TWENTY-SIX

MAVERICK

"I CERTAINLY DID, MY BOYS."

Our heads whip around towards the new voice in the room, and my eyes widen in horror when I see our mother standing before us. My mind and body completely lock up, and I can't help but feel like a scared little boy.

She's nothing like how I remembered; she's older, more jaded, and stone-faced. She's dressed in skinny black jeans, black knee-high boots and a leather puffy coat, the hood lined with fur. She's clearly trying to pull off a youthful look, but all I can think of when I look at her, is mutton dressed as lamb. Her hair is scraped back in a ponytail, looking oily from the excessive amount of hair products. Her face is pinched together in a stern expression, inspecting us before quickly dismissing us with a look of disgust.

Finally snapping out of it, I notice my brothers have moved at my side. Mason and Myles stand off to my left, Malik and Max to my right, leaving me in the middle, glaring down at the woman before me.

I eye her warily, not wanting to underestimate her. Not again. All week while I've been inside working, Evan has been outside watching and waiting for her to show up. It was the only plan he could come up with, to trap her in a place where we knew she'd most likely come—the club. But she's chosen the one day Evan isn't here watching, like she had someone watching us as well.

"Myles, call the cops," I demand, not taking my eyes off her. Just then, four men step into the room, all wearing deadly expressions.

"I wouldn't do that if I were you," she warns, and I feel Myles stop, his eyes burning into the side of my head.

"And why's that?" I ask, my voice hard, cold.

"I have something you'll want, and you have something I need. I think we can work out some sort of arrangement to make sure we both get what we want."

"Yeah, that's not going to happen. There's nothing you have that I could possibly want... except for you to fuck off."

"Oh, but I do."

"Pretty sure we've all outgrown breastfeeding, Mother," Max tells her sarcastically.

She turns her head, looking at him distastefully. There's no emotion in her eyes, not even a flicker. You'd think a mother who hadn't seen her sons since they were babies would show *something*.

Not her.

"And which one are you?" she asks, sticking her nose in the air.

He laughs, throwing his head back. I've already had enough and take a step forward. Her goons move into a protective stance beside her and I sneer.

"I wouldn't do that if I were you," Malik bites out. I can tell he's barely checking in his anger, and I can't say I blame him. I'd never hurt a woman, but the drive to wrap my hands around her throat is compelling.

"I just want what I came for. Then I'll be on my merry way." She sounds smug, like she really believes she'll get it.

"You'll be getting fuck all from us," I tell her before turning to Myles. "Call the police."

"Calling them won't help your sister," she says.

My eyes narrow as I take a menacing step forward. "We don't have a sister."

"Yep, pretty sure we all got dicks," Max mutters.

"Debatable," she snarls, shaking her head. "But you see, you do have a sister. A half-sister who is three-years-old. So, are you ready to listen?"

I shake my head, not trusting anything she has to say, though her expression indicates she's telling the truth. "I don't fucking believe you. Why should we?"

"You'd have called the police the minute I told you if you didn't. But if you want proof, I have a picture." She takes a step forward, holding her phone out to me. I glance at the picture of a little girl, huddled in a dirty blanket, sleeping. Her face is barely visible, her brown hair knotted around her face and a ratty teddy cuddled to her chest.

"That could be anyone's kid," I scoff, stepping back. I try to come off as blasé, hoping she can't tell how much her confession has really gotten to me.

"Oh, but she's not. And you five should know by now that I don't do kids."

Malik curses under his breath, stepping forward. He doesn't get far before one of the men take a step towards him.

Before I have chance to stop him, Malik's throwing a punch at the bloke closest to him.

"Malik," I shout, just as another goon steps forward. I growl, punching him in the jaw and knocking him to the floor. I jump over him when Malik and the guy fall into the hallway, landing punch after punch. "Stop!"

They don't listen or they can't hear me, so I grab the guy fighting Malik, throwing him behind me. I watch as he stumbles into the wall, falling to the floor with a thud. I turn to make sure Malik is okay when a punch connects with my jaw. Wincing, I rub my throbbing jaw, frowning at my brother.

"Fuck!" he roars, pulling at the strands of his hair, his face red, seething with anger.

"Myles, call the fucking police," I shout and pull Malik back into the room, past our mother and the other guys to stand beside Mason and Max.

"Well then, I guess I'll sell her to the highest bidder," she mutters, like it's a hardship. Myles puts the phone down, looking at me pleadingly, and I sigh. I know that, no matter what, I couldn't let her sell a child, even if she might not be my sister.

Turning, I step forward, getting in her face. "What the fuck do you want?"

She smiles wide. I'd love to wipe it from her smug, grimy face. "Now that you've asked, I want twenty grand."

My eyes widen in shock and I splutter, stepping backwards. "I-I don't have that kind of money."

"You're fucking sick," Mason growls, the first time he's shown any sort of sign that he knows she's here. He's been frozen since she walked in.

"Thank you." She smiles at him before looking at me. "And you do have the money. I've been watching you a long time, so don't lie to me, son. You have properties you could sell."

Hiding my shock at her knowledge, I blank my expression. "I have a mortgage, not fucking money. I don't know what you expected, but we don't have that kind of money lying around. You've come to the wrong person if that's what you're after. And just so we're clear, I'm not your fucking son."

Her eyes flash for a second with annoyance and anger. Something tells me it's not from me telling her I'm not her son, but more to do with the fact that I said I don't have the money.

"You'll find it if you want your sister kept alive and safe. I'm sure she'll be sold pretty quickly. It's a shame your daddy isn't alive. He would've loved her." She grins wickedly.

The image of the little girl on the tapes flashes in my mind and I growl, my fists clenching. "Careful. You wouldn't want to end up how he did, now would you."

Her eyes flash in surprise before she grins. "So the rumours *are* true. You killed your dad." When I don't say anything, she just stands there, shaking her head. "Looks like we're at a standstill."

I give Mason a look and he closes his eyes, seeming to be in thought. When he opens them, they're cold, trained on Maralynn. "We can round up eight grand at the most."

"I owe twenty," she yells, then realises what she's just let out, her face full of shock and surprise.

I smirk, clicking my tongue. "So you need *us* to bail *you* out," I state. "That's all we've got, so take it or leave it. It's not our fault you owe some scumbag money."

"I'll just sell Lily," she says, playing it off. Something tells me that it's the last thing she wants to do. Not because she cares for the little girl in the picture, but most likely because she can't get the money she wants.

"You got to play that card once, and let it pass, but if you threaten her or another kid again, whether she's our sister or not, I'll fucking kill you myself," Malik grits out, his whole body trembling.

She eyes Malik in distaste. "You were always the angry one. No wonder you were chosen to be beaten." She giggles. His fists clench. "But I'll threaten her all I like. Until she's sold, she belongs to me. Plus, I could always sell your baby. You boys have good genes."

Malik steps forward, but this time I have time to grab him.

Just as I do, the place is swarmed with police officers. I notice Barrett in the mist, standing at the door issuing orders. There's yelling to get down onto the floor and my eyes widen in horror, not for my mum being arrested, but for the little girl in the picture. We'll never find her if she's locked up.

"No!" I yell, and step forward, my eyes colliding with Maralynn's. Her eyes are dilated in a cold, menacing look, and I know there's going to be retribution.

"You're going to regret this, you stupid fucking boy," she yells as a police officer handcuffs her arms behind her back.

"Tell me where she is," I rush out, stepping forward.

She laughs at me before spitting in my face. The officer pulls her roughly, warning her to behave. Lifting the bottom of my shirt, I wipe the spit away, inwardly gagging. "You think you'll have her now? She'll die without me. You'll never find her."

"Tell me where the fuck she is," I roar, and Mason steps next to me.

"We'll find her," he says, giving our mum a cold look.

"No, you won't," she taunts before being pulled away.

Evan steps into the room and I rush over, pulling him out of earshot of the other officers. "You need to do something. Stop them!"

"What?" he asks, eyeing me like I'm on drugs.

"She's saying we have a sister out there, and she threatened to sell her."

"She could be lying to get what she wants," he tells me, seeming unsure with his answer.

I know how it sounds, and yeah, she could be lying, but the sharp pain in my chest and a gut feeling are telling me otherwise.

I shake my head. "She showed me a picture. She wanted us to give her money in exchange for her. She was blackmailing us because she owes someone money, Evan. The little girl is clearly not with them, so she's left her somewhere alone. We've been searching a week for Lynn with no luck. If we couldn't find her, what makes you think we're going to have a chance at finding a kid? She'll starve to fucking death and with *our* mum, who even knows when she was last fed."

His eyebrows scrunch together but his face hardens, finally taking what I'm saying seriously. "I can't stop the arrest. Your mum is a wanted person. I'll see if

Barrett will let me in on the questioning. I'll get her to talk," he tells me, but I feel helpless.

"We need to find her now," I growl.

"Just let them do their job," Mason says, giving me a look. Reluctantly I nod, running my hands through my hair as a ruckus by the door grabs my attention. Denny, Harlow, Lake and Kayla come rushing into the room, all with panicked expressions.

"Oh my God, what happened?" Denny gasps, moving over to Mason and hugging him.

"Harlow, you can't be here," Malik says, panic written across his face.

"Why?" she asks, but I tune them out when Teagan comes running into the room. She glances around the room before coming to me, tears falling down her cheeks.

Fuck! How I landed someone like her, I'll never know. I don't deserve her, but I'm too selfish to let her go. I've never had anyone care for me the way she does.

Her scent envelops me as she runs to me, making goosebumps rise up my neck. Wrapping my arms around her, I pull her close, breathing her in.

"Are you okay? I saw her. She's in a police car," she tells me, then pulls back, searching all over for any signs of injury.

I place my hands on her cheeks, tilting her head until she's looking at me. "I'm fine," I whisper, kissing her softly. "But we have a problem."

"I know! We figured it out. Well, I think we have. We were talking and one theory led to another and then bam," she rambles, smacking her hands together. I try to keep up but I'm lost.

"Wow, calm down and explain... slower."

"We were at the spa and I was worried. We got talking about everything and came up with a theory. We think she's got a hidden agenda. She clearly wants money, and she must have known the police would eventually get involved, right?" I nod. "In that case, she must have something to bargain with, something to use to get you to comply. Because let's face it, she's not winning any Mum of the Year award, so it wouldn't be like you'd do it out of love."

She's still rambling but I couldn't be more in love with her than I am right now. They were able to come up with this in a day, something Evan and I have spent a week trying to figure out.

My woman is incredible.

"I know."

"So it's true?" she asks, tears slipping down her cheeks.

"Hey, it's okay. We'll find her," I tell her, wiping them away.

"Find her?" she asks, her nose scrunching up adorably. "I swear I just saw her being put into the back of a police car."

"Um, you did. Apparently, we have a sister."

"A what? Come again," she splutters, shaking her head as she pales. "Oh Lord, we have to find her."

"What did you think I meant? I thought you figured it out."

"No, I thought she had tapes of... you know," she says under her breath, and my face pales. She didn't mention those tapes and if she did, I think she really would have been killed, brought back to life and then killed all over again by each brother.

"She didn't mention them," I whisper.

Mason, who's hugging Denny next to me, must have been told the same thing because he turns to me sharply.

"I know we said we wouldn't look, but I think it's best that we do. We're parents now. I can't have that out there." The pain in his voice causes my stomach to turn.

"I'll sort something," I promise, although I don't know what I'll do since I have no fucking clue where to start. Only someone sick would know how to get their hands on something as mundane and twisted as that.

"About that...," Denny starts, shifting uncomfortable.

"What?" Mason asks, eyeing his wife warily.

"Well I... uh, I went to Evan for help. I just wanted to help you. I knew it was eating away at you even though you never said anything. I just wanted to make it go away for you. I'm so sorry," she sobs.

Mason looks down at her with a soft expression. "Fuck, I love you so much," he whispers, pulling her against him and kissing her. I look away, smiling, but Malik getting into it with Harlow across the room holds my attention.

Keeping Teagan by my side, I walk over, frowning when I see tears falling down Harlow's face.

"I'm not leaving. We're getting married," she pleads with him.

"It's not safe, Harlow, don't you get that? She knows you're pregnant and has already mentioned making a profit. I'm not risking it."

"She's just been arrested," she cries, throwing her hands up.

"Please, Harlow. It won't be forever, just until I know it's safe," he begs.

"Malik, think about this, bro," I interrupt, placing a hand on his shoulder. He shoves it off, his eyes lost, dull.

"I have thought about it, Maverick. I'm not risking their fucking lives. If it were Teagan, would you want to keep her safe?"

I growl, pulling Teagan tighter against me. There's nothing I wouldn't do to keep her safe but Harlow's right; Maralynn's just been arrested. There's nothing she can do to us now.

"Malik, we need to stay together. We're safer together. Not that I think she'll do anything now, since she doesn't have a leg to stand on. You're getting married this weekend, and the twins will be born in a few weeks. Do you really want to miss that?"

He looks torn, staring at Harlow helplessly. "I can't lose you."

"You're not going to lose me, Malik. I know you'd do anything to keep us safe. I've never doubted that, and you shouldn't either."

"We need to concentrate on finding out if we really have a sister and where she is," I tell him. Malik is loyal to the bone; if anything can get him motivated, it's family.

"A sister?" Harlow gasps, then winces, her hand going to her stomach.

"Are you okay?" Malik panics, moving to her side and guiding her over to my desk chair.

"Yeah, just a sharp kick," she says, breathing heavily.

"Are you sure?" Teagan asks, kneeling on the other side of Malik. "You look a little pale."

"Let's get you home so you can rest," Malik tells her, then looks to me. "Do you have your car?"

"Yeah, I'll drive you two back. Let me just talk to Evan."

He nods before turning back to Harlow. I look down at Teagan, getting her attention. "I'll be back in a minute. We'll drop these two off and go get Faith, okay?"

"Sounds good." She smiles before turning to Harlow. "Do you need some water?"

A few officers remain, talking to Barrett and Evan. Myles and Max are on opposite sides of the room, Kayla and Lake in their arms, whispering to each other.

Max looks angry, ready to kill someone, whereas Myles seems sad, withdrawn. It looks like Kayla is having a hard time reaching him.

I walk over, interrupting whatever Kayla was whispering to him. "Hey, how you doing?" I ask, knowing seeing our mum for the first time must have been hard on him.

"I don't know. Mav, I know you, Malik and Mase didn't believe her, but I think she was telling the truth about Lily," he whispers, looking away.

Hearing her name causes my chest to tighten.

"Yeah, me too." I sigh. "Evan is going to question her, see if he can get anything out of her."

"What will happen if they find her? Will she be able to stay with us?" he asks, seeming worried.

"Yeah, kid. She will," I promise and he nods, a little colour coming back to his cheeks. "I'm going to check on Max. We're heading back soon, so if you want, you can go and meet us back at the house."

He nods and I clap him on the back before walking over to Max, his face tight with frustration.

When I'm close enough for him to notice me, he turns, glaring. "I want to fucking kill her. We need to find that little girl. I don't care if she's not our sister, Mav. She's a little fucking girl, and I know I only got a glimpse of the picture but still, she looked uncared for. She's a fucking monster for doing this. The doctors should have neutered her. Fuck, Nan and Granddad should have aborted the bitch the second they found out they were pregnant," he fumes. I can understand where he's coming from, but he needs to rein it in. He's scaring Lake, for one. She's never seen him like this before, so it must be hard for her.

"Bro, we're gonna find her, but I need you to calm it down. I know you're hurting and I understand, but Myles needs you. You can be mad later. Go home together and we'll meet you there," I tell him.

He looks over at Myles, his eyes saddening when he sees how hurt his brother is. I'm just glad he's calmed down a little, his fists now unclenched.

Lake smiles at me gratefully before taking Max's hand. "We'll see you back at home," she tells me. "Max, let's go to Myles. I'll order you some food when we're back."

He looks down at her lovingly, his eyes softening. "Yeah, I am a bit hungry."

I watch them leave before turning to Evan. He looks in my direction and meets me halfway, both of us talking in low voices.

"How did you know to come? I thought you were out working a case today?"

"I was meant to, but it got cancelled last minute. I was at the office so I logged into your security cameras and noticed it was being hacked. As I was calling Barrett, I had a message from Denny telling us to come here. I thought they were connected, so I raced over."

"What are we going to do if she doesn't talk?" I ask, changing the subject.

"She will. But even if she doesn't, we have more to go on. Not only do we have her but we have her henchmen. One of them will talk, and we'll be able to look into their backgrounds."

"Sorry to interrupt, but we should get Harlow back. She's throwing up in the bin," Teagan says. Grimacing, I look over her shoulder to where Harlow and Malik are, finding her bent over the bin, throwing up.

"I'll talk to you later," I tell Evan, taking Teagan's hand in mine.

"I'll call you with any new information," he tells me, walking back over to Bennett.

When we reach Harlow and Malik, she's wiping her mouth, groaning. "I've been sick."

"I can see that," Malik tells her, holding her hair back.

"Me too. It's making me feel sicker, Malik," she whispers, closing her eyes.

I chuckle, grabbing my keys off my desk. "Let's get you back home."

"Can we get some food? I'm hungry," she asks, her eyes wide and hopeful.

I burst out laughing, along with Teagan. Malik doesn't know whether to laugh or be worried. Instead, he helps her up, telling her she can have whatever she wants.

This... this is what family is all about. We've just had our world turned upside down and yet, together, we've come out stronger, closer. And that's why I'll do whatever it takes to ensure they never have to go through anything like this ever again.

TWENTY-SEVEN

TEAGAN

When I moved out of my flat, I thought that would be the biggest thing to happen to me this year. I wanted a fresh start, a new life with my daughter. Never once did I believe I'd end up in a relationship with the hottest man I'd ever laid eyes on, *and* somehow move in with him. Love most certainly wasn't in the cards for me either, but I've found it.

My life has changed drastically, and I don't just mean from finding out that my psycho uncle's ex-girlfriend is also my boyfriend's mum.

Lynn coming into our lives could jeopardise all that I have, but I've been beaten, run out of my own home and threatened. If none of that has managed to destroy what Maverick and I have built together, then nothing will.

Even with all that going on, I can't deny that I'm stupidly happy. I feel like I finally belong, that I have a place in the world, one where I'm accepted and surrounded by people who actually care for me. They've become my family, and I'd do anything for them.

Which is why I did something stupid the other day. I went to visit Lynn, hoping I could somehow get her to talk.

She claims they have a three-year-old sister, but no one has been able to locate the little girl or get her vile mother to talk. I'd like to say I don't think she'd actually leave her unattended on her own, but this is Lynn we're talking about. I wouldn't put anything past her.

I tried to get her to talk, even offered her money—which she knew I never had. She laughed in my face the whole time, taunting and warning me that this wasn't over.

I'd like to think I at least helped in some way by trying, yet ever since I walked out of the building, I've felt nothing but dread.

Not telling Maverick what I did has been eating away at me. But how do you tell the man you love that you've made the situation a whole lot worse?

In the four days since Lynn was arrested, the boys have slowly been going out of their minds with worry over their sister. The only thing keeping them from losing it is Malik and Harlow's wedding. Harlow tried to cancel it, feeling this wasn't the best time, but Maverick put a stop to it, telling her it's still on and for her not to worry about anything except walking down the aisle.

"Hey, babe, Faith has decided she wants to come dress shopping with us," Maverick says, walking into the room.

Lifting my head in his direction, I give him a small smile.

I can't hold this in anymore. I need to tell him before it all becomes too much. I just pray he doesn't hate me when I do.

"I knew she'd change her mind," I murmur.

"Are you okay? You've been really distant the past two days."

This is it. This is my chance to tell him. Straightening my back, I shake my head, willing my eyes not to start watering. Already I can feel the tears burning at the back of my throat.

"No. Maverick, there's something I need to tell you," I whisper, ducking my head.

He sits next to me, taking my hand in his. I give him a squeeze before making eye contact, trying to mask the sadness I'm feeling.

"What's wrong?"

"You know the other day when I told you that I had to go into work to sort out a delivery for my nan?"

"Yeah." His voice is cautious now, wary, and I hate that. I never wanted him to be wary, not of me.

My hands start shaking, my eyes filling with unwanted tears. "I lied. I went to see Lynn. You were all so torn up, not sleeping and always worrying about Lily. I hated seeing you in so much pain so I went to see her, to see if I could make her talk. I'm so sorry I didn't tell you. I really am. I never wanted to lie to you, *ever*, but I knew you'd never let me go if I did," I rush out, the first tear slipping free.

His eyes bore into me, narrowed as he grits his teeth. Turning away, he roughly pushes his fingers through his hair, leaning forward with his elbows resting on his knees.

"I really am sorry," I whisper, scared I'm going to lose him. "If you want me to go, I will, but please know I only did this to help. I didn't mean to hurt you."

When he still doesn't say anything, the pain in my chest becomes unbearable. Standing, I try to shake it, unable to look at Maverick.

I'm so angry with myself. I should've listened to my gut instead of rushing in there, not thinking it through. I knew there could be a chance I'd lose him when I made the decision to go see her, but I was willing to do anything to find Lily and help Maverick.

I go to leave, a strangled sob escaping. But then he reaches out, pulling me down into his lap. Wrapping his arms around my waist, he presses his head into the crook of my neck and more tears fall. He only ever does that when he's seeking comfort.

I'm puzzled by his actions, wondering why he isn't yelling at me.

"Maverick?"

"You shouldn't have kept this from me, Teagan, but most importantly you shouldn't have gone. Someone as pure and good as you shouldn't be stepping into a place like that. Something could've happened," he stresses, running his palm up and down my thigh.

"I'm so sorry," I whisper, dropping my forehead against his.

He sighs, kissing me briefly. "Did she say anything?"

"No. She just laughed. She kept taunting me, saying it wasn't over and that we had what was coming to us. All the usual mumbo jumbo crap."

"Hopefully she's all talk, but until we find Lily, I don't want to take any chances. The cops have put out an alert, but with only a name, no picture, and Mum's mugshot, we don't have much to go on. The calls coming in are from all over the place, but they're all dead ends."

"We'll find her," I tell him, cupping his jaw. "God wouldn't bring you a sister if he didn't mean for you to have her in your life."

"Mummy, Da— I mean, Maverick, can we go now. I'm bored," Faith asks, walking into the bedroom with her doll. "Sally wants to go for a walk."

Maverick tenses underneath me, and my breath catches in my throat. It's not the first time she's slipped up and started to call him Daddy. The first time, his face went soft and he lifted her in his arms to give her a kiss before carrying on with what they were doing. I, on the other hand, must have messed up big time because I told her he was Maverick, not her daddy. I didn't mean it the way it came out, but nonetheless, it hurt his feelings. I could see it in the way he looked at me afterwards, his eyes drawn and sad.

As much as I'd love for him to be her father, because he would be a great father, I don't think we're ready for that. Maybe farther down the line, when the time is right, we'll talk about it, but at the moment, I think we just need to see where this is going. He could get bored of us at any moment and ask us to leave. Then I'll be the one left mending my little girl's broken heart and explaining to her why he wasn't her daddy anymore.

"We're not taking Sally and her pushchair, bug," I tell her, getting out of Maverick's lap but not before giving him a quick kiss. He relaxes, smiling at Faith.

"But I want to take Sally." She pouts and Maverick chuckles. I finish tying my hair up in a ponytail before facing her.

"I said no."

"But—"

"She said no, squirt," Maverick chimes in.

"Oh, okay then," she sulks, stomping out of the room.

"You ready?" I ask, wrapping my arms around his neck.

"Yeah, let's go get you girls some dresses."

Leaning down, he captures my lips in a scorching kiss and I begin to wish Harlow hadn't asked me to be bridesmaid. I want to stay here and get back into bed with him.

We stay like that, wrapped in each other's arms until Faith comes back in, demanding we hurry up. We chuckle, watching as she runs back down, telling everyone down there we were kissing.

"Come on, there's only two more days until the wedding. We need to get going," he says, pulling me behind him.

My feet are killing me; it's like walking around on bruised feet. My arms aren't much better, aching from the amount of dresses I've had to try on, but I've finally found the perfect one to wear to the wedding Saturday.

When Harlow insisted we pick out our own bridesmaid dresses, only giving us a colour theme, I thought it would be a quick grab and snatch.

Boy, had I been wrong.

Although, Maverick's appreciative glances were *kind of* worth it.

Faith's dress, on the other hand, had been a walk in the park. We walked into the kids' party dress shop, Faith laid her eyes upon a puffy, pink sequined dress and demanded we buy it. Maverick and I then spent ten minutes arguing who was going to pay for the darn dress. He won.

My phone beeps, so I step away from Maverick where he's paying for my dress. I'm still a little annoyed with him for buying it, but I can't help the butterflies in my stomach at the romantic gesture. I've never had anyone but my nan and Tish look out for me the way he does.

"Who was it?" he asks, coming up behind me and making me jump. I've been jumpy ever since the attack, and trying to adjust has been hard. But with Maverick there for me and the culprit behind bars, it's becoming easier.

"Kayla. They're all going out for dinner and wanted to know if we're joining them."

I giggle when I find Faith struggling with the bag her dress is in, dragging it behind her.

"Give me that, squirt." Maverick chuckles, holding his hand out.

"No! It's *my* princess dress," she tells him, her face strained and full of concentration.

"I thought princesses got other people to carry their bags."

Her eyes widen adorably at Maverick's statement, making me giggle. "Oh yeah. Here you go. It was getting pretty heavy." She puffs out a sigh of relief.

Another message comes through, and I laugh when I see it's from Max.

MAX: ??? I'm hungry.

"What shall I tell them?" I ask, showing Maverick the message.

"When isn't he?" he chuckles. "Tell them we're good, we're eating out so to go without us."

"You sure?" I ask, typing back to Kayla.

"Yeah, I want to spend some quality time with my girls," he says, giving me a heated look. My stomach flip-flops. I love it when he gives me that look; it makes me feel warm inside.

Once I've put my phone away he pulls me into his arms, dipping his head to kiss me.

"Mummy, stop kissing. People are looking," Faith whispers loudly.

"Okay." I giggle, pulling away but staying close. Looking up at him, I smile. "What did you have in mind?"

"There's a wacky warehouse twenty minutes from here. I thought we could go for dinner, let Faith run around and blow off some steam before we head back. What do you think?"

Ha! He has no idea what he's getting himself into. "You do know there are going to be other kids there, don't you?"

He scrunches his eyebrows together in confusion. "Well, yeah. Faith can play with other kids."

"They'll be screaming... loudly."

"It can't be that bad," he scoffs and I laugh, throwing my head back.

He really has no idea.

Two hours later, Maverick is eating his words. Not only did he complain during the meal about the noise, but a kid sitting behind him with his parents did nothing but throw his food at Maverick's head. I'd laughed every single time, even snapped a photo and sent it to the others.

But the worst part is what happened after we ate our dinner. Faith had batted her dark eyelashes, using her brown eyes to get her way, dragging him into the play area. Maverick, not being able to say no to my daughter, went along.

Now he's stuck, wedged between four rolling pins that he followed Faith through. His large frame isn't made for such a tight space; how he didn't see that when he struggled through the first two is beyond me. No matter how hard he tries, he can't get through the last two pins and instead of being any help, I've only stood here laughing.

"Teagan," he hisses down at me.

"I'm sorry. Give me a minute," I wheeze, holding my stomach.

"People are staring," he tells me wide-eyed.

Yeah, people are staring, mostly the female variety. I can't say I blame them either. With his black leather jacket thrown over his white T-shirt, dark denim jeans, and his unshaven jaw, he looks incredibly hot. It's such a shame that he's currently wedged between pins in a kids' play area.

"I'm going to try to pull you back, so push back as hard as you can, okay?"

"Just get me out of here," he moans, and I laugh all over again. "Teagan!"

"Okay, okay, sheesh. Keep your pants on." I chuckle, grabbing his broad shoulders.

"I'll push," Faith yells excitedly, standing in front of Maverick.

"Sir, we're going to have to ask you to leave the play area. Parents are complaining about bad language," a squeaky voice says. I look down to the waiter, giving him a smile and a wave.

"Don't you dare tell him I'm stuck."

"We'll be down shortly. He's in a bit of a situation at the minute," I shout, causing Maverick to groan.

"Is everything all right?" he asks worriedly, looking Maverick over. From his angle he probably can't see much, just some bloke standing awkwardly.

"Don't," Maverick warns me, still struggling to free himself.

"I'm afraid not," I muse. "He's stuck between the rolling pins."

The waiter looks at Maverick again with wide eyes before turning to me with a grim expression. "That's never happened before. Let me see if I can help."

"I can't believe you told him," Maverick growls.

"We're not exactly having any luck getting you out, you big turd. He might be able to help," I whisper.

"Oh dear, you are in a pickle," the waiter says. "I'm Sam by the way. Can you turn?"

"Hi, Sam, and we've tried that. Doesn't work," I answer, grinning.

"Hmm, okay. Let's try this. You go around the front and push, and I'll try to pull this pin away from his shoulders," he tells me, pointing to the rolling pin blocking Maverick in.

I nod, ignoring Maverick's whining. Moving to his front, I look up at him with a smirk.

"You could stop enjoying this so much," he mutters. I giggle, sticking my tongue out at him.

"Ready? On three. One, two, three," Sam says, then starts to pull the pin away as I push Maverick.

After three more tries, I give up, sighing. "We need to call the fire department."

"No!" Maverick shouts, horrified.

"Let me film him for five more minutes," we hear a familiar voice say, and I look up at Maverick with a sheepish expression.

He closes his eyes, ducking his head. "Please tell me you didn't."

"Um...."

"Tell me I'm hearing things." He glares at me, making me wince.

"What?" I ask innocently, holding my hands up. "They asked us why we weren't back yet, so I explained what was going on."

"This is fucking ridiculous. I'm never going to live this down," he mutters before looking through the ropes to where the gang is standing. "Max, stop fucking recording."

"Sir, can you not swear? There are children around," Sam says, sounding fearful as he steps away from Maverick.

"Get me the fuck out of here, now."

"Calm down. Lads, come help," I shout.

"Pleasure. Mav, don't go anywhere, I want to get a close-up," Max shouts, then kicks off his shoes and enters the play pit.

"If he comes anywhere near me with his phone, I'm breaking his neck."

"Mummy, can I go play with Auntie Denny and Hope?"

Looking down at Faith, I smile, running my hands through her hair. "Of course you can, darling. I'll be down soon."

As she runs off, Max and Mason walk up to us, both laughing their heads off. "How the hell did you manage this?"

"Mason, I swear to God, shut up. Just get me out of here," Maverick orders

"Wait!" Max laughs, moving so he's standing next to me.

"Max, get that fu—phone out of my face before I shove it down your throat."

I giggle, hiding my face when Maverick's glare turns to me. Max laughs harder, smacking his knee when Maverick struggles.

"Awe, is Mavy getting all worked up?" Max asks in a baby voice, goading his brother. He steps forward, tickling Maverick's stomach. "Be a good little boy and stay still."

"Max, I swear on all that is holy, I'm two seconds from throwing you off the side," Maverick growls, struggling harder.

"Like you could get me," Max scoffs, holding his phone up. "Say 'stuck'."

The flash goes off but then, without any warning, Maverick flies out of the pins, landing straight on Max with a thud.

"There are kids around," Max squeaks, his hands palms in surrender.

Maverick looks around, noticing all the kids watching, and drops his head, muttering something to Max, who pales.

Getting up, he walks over to me, straightening his clothes out, a predatory look in his eye. I step backwards, fighting the laughter trying to bubble free.

"Calm down," I tell him, a grin spreading across my face. "I didn't get you stuck. You did that all on your own."

"You owe me," he growls, still coming for me. I shake my head, denying him. When he reaches me, he backs me into one of the foam poles, crowding me in. "You owe me big. Tonight, when Faith is asleep, I expect to be paid. You're also getting a tanned ass for telling my brothers."

My mouth drops open at his words, my thighs squeezing together. His gaze darkens, flickering to my lips and staying there. When I bite my bottom lip, he groans, pressing into me.

"I didn't tell your brothers, I told Kayla," I whisper, lost in his eyes.

"Don't care. Your ass is mine tonight," he tells me before walking off, finding his way back down to safer ground.

Breathing hard, I look around, noticing Mason, Max and Sam have disappeared. When I look down, my eyes find Maverick's, lost in the promise he just gave me. He hasn't touched me since the attack, and hearing him say those things, knowing I'll have him inside of me again, is turning me on more than I like to admit, especially in a kids' play area.

Shaking myself out of it before Sam comes back up to get me down, I head towards the stairs, praying Faith tires early so I can spend the whole night alone with him.

Tonight can't come quick enough.

TWENTY-EIGHT

MAVERICK

Watching Malik, of all my brothers, get ready for his wedding is bizarre, but it's happening and I couldn't be happier for him.

When Harlow moved in next door, not only did she change Malik's life, but she changed ours too. She gave Malik a purpose, a reason to live.

She completed our family.

Even though we've always been one, it wasn't the same as the one we are now. Harlow is to thank for that, they all are, but she changed not only Malik's view on life, but ours too.

He looks dapper in his black suit, a gold tie adding some colour. The rest of us are wearing a light grey tie.

He struggles with his, trying to loosen it from around his neck.

"Stop messing with it," I scold him.

He growls, annoyed. "Why the hell am I wearing a fucking tie?"

"Because Harlow wanted you to."

His eyes soften as he curses under his breath. "Yeah."

"Come on. Let's go join the others outside. Mason bought a drink to celebrate," I tell him.

"I need one if I'm going to get through today wearing this," he mutters, following me out.

"Are you nervous?" I ask as we stand outside in the garden. He's not giving anything away, so calm and collected. If anything, he looks like he's done this a thousand times.

"Nah, why would I be?" he asks.

"Um, because you're getting married?"

"To the woman I love and am going to spend the rest of my life with. I'm not thrilled about talking and shit at the registry office, but I'll get over it."

"It's not that bad. It wasn't until everyone started clapping that I realised we were in a room full of people. All I could see was Denny," Mason tells him.

"I'm grateful she only wanted family at the actual reception. Don't think I'd be able to do it with a bunch of people I don't give a shit about watching," he mutters as Mason hands him a drink.

We all take seats on the lawn chairs, looking over the overgrown grass none of us have had time to cut. We're all at our place while all the girls are over at Harlow's and Malik's getting ready.

When I glance in Malik's direction again, he's lost in thought, something he's done a few times since he woke up this morning.

"Something's bothering you. What is it? You keep spacing out."

He hesitates before turning to us with a grim expression. "I know you said not to think about it until after the wedding, but I can't. She's out there somewhere, and we have no fucking clue if she's been looked after. I feel guilty for being happy when she could be suffering," he admits, running a hand through his dark, unruly hair.

The five of us fall silent. I knew telling them to try and forget about everything going on would be pointless. Hell, I haven't even been able to take my own advice. Lily has been on my mind since we first found out about her, and she's going to be there until we find her.

The police are no closer to finding her and the last word I got from Evan was that they were searching the family homes of the men who were arrested along with Lynn. If they've been keeping Lynn hidden and protected, then they could have something to do with why we can't find the little girl.

"I know it's hard, bro, I really do, but we'll find her. When we do, we'll spoil her with love and give her a home. She'll never have to suffer another day in her life, I promise you that."

He turns to me and nods. "It's all a fucking mess."

"It is. I wish there was something more we could do, but there's fuck all. We're doing all that we can."

"I know. It just sucks."

"I'm still trying to come to terms with the fact that we have a sister and that girls are now ruling this family. Have you noticed that it used to be us five and Granddad, but now we're surrounded by women? We're outvoted. We can't even add Splinter in our favour because the thing ain't normal." Max shivers.

"That's actually true. And if Harlow has girls, we'll be beat twelve-to-six," Myles chuckles, holding his drink up.

"Got to admit it though, boys, you'd be nothing without those girls," Mason says.

"Too right. I'd have to do my own washing." Max grins.

"I think she'll have two boys." Malik gulps, looking pale as we all clink our glasses with his. We laugh, patting him on the back before sitting back in the garden chairs.

"I know life hasn't been easy on us, but having Harlow, Denny, Kayla, Lake and now Teagan has made it breathable again. We're family. And even with the current shit happening, I couldn't be happier for you guys. I've watched you grow into men, seen you through some pretty tough shit, and I couldn't be prouder," I admit, looking at each of them.

"Emotional shit, really? It's me getting married," Malik mutters, but I can see my words have affected him.

"We wouldn't have gotten this far without you," Myles says.

Looking up from my glass, I notice everyone agreeing and I shake my head, smiling.

"He's right," Granddad says, coming out. "You boys have turned out to be the best men I know. You've all come so far and to see each of you settling down, one married and one getting married, it makes my heart full. I'll be able to leave this world knowing my grandkids are loved, taken care of and happy."

I swallow thickly at the sincerity and pride in his eyes as he looks over each one of us.

"Granddad, don't talk about popping your clogs. You'll outlive all of us fuckers." Max chuckles, pouring him a drink.

"You know what I mean. I never thought I'd see Malik settled down, let alone getting married and having babies. If your nan were alive, she'd be so proud of you. All of you. She'd love Harlow too."

"Wouldn't like Joan much though," Max mutters and we all chuckle, watching Granddad blush.

After our mum's mum left him, he met Nan and fell in love. She was so protective of him and hated all of the other women who tried ogling him. Its why she never had many friends, though everyone loved her.

"Yes, well, things happen for a reason. Now, let's toast to the groom. May he live a long and happy life blissfully married."

"Hear hear," we toast, clinking our glasses together.

"Not to speak of the devil, but have they told you when her sentencing will be?" Mason asks.

"No, they're still gathering evidence. Why, I have no idea. They have enough shit on her to lock her away for two lifetimes," I tell him.

"Let's not talk about her. Not today," Myles growls.

"You're right. Let's enjoy today. We'll deal with everything else tomorrow," Mason says, pouring himself another drink.

My phone beeps in my suit pocket. As I pull it out, all of my brothers give me a pointed look. "What?"

"That better not be the club. If something's wrong, I don't want to know," Malik says, downing his drink.

Looking down at my phone, I chuckle. "It's Teagan."

TEAGAN: Need a huge favour!

MAVERICK: What's up?

TEAGAN: Harlow's hungry. She's craving a double cheeseburger, six nuggets, a chicken wrap and a McFlurry. She's going out of her mind. Please can you go get her food?

MAVERICK: I'll leave now.

TEAGAN: Thank you. You're a lifesaver.

"I need to go," I tell the others, getting up.

"Why? What's wrong?" Malik asks, getting up to follow me.

"Harlow's hungry. She's craving McDonald's, so I'm going to get her some." I chuckle.

He takes his phone out, frowning. "She hasn't texted me."

"That's because it was Teagan who text me. I won't be long."

"Harlow's always hungry," Max mutters. "Will you get me a chicken deli and six nuggets?"

I shake my head, not knowing who's worse for eating when it comes to those two.

"I'll come with you," Malik says, but I shake my head, pushing him back down his seat.

"No, you stay here. If you come with me, you'll want to take the food in to her to make sure she has everything she needs," I tell him, amused.

"And? What's wrong with that?"

"You're not supposed to see the bride before the wedding," Max mutters dryly.

"Bollox, I want to go," he whines.

"Son, sit down and have a drink. Let Maverick go sort out the food. The more you gripe about it, the hungrier Harlow is going to be," Granddad tells him.

Malik sinks back in his chair, the fight leaving him. He still doesn't look happy, but he can't exactly argue when he knows Granddad's right.

"I'll be right back." I pat Malik on the shoulder as I pass.

"Don't forget my food," Max shouts as I walk through the back door to grab my car keys.

Twenty minutes later I'm back at the house, grabbing all the bags. The second I left, I had another message off Teagan with a food order for everyone.

I'm not even to the door when I hear Harlow shouting. "Food! I can smell food."

Grinning, I step up to the door. It swings open and I nearly drop my bags when I see Teagan in front of me, her silver, fitted dress falling down to her ankles with a long split up her leg, revealing a lot of thigh. Her hair is pinned to the side in curls, her make-up flawless and natural-looking.

She looked beautiful in it the day she tried it on at the shop, but today she's breathtaking. My eyes rake over her, taking in every inch. She's truly stunning.

I can't believe she's mine. All mine.

"Wow," I manage to choke out when I reach her eyes. She blushes, ducking her head. "You look beautiful."

"You don't look so bad yourself." She smiles.

"Yeah, yeah, stop eye-fucking each other. I'm hungry," Harlow whines out of nowhere before snatching a bag of food out of my hands. "Thanks, Mav."

I chuckle, handing Denny the other three bags before turning my attention back to Teagan, speechless. Pulling her into my arms, I smile down at her. "You look gorgeous. But I have a question," I tell her, running my hands up her sides.

"You do?"

"Yeah," I whisper, peppering kisses along her jaw. "Are you wearing any knickers?"

She moans, arching her neck to give me better access. "No," she whispers back and my hands tighten on her ass, squeezing her against me.

"Fuck!" I growl, pinning her against the wall next to the front door. Lifting my head, I smash my lips against hers, kissing her with ferocity, stealing her breath. She clings to me tighter, one leg lifting and hooking around my thigh. "Are you wet?" I murmur, my voice husky as I rest my forehead against hers.

"Why don't you find out?" she pants, her body arching into mine.

My hard dick twitches as I press against her, rubbing my hardness into her core, making her moan. I look down at the split in her dress, my finger running up her bare thigh. "I like this dress," I tell her, wanting to plunge my fingers inside her.

"I can tell." She grins, lifting her leg higher for me.

"Please, no more. You're going to give Joan and Mary ideas," Kayla says.

Teagan squeals, pulling her dress down, and I growl, wishing we were in my bedroom. I took her this morning, but it's not enough. I can never have enough of her.

"Please tell me they weren't watching," Teagan groans, pressing her head onto my shoulder. I turn to Kayla, finding her in the doorway wearing her own silver dress, with a lace top and silk bottom.

Kayla smirks, looking over her shoulder before glancing at Teagan, shrugging sheepishly. "We didn't realise what they were up to until it was too late."

"This is so embarrassing. Can I come hang out with you?" she asks me, optimistic.

"Sure." I grin, thinking of how I can sneak her up to our room so I can see if she really is wearing knickers or not.

"Nope, you can't. Sorry, Teagan, but we're about to have our photos taken, so get your butt in here."

"But—"

"Nope, come on," Kayla says, dragging her away from me.

"I'll see you later." I chuckle as she's pulled through the door.

"Yeah, bye," she grumbles, just before the door is slammed.

Making my way back to mine, I let myself in, finding them all still sitting in the garden, shooting the shit.

"Did she get her food?" Malik asks.

"Yeah." I move to grab another chair.

"Dude, cover that shit up," Mason tells me, throwing a beer cap at me. Growling, I throw it back and adjust my semihard cock in my trousers.

"Never mind his dick. Where's my food?" Max asks, frowning.

"The girls took it all." I shrug, having forgotten his order anyway.

"You fucking suck."

"Fuck off. Are you ready? We need to get to the hall soon," I say, looking at Malik.

He smiles. "I was born ready."

TWENTY-NINE

TEAGAN

"They're not going to let me live this down, are they?" I whisper to Kayla. She giggles, covering her mouth behind her hand as she shakes her head.

"They love this. Sometimes I swear they're a group of horny teenagers locked in old people's bodies. I've never met anyone with more life inside of them than those three," she says, looking in Mary, Joan and Nan's direction. They're all complaining at the moment about Harlow not being able to have a 'real' hen party. Apparently they weren't allowed to Denny's so they were hoping Harlow would have one, with strippers. Now they're conspiring with my nan to make sure I'm given strippers for my hen party. When I explained that I wasn't getting married, they just looked at me and grinned.

"They're nuts," I say, shaking my head when I hear Nan tell them she has my dress already picked out.

"The cars are ready," Mark calls out, stepping inside.

"Has Malik left?" Harlow asks, struggling to stand.

She looks beautiful in her gold silk gown that flows elegantly over her huge bump. The top encases her chest, the lace trim giving it character and style. Her leaf-brown hair is curled up into a bun at the top of her head, a gold band completing the goddess look. Her skin is glowing, as are her brown soulful eyes, which are glistening with happiness. Her full, pouty, rose-coloured lips are tipped up into a smile. I've never seen her look so radiant. Getting married and being pregnant really do suit her. I wish I looked that good when I was carrying Faith; I just looked like a whale in distress.

"They all left fifteen minutes ago." he looks at her lovingly. "You, my darling girl, are absolutely breathtaking. Malik isn't going to know what hit him when he sees you."

Her eyes water as he helps her to her feet. "Really?"

"Really," he says softly, running his finger down her cheek. "You've made an old man very happy knowing his grandson has someone as kind and loving as you in his life."

"You're going to make me cry," she croaks out.

"Don't make her cry," Denny squeals, rushing in.

"Sorry." He chuckles before pulling Harlow in for a hug.

"Mummy, can we go show Maverick my dress now?" Faith asks, walking in holding hands with Hope. The little girl looks adorable in her pink dress similar to Faith's. She toddles in, still a little unsteady on her feet with a look of wonder on her face as she giggles up at Faith.

"Me, me, me," she chants, making Faith giggle.

"We're going now, sweetie. Why don't you get your coat and find Nanny," I tell Faith. She nods, taking Hope with her.

"Are you ready?" I hear Denny ask Harlow as I get up.

"More than ready. I feel like I've been waiting for this day my whole life," she whispers, her eyes shining.

"I meant have you got everything, but I'm glad to know you're ready to get married. That would've been awkward."

"Oh." Harlow giggles, fanning the tears threatening to spill. "I don't know if I'm going to last, guys."

"Bit of a good job that we used waterproof makeup." I chuckle, handing her a tissue.

"Sweetie, before we go, there's something I've been meaning to give you," Joan says, stepping into the room with a box in her hand, something I've been waiting for her to do.

"You didn't have to get me anything, Grams."

"Oh, sweetie, I didn't get it. I already had it," Joan says quietly, stepping closer to Harlow.

"Grams, is everything okay?"

"Ignore me. I'm just being emotional." Joan waves at her, wiping under her eyes. "I wanted to give you this. It's something I wanted your mum to have when I found out she was getting married, but I never got the chance to give it to her. It was given to me on my wedding day, my mothers, her mother, and now it belongs to you," she tells Harlow, choked up as she hands her the box.

"Grams," Harlow says, her voice filled with emotion as she lets the tears slip free. She opens the box and we all watch in anticipation, gasping when she pulls out a light rose-coloured pearl and crystal hair brooch. "Grams, this is beautiful."

"And so are you. Your mum and dad would be so proud of the woman you've become," Joan whispers, taking the brooch from her and adding it to her hair, completing the look beautifully. "This is your something borrowed."

"This is your something blue," Lake and I say, handing her our box. She opens it, laughing as tears fall free.

"I don't know if this is to torture me or Malik, 'cause I can assure you, there's no way I'll be able to get that on." She laughs, holding up the gold garter with blue crystals for everyone to see.

"Here." I giggle, bending down on one knee. She passes it to me, her eyes twinkling with an overwhelming happiness that it brings tears to my own eyes. I roll it up her leg, fitting it in place before stepping back, letting Kayla and Denny step forward.

"This is something new," they say, handing her another gift box.

"Guys," Harlow whispers, choked up. She opens the box, revealing a pair of pearl earrings. "Thank you. Thank you so much."

"There's one more," Denny says, tears running down her cheeks now too. "Malik wanted me to give you this."

Handing her a letter with another gift box, Harlow takes a seat. Upon opening the letter, her hand goes to her chest.

"Read out loud, woman," Joan says, sitting on the arm.

"It says 'Harlow, today I get to marry the woman of my dreams, my soulmate and my best friend. I've fucked up a lot in my life and I don't want my vows to be one of them. I'm not good with spoken words, so I wanted you to know them so that when you're looking at me as we exchange our vows, you know I mean forever.

"Before you came into my life like a tornado, blowing me off my feet, life meant nothing to me. But you came, showing what love truly was, what it meant to love and be loved. And I promise until my dying day to show you how much I love you. Because I do. I've never loved anyone or anything as strongly as I love you.

"So remember, when you're walking down the aisle, that I love you unconditionally, and that there's no other love out there as strong and as powerful as my love is for you. Yours always, Malik!." She chokes up before continuing. "P. S. You're the strongest person I know and because of that, I know you won't admit that you're also hurting today. I know how much you wanted your parents at your wedding, and as much as I wish that I could bring them back, I can't. But I wanted to try easing some of that pain for you. With this gift, I hope it brings you a little of them back, knowing they were a part of your wedding day even if they couldn't be here. I love you."

Harlow's a sobbing mess as she opens her last gift, taking the chain out of its box, hiccupping when she sees the locket attached to it. She opens the locket, then starts crying into her hands.

"I love him so much," she sobs. We all step forward, but it's Mark who kneels in front of her to comfort her. "He... he gave me my parents."

"Hey, girlie, calm down. I think he'd be kicking himself in the nuts if he knew you were crying. You know he hates to see you cry."

"He does." She nods, wiping her cheeks.

"So much for waterproof," Denny mutters, stepping out of the room, while wiping away her own tears.

"Why don't we put this necklace on and get you cleaned up so you can go marry that grandson of mine?"

She nods again, sniffling. "Okay."

"Let's get this show on the road," Denny announces, walking in with her make-up bag and some tissues.

"I'm getting married," Harlow tells her.

"I know, girl."

"I'm getting married," she squeals, smiling wide.

"That was touch-and-go for a minute. I didn't think we'd calm her down," Kayla whispers and I giggle, wrapping my arm around her shoulder.

"Someone needs to tell the boys we're going to be late. It's not just Harlow's make-up that needs fixing." I chuckle, gesturing to our own.

MARY, JOAN AND NAN TAKE Hope and Faith into the registry office while the rest of us gather outside, waiting for the photographer to take the last of the photos.

Once we're finished, I watch as Harlow takes a deep breath before a huge smile breaks out across her face.

"Let's do this," she tells Mark, hooking her arm in his.

Lake and I walk through first, heading to the hall they're getting married in.

The music starts and a nervous flutter kicks up in my stomach. It intensifies the second the door opens and my eyes find Maverick's. Even from here I can see the smouldering look in his eyes. I can't look away, not even if I wanted too.

Please don't trip.

Marriage has never crossed my mind before—Faith has always been my primary focus—but seeing him standing there so hot in his suit, has me picturing if this is how he'll look at me if we ever got married. The intense stare is burning into me, setting me on fire.

As we make it to the front, we break eye contact, but the second I'm standing in front of my chair, I turn to face him. His eyes hit me like a rock to the head, nearly knocking me off balance.

Lake nudges me and the rest of the room comes into focus. My cheeks heat when I realise Kayla and Kennedy have already made their trip down the aisle and Harlow is now walking in, her hand looped through Mark's. Denny trails behind her, looking just as beautiful.

A snigger behind me has me turning around. My nan stands next to Mary, a smirk firmly on her face as she winks at me, then glances to Maverick. I narrow my eyes, sticking my tongue out at her. It may be childish but who cares; I just got caught ogling my boyfriend in a very intense way.

Malik, in all his glory, stands frozen at the front of the aisle, watching his soon-to-be wife walk towards him. He pinches the bridge of his nose and I watch, overwhelmed and mesmerised when tears fill his eyes. It causes my own to water, and my heart fills with happiness for the both of them.

Harlow's stuck between smiling and crying, and I can't help but be inspired by her bravery, her will to love unconditionally, even after everything she's been through. I've heard her story, felt it deep in my bones, yet she walks down the aisle filling the entire room with light and happiness. She's truly an incredible woman.

"You look beautiful," he tells her, choked up.

"You too—handsome, I mean," she says, tears spilling over her cheeks.

Taking each other's hands, they stand in front of the registrar, who then starts the ceremony.

Words fail to describe what I'm feeling right now, witnessing two people I've not known long but well enough to know they belong to each other, get married. A lump forms in my throat and I can only pray that my time will come when I'm the one walking down the aisle.

"Harlow informed me that she has something she'd like to say," the registrar says, smiling softly at Harlow.

Gulping, she clears her throat, taking Malik's hands in hers. "I choose you. I choose you as my best friend, my family, my lover, my husband and the father of my kids. I choose you above all else because I truly believe God sent you to me.

"I love you. I love you unconditionally, with my whole heart, body and soul. I vow to help you love life, to help you smile when you frown, to speak when words are needed and to be silent when they're not. I promise to stand by your side, no matter what challenges life throws at us, but most of all, I promise I'll always be yours."

Her words are clear despite the tears running down her cheeks. Not that I can blame her. There's not a dry eye in the house. Even the brothers look close to losing it.

"Malik, is there something you'd like to say?"

He clears his throat, pulling Harlow against his chest, his eyes glistening with unleashed tears. "Mine, forever and always."

She giggles into his chest, a happy sob breaking through. We laugh at his short answer, knowing he's already shared his undying love for her. Not that words are needed with these two; their everyday actions prove their love and devotion towards one another.

The registrar continues the ceremony, guiding them as they exchange rings. Then it comes to my favourite part, the one in the movies that always made me feel girly, made me believe in true love.

"You may kiss the bride," she announces.

Malik wastes no time taking Harlow in his arms, crushing his mouth against hers in a scorching, wet, kiss.

We all stand, cheering with tears of joy slipping free as we all congratulate the bride and groom.

Out of nowhere, Maverick slides up to me, wrapping his arms around me from behind.

"Hi." I smile, dabbing the tissue under my eyes.

"I can't wait for the day you marry me," he whispers against my ear.

My mouth hangs open in shock, but before I can turn around to see if he's serious, he's gone, walking over to his newlywed brother and smacking him on the back.

What the hell just happened?

THIRTY

MAVERICK

STANDING OUTSIDE OF MC5, where all of our friends and family are gathered waiting for the newlyweds to arrive, I search for Teagan.

From the moment I said those words to her back at the registry office, I've been mentally kicking myself. I don't know what came over me. One minute I was lost in listening to Harlow's vows, and the next my eyes were drifting back over to Teagan, mesmerised as she cried in happiness. It was in that moment that I knew—I was going to marry her. I felt it with every fibre of my being. But it wasn't until I looked at her, *really* looked at her, that it hit me, literally knocking the breath out of me.

I love her.

I love her more than life itself, and I want to spend the rest of my life with her. No one gets me the way she does. She sees the darkness clouding inside me but is with me anyway. I find myself talking to her in ways I've never spoken to anyone in my entire life. I can confide in her, be the me I've always wanted to be without actually changing who I am.

She gets it.

She makes me feel worthy. And I know I'll never be able to feel this way with anyone else. She's special, and I know I'll spend the rest of my life showing her just how special she truly is. I'm not sure how I made it this far in my life without her.

I've been trying to get five minutes alone to tell her this, but each time we've gotten close, one or both of us have been pulled away.

Finally, in the crowd of people, I find her standing next to her nan and Mary, searching through the crowd for someone.

The car pulls up with Malik and Harlow as I start my way over, and people get in my way as they fight to greet the couple, wanting to throw confetti. I groan, pushing my way through, crossing paths with Faith on the way.

"Hey, squirt. Where are you going?" I ask, catching her around the waist and lifting her into my arms.

"I want pretty snow on me," she pouts, looking over my shoulder, her eyes full of excitement and envy.

"Okay, but stay away from the road."

She nods, wiggling to get down. I watch her run over to Malik and Harlow, spinning in a circle when confetti is thrown.

Smiling, I continue over to Teagan, pulling her into my arms when I reach her. "Hey, beautiful."

"Hey," she greets shyly. "Faith is having so much fun."

Watching Faith smile and laugh always makes my heart jump. From the minute I met her, she's had me wrapped around her little finger. When I look at her, all I think is *mine*. I can't explain how or when, but she's mine.

When I look again, she's holding hands with a little boy, making me frown. "Yeah, I wish we could get gun permits. She'll give me an aneurism the first time she brings a boy home," I grunt.

Teagan's silent, so pulling my eyes away from Faith, I glance down at her. Her face is soft, but hidden in the depth of her hazel eyes, I can see uncertainty.

"You okay?"

She sighs. "That's the second time you've mentioned the future," she says, trying to gauge my reaction.

Glancing away, I quickly make sure Faith is okay. When I see her with Max, I pull Teagan off to the side, away from the club windows and prying eyes.

"We are serious, Teagan. Why wouldn't I think of the future?" I ask, tucking a loose strand of hair behind her ear.

"I don't know. I guess I... It's just that earlier you mentioned marriage and now you're talking about being with us long enough to scare off potential boyfriends. I didn't think you felt so strongly about us," she whispers, then ducks her head.

Bending, I meet her eyes. "Teagan, you have no idea how strongly I feel about you and Faith. You both mean everything to me. I thought I made that clear."

"You're talking about a huge commitment, something I didn't think you even wanted. First you move us in—without even asking—and then you throw marriage at me in the middle of a wedding. It's a lot to handle."

Panicked that she doesn't feel the same, I pull her close. "What's a lot to handle?"

She pushes away from me and begins to pace, her hair blowing in the wind. "Everything! We've not been together long, not nearly long enough for me to have these feelings for you. I love you so much—so bloody much. But what if you get bored of me? What if you change your mind about being a one-woman man or being a father figure to Faith? I don't think my heart could take the pain of losing you, Maverick. I'm not strong enough to overcome that kind of loss," she rambles, her eyes beginning to water.

"What did you say?" I growl, stepping closer. She lifts her hands, palms up, warding me off. Not liking the distance, I move her hands away, pulling her against me. "What did you say?"

She pauses, her breathing hard as she looks up at me. "Maverick, I said a lot of stuff. You need to be more specific."

"Cute," I mutter, rolling my eyes. "I'm talking about the three words you just said to me. Say them again."

Her cheeks take on a rosy pink colour when she looks up at me this time. "I don't remember."

Stubborn girl.

"You love me." My voice is quiet, stunned. I never expected to hear those words. I know I love her and I'd hoped she loved me back, but I never believed she would.

Her body sags into me, her hands going to my shoulders for support. She gazes longingly into my eyes, hers glistening with unleashed tears. "I do, Mav. I really do love you."

A smile breaks out across my face and I pick her up, swinging her around. Putting her down, I cup her jaw, lowering my head until my mouth is hovering over hers. "I love you too," I whisper, and before she says anything, I press my lips to hers.

The kiss is soft, and I pour all my love into it. When we pull apart, we're both breathing heavily.

"You love me?"

"I do," I answer, leaning down to kiss her again, but she pulls back, giving me a watery smile.

"You love me?"

I peck her on the lips quickly before pulling back to look into her eyes, showing her how sincere I am. "Yeah, baby, and you love me."

Dropping her head to my shoulder, I hear her take in a jagged breath. "You have no idea how long I've waited for you to say those words."

"Yo, bitch, what you doin' back there?" I hear shouted behind me. Glancing over my shoulder, Tish is grabbing her change from the taxi driver.

"Way to ruin our moment," I grumble, earning a slap to the chest from Teagan. "Shush."

"Sorry." I grin, bending down to kiss her.

"God, I feel like a dead badger," Tish mumbles when she reaches us.

I turn so we're both facing her, chuckling at how rough she looks.

"What on earth? What happened to you?" Teagan asks, trying her hardest not to laugh.

"I went out for the hen party," she answers, cursing.

"Whose hen party?"

Tish gives her a dry look, pointing inside. "Harlow's."

Confused, I look between them, wondering if I'm missing something. I'm pretty sure they already had their hen party—a relaxing day at the spa. "Um, Harlow didn't have a hen party."

"Yeah, I know. I had one for her."

Teagan giggles, covering her mouth. "How was it?"

"Rough and kinda shit. I remember when I went out at seventeen and clubs were so packed you were sure to end the night with a few fag burns and drink stains down your dress. Now you could do fucking snow angels and a Mr. Bean dance and still not touch a thing. It was dead."

Teagan nods in understanding, laughing. "So you won't be drinking today, then?"

"Course I'm fucking drinking. It's free," she says, rolling her eyes.

"Guys, come on. We're waiting to open the food," Max moans, sticking his head outside the door. He sees Tish with us and his eyes widen, taking a step back behind the door. "Or take your time. It's fine." And then he's gone, disappearing behind the door.

"Babbie ass," Tish mutters before turning to me, her expression serious. "Any single men in there?"

"U-um," I stutter, looking down at Teagan for help.

"Well?" Tish snaps, getting impatient.

"C'mon, I'll introduce you to Matt, their bar manager," Teagan says.

I sag with relief. Then I picture Matt's face when he meets Tish and I burst out laughing. *He's so going to hate me when tonight is over.*

As they reach the entrance, Teagan looks over her shoulder, meeting my eyes. "I love you," she mouths.

She turns before I have a chance to reply, leaving me with the goofiest grin on my face.

THE WEDDING PARTY IS underway. Everyone is in high spirits, drunk off the atmosphere, or alcohol. Either way, everyone is having the time of their lives.

I've never seen Malik look so happy. He's talking to Matt and a few friends from motocross, laughing and joking like he doesn't have a care in the world. It's a good look on him.

It's the first time I've seen him step away from Harlow, although his eyes flicker over to her every few seconds, making sure she's still there.

Looking over at her, I can't help but chuckle. She's still shoving wedding cake in her mouth. She's practically glowing, and every time I've glanced her way tonight, she's been wearing the same smile, her face shining with so much happiness, it's blinding.

I turn my attention away from her when someone knocks into me, my drink sloshing over the sides of my glass.

"Whoa." I shake droplets of JD off my hand.

"Good! It's you," Matt says, paler than I've ever seen him look and that's saying something since he's naturally pale. "You need to help me."

Looking over his shoulder, Tish is standing not too far away, fluffing her hair and lowering the top of her dress to show some more cleavage.

Grimacing, I turn back to my friend. "What's wrong?"

"Look, I like your girlfriend, I really do, but did I do something to piss her off?" he asks, glancing nervously over his shoulder, his whole body shuddering when he makes eye contact with Tish.

Smirking, I fight back a chuckle. "No. She thinks you're cool, why? What's made you ask that?"

"Because," he says, swallowing forcefully. "she introduced me to her friend when we got here. That was what... three hours ago? In that time, she's told me about every sexual position she's ever tried, asked what my favourite was and when I wouldn't tell her, she thought I was being shy. She thought getting me 'in the mood' would spark some enlightenment."

"Why don't you just ditch her?" I ask when he takes a breather.

He's clearly not amused. "I've been trying to ditch her all night, Mav. But she's there. All the time."

"You seem to be doing all right now." I chuckle.

He blushes, looking back over his shoulder before turning his attention back to me. "I kind of told her I needed to get some condoms from you."

I splutter, spraying my drink all over the place. I laugh, throwing my head back. "What?"

"What?" He throws his hands up in the air. "I went for a piss and the second I had my pants down, she was there."

"And...?"

"And then she blew me. I got caught up in the moment and said the first thing that popped into my head," he says, freaked out.

"Which head?" Max chuckles. I hadn't even seen him walk up beside me. "You're so screwed."

I nod. "Literally."

"I'm glad you two find this amusing," Matt mutters.

"If it's any consolation, I'm actually scared for you," Max says, shuddering.

"Please, Mav, you need to do something."

"Like what?" I ask, laughing at his pleading expression.

"I don't know. Tell her I can't," he says, exasperated.

"What, can't perform?" Max asks seriously, looking down at Matt's crotch.

He splutters, looking at Max in disgust and fury. "*What?* I can perform perfectly fucking fine, thank you."

"So... go perform," I tell him, wiggling my eyebrows.

"Ahh, fuck. I'm going to hell," he mutters, before sulking off, Tish following smugly behind.

Max and I turn to each other, pausing for a moment before bursting into laughter. My stomach hurts and I have to bend over to get my bearings.

"What are you two laughing about?" Teagan asks, smiling as she tucks herself under my arm. I pull her close, kissing the top of her head.

Lake isn't far behind, her face bright as she skips up to Max, kissing him on the cheek.

"Nothing." I chuckle as Max turns to Lake, smiling.

"Was everything okay?"

"Yeah, Mum said to tell you that she'll see us tomorrow, and to thank Malik and Harlow for the invite. The music and excitement were too much for Cowen to handle, so they decided to take him home."

"Still pissed he beat me at that dance-off," Max frowns and Lake giggles, shaking her head.

"Can the bride and groom make their way to the dance floor for their first dance," the DJ booms. Turning towards the stage, I pull Teagan to my front, holding her close.

I catch Denny taking food off Harlow, helping her off her seat. Malik is struggling with Mason, growling something at him, most likely threatening to kill the DJ since he said he didn't want to dance. Verbally, Harlow agreed, but what Malik didn't see—but I did—was her fingers crossed behind her back.

Mason says something to Malik that has his head turning to the dance floor, his eyes softening. Following his gaze, I see Harlow standing in the middle, looking as beautiful as ever.

James Arthurs, "Say You Won't Let Go" starts playing and I smile at how quick Malik relaxes, pulling Harlow as close as she can get with the huge bump between them.

"They're so happy," Teagan whispers, resting her head on my shoulder. I look down to find her eyes shining bright, happiness pouring out in waves.

Movement to my left catches my attention and I find Max being pulled onto the dance floor, Lake laughing at something he says. He smiles at her, love and happiness filling his eyes, burning my chest.

The same thing can be said for Myles and Mason as they drag Kayla and Denny out to the dance floor. Seeing them like this makes everything I endured worthwhile. I'd do anything if it meant they got to where they are now.

"Come on." I smile, taking Teagan's hand and pulling her over to the dance floor.

Her arms wrap around my neck, her body fitting perfectly against mine. The last time we stood like this was at Denny and Mason's wedding. So much has changed since that day, but I wouldn't change a thing if it meant I got to be here with her in my arms.

"I love you," she whispers, her eyes sparkling. I don't think I'll ever get tired of hearing her say those words.

The way she looks at me, like I hung the moon and stars, has a flurry of emotions fighting their way out. My heart is full, the hole and ache that once consumed me no longer there.

"I love you too," I tell her, leaning down to capture her mouth.

Grinning against her lips, I pull back before twirling her around, lifting her off her feet. She laughs, throwing her head back, never looking more breathtakingly beautiful than she does in this moment.

Slowing down, I slide her down my body, swaying to the soft flow of the music as we become lost in each other's eyes.

I'm snapped out of it when I hear Faith giggling. I turn to find her dancing with the same kid from earlier—a little too closely if you ask me.

"Oh, hell no!" I growl, taking a step forward to warn the kid, but Teagan pulls me back, giggling. I'm about to argue but my name being called over the music gains my attention.

Evan is on the edge of the dance floor waving me over, his phone against his ear. His expression is hard, and I know whatever it is, isn't going to be good.

Everything happens at once after that.

I lift my foot to take a step towards him, my eyes never once breaking contact. The next thing I know, I'm flying through the air, my ears ringing from what could only be an explosion.

THIRTY-ONE

TEAGAN

ALARMS BLARE, COMING FROM ALL directions, the ringing in my ears deafening me. My body trembles as I sit up, rough fragments of stone and glass falling from my bruised body. I look around in a blind panic, my vision murky due to the smoke and dust stinging my eyes. My eyes widen, taking in the destruction and carnage going on around me.

How did this happen?

One minute everyone was smiling and dancing, and the next I swear I heard a bomb go off at the same time the floor shook and rumbled beneath me. Then there was nothing; everything went black.

I swallow the vomit crawling up the back of my throat, trying to remain calm when I'm anything but. I want to believe this was all a mistake, that this was all a bad dream, but I know better. Everything felt too real—the pain, the panic, and the unbearable fear.

A sick feeling worms its way around inside me as my gaze flickers across the room to where I last saw Faith.

My heart stops when I don't see her.

Oh God, Faith!

"Faith!" I cry out, stricken with fear when I see a tiny form trying to get up from the floor.

With shaky limbs, I go to stand, but my vision blurs, dizziness causing the room to spin. I fall to my knees, shards of glass cutting into me.

"Faith!"

Everyone around me is as scared as I am, some stopping to help other guests, others stepping over the more seriously injured, frightened as they fight their way to the exit. Everywhere I look the scene becomes more horrifying—blood pouring from open wounds, terrified expressions on everyone's faces—but it's the screams that will forever be burned into my memory.

Crawling across broken glass, I get closer to the small huddle, my stomach dropping when I realise it's not her but Sam, the little boy she had been dancing with before the explosion.

When I reach him, I hold his head in the palms of my hands, gently checking him over for any injuries, seeing nothing but a few minor cuts on his arms and face.

"Sam, sweetheart, have you seen Faith?" I ask shakily.

"I want my Mummy," he cries, clinging to my torn dress.

My heart breaks for him. Looking around, I see a man close by. "Hey, you! Excuse me!" I shout. He turns, his eyes unfocused and glazed over. "Please help me. Take him to safety."

He shakes his head in a daze, looking towards the exit and then back to me.

Just then an explosion shatters the optics along the bar and a spray of glass rains down on us. I cover Sam with my body, protecting him as a scream tears from my throat.

When I turn back towards the man, he's gone, wobbling his way over to the exit.

"No, no, no," I scream, glancing around for my daughter. "Faith? Faith! Please, someone help me."

"Teagan?" I turn to Max, but something in the rubble has me pausing and I look back.

Then I see it.

Her shoe is poking out of the rubble, lying at a weird angle. Putting Sam down, I leap across the wreckage, trying to get to her as quickly as possible, my heart in my throat.

"Faith," I sob, my vision getting blurrier by the minute. A wave of dizziness makes me sway, but with as much strength as I can muster, I begin picking through the debris.

"Please, God, no. No, no, no," I chant, trying to uncover her body.

A hand falls over mine, warm. I scream, ripping it away to get to my girl.

Please no!

Those same hands help lift the rest off her. The minute the last piece is taken away, I get a good look at her. I fall back on my heels, an agonising, blood-curdling scream ripping from my throat.

Pain like nothing before fills every fibre of my being and I struggle to breath.

"No!" I scream.

The last thing I see is Maverick, his dark eyes locking on mine, witnessing the devastation and pain inside me.

I open my mouth but no sound escapes, not even a puff of air.

Then nothing once again.

I succumb to the darkness.

MALIK

"Malik."

Why the fuck is Harlow screaming... and right in my ear?

"Malik!"

Coming to my senses, I open my eyes, smiling when I see my beautiful wife. Then I register the suffering and alarm in her eyes, and everything around me comes into focus.

My eyes widen at the state of the room. There's a huge gaping hole in the ceiling not too far from where I'm lying. A fire burns in the far back, everyone running around in a panic. I cough, stunned and shocked.

"Malik! Malik!"

Harlow.

"Fuck, babe, we need to get you out of here," I say, my chest squeezing painfully with pure fear, needing to get her and our babies to safety.

"No. *No.* I... Malik... the babies," she pants, her face scrunched in agony.

Fuck no.

"What's wrong?" I ask, swallowing back my fear.

"Oh God, it hurts so much!" She screams. My eyes widen in horror when she hugs her stomach, her face tight, reddened from pain.

Looking around, I see Max close by helping a crying and scared-looking Kayla and Lake to their feet.

"Max, help," I yell, wiping my burning eyes with my sleeve.

Hearing the desperation in my voice, he turns. I curse when I see the side of his face is covered in blood. His eyes flicker to me, then to Harlow before he turns back to the girls, yelling something over the roaring chaos of the room. He hands Kayla off to Lake, pushing them towards the door.

"Please make it stop. My babies," Harlow sobs.

I brush her hair back, resting my forehead against hers, trying to push aside my alarm and dread. I hate seeing her like this; having my insides ripped out would be less painful.

"We need to get out of here. The fire is spreading," Max says, coming up on the other side of Harlow.

"Help me." I order him to take her other side. Together we try to help her to her feet, but then another agonising scream escapes. Her back bows in pain, leaving us no choice but to lower her back to the floor.

"What the fuck. Where are you hurt?" Max asks, looking over her body, his eyes round.

"Oh God, no," she moans.

I clutch her hand in mine. "What is it, baby?" I ask, a fear so brutal filling me, it's suffocating. I run my hand through my hair, everything inside me trembling as I think of what to do.

My brain can't focus on anything but her.

I can't lose her.

"My waters just broke," she pants, a sheen of sweat lining her forehead.

"You're having your babies?" Max yells, his eyes nearly popping out of their sockets. "Here? *Now?*"

"Max, get some fucking help, now!" I roar, pushing him away.

MAX

THE LOOK ON Malik's face is enough to make any grown man piss himself, but I can understand his urgency. Harlow doesn't look good at all, and the way she's clutching her stomach....

I shake my head.

Please let my nieces or nephews be okay.

But it's not just about her being in labour. The place is on fire, the smoke getting thicker by the minute, and everyone is screaming; it's pure and utter chaos.

"I'm going to get help," I assure him, getting up.

The minute I turn, I run straight into Mason. His face is covered in blood, his eyes red and wild as he looks around with jerky movements, his arm held tightly to his chest.

"Where's Denny? Hope?" he shouts frantically.

Grabbing his shoulders, I give him a gentle shake, getting his attention. "They're fine. Hope wasn't in here. She was outside with Mary," I remind him.

He sags against me, swaying slightly.

"What about Denny?"

"She's outside. She left with Kennedy," I tell him, hiding the fact that it took me and a few others to drag her out. She'd been hysterical when she couldn't find him. "We need to get Harlow out of here. She's in fucking labour. We can't find Mav either. Myles is trying to search for him whilst helping others get out." I cough into my hand, the smoke becoming thicker.

"Holy fuck," he breathes when he sees Harlow.

"Get some fucking help," Malik roars.

I start to go, but Mason stops me. "I'll see if the medics are here and bring in a stretcher."

I nod, watching him leave before turning back to Malik.

"Faith? Faith! Please, someone help me."

I turn to the voice, squinting through the grey clouds of smoke. "Teagan," I shout. Her head turns in my direction but she stops, turning back to look at something.

Time seems to stop and dread fills my stomach when I see what has her attention—a small arm hanging limply through the plaster and stone.

Fuck no!

"Myles," I shout, my eyes wide from fear, my gut twisting painfully.

MASON

Rushing out of the club and into the night's cool air, my lungs burn painfully, coughing uncontrollably as I clutch my useless hand to my chest.

In the middle of the street are six ambulances, all with crowds of people surrounding them, fighting to get medical assistance. Running to the closest one, I push through the crowd, grabbing the shoulder of the first paramedic I see.

"Sir, you'll have to wait," he says, turning back to treat someone I don't recognise.

"No. My sister-in-law is in labour. She's carrying twins and is in too much pain for us to move her."

He glances over at MC5, smoke pouring out of it, and shakes his head, looking scared.

"The fire brigade will be here any second," he informs me, swallowing when he sees my stormy expression.

"We don't have time. She needs help now," I yell, grabbing him by the collar and shaking him. He opens his mouth, but he doesn't need to utter a word for me to know what he's about to say. "Fuck this."

Shoving him out of the way, I move through the crowd, reaching the ambulance. I'm filled with relief when I see a stretcher near the backdoors, blankets folded on the top. I throw them in the back before pushing the bed through the crowd, wincing at the unbearable pain in my arm every time someone knocks into me.

"You can't take that," the paramedic snaps as I pass him.

"Watch me," I shout, not even looking in his direction.

"Mason," Denny yells. When I turn, she's rushing towards me, tears streaming down her face. I catch her with my good arm, pulling her close and breathing her in. "Thank God you're okay."

She sobs against my chest and it kills me to pull away, but Malik and Harlow need me more right now.

"Denny, I need to go back inside, Harlow's in labour."

"Harlow's in labour?" she asks, paling. "C'mon, we have to help her."

I stop her, folding her against my chest. "Go be with Hope. We'll get her out, but I need you to be strong and stay here where I know you're safe."

I can tell she wants to argue, but she must see the desperation on my face because she nods, leaning up to kiss me.

"Go. Hope and I will be here waiting."

Fuck, I love her.

Grabbing the back of her head, I slam my lips to hers in a quick, passionate kiss, relieved she's really okay and I've seen it with my own eyes.

Life without them isn't a life worth living.

"I love you," I breathe against her lips.

"I love you more. Be safe."

With those words, I rush back into the building, practically dragging the stretcher behind me over the debris.

"Thank fuck," Malik says when he sees me, his face pale, looking scared and vulnerable for the first time in his life. My heart hurts for him.

"C'mon." Moving, I help him get Harlow on the bed, her screams turning my stomach. She doesn't look good, her expression dazed and her skin awfully pale.

We turn when a thunderous roar echoes around us. My eyes widen in horror when I see Maverick holding a limp Faith in his arms, tears rolling down his cheeks.

Please, no.

MYLES

"Get him out," I shout to the two men who came in off the street to help with the casualties.

I take one last look at Evan, praying he'll be okay before moving to help the next person.

"Myles!"

Turning, my eyes land on Max. He coughs, pointing across the room. I see Teagan knelt over something, distraught. Not far is Sam, the son of one of Malik's motocross friends, crying.

"You," I yell, grabbing the first capable person I see. "Get that boy out of here."

He nods, moving quickly to get to Sam, as I head over to Teagan.

When I see what has her so torn up, my stomach turns and I fall to my knees in front of her. Covering her bloody hands with mine, I try to get her to let me help, but she slaps my hands away, not stopping as she frantically tries to free Faith.

Please let her be okay.

A wave of panic hits me and with quick movements, I lift the larger piece of debris. Faith's face comes into view and I gasp, stricken by the horrifying sight.

"Teagan," Maverick yells, but his voice is drowned out by Teagan's gut-wrenching cries.

"Teagan, baby.... No! Teagan," he shouts as I watch, my heart aching as she falls to the floor unconscious. "Myles?"

I meet his eyes, my body frozen, not knowing what to do as I give him a pained look. How do I tell him? This will break him.

Then he sees her.

His face... God, I've never seen such sorrow and grief in all my life. Tears flow freely down my cheeks as he falls to his knees, pure despair in his haunted eyes.

He leans forward, pulling a limp Faith into his arms, a roaring cry tearing from his chest. I feel it in the depths of my soul.

"Get Teagan out, now," Max yells, his breathing ragged and hard as he steps past me to Maverick. In a daze, I move over to Teagan, who is still unconscious.

"Maverick, you need to get Faith to a paramedic," Max orders, his voice gentle yet firm. "Now, Maverick."

His head lifts, his eyes red with tears pouring down his face. He nods at Max, cradling Faith in his arms before getting her out, his body hunched over hers in a protective stance.

Turning to Max, I let him see the fear in my eyes. "Max."

"Everything will be okay," he says, looking away.

Please let everything be okay.

THIRTY-TWO

MAVERICK

Life is made of moments, of memories, some good and some bad. But those moments, those memories, they have the power to either make or break us. They shape who we are, no matter what we try to do or say.

But what do my moments say about me? That I'm a broken man destined to live in torment and pain.

Because that's what I am in this moment.

I'm broken.

I can't wrap my head around the reasons as to why fate would bring someone as remarkable as Teagan and Faith into my life, just to have them taken away, causing so much misery and despair. It's not fair.

Have I not been through enough in my life? Is this my destiny? To suffer, tormented?

I'm shaken from my dark thoughts when the curtain slides open. The nurse walks in and I sit up, hoping she has some good news for me.

"The test results have come back clear."

"So why isn't she waking up?" I ask, looking over at Teagan's pale face.

I need her to wake up. I can't live without her. I can't go back to that lonely existence before I met her. She's everything to me.

"Patients who have gone through a traumatic event sometimes shut down to give themselves time to recover mentally. I promise she's fine. I'll be back in a little while to check in on her, " she tells me, putting her clipboard back in the pocket at the end of the bed.

Turning back to Teagan, I bring her hand to my lips. "Please wake up. I need to know you're really okay," I whisper.

I don't know how much time passes, but when her hand twitches in mine, I shoot up off my seat, leaning over her.

"Come on, baby. Open your eyes for me," I breathe. Slowly, her eyes flutter open and my shoulders sag with relief. "That's it, baby."

Sliding my thumb across her cheek, I lean down, kissing her forehead. "I love you. I love you so much," I murmur, tears falling from my eyes.

"Faith," she croaks, and like a switch has been flipped, she tries to sit up, her eyes wide and filling with tears.

"Calm down. You need to calm down," I warn, pushing her back down on the bed, mindful not to hurt her.

She shakes her head, tears falling heavier. "She was... she was... Oh God, my baby," she sobs, her body shaking uncontrollably.

"No, no, Teagan. Faith is doing okay. She's in the children's ward with your nan."

"No, I saw her." Her chest is heaving, but I can see the hopeful look in her eyes.

"I know, babe. I saw her too. She's lost a lot of blood and has broken her leg in three places, but she'll be okay."

When the paramedics told me she had a pulse but it was weak, I collapsed onto the floor, my weight giving way. I believed I'd lost her and everything in me tore wide open, my insides ripping apart. It hurt so much that I couldn't hear or see anything, nothing but those words on repeat. It was like God had answered my prayers for the first time in my life.

"I need to see her," she tells me, her voice rough.

"Let me get the nurse to make sure it's okay."

I move to the curtain only to bump into Mason and Detective Barrett.

"How is everyone?" I ask Mason, wincing. I feel like shit for not checking in, but as soon as I got the all-clear with Faith, I left her with Tish and Connie,

Teagan's nan, and came straight to my girl, not wanting her to wake up alone. I haven't left the room since. I even had the nurse treat me whilst I sat next to her, holding her hand.

"They won't tell us anything about Harlow. All we know is she got rushed into theatre for an emergency C-section not long after arriving. Everyone else is okay, just minor cuts or injuries. But...."

"But?" I prompt, swallowing.

He sighs sadly. "Evan isn't in good shape. He was the closest to the blast and has a piece of glass wedged into his back. He's in the ICU upstairs."

"Fuck." I run a hand through my hair, worrying about my friend. "What happened? Who did this?" I ask, looking at Barrett.

He winces. "Your mum."

My fists clench and I grind my teeth together, my hatred for her only intensifying. "How? She's in fucking prison."

"She made a phone call two days ago. They're recorded, and we were concerned about the context. She only said two words: 'Go ahead.' We found out earlier today that the call was made to a gang member who deals with explosives. I'd just called Evan—"

"Wait," I say, holding my hand up. "Just before the blast, he called me over, trying to tell me something. Was that you getting him to warn us?"

"Yes and no. I hadn't gotten that far into the conversation and had no idea it was your brother's wedding. I'd actually called him when I couldn't get in touch with you so he could inform you that we found your sister."

Holy shit.

I know I should be asking other questions, getting answers, but I can't concentrate on anything other than this and my girls. They need me.

Mason looks as shocked by the news as I am. "Where is she?" I demand, hoping they've got her.

"Here. She's being treated at the moment. She was severely underfed, and the crack house we found her in... well, let's just say it wasn't clean. They've taken bloods to make sure she hasn't picked anything up."

"Can I see her?" I ask, hope flaring in my chest. I've not even met her and yet I already feel protective over the little girl.

"Yes, but she has social services in with her at the moment. I know you're all eager to meet her, but at the current time, I think it's best if it was just you."

"Is that okay?" I ask Mason.

"Yeah, we'll have our chance. Just make sure you tell her we're here and that we love her already."

"I will. Teagan wants to go see Faith, so we'll be in her room," I tell Barrett, then turn back to Mason. "Can you get a nurse for me?"

"Yeah, bro," he says, slapping me on the back. For the first time, I notice his hand is in a cast.

I want to find my mother and strangle the life out of her. But first, I need to get my woman to our girl.

TWENTY MINUTES LATER, I'm pushing Teagan into the ward Faith is staying on. Connie stands up when she sees us, her eyes on her granddaughter, tears spilling down her cheeks.

"Teagan," she whispers, covering her mouth with her hand. "You're okay."

"T?" Tish calls, standing up. Her eyes widen when she sees Teagan, and she flies past Connie, engulfing Teagan into a hug.

"Careful," I snap.

"Don't ever scare me like that again, girl. I can't lose either of you. You're my family," Tish says, breaking out into a sob. I rear back in shock. From what I've seen and what Teagan has said, Tish isn't good at expressing her feelings. Seeing this side of her is like looking at a completely different person.

"I'm not going anywhere. Promise," Teagan whispers, her voice filled with emotion.

"You scared me to death, child," Connie says, running her hand over Teagan's hair when Tish finally moves away.

"I'm sorry," she starts, but then her eyes land on Faith and a strangled cry leaves her mouth. "Oh my God."

"She's doing well. She's a fucking fighter, that one. She woke up a few times asking for you, but she was never awake long enough to hear us," Tish says hurriedly to reassure her, but I can see she's finding it hard to see Faith hurt.

"Push me closer," Teagan tells me.

Doing as she asked, I take a closer look at Faith, my gut twisting. She still looks like death, but I have to admit there's more colour in her cheeks than when she first arrived.

My heart hurts seeing her look so broken. It should be me lying there, not her. I'd give anything to take her place.

"Oh, sweet girl," Teagan cries, running her fingers gently over Faith's head. "Mummy's here. Everything is going to be okay."

"Sir, are you Mr. Carter?"

I turn and a woman in a pinstriped suit walks up to me, her expression unreadable.

"Yeah, that's me."

"We were told you wanted to see your sister, Lily?"

Realisation dawns on me and I take a small step towards her. "Yes, please. Is she okay?"

"With a lot of love and care, she'll be fit as a fiddle before we know it. We do have some concerns over her development though. She hasn't spoken to us yet and has only been able to communicate through nodding or shaking her head. If I were to guess, she was either never taught, or is too scared due to her upbringing."

I grit my teeth together, hating that she went through anything at all.

"Is there anything I should know before going in there?"

"We aren't sure how well she'll react to a male in her presence, so I'd advise you to take it slow."

I nod and kneel in front of Teagan, taking her hands in mine. She's been listening to the whole conversation, but I'm still worried about leaving her, knowing she needs me.

"Go. I'll be here waiting for you. If you need me, come get me and I'll be there."

"I love you," I tell her, kissing her head.

"I love you too," she says, tears dropping onto our joined hands.

"I won't be gone long."

Following the lady, we don't walk far down the hall until we come to a private room.

"Come on in," she says, and I realise I'd been staring at the door, shaking with nerves. I don't know what to expect when I walk in there, and that frightens me.

This is one of those moments that can change our pasts or our futures. In this phenomenal moment, I get to meet my sister for the first time, a sister I knew nothing of until recently.

Swallowing down my nerves, I take a shaky step into the room, my eyes shooting straight to the bed. Sitting in the middle of the small bed is a little girl, her knees tucked into her chest.

I pause, just staring, my heart opening with vulnerability when I look into her eyes.

Eyes I've seen before.

Then it hits me.

Jesus Christ.

She was the little girl I saw at the house I found Teagan's attacker hiding out in. Guilt wraps around me like a snake choking me.

I could have helped her.

She was right there.

The doctors have cleaned her up, but it's definitely her. I don't know how I didn't see it then, but she has our brown eyes—expressive, big and round like an anime character's. What I thought had been brown hair is actually a dirty blonde.

She looks at me hesitantly, her eyes flickering to the woman sitting next to her. I hadn't noticed her when I walked in. She's dressed in a suit too, her eyes soft as she watches Lily.

"It's okay, Lily. This is your brother, Maverick. Can you remember me telling you about him?" she asks her gently.

Lily nods slowly, still seeming unsure about me. "Hey," I say, my voice gruff.

Get a grip before you scare her half to death.

Seeing the stuffed rabbit in her hands, I take another small step towards her. "I like your rabbit."

She pulls the rabbit closer, but I see in her eyes that she's curious about me.

"Does she have a name?" Hesitantly, she nods, a small smile tugging at the corner of her mouth. "Can you tell me, or is it a secret?" I whisper expressively.

She full-on smiles at that, and it transforms her entire face.

She's fucking beautiful.

She nods again, putting her finger to her lips.

"Can I sit down?" Another nod, but when I move closer, she frowns, pointing to my face. I know she's referring to the cut above my eye and most likely my torn clothes.

"Me, your other brothers, my girlfriend and her daughter were in an accident. We're all okay though," I assure her when her eyes go wide.

She rocks her arms side to side as if asking me something and I'm confused. Then it clicks.

"No, Faith isn't a baby. She's actually a little older than you. She's poorly at the minute and sleeping in a room down the hall. Would you like to meet her? She'd love the company when she wakes up."

She nods furiously, her whole face lighting up.

"Maverick," the woman behind me calls and I turn, giving her a look not to argue with me on this. I've just got her; I'm not letting her out of my sight ever again. She's family—our family—and family sticks together no matter what. Lily will soon see the true meaning of the word, and I intend to spoil her rotten.

"Can she be moved into the same room as Faith? That way my girlfriend and I can watch over her." She pauses, thinking about it, then nods. "Thank you," I say, relieved. I'd expected an argument, and I'm seriously not in the fucking mood.

There's a knock at the door and she walks over, stepping outside. Muffled voices come through the small gap, and a few seconds later she walks back in, closing the door behind her.

"Your brother Max needs you upstairs. He says your sister-in-law is back in her room."

I nod, turning to Lily. "I'll be back, but these two ladies are going to take you to Faith and her mum, Teagan, okay. She's really nice, I promise."

She nods, smiling, so I give her a smile back, wishing I could pull her in my arms and hold her. I want to promise that I'll make her life better and that she never has to be scared again, but words won't mean anything to her. I intend on showing her how loved she already is.

"I'll be as quick as I can," I tell her before reluctantly leaving.

Max is in the hallway when I step out. He sees me and kicks off the wall, frowning. "Why couldn't I come in and see her? Kids love me."

I roll my eyes. "Dude, you look like you've been on a killing spree," I say, gesturing to his bloodied clothes. "And she's not good around people. She doesn't even talk."

He nods, understanding. "What's she like?"

I smile. "She's fucking beautiful, and she has our eyes."

"I can't wait to meet her." He smiles, looking over my shoulder at the door. "Is everything okay? She mentioned Harlow."

"Oh yeah, Malik wants us to meet the babies. They're both doing fine and healthy. So is Harlow."

"What she have?"

"Fuck knows. The bastard wouldn't tell us." He chuckles.

"Let me tell Teagan they're going to put Lily in the same room as Faith, and then we'll go up."

He nods and walks beside me as we head down the hall. Before we reach the room, I put my hand out to stop him, turning to face him.

"Mason told me what you did tonight. You did really fucking well. You took charge, stayed calm and got everyone to safety. I'm really fucking proud of you, Max," I tell him, giving him a hug. I don't care if we get caught; when Mason told me how amazing he'd been, I knew I couldn't let it go unsaid. He stepped up tonight and saved lives. I'll never forget that for the rest of my life.

"It was nothing. Anyone would've done it," he says, shifting uncomfortably on his feet.

"But they didn't—you did." His eyes water, his throat bobbing up and down. "Are you crying?" I chuckle.

He rears back, wiping his eyes. "Fuck no. It's the dust getting to me."

"Yeah, yeah." I laugh and walk into see Teagan, excited about meeting the new additions.

WALKING DOWN YET ANOTHER sterile hallway, we come to the maternity ward, both Max and I peeping through the glass window in the door to see if anyone we know is in the waiting area.

"I don't see anyone," I mutter, but then the door opposite opens and Mason pokes his head out, frowning.

"Will you two fucking hurry up? I want to meet my nephews."

"They could be nieces."

He waves me off, giving me a look that says 'that will never happen'.

When we walk in, everyone is gathered outside a room, talking in low voices. I'm immediately bombarded with questions, so after giving them all a hug, I fill them in on Teagan, Faith and Lily, letting them know they're all fine.

"Before we go in, do you have any news on Evan?" I ask Denny, and the mood dims.

"I've just got back from there. He's just gotten out of surgery and they're pleased with how it went. It's going to be touch-and-go through the night though. He lost a lot blood, so he needed a transfusion," Denny says, her eyes glistening with tears. Mason pulls her against him, kissing her forehead.

"I'm sorry," I say, closing my eyes briefly. "Is Kennedy doing okay?"

"She's okay at the moment. Her friend came to get Hope and Imogen for the night so we could stay here. Dad and Nan are with her, and I'll go back down after."

"I'll pop by tomorrow. Max said he wasn't allowed any more visitors," I say, not wanting her to think I don't care.

She laughs dryly. "No. They made us get changed into these before we could see him," she says, touching the blue scrubs.

"He'll get through this. He's strong."

"Yeah, he is." She smiles and we turn to the door when Joan sticks her head out.

"Come on guys," she says, beckoning us in.

We all pile into the room. My brother's sitting on the bed, holding a baby in his arms. He's a sight for sore fucking eyes. He's been crying, I can tell, but I can also see how relaxed and happy he is as he stares down lovingly at the bundle in his arms.

"Hey, guys. Meet my daughter, Madison Joan Carter," he says softly, his voice filled with pride.

"A girl?" Max gasps, pretending to be horrified.

"Can I hold her?" Denny asks, then goes to take a step forward.

"No," he growls, narrowing his eyes, and we all laugh. My eyes fill with tears watching him. They're five minutes old and already he's a big old lion protecting his cubs. He's going to be an amazing father; seeing him with her in his arms, the look on his face as he holds her, just proves it.

"And what have you called this one?" Kayla asks softly. I glance over, noticing she looks awfully pale as Myles fusses over her.

"This is Maddox Mark Carter, our son." Harlow smiles and we all hoot, congratulating the both of them.

We all take turns looking at the babies, as Malik wouldn't let us hold either one of them.

"Why do you keep fussing over her?" Max snaps at Myles, and I turn from looking down at my niece's face to see what's going on.

"Because, dickface," Myles snaps, glaring at Max.

"She's fine. She's told you that," Max says back, mystified.

"Yeah, but she's carrying my baby," Myles blurts out, his eyes rounding when he realises what he said.

"Myles, you said we wouldn't tell them," Kayla gasps, narrowing her eyes.

"No way. You too?" Mason says and I swivel my head in his direction, feeling like I hit my head harder than I thought.

"What do you mean, *him too?*" I ask.

Mason looks at Denny sheepishly. She rolls her eyes. "I'm twelve weeks pregnant. We found out three weeks ago but with everything going on, we decided to wait to tell you."

"Congratulations, both of you," I beam, and everyone joins in, hugging each other once again.

"Why didn't you tell me?" Max asks, hurt, when everyone settles down.

"We *just* found out. They ran some tests because her blood pressure was low. It came back positive. She's about four weeks, so we wanted to wait," he tells his brother, his face softening.

"Oh good. At least you didn't wait long. Next time, tell me right away. The minute my sperm hits Lake's eggs, I'll be calling."

"Max!" Lake screeches, rolling her eyes.

"What?" he says, looking at her quizzically. "It was your brother who gave me the idea. He said he'll call me when it happens with Marybeth."

"Oh God," she says, laughing.

"Sorry to interrupt, but visiting hours are over," a midwife says, coming into the room.

"We'll go and let you get some rest. I'm on the children's ward if you need me," I tell Malik. He nods, but doesn't seem to be paying attention as he coos down at his daughter, smiling.

Giving everyone else a hug goodbye, I make my way back to the children's ward, stopping just inside the door when I spot Lily asleep on Teagan, her head resting on her chest. She looks so small, frail. They all do. I know right then that I'll do anything in my power to protect them.

Teagan rocks the recliner back and forth, running her fingers through Lily's hair and holding Faith's hand.

I've never seen anything more beautiful in my life.

Stepping into the room, Teagan jumps, turning towards me. "How is everyone? Are the babies okay?"

"Harlow had a healthy baby boy and girl, Maddox and Madison." I smile.

"Oh my God, I can't wait to meet them. I bet they're so cute."

"Yeah they are, but I only got a glimpse. Malik wouldn't let anyone near them." I chuckle, rolling my eyes.

"Aw, he's protective already."

"Seems you've made a friend." I grin, looking down at Lily in her arms. I still can't believe she's my sister. She's so innocent, so tiny.

She smiles softly. "Yeah, as soon as they introduced us, she came and sat on my lap, handed Faith her rabbit and laid her head on my chest. She fell asleep not long after, and the two women left. She has your eyes," she says, kissing Lily's head. I can tell she's in love with her already, just like me.

"How's Faith?" I ask, moving to the chair between the recliner and the bed. I kiss Faith on the forehead, running my hand over her hair before sitting down.

"She woke up a few times. The drugs they have her on are making her drowsy. The doctor came by earlier and is happy with her recovery. He said she'll be able to go home in a few days if she continues improving."

"Thank God," I breathe in relief. "I don't know what I would've done if I had lost either of you."

"You haven't. We're here," she says, grabbing my thigh.

I take her hand in mine and face her fully. "You don't understand. There was a minute back there where I thought I lost the both of you. I felt empty, broken. After having the smallest taste of what it would be like without you, I never want to feel like that again. I don't want to look back on life and wish I did things sooner. I don't want to be scared to take chances, not with you. You woke me from a deep slumber and gave me life. I want to marry you, Teagan. I can't breathe without you. You and Faith are my life. I never want to be without you, so please, *please* marry me."

Tears falling, her mouth hangs open as she stares at me in shock.

"Please say something," I plead, kissing the palm of her hand. I know it wasn't the best proposal—I don't even have a ring—but I love her without a doubt. I know there's no one on this earth that I'd want to spend the rest of my life with. Fuck, I go to sleep thinking about her and wake up the same way, my head swimming with happiness for the first time in my life. There's nothing I wouldn't do for her.

"Yes, yes, I'll marry you," she cries.

I let out a breath I didn't know I was holding, relief coursing through me.

Leaning forward, I kiss her deeply. My heart is full for the first time in my life, so full I feel like I'm about to explode.

Life can't get any better than this.

"God, I love you so fucking much," I growl, kissing her once more.

"I love you too. Always," she whispers, her eyes glistening with happiness.

THIRTY-THREE

TEAGAN
6 MONTHS LATER

With the warm sand between my toes and the sun beating down on my chest, I relax on my beach towel, eyes closed as I think over the past few months.

So much has happened in such a small amount of time. It's been hectic, one thing after another so that none of us has had much time to breathe until now. Reflecting back on what happened, it's hard to know where to begin.

Everything has slowly been coming together for each of us. We've had to fight to get to where we are, but we did it—together. It's one thing I've come to know about the brothers: they're at their strongest when they're together. It's the same with all of us.

We've had to overcome so much, but we're definitely stronger for it.

Lynn was charged and sentenced a month after the explosion after the police gathered as much evidence as they could get, her charges piling up. She'll basically be doing life in prison which is good; it helped us in our case for custody of Lily.

Lily is now officially Lily Carter, mine and Maverick's adopted daughter. She's been a fight none of us has been willing to back down on, no matter what social services said. We proved them wrong. They were unsure whether our household was a safe environment for Lily since so many of us lived under one roof, but we assured them that once the time comes, we'd be getting our own place. Then they argued that we didn't have what it took to raise a troubled child—not that any of us think she's troubled. But we proved them wrong on that. She's the happiest we've ever seen her.

Her development improves every day and she's picked up a few words along the way. Her interaction with people is getting better; she's still wary around strangers, but with her upbringing, who wouldn't be? I'm proud of her. She's really come out of her shell, and I'm honoured to call her my daughter.

I knew the moment I met her that I loved her and would do anything for her, so when Maverick asked me to marry him, he also asked me to adopt Faith. I said yes on one condition—we adopted Lily too. She deserved to have a real home where she was surrounded by love and family. She needed stability, to feel safe, and we give her that every single day.

But since we had to fight to get custody, the adoption was only given the all-clear just under a month ago. And surprisingly, we're adjusting fine. Even the brothers who thought they'd have a sister have gotten used to her being their niece now. They're all attentive and overprotective towards her.

She's loved every minute of it and has each brother wrapped around her little finger. It melts my heart when I see them all together, knowing they've missed out on so much.

Two months ago, Maverick and I got married. We didn't do the whole wedding party business, not after the last one turned out so great. Instead, we jumped in our car with the girls and our family and drove to Scotland, where we got married off the street and finished with a meal at a pub close by. It was simple, no fuss, and the best day of my life. It was perfect.

It's still hard to imagine that six months ago we were all scared for our lives, fighting to be free. Life is so unexpected—you never know what will happen next—but for us, that night changed us. It doesn't define us, but it certainly made an impact on our lives and our hearts.

Although, if I'm honest, my life changed the day I met Maverick. Yes, a lot of bad happened, but in between those moments we grew closer, connected, became one. We got to know each other in a way other couples dream of knowing their partner. I don't mean knowing what his favourite colour is, or his favourite movie, but *him*. I got to know his darkest secrets, his inhibitions, his goals, and how he thinks. I got to know the man inside.

And what a man he is.

The biggest news was finding out I was pregnant.

Yes, pregnant.

I'm not the only one though. Kayla, Denny and Kennedy are too, and we're all due a week after one another—apart from Denny who's due any day now.

My life couldn't feel any more complete. After losing my mum and living with that monster, I never thought I'd reach this kind of happiness ever again. There was always an ache in my heart, a void that could never quite be filled, but over time, Nan, Tish and then Maverick and his family have filled it with so much joy and happiness.

"What are you thinking about, baby?" Maverick whispers, kissing my bare belly. My belly dips seeing him topless, his ripped muscles flexing in a way that makes me drool. I don't think they'll be a time I don't get butterflies when I see him.

"Life, how good it is, how much has changed, how we've changed," I tell him, smiling when he starts rubbing my bump affectionately.

"Yeah? It doesn't get much better than this, does it?" he asks, lying on his side next to me.

"No, it doesn't," I agree, looking out on my family.

Evan is playing with Imogen, Faith and Hope in the sand, building castles. Kennedy is close by shielded under an umbrella, the sun getting to her. Her pregnancy hasn't been as straightforward. She's had morning sickness non-stop and I really do feel for her. Those first two months for me were a nightmare.

It's still a shock to see Evan up and about. He's recovered from his surgery fairly quickly, but he had to undergo some major therapy for his back and legs.

It was hard seeing such a strong and confident man struggle for those first few months. It was hard on everyone, especially Kennedy. Maverick helped out whenever he could, not only because Evan is his friend but because he felt guilty over what happened to him. It's taken a long time for me to convince him that he isn't to blame, that it was all his mum's doing.

Turning my attention away from Evan, I glance over to Myles fussing over Kayla, making sure she's out of the sun. I giggle, loving this side of him. He's been like this ever since they found out she was pregnant and it's driving her batshit crazy. I'm pretty sure I heard her threaten to leave him last week. Still, I know she wouldn't have him any other way.

I glance out to the sea where Max and Lake are swimming, hopefully not doing what Max suggested they do. As much as he's grown up since the explosion, he still has the brain of a child at times, always up to no good, but with Max, we wouldn't want him any other way. What he and Myles did for me that day can never be repaid. They saved our lives, as well as most of the lives of the guests'.

Smiling, I turn away, looking over to where Malik and Harlow have settled under the gazebo. I try not to laugh when Malik fights with the twins, who are giggling and shoving sand in their mouths. He's such a good dad, and each and every day I see a change in him. The hardness around his eyes is gone, replaced by a glow, and his features are softer. It's such a drastic change from the Malik I first met.

"Oh God, Malik is gonna demand we go inside, watch." Maverick chuckles, hiding his face against my neck.

"Nah, they're having too much fun. The minute he tries to take away the sand, they'll cry. You know Malik, he'll give in and give it back." I smile.

"True," he says, and I watch as he takes everyone in around him. His eyes soften, his lips tipping up into a smile. "Who would've thought we'd be here. There were so many times I thought I'd never get this."

"Well you do have it, and you deserve it honey."

"I'll never be worthy of it or you, but I'll try my hardest every damn day to prove I am. You guys are my world, my life, and after everything we've been through, I'm fucking lucky to have each and every one of you. You bring out the best in me, the real me. I feel like I've been given a second chance at life, no longer haunted by my past. I've moved on, with you, with Faith and Lily, and my family, but it's you and the girls who complete me," he says, looking lovingly up at me.

I melt, his words causing a lump in the back of my throat.

"Kiss me, you stupid fool," I rasp, hiding the effect his words have on me because, truth be told, he's the one who completes *me*. I loved my life before, don't get me wrong, but all I did was work and go home. Then he came into my life. He made me feel needed, wanted, loved. I had never before experienced the love he's given me. He made me realise I wanted more from life. He taught me to trust again, to open my heart.

Tugging at the hair on the back of his neck, I pull him closer. He kisses me, then deepens the kiss and I grow wet, arching into him when he leans across me to get a better angle.

His hand glides down my side, over my bump and down to where my bikini bottoms are, his fingers smooth, leaving a trail of goosebumps. I pull back, a little breathless, and stare up into his mesmerising eyes, lost in the intensity.

"You can't. We're at the beach," I scold, but it holds no meaning, my voice low and scratchy.

His eyes darken as he hovers over me. "I need you."

"You had me this morning," I remind him, running my fingers through his silky hair.

"I'll never get enough of you," he growls, looking deeply into my eyes.

"Then take me home, husband." I grin, squealing when he picks me up bridal-style. I duck my head when everyone wolf whistles, calling us out.

"I'll watch the kids," Evan offers and I groan, embarrassed.

"Cheers," Maverick replies, then carries me over to the cottage we rented for two weeks.

"Let me go," I scold—well, try to since I can't wipe the smile off my face.

He looks down at me, his expression intense, smouldering. "Never."

EPILOGUE

MARK
TWENTY YEARS LATER

THE SUN SHINES BRIGHTLY, high in the sky. The smell of the barbeque and freshly mowed grass fills the air, and the sound of everyone's laughter and banter is like music to my ears.

Today is a good day.

Watching my grandsons as they all stand around the garden with their wives and children, I've never been more proud of them than I am now.

They all had a rough start in life, including their wives, but they found each other along the way. They didn't fix each other's broken pieces; instead, they replaced those pieces, giving the other the love and life they deserved. It's a rare commodity, to have what they have in life, but not a one of them takes it for granted.

"Grams, can you talk some sense into Dad for me please? He won't let me date," Madison, Malik and Harlow's eldest daughter, says, looking so much like her mother.

"We've discussed this. You're not dating until you're thirty," Malik tells her sternly, leaving no room for an argument.

"No, Dad, you discussed it with yourself. Maddox and Trent date everything in sight. Sheesh, Maddox has slept with *all* my friends."

"He's a male," he replies, pulling Harlow into his lap and kissing her neck.

"This is so unfair. I'm twenty, not two, Dad."

"She's got you there." Joan chuckles, but it soon turns into a coughing fit.

"I'm with your dad on this one. Anyone gets near my girls and they're dead," Mason grunts, sitting down in the lawn chair opposite Malik.

Hope huffs in agreement, not happy with her dad. I don't really blame the poor girl; he's threatened any boyfriend she's brought home with bodily harm.

"Dad, you took a baseball bat to my last date," Ciara, Mason and Denny's youngest daughter, pipes up, rolling her eyes.

"Fuck deserved it too," Ashton, their youngest son says.

"Isn't that the lad who was talking shit about her?" Landon grunts, looking at Ashton in agreement.

"Yeah, but we didn't need your help. I sorted him out myself," Hayden says. Her brothers Landon and Liam, two of the triplets, laugh, clearly remembering what Hayden had done. Landon is actually the calm one of the three, but Liam, he gets all his attributes from his parents, Max and Lake. He's always egging Hayden on with her mischievous ways, wanting to get her into trouble. Although, in Max's eyes, Hayden walks on water. She's really a daddy's girl, even though she won't admit it.

"What's wrong with Faith?" Joan asks and I look over the garden, seeing her sitting on a blanket talking to Lily in hushed tones. She doesn't even turn around when she hears her name.

Since Maverick and Teagan adopted Lily twenty years ago, she and Faith have become more than sisters—they became best friends.

"Fuck knows. She kicked me out the other day before she had the chance to feed me," Mark, Maverick and Teagan's eldest son, whines.

"Yeah, she wouldn't make me any chocolate cake either. She texted, telling me to go and buy one," Aiden scoffs, looking at his sister, hurt.

"It's probably just work," Teagan murmurs, but I can see she's concerned for her daughter too.

From the corner of my eye, I notice Maverick staring intently in the girls' direction, a frown creasing his forehead.

I dread the day that boy finds out what's up with our girl. I just hope she finds the courage to tell them all soon. I can see she's hurting and I wish I could make it better for her, but as time has proved, only she can do that.

"Uncle Maverick, did you put some veggie burgers on?" Charlotte, Myles and Kayla's eldest, asks quietly, her cheeks turning pink. She's so much like her mother—quiet, soft-spoken and as shy as they come, and she'd go out of her way to do anything for anyone.

"Yeah, girl," he answers just as softly, and she smiles wide.

"I don't know how you eat that crap," Jacob, her brother, mutters, looking disgusted. I chuckle, knowing the growing boy needs his meat.

"Well, I don't know how you eat meat," she mutters back, making me smile.

"Food's ready," Myles calls. They all move to the table where the food has been laid, grabbing their plates.

Joan coughs once more and my chest tightens. I rub her back soothingly, wincing when I see spots of blood come away with the hanky she was coughing into.

"We should tell them, dear."

She turns to me, her once bright blue eyes now a dull grey. Her skin is pale and pasty, and when I take her hand in mine, it's freezing.

"No. They can't know. They're not ready."

"They're stronger than you give them credit for. Look at them, my love. They have each other. They'll be fine."

"You okay, Grams?" Hayden asks, walking over with her plate of food.

"You do look a little pale," Harlow mentions, looking concerned.

"It's just the heat getting to me, sweetheart. I think I'll go lie down for a little while."

"I'll come with you," I tell her, squeezing her hand gently.

"Want some help up the stairs?" Maverick asks.

"No, no. I'm fine. I have my man," she tells him, forcing a smile.

The exhaustion is clear on her face. How she's managed to hide her sickness this long is beyond me, but as always, my woman is stubborn and gets her way. I'd give her anything as long as it made her happy. It just doesn't mean I agree.

As we stand, her legs wobble before giving out. Liam moves quickly, helping her to her feet before she can reach the floor, and I let out a breath.

"I'd say no to his ugly mug too, but you wouldn't say no to your favourite grandson, now would you?" he pouts.

"Oh, you charmer." She giggles, slapping his chest.

"Such a suck-up." Hayden laughs, and Liam flips her off.

"Come on, milady," he says, looping one arm around her waist, taking her hand.

After helping me escort Joan to bed, Liam turns to me, his face pinched with worry. "I'll be up in a little bit to check on you."

"We're good, son. You get some grub in you before the others eat it all."

He shudders at the thought. "I'm not eating veggie burgers again. That shit was nasty."

I chuckle watching him rush from the room like his ass is on fire. Seconds after I hear the back door slam shut, I hear him shout, "Who swapped my burger for a fucking veggie one again?"

Laughter echoes up through the open window, making me smile as I walk over to the bed. Joan gazes at the window, a small, tired smile on her face.

"They're all so happy."

"They are," I agree, lying next to her on the bed. I turn on my side so we're facing each other, linking our hands together between us.

"We did well, huh?" she says, her voice weak.

"We did, my love. They're great people, fantastic partners, and have raised amazing children. They've all overcome so much, but they're stronger for it. They're a family—*our* family."

"I'll miss them."

"They'll miss you too, sweetheart. But I firmly believe our souls are all joined together, that we're destined to find our way back to each other. One day we will. We won't be apart forever."

"I'm tired," she tells me, fighting to keep her eyes open.

I watch her chest closely, rising and falling slower and slower as each breath shallows.

"Sleep, my love," I tell her, kissing her forehead.

I keep watching long after her eyes close, my own growing heavy. I watch the last breath leaves her body, my eyes closing as a lone tear drops, slipping down my cheek and dropping between us.

"Forever, sweetheart," I whisper, not wanting to say goodbye to my one true love.

That day, I died in my sleep, next to the woman I love, and forever belonged with.

The End...
Or is it?

ACKNOWLEDGEMENTS AND SURPRISE REVEAL

No matter how much I've tried to end this series, I can't. I've written the ending about a million times, but nothing ever felt right. It needed to be epic, to be brilliant... but no matter what, my heart wasn't in it. I just couldn't let them go, and I think that's why it took me *forever* to write.

I really, really hope you guys loved this book, and that I did Maverick's story justice. Out of all of them, he really did deserve it.

But it won't be the last you hear of the boys.

I'm proud to announce that the *Carter Brothers* will continue as *The Carters, Next Generation*. The books will be set twenty years later, with each of their children grown up. Although they won't be focused solely on the brothers, you'll still get to see them and learn what has happened over the past twenty years.

I mean, aren't you wondering what job Max got, or Myles for that matter? Are you not wondering if Lily ever finds out about her dad actually being her brother? Well, this is why I couldn't simply finish the book off the way many of you probably hoped I would. The answers you want will be in the new series.

I don't know when I'll publish the first book, but I do have it planned out. As some of you may have guessed, Faith's book will be the first—that much I *do* know.

I want to thank all my readers from the bottom of my heart for letting me continue these books. Your messages, reviews and kind words are what kept me writing. You gave me the inspiration to put pen to paper when I struggled for words.

You are the reason I get to live my dream.

So thank you. Thank you for supporting me and believing in me.

I want to thank everyone who has played a huge part in this series and getting Maverick's book out there. There are too many people to name, but you know who you are and I love you. Without you, I'd be a complete mess, rocking in the corner, wondering what I'm supposed to do first.

If you liked Maverick, please leave a review on Amazon or Goodreads.

OTHER BOOKS BY LISA HELEN GRAY

Carter Brother Series

Malik ~ Book One
Mason ~ Book Two
Myles ~ Book Three
Evan ~ Book 3.5
Max ~ Book Four
Maverick ~ Book Five

Forgiven Series

Better Left Forgotten ~ Book One
Obsession ~ Book Two
Forgiven ~ Book Three

Whithall Series

Foul Play ~ Book One (Willow and Cole's Book)

Wish It Series

If I could I'd Wish It All Away ~ Book One (Standalone)

ABOUT THE AUTHOR

Lisa Helen Gray is Amazon's bestselling author of the Forgotten Series and Carter Brother series.

She loves hanging out, but most of all, curling up with a good book or watching movies. When she's not being a mom, she's been a writer and a blogger.

She loves writing romance novels, ones with a HEA and has a thing for alpha males.

I mean, who doesn't!

Just an ordinary girl surround by extraordinary books

Printed in Great Britain
by Amazon